A SMUGGLER'S BIBLE

JOSEPH McELROY

 A BARD BOOK/PUBLISHED BY AVON BOOKS

The author wishes to thank John Murray (Publishers) Ltd. for permission to quote, on page 21, the lines from "Thoughts Occasioned by Hearing the Church of England Bells of Magdalen Tower from the Botanic Garden, Oxford, on St. Mary Magdalen's Day" and those from "Essex," both by John Betjeman, from *Collected Poems*, 1959; Thomas Yoseloff, Publisher, for permission to quote, on pages 55 and 56, the lines from "The Golden Peacock," from *The Golden Peacock*, by Itzik Manger, compiled, translated and edited by Joseph Leftwich, 1961; Holt, Rinehart and Winston, Inc., for permission to quote, on page 341, the lines from "The Star-Splitter" from *Complete Poems of Robert Frost* (copyright 1923 by Holt, Rinehart and Winston, Inc.; copyright 1951 by Robert Frost).

AVON BOOKS
A division of
The Hearst Corporation
959 Eighth Avenue
New York, New York 10019

Copyright © 1966 by Joseph McElroy.
Published by arrangement with the author.
Library of Congress Catalog Card Number: 66-22283.
ISBN: 0-380-01687-7

First Bard Printing, May, 1977

BARD TRADEMARK REG. U.S. PAT. OFF. AND IN
OTHER COUNTRIES, MARCA REGISTRADA, HECHO EN
U.S.A.

Printed in the U.S.A.

Nature has made all her truths
independent of one another.
Our art makes one depend on another,
but this is unnatural.
Each has its own place.
—David Brooke, quoting Pascal

CONTENTS

the principal parts of david brooke

He doesn't know what I am, but he knows I'm in him and behind him. His name is David Brooke, and he and his meddling English wife are aboard the *Arkadia* bound east. For Form's sake I'll grant that he and I've been (as old Reverend Mann would say) put here by a Creator (one, of course, whose distance from us and whose flair for style are consonant with my own independence and outrageous intelligence). David gets uppity, but sourly he senses that I—*I*—am his propulsion. If he turns round suddenly, with that noise he makes—"kaa-kaa, kaa-kaa," hissing schoolboy pistol shots—he won't find me in this stateroom. He will get up—yes, he's doing it now, opening the closet—but he won't flush me. I inhabit him.

His wife is in an after lounge playing chess with a little boy from New York. David wonders where she is. But he's thinking about the eight manuscripts in the East Lite Box-File (with Lockspring) on the stateroom table.

He feels, rather than hears, the deep presence of the ship's engines. This, and the movement which even in a calm sea and inside a stateroom the sitting passenger, moving like the ship at twenty-odd knots, can feel, lure David to put down the book he thought he would read. Was it Peter St. John who said never try to read anything serious on a voyage? On the voyage home from England in November, 1960, David read the same eight manuscripts. Well, not quite the same.

On the lower berth *House Beautiful* is open at an ad telling how to "Take Off Bunion in 7 Days." Beside lies a recent copy of *Elle*, which David's wife Ellen bought the day before in Montreal. David has tried to get through the piece in it by Madame Malraux, *"Apprendre à Vivre."* Then he

1

started to read the Simenon mystery he had stolen from Peter St. John in Brooklyn. "For sale in U.S.A. only."

But there is only one task. It lies on the stateroom table. Unless the manuscripts—the memories—can be made one manuscript, one memory—then David's project founders. In London the old man he hardly knows waits to be given the manuscripts—or so David believes.

He will write now. Yes. On a page of a red hard-cover ledger-type notebook David writes: "There are two forms of suicide; one brings LIFE."

Here's what he's thinking: Are the manuscripts one manuscript simply as they now stand? After all, they're crawling with links. Words in one MS recognize words in others, intransitive, transitive. There must surely be one substance the eight memories together make. And if not? If not, then David has barely a week to join them.

In the red ledger-type notebook—under the heading "LINKS CLASSIFIED"—the links seem more than mere haphazard options, seem undeniable parts of the memories his manuscripts record. Item: In each manuscript a dark-haired young man with a plump, pale, puzzled face may perhaps be found reading and may come on the word foudroyant ("shocking") and know he has looked it up twice already and curse himself for a fool and shrug along into the next sentence hoping the sense of foudroyant will revisit his flirtatious memory. (This could be one link David might add to the manuscripts; this might bring them closer together.)

Item: Each manuscript can be made to represent a nation or national grouping, and at the end of the eight manuscripts David can show these nations uniting in a psychic federation that will insure the planet against nuclear loss.

Item: Let a yellow vaccination card turn up again and again in these manuscripts, and again and again slip out of sight. (David writes in the margin, "Let it appear and then seem to disintegrate among the words of the succeeding sentences—let the letters y-e-l-l-o-w-v-a-c-c-i-n-a-t-i-o-n-c-a-r-d be seeded among the succeeding words and sentences, separating, being briefly seen, then dissolving.")

Item: Upon each of these memories impose a famous

myth. On the other hand maybe these myths already exist in the eight manuscripts. David writes, "Select myths, then see if they can be found in the manuscripts."

Item: The Eight Wonders of the World. But why not use the idea of seven, and make the eighth manuscript a release?

Solitaire, the Seven Hills of Rome, the Seven Against Thebes, the Seven Gates of Thebes, the Seven Stones of the Channel between the Scilly Isles and Land's End. ("Double solitaire" I put into David's mind, and he writes it down.)

But to find the unity of these eight manuscripts, shouldn't he review the origins of the project? The thought scares him, and he makes his whispering "kaa-kaa" sound.

He still hears that intimate mechanical voice—my voice; it spoke to him from one of those experimental weighing machines in the exhibit at the New York Coliseum; it said words to him that seemed impossibly important: "One hundred sixty-five pounds; project yourself into the lives of others. Project, reorient-ate"—an electronic quiver made the voice seem all the more certain—"analyze, synthesize, assimilate; project yourself." And David decided to do just that.

But there were other origins. David hardly dares think how insubstantial, how equivocal they were.

He gets up and moves to the door, opens it, and steps over the threshold into the passageway. Two boys, thirteen or fourteen, brush by. One is saying, "It simply isn't so; you don't meet a cross section of people on a ship." David doesn't like to hear that.

Up the passage the huge blond zoologist lurches out of his stateroom and disappears into the men's toilet. Judging from grunts David and Ellen have heard him give his little plump wife, and from the twittery, liquid replies she returns to him in her own marital shorthand, the couple must be Dutch or Swiss or German. Is he working with those great jars again? David abandons the idea of studying his manuscripts and goes to the men's toilet.

Again he finds the giant zoologist changing the water in his jars. The man looks up into the mirror balefully as David enters. The long, tan, jowly face, as if detached from its body, glowers from the mirror. His big jars are planted in

3

the four basins. This morning he grumbled when David and another man, an old Irishman, wanted to shave.

The zoologist—if he is a zoologist—seems to be in a hurry as he peers intently from jar to jar. He seems to be in a hurry to grow something in them. All one can see in them are mists of infusoria.

Now, David, feeling a dragging pitch meet his feet and weight them as he crosses from urinal to door, hears the man cry, "Aiee! Aiee!" And when David turns at the door, surrendering to curiosity, the man greets him in the mirror with an eyebrow-raised "Ha!"

Jar in hands, he half turns to David to report some development. But halfway round, jar in hands, his face almost confronting David, the man loses whatever words he needed, and with another "Ha!" turns again to the basin and gives David a dark reflective look in the mirror.

Back in the stateroom David sits at the small writing table arranging and rearranging the bulky typescripts. He returns them, in a new order, to his East Lite Box-File. Ellen has never read them.

(And if I have my weigh, Dave will see she never does; for she could not sense the over- and understatement within which the ark of my incandescent current lives in David secret and luminous and prophetic. She can't appreciate what I do for Dave, what I *am* in Dave, for all she detects of me in this many-sidedness she observes in Dave: what I *am* quite ravishes me (how lucky David is to have me!): I am (yuk yuk)—)

The intimate mechanical voice that spoke from the weighing machine at the New York Coliseum said words to him that he now for a moment thinks were the neutrix of these manuscripts. "Project yourself into the lives of others. Project, reorient-ate." Instead of a fortune, a prescription—like most horoscopes.

David puts the East Lite Box-File on its side under the lower bunk. He has left the door hooked a few inches open. He hears a mumbling gabble come along the passage. An "obviously-of-course" voice—a girl's—addresses a companion-silence, and now the words are bared as the voice passes David and Ellen's stateroom: "So he said, 'A *scène à faire* is what I need,' and I asked, 'You have to write the

4

scène à faire?' and he said, 'I gotta find out what a *scène à faire is,* do you happen to have a French-English dictionary in your stateroom?' so I said, 'What *is* a *scène à faire?'* "

Then they were past: one voice, two presences. David has heard the voice before. It's a drawling, nasal, comradely, middle-Atlantic, anticommunist, junior-year-abroad voice: dealing skilled casual bridge in the bar with a girl friend and two weathered boys who call each other "Dad"; twisting nightly from nine to eleven on the gently moving floor of the Mycenaean Room; coolly contriving stateroom swaps at midnight; appearing in the bar the following noon to sit with freshly washed, faintly stiff face sipping sherry flips and, with the girl friend and the same boys, playing bridge. But a sensible way to travel—an identifiable way.

David wants to get together with Ellen—where is she?—to tacitly forget their brief frigid fight just after lunch. But, reaching the promenade deck, he thinks he will have a look along the outside starboard passage, where he knows he won't find Ellen. He strolls aft. I'm not only *in* thee, but also *near* thee, D.

At the rail. Scalloped wavelets of the strong, moving sea make steely violet shadows. Everywhere.

A man is beside him before David even knows he has been approached. The man foregoes the customary transition—the moments of half-expectant silence at the rail after which limited conversation can get under way. The man has simply begun to talk.

He's English. David resists the impulse to say that his own wife is English. ". . . but the amount of smuggling that gets carried on even on a ship like this!" The accent carries a hint of cockney; but the echo of a Dorset roll gives the *r*'s a south-country swell. "Look at that man there with his feet tucked up." David's companion nods over his shoulder. "Today's smugglers are just your deck-chair dozers. And the best of 'em today wouldn't know a false heel from an old Cornish hide. They just carry their goods in a pocket or two."

"A Cornish hide?" asks David. "Under a skin, you mean?" He eyes the man sideways and wonders how to get away.

"A place *to* hide something. Now, to hide what? Well, a

hundred and thirty years ago it could have been an anker of spirits or a box of tea or silk."

"How did we get onto smuggling?" David asks.

From under his fake captain's cap the man winks blond eyelashes and says, "Are we ever far from smuggling?" The man is taller even than David and must be about fifty. His full brown face—its long rich cheeks and the care with which it purses its darkish lips—seems to insist on being in touch with David.

"I mean smuggling of every sort. Every imaginable." The man laughs abruptly. "Now there's a thought."

David mumbles, "Sorry, I have to look for my—" and he exhales quietly, dramatically. "We'll pursue this another time."

"My card," says the man, with a sober, probing look, but David has turned away and pretends not to hear.

He passes through a lounge, from starboard to port. Then, as he walks slowly along the port pasageway, he hears the man's voice in pursuit: "Y'see, the smuggler disguises or hides something of value in order to—"

"Oh, hello again," says David; "I haven't been able to find my—"

"Here," says the man. "I offered you my card."

David takes it and slips it into his jacket pocket. "I'll have to look below," he says, trying to be polite. He and the man reach the door of another lounge, and David pulls on it hard, just as someone pushes from inside; the man in the captain's hat steadies him by placing his palms on David's shoulder blades.

Back in the stateroom. Clipped to the first manuscript, a list of names: people prescribed for treatment.

Why is the first manuscript first? David begins to make certain additions. He snooped and lied to get what he wanted —the data, the secrets.

In this memory—number one—Peter St. John should be less emphatically English. Why? Because he is in fact English? Or because David wants not to seem to be making a point?

He presses one sentence hard: An adjective and several hopeful syllables are neatly squeezed out; he hates to waste them; he copies them hastily onto a page of the second manuscript. Delete "badge," penultimate page; delete "cf."

Now the phrase of his mother's—that a ship is a bridge forever making and destroying itself. The phrase, in the manuscript as it stood, was, alas, apropos of nothing. He writes the phrase (abbreviated) on a random page of the third manuscript.

Returning to the first he cuts off a few of his cops-and-robber shots *sotto voce:* "Kaa-kaa, kaa-kaa, kaa-kaa." Use that.

He feels me near him in the stateroom. Yet not in the same way I sometimes feel the nearness of our ostensible Creator, D.'s and mine; for if (out of his many-splendored wardrobe) my—if He *is* my—Creator has seen fit to give me for a body only David's, and if, moreover, in those infrequent manipulatory intimations of His touch upon me He tells me I'm merely a subordinate (let us say, *egotic*) part of David's personality, or an accredited envoy to David's mind, in reply I trump my would-be Papa-Doom by pointing out that as an accredited occupant of David's mind I qualify as *bodiless,* and thus, free. Therefore, while I do feel this Creator's touch, I and dear David will not doubt *my* genial touch (now up now down) in, on, and around dear dour dire *Dave.* One day when I was hiding in David's closet, I heard a voice on the other side of the door say to me, "You are a part . . ." (in D's hair, I joked back) . . . "of David's mind." Was that presumptuous voice to be believed? *Look* at David.

He removes two lines of dialogue at the end of the first manuscript. The lines were verbatim as spoken; but to leave them in will make the memory, at what ought to be its end, head off in a new direction.

David begins rereading the first page. He is enjoying it.

I

THE SHADOW

FIRST, that boy in the corner of Peter St. John's eye was a tentative shape, a part of the summer landscape of Brooklyn Heights. The boy was never ahead, always behind, always bouncing his ball. Late-afternoon heat seemed to mute and clarify the natural city sounds—car engines revving, a hotel doorman whistling up Clark Street for a cab, even the Moran tugs hooting in the harbor. On his way home St. John would pause at the foot of Pierrepont for a look across the East River at downtown Manhattan. Ever since he had come to America those gray towers had surprised him, for although they stood overshadowingly near, they seemed by some optical trick to have been charmed to the scale of models. Friday the second week of August St. John paused as usual to pay his respects to this great reassuring vision. Glancing back as he turned to go on home, he saw the unknown but familiar boy a block away apparently watching him.

Next day he saw the boy again. St. John had stopped to post letters to his wife in Maine and his father in London. Looking back he saw the boy pause by a green Jag and peer in as if to inspect it. A dog locked inside started barking, and St. John continued home.

On succeeding afternoons he would spot the boy by the druggist's across the intersection from the paper store. Between St. John's bookshop and the paper store three blocks away, he never saw the boy. But soon after he left the paper store he would find the boy walking behind him.

Wednesday the third week in August St. John closed his shop—WALDMAN'S ANTIQUARIAN BOOKSHOP—at five, and so arrived half an hour early at the paper store. Leaving there he saw the boy across the intersection. And again the boy followed.

To be absolutely sure, St. John planned to close even earlier Thursday. But his young friend David Brooke, lounging and nervous, had come in at three and seemed ready to stay all afternoon. At the rear of the shop St. John typed the catalog he hoped to get to the printer by Labor Day. But the mystery of the boy dodged through his mind and, fearing that David might not leave, he wondered how to get rid of him. He didn't want David coming home with him.

A whispering explosion broke David's silence as he edged along the walls of books. "Kaa-kaa, kaa-kaa." David was shooting one of his parents' friends, or mowing down members of that silly Brooklyn Heights club—Iroquois—or plugging one of his old school pals who at thirty-two had been playing the same bridge foursome twice a week for twelve years. Lately the "kaa-kaa" went tracing off after the generation of young marrieds who, with their first babies and their Readers' Subscription books and their garlic presses, were infiltrating the Heights now that it had got to be better known. David sneered at the Heights, but with the proprietary insight of an old resident. At twenty-eight he stayed on in his parents' flat, playing indoor tennis on a canvas court at the Heights Casino, taking the subway to Columbia, fitfully planning to go abroad. St. John told him to get a room up near the university, live like a man. David loved being given advice.

Today St. John was tempted to tell David about the boy. But he wanted to keep it to himself, and anyway David would have some outlandish explanation. He would say it was a plot against foreigners on the Heights. To David, St. John remained the clever, calm Englishman, alone, resigned, and skeptical. Why did he like David?

David assumed that in England men always used surnames—"St. John" this, "St. John" that. And like a respiratory habit that damned phrase "As an Englishman you must feel" often prefaced David's solemn comments. There it was again: "As an Englishman you must think it unfair for our universities with all their money to plunder the foreign book market."

Ignoring this, St. John typed another line: "Full tree calf. Trifle foxed, else fine . . . $37.50." The bell tinkled and he sliced the carriage back too hard.

Why had that boy been following him? And why the hell didn't David go?

"Now, Delacroix's *Journal*," said David, "what about Delacroix?"

After a moment St. John murmured, "Intriguing view of shade and color." This was all he knew about Delacroix.

He erased "As new" and typed in "Trifle worn." Getting careless. David was watching him; he wished David would go.

David sighed. "I'll stop in or phone tomorrow, St. John. I'll come down here and haunt you."

St. John raised the paper clamp to see a line of type, then looked up as if surprised. "Yes, be in touch."

He wondered if the boy would be waiting in the same place.

David had turned away and was shuffling, tall and round-shouldered, toward the door. As he passed the long table on which St. John displayed sale-books, David picked up a green paperback and slipped it into his jacket pocket. Then he opened the door and left.

St. John had seen David steal books before. Was it a game —some intimate gamble that pleased David? St. John often gave him books, and David often bought. Once St. John had sold him a deluxe Eleventh Edition of the *Britannica* for sixty dollars.

David was pedantic. Drop David only a casual fact—like the Delacroix—and soon after, David would know more about the subject than St. John. Well, a bookseller's head was cluttered with hard, unsatisfying facts—hollow-back bindings, bastard titles, press marks, issue dates. (Now what was the difference between Carolingian script and insular? St. John thought he'd check that tomorrow.) Once he had mentioned to David that Le Brun had practically thought up the myth of *Le Roi Soleil;* a week later David was comparing Le Brun's drawings and Watteau's pictures of Hector and Alexander.

St. John straightened his papers, then pulled down the door shade and locked up. He wondered if he ought to change the name of the shop. But it had been known for fifty years as WALDMAN'S ANTIQUARIAN BOOKSHOP—silver letters on a black background.

Arriving at the paper store, St. John saw the boy across the intersection. He paid for his afternoon *Post* and a new Simenon thriller—*Maigret's First Case.*

Outside the paper store he read the headlines. The boy

10

stayed where he was. St. John moved on.

At the foot of Pierrepont, St. John paused to watch a police helicopter patrolling the Brooklyn docks. Tail slightly swaying, it dipped off and made slowly toward the Battery. St. John looked back up Pierrepont. A block away the boy now started to bounce his ball, whipping it down, halting it waist-high.

When St. John reached his house on Columbia Heights and started up the brownstone steps, he looked back once more. The boy came on, bouncing his ball, side-arming it into a stoop, dribbling it low like a basketball. St. John didn't wait.

II

Friday he stuck at the catalog. First, Lowndes (older prices); then the red *Book Auction Records;* then, as it happened, the *Oxford Dictionary of Quotations* (just to see who had said that about the Statue of Liberty); then (just to see the type again) his Baskerville *Milton;* then wearily to *American Book-Prices Current* to check the *B. A. R.* prices; but then—almost rhythmically—through several books already cataloged and shelved: (rhythmically) White's *Selborne* (beige and gilt) (ed. Jesse), a great old grab bag; Stewart's *Scottish Coinage* (yes, yes); Sartre's *Nausea* (now where was the French? "devoid of secret dimensions," Sartre said—not the language, but . . . we? well, anyhow, "devoid of secret dimensions"); the Repplier edition of Howell's *Familiar Letters* (with the French engraving of J. H., floppy-booted, spurred, and cloaked, ruminating against a forest tree, left hand to cheek-whiskers, roots and branches grace-fully everywhere—oh, what did *Heic tutus obumbror* mean? "Go to the dictionary," his father used to say—in the pub-lisher's oval on the title page sat a naked chap on a stool made out of the top of a capital—Ionic, Corinthian?— tooting a two-barrelled pipe that stuck out just above "TOUT BIEN OU RIEN" . . . well, Riverside Press might have done better than that, even as early as 1908); then the Philadelphia translation of the Jewish Bible (ah, the Masoretic text) from Genesis to Second Chronicles (ordinary black cloth)—that Reform rabbi from Bay Ridge gave him this a year ago and now St. John was selling it—well; "sell"? He returned to the

11

ODQ, passed on to the *Oxford Companion to French Literature* and, after a peek at the Acropolis ground plan in the *Blue Guide to Athens,* and before returning to the *B. A. R.* to look up a price he'd already looked up, he went to the parchment *eroti . . . cum* (?) he had once thought Ian Harper would buy: *The Emperor Chooses His New Concubine.* Maybe sell it to that gray-jowled Columbia professor, that translator.

At four-thirty St. John felt strangely spent; was he worrying too much about the mystery-boy? Not exactly. But he must close up now.

Leaving the paper store St. John looked for the boy but didn't see him. At the corner of Pierrepont and Hicks he stopped to post a letter to his father. He looked back. But he didn't see the boy.

He passed down Pierrepont, paused to admire the skyline, and without glancing over his shoulder turned into Columbia Heights. Just before he reached his house he felt sure the boy was behind him.

St. John wheeled round so fast that for an instant he didn't see the boy, who was there, confronted, a hundred yards away. But then, as naturally as if he had just looked up from his game, the boy turned and threw his ball against a stoop.

St. John went on in. He went up to his daughter's room on the street side. Joan's room was dark and musty, haunted by the stripped bed sleeping under a white summer spread. St. John tilted a slat of the blind and peeked out.

Now the boy appeared on the other side of the street. Had he crossed over to get a better look at the St. Johns' house? Could he see the dark line of the tilted slat? He eyed the house, then turned and began to play stoop ball. The ball hit the edge of a step perfectly and shot back over his head, across the street toward the St. Johns' house.

The phone went, and St. John took it in the bedroom on the harbor side. It was old Mulcahy, the printer. He'd tried the shop. Could St. John get the catalog to him before the end of the week?

When St. John returned to the window in Joan's room, the boy was gone.

Today there were letters from his father in London and Sally in Maine.

At the end of his July holiday St. John had decided to

spend the August weekends in town rather than fly up Fridays. He had told Sally that cataloging the library he'd bought upstate in Gipsy Trail would take every minute till Labor Day, if he was going to offer it in his autumn list. He had known this was a poor excuse; Sally knew he could work very fast if he wanted to.

He read slowly into her letter; then he lost interest. She stuffed her prose full of breathy *aperçus*. Did English wives write letters like this? What he wanted in a letter was news. Instead, Sally gave him "the sandy damp skin of great derelict beams" washed up on the beach, and "shimmering arabesques" on the water of Casco Bay. Joan added six kisses at the bottom of the page.

St. John slit open his father's letter. Again the old man wondered if they could fly over for Christmas; again he regretted he wasn't up to visiting New York; again he regretted they hadn't come for part of their summer.

St. John couldn't tell his father that Sally assumed that four trips to England in thirteen years suspended the duty indefinitely. It was, of course, a duty to her English husband, not his English father. She and Joan loved the gray house in Falmouth Foreside. Furthermore, if the three of them spent the summer in England, the days would be so precious for his father that they couldn't think of taking a fortnight in France or Italy. Hugh St. John knew, perhaps by the frequency with which Peter wrote, that they simply didn't feel like coming over to see him.

Two years ago the old man had sensed Peter's new slant on London. "Did you see the new supermarket in Junction Road? They've dressed the manager like a city director. You must show Joan Waterlow Park and Highgate Cemetery; they've stuck a great horrid bust on Marx's gravestone." The words had sounded both urgent and perfunctory.

Still, London hadn't changed that much since the war. That wasn't why Peter St. John had felt that strange pang of indifference. No matter that the old man had had to have the almond tree in the garden uprooted and taken away. (Joan called the garden a backyard and argued with her grandfather, really rather tediously, that what he called the pavement was the sidewalk.) No matter that the off-license in Archway Road had changed hands, or that the new manager had installed against one wall a beer cooler (or that this beer was sold in cans). The hospital in which Peter St. John

13

had been born still stood halfway up Highgate Hill. He had shown Joan the place on the hill where Dick Whittington had turned round three times; staring at the sidewalk milestone boxed by low railings, she had said, "I thought it was only a story." He had shown her Highgate School at the top of the hill; it hadn't meant much to her that he had gone to a public school.

London, and within it, Highgate, and within Highgate the old house in Cromwell Avenue, hadn't moved. The whole thing was still there. Maybe that was the trouble; it was as if London had refused to be changed by his absence.

In '45 he had come to see America and have a look at the American antiquarian trade. And instead of leaving old Waldman's bookshop after a year, he had stayed. Brooklyn Heights had become his home. That was simple enough.

But perhaps it was no simpler than the lie he had told Sally about why he wanted to spend the August weekends in the city. All this had started in early March, during a week of spring days—an early, London spring. For years St. John had loved the Heights because it was foreign. He had felt, from block to block, the solid architectural presence of a foreign city.

But then, all that balmy week this past March, St. John had known he was walking through a neighborhood newly strange. Walking down Pineapple from Henry to Hicks, he had suddenly stopped: he couldn't hear the great humid vents humming at the back of the St. George Hotel. Then, when he concentrated, the humming turned itself on in his ears.

The next day when he had passed the barber shop the same thing had happened. A few yards past the broad window, he had realized he hadn't noticed what he always noticed—hadn't turned to nod to the three heads that, at different distances from him, would ordinarily be visible above the curtain that covered the lower half of the window —visible if they were all working—which, he had suddenly thought, they always *had* been, when he passed. He had failed to notice not only those three barbers but also the neuter, ecstatic, staring papier-mâché head that stood in one corner of the window in front of the curtain, skin creamy, black hair shiny and trim.

And the next day, passing Plymouth Church of the Pilgrims on Orange Street, he had looked in at the statue of

14

Beecher in the ample courtyard garden as if this church were like others on the Heights.

The same with the fine, myopic brownstones.

And when he passed the place where that snooty old damsel had had her exclusive garden for children of five or under, he hadn't given a thought to the tall yellow block of flats now standing there.

At first, years ago, strangeness had bred curiosity, and curiosity closeness. The feeling had lasted, or seemed to last. Indeed it had been part of his love for Sally, her mild West Virginia accent, a certain warm, joking savvy she might have picked up at Smith College. But now he felt that by becoming familiar, Brooklyn Heights was failing him. Was it just a foggy idea? Because of it he had decided to stay in town the August weekends.

At the age of nine or ten he had been in the habit of reading all night once or twice a week. He was a reader, true; but the real reason had been that everyone in London had been asleep—schoolmates, masters, the people who bought books at the stalls near Leicester Square.

And now, after his July holiday, St. John had wanted to be, as it were, alone with the Heights. To find out what had happened. Sally and Joan were in Maine; Ian Harper and his wife had a house in the Berkshires; Monica Flower in Buck Hill Falls. The Heights wasn't exactly deserted, but it was different. David Brooke stayed in town, plodding through his thesis, visiting St. John some evenings.

And into this neighborhood that had become so disconcertingly familiar, had come the boy. It was all very confusing.

From his armchair in the living room St. John watched the harbor. A commuters' helicopter near the Coast Guard pier lifted off slowly into the soft evening light.

St. John raced through a few pages of his new Simenon mystery. Shortly afterward, knowing he would walk for a long time, he went out.

III

Saturday he spent half the afternoon staring at a calf quarto, pondering whether or not to sell it. It was the Bouchet, dully glistening; he'd had it on this desk for years.

15

He'd had plans for the Bouchet. One was the essay on Francus, reputed progenitor of the French kings, reputed son of Hector. St. John had never actually started the essay. He had entitled it "Bouchet's *Genealogies:* History as Facetious Chauvinism and Chauvinistic Fancy," whatever that meant. As for the other half of the Bouchet project, the translation, he'd got well beyond the title. But then somehow he had put it aside. In the bottom drawer of his desk his manuscript waited for him: *The Genealogies, Effigies, and Epitaphs of the Kings of France.* Jehan Bouchet d'Aquitaine. In April he had treated the Bouchet with lanolin; the joints had got dry and thin. He had known, of course, that one day he'd give up and catalog the wretched thing. "Source of Ronsard's unfinished epic. Contemporary calf, 1545." A nice copy, colophon, title page—he could ask three hundred for it.

But he would write that essay; he'd write it if it took him ten years.

That gray-jowled professor, the translator, had once said to St. John that proper translating was like kissing the author, kissing deeply; and St. John had wished to speak of Bouchet but instead had said, "I'm afraid I'm just a browser," and that gray prig, with hepatitic shadow-bags under his eyes, had said, "We need our browsers." And who was "we"?

At four-thirty St. John closed, and five minutes later he reached the paper store. But the boy hadn't come. Yet when St. John stopped to post a letter at Hicks and Pierrepont, he did see the boy—again a block away, again bouncing that rubber ball. St. John passed on down Pierrepont.

Then, instead of pausing to look at the skyline, he turned into Columbia Heights and suddenly started to run. Fifty yards along he pulled up and ducked into an areaway. He was going to know for sure.

Below street level, slightly ridiculous, his head just blocked by a brownstone pier, St. John wondered if it would indeed be possible to ambush the boy. He had seemed so fixed in distance.

But now the steps came, light sneaker steps mingled with the clear slap of the ball.

When, a moment later, as the boy passed into view on the pavement above, St. John moved toward the areaway gate to arrest him, he suddenly felt he was taking a risk, spoiling

16

something. And as he said, "Excuse me," he thought, "This boy is just a boy walking."

The boy had seen or sensed him a second before he spoke. Turning to St. John, he looked less scared than curious. His brown, mussed hair was rather long—not the typical summer brush cut. He wore khakis, a dark blue short-sleeved shirt, and a western belt with a big silver horseshoe buckle.

"Excuse me, but do you know me?" St. John opened the gate and stepped up onto the pavement. "I take it you know me."

"No," said the boy.

"Have you or haven't you been trailing me?"

"Yes."

Resignation deadened the boy's eyes. He was staring at St. John's face, not cheekily, but as if he were examining it.

"Well, what do you think you're doing?" St. John wasn't handling him.

The boy shook his head. Hair both thick and fine, ordinary brown, St. John's color.

"Is it some joke? Are you having me on?"

The boy shook his head. Did he take St. John for a crank?

"Come on, then, we'll walk along and you can tell me." St. John took a few steps, felt like some kind of group leader, paused, then went on.

The boy came up with him.

At the house St. John turned to the boy, who looked straight into his face.

"If I tell you why I've followed you, you won't get mad?"

"Well, as a matter of fact, I don't think I will."

"I have a summer job at the florist's on Montague Street."

"I know, near Clinton Street."

"My mother's gone there for years. It's just a summer job. I get off work at four-thirty and I come up Montague Street and stop at the drug store. We live on Grace Court."

"So Columbia Heights is out of your way."

"But one day I came out of the drug store and I was turning to go home when I saw you. That first day I didn't know you'd come from the paper store. I saw your face. And I followed you. Up to Pierrepont and then down past Willow to Columbia Heights and around into Columbia Heights. You didn't see me. The next day I followed again. After you stopped at the foot of Pierrepont to look at something, you

17

looked around toward me, but I don't think you noticed me."

"But I still ask, *why?*"

"It was so funny. And now I see you close up . . . it's so hard to understand." The boy's mouth grew fixed and his cheeks tense.

"What is it about me?"

"Nothing. It's so stupid."

"Look, this is silly. Come in here . . . and have a ginger ale and you can tell me."

The boy looked back down the street. "Yes. I should." St. John felt the aloof propriety of the phrase. Somehow the boy had kept himself free.

Following the boy into the house, St. John found himself wishing he had kept their relation on its original footing. But what had *been* its footing. Did he wish not to know?

The boy sat in St. John's chair by the harbor window staring at his glass.

"Now explain."

The boy shrugged, shook his head. "It was your profile."

St. John sipped his beer.

The boy finished his ginger ale in one slow series of swallows. "My father died in April." Again he seemed to be noting St. John's face. "It's so stupid," he said again, but now with a bit of relief.

"I'm sure 'stupid' is the wrong word."

The boy tried again. "You look like him." And now the boy's face turned stiff and his voice became delicate. "No, I mean . . . I thought . . . you were. . . ." He brought out the truth simply: "I just thought I was sort of seeing my father."

Slowly enough to show seriousness, St. John said, "Well, what's stupid about that?"

"I mean I thought I really was seeing him."

St. John, feeling his own fear frivolous, couldn't face the boy, and rose and went to the harbor window.

"Do you want to hear?" the boy asked. But when he went on, he seemed hardly to be addressing St. John. "After he died I used to read the newspaper every morning. He always said to study current events. But I was reading the paper to see if there was something. I mean a clue." He moved securely within his story, and St. John turned back toward him. "A clue to what I kept thinking . . . might have happened. That it was. . . ." The boy spoke very softly. "Oh Jeez, we . . . *you* know."

18

"No," said St. John quietly, letting amusement run up his voice, "I *don't* know."

"What I mean is, I hoped . . ." Then the boy sounded almost defiant. "I hoped he'd been sent on a secret mission. To Russia or somewhere. And that they couldn't tell me or my mother because it was so . . . *you* know, secret. And that he'd come back. He *would come back.*" The voice wavered sternly. "Come back after a while. I dreamt about it."

Covering his face with his hands, the boy held in his sobs. He was crying. He stood up and stood stiffly, and St. John, also standing, felt that he was honoring the boy.

St. John had to say something. "What was your father?" Strangely the question seemed important.

"He worked in Wall Street."

"A broker?"

"An investment counselor." The boy had recovered himself. "He was always reading, and always saying I mustn't be like him because he hadn't done what he wanted to do even though he never found out what it was he wanted to do." The boy paused, then said, with formality, "He was forty-one. He used to say to me 'The world is your oyster.'"

"I'm forty-two," St. John said.

The moment had not lost a suspense that had seemed to bind them. The boy's name was Walter Roy—rather an old name for a boy. St. John wanted to know about the father, William Roy, but Walt's answers were shy and skillful in their brevity. Walt seemed to feel in these questions something more—or less—than sympathy. Or did St. John merely imagine that?

"Got a picture of your dad?" The words weren't right.

And Walt obviously wanted to leave. "Your accent, you have an English accent."

As if at a distance little pompous phrases puffed into St. John's mind—"retain some bad habits . . . would say *in* Grace Court whereas you'd say *on* . . . still say first floor instead of second . . . European custom . . ."—but he kept silent.

Though eager to go, Walt wished to go smoothly. From a bottom shelf where Sally had put the art books, St. John pulled out the *Oxford Illustrated Atlas*. But then he was afraid giving it to Walt would seem awkward.

He was taking Walt to the front door—down the hall, from the back of the house to the street side. And Walt was promising to visit the shop. And St. John was thinking of fifty things he wanted to know about William Roy.

"Off you go, then." St. John was matter-of-fact.

As the boy passed through the doorway he turned to give St. John the slightest stiff bow.

On the outside landing, the boy turned. "Who else lives here?"

And St. John replied quickly and naturally, "I'm by myself."

St. John heard the queer question in his head: wouldn't Walt be following him any more?

IV

Their walk together had become almost customary: past the old brick apartment house (what color was it?) and then between lines of brown and gray stone houses with high stoops Joan had loved to tiptoe up and race down when she went ringing doorbells on Halloween (until she was eleven she had made him come with her, and after she had pressed a bell she'd rush down the strange steps and scurry round the block to where he waited, and they two would peek round to see if anyone was home); his walk with Walt had become strangely natural. Well, the mystery of Walt had been solved: that was the point.

But what about the father?

Back in the living room St. John looked up the Roys' number. If Walt could drop in to the shop tomorrow, Saturday, perhaps. . . . Perhaps he wouldn't find the atlas such an awkward gift. Some young people took that sort of thing without a surprise. Maybe even that Ackerman? Such an expensive gift? As a token of something or other.

It would be crazy to call up the Roys. Walt wouldn't be home yet anyway. This dim person William Roy filled that apartment on Grace Court more masterfully than he ever had in life. St. John looked like him. Same age. (Same doubts?) Bookcases? *Business Week?* A Republican who had voted for Stevenson? Had William Roy gone to college? He wouldn't have known about Ackerman but he would have recognized its value.

There it was, down among the art books. Sally didn't think much of it. That thin, heavy buckram folio had once been the start of a collection. St. John had abandoned the idea.

One day he had realized, with a shock that had made his insight feel subtle, that the charm Ackerman plates had was the charm bookselling tradition gave them. Of course, the silhouettes and rinsed colors did say something, laid out for the right reader the sort of past one found in a Betjeman poem. Now why recall *those* lines? He didn't even like them.

> I see the urn against the yew,
>   The sunlit urn of sculptured stone,
> I see its shapely shadow fall
> On this enormous garden wall
>   Which makes a kingdom of its own.

The Ackerman plates had a nagging clarity. St. John hadn't a Betjeman here or in the shop—

> Edwardian Essex opens wide,
> Mirrored in ponds and seen through gates,
>   Sweet uneventful countryside.

He hadn't collected Ackerman. Nor had he made that collection of the great Elizabethan and Jacobean translations—Golding, Harington, Fairfax, Sandys (he had the *Metamorphoses* in the new catalog).

He liked to own the books he'd read. But his trade turned over so many he'd read, or half-read, that at last he had let himself catalog most of his own volumes. So the library at home became largely whatever he had lately felt like reading. Secretly, St. John believed in some intellectual osmosis—as if he, a strange middle creature, lived on schools of cultural infusoria passing through him.

He should have gone to university. The old man, out of his earnings from the art supplies shop off Lower Regent Street, had sent him to a first-class school. But Peter St. John had ended by disappointing his father. Despite being such a reader, he hadn't come high enough on his matric. Even at twelve or thirteen he'd spent hours and hours standing in West End book stalls. Failing to make a university, he had found his way into antiquarian bookselling. Well, at least he had the consolation of finding himself among books. He had always been a browser. As he had told his father, he had gone to browse and he had stayed. It seemed to him now, as he looked across the harbor, and thought of Highgate

School and Sally and Joan and David Brooke and the boy Walt and Walt's father—that he had spent most of his life near that special sweet dusty scent of old book boards and brittle, foxed paper.

Yes, he *would* call the Roys and ask Walt to visit the shop tomorrow.

What had William Roy wanted to make of his life? From college he had gone to war. Later he had found himself following a couple of his college friends into Wall Street. Year after year he had imagined another life.

St. John caught himself confusing what the boy had said with what he himself was guessing. A similar thing happened with books he knew a lot about but hadn't read—books that had turned up in his catalogs for years, books he had read about and heard discussed, books seemingly so familiar.

Perhaps the Roys had put off buying a summer place; perhaps they had rented. Had they lived long in Brooklyn Heights? Had they kept the same flat? Probably they had moved to a larger one. Eventually they'd have needed another bookcase. Somewhere they'd have those volumes of Churchill, with the bright dust jackets. Was Mrs. Roy blonde, like Sally? How long had it taken William Roy to die? St. John pictured the scene in Brooklyn Hospital, where Joan had been born: Mrs. Roy speaking quietly to the nurse; William Roy, solid and real, in the fragile oxygen tent, smiling wearily at the boy, who stood lost at the bedside. But why imagine him in that hospital? Why imagine the oxygen tent?

St. John sat down by the phone. He dialed the Roys, and waited. At last a woman answered. Unable to say anything, St. John hung up.

V

Monday he dreaded the walk home. It would seem so short.

But then, at four, Walt Roy came in. St. John got up from his desk.

"I was going to phone," he said, and then wished he hadn't spoken.

Walt had seemed prepared to say something, but now

22

seemed embarrassed. He put a hand on the sale-books on the table beside him.

"I wanted to ask you . . . not to tell about Saturday."

"Could you imagine I'd tell?"

"I'd hate my mother to know."

"She shan't."

"But more than that. I couldn't study last night. I missed my finals in June and I'm making them up in two weeks. I couldn't study last night because I thought I'd done something awful."

"Telling about your dad?"

"Saying you looked like him. Because you don't." Walt walked toward the desk.

St. John felt a chronic falseness in his own voice as he said, "It doesn't make any difference. Forget the whole thing." Then, from the desk he took the *Oxford Atlas* he had brought from home. "Will you do me a favor?"

"Well, what is it?"

"Let me give you this book."

Uncertainly, Walt thanked him. He opened the atlas and looked blankly at a map. "It's great," he said. "But I shouldn't take it."

"But I have thirty thousand books!" Yet, no, that wasn't what he had wanted to say to the boy.

"I can't take it."

St. John felt the forced genial bullying in his voice: "You *must* take it."

"I don't see why." The boy was surprised at his own words.

"Do you have an atlas?"

"Nope." Walt was trying to seem phlegmatic rather than obstinate.

"Look, you began all this by following me."

Walt spoke almost in a mutter: "All right, I'll take the atlas if you're giving it away."

"I'm not giving it away; I'm giving it to you."

"My father gave me a hundred books."

St. John countered quietly. "I should *like* to have been your father."

"*Don't* say that!" Walt cried. "Don't say that!"

"I only mean—"

"Who cares what you mean? Oh, I wish . . . you're OK. But I'd rather. . . ."

"Rather forget about your father?"

"God, no! No! Why do you say things like that? I'd rather . . . have him dead and have him *him* than have him back and have him *you!*"

The instant after these words, St. John and the boy were speaking together: "Yes, of course you would"—"What am I saying!"

They were silent, not looking at each other. Was the conversation going to go on?

"Do take the book."

"No." Walt put the atlas down on the sale-books that stood spines up on a broad table as if in a horizontal bookcase. "I'm leaving it. I have to go. I'm sorry I made a jerk of myself. It was probably all my fault."

At the door he turned, and for a second, his smile, though theatrical, was poignantly polite. "Goodbye."

St. John could only nod.

VI

He passed the barber shop; the men were all up working, and he nodded to the one-two-three grins that appeared above the curtain, and he glanced at the papier-mâché head. David Brooke had had his hair cut in those chairs ever since at the age of five he'd graduated from the merry-go-round steeds in the children's barber shop at A&S. (St. John hardly associated "hair-dresser" with a barber anymore, except to recall Joan once calling the English appellation sissy.)

Had William Roy walked along Columbia Heights? St. John's father sometimes mixed it up with Brooklyn Heights. Down this home street, St. John glanced up at familiar doors behind which lived people he didn't know. Late-summer warmth, untouched by the hour, gathered close the muddled sounds of steps and abortive muffled voices and locks latching and car motors accelerating. Had William Roy had a car? Perhaps not—inconvenient in the city. Unless he had had a very good salary and could afford thirty dollars a month for a garage. Sally's friend Monica Flower had once implied that Sally must have money of her own—booksellers didn't own a brownstone on the Heights and a house at Falmouth Foreside. That showed how much she knew. Perhaps William Roy hadn't been doing so well. On the other hand, Walt went to that expensive school in Bay Ridge.

When St. John entered his house he wanted to hear Sally and Joan talking in the kitchen downstairs.

Through the evening his actions seemed to be taken in order to break his mental ramblings arbitrarily into sections. He rubbed lanolin over the boards and spine of a high folio of Hooker. Why keep the damn thing? He would never read it. He rubbed the lighter calf of Demonde's eight-volume *Notes on the Hindu Mandala*. (He would give this to David, who had once observed, as he idled through the books, that he had studied the bearing of mandalas on racial memories and would be glad to take the Demonde off St. John's hands. Thereupon David had drawn a mandala, a free octagon full of triangles and circles and squares.)

At ten, St. John picked up the telephone receiver and dialed the Roys. After the first ring at the other end, he lowered the receiver, but then a woman answered. He didn't bring the receiver up to his ear. He held it, listening to her repeated "Hello? . . . Hello? . . . Hello!"

She wasn't hanging up.

"May I speak to Walt, if he's there?"

"Who is it?"

"Peter St. John." Feeling a simple adequacy in the answer, he added nothing to it.

"Just a minute."

As he waited, St. John suddenly thought, "He must have had a moustache."

Then Walt's husky voice: "Hello."

"Walt. I'm sorry I said anything this afternoon to embarrass you. I called just to ask you to meet me for a short walk. On the Promenade." The words were coming out—he couldn't hold them. "Just one or two things. Will you meet me on the Promenade? Just a half-hour break from your studies."

St. John heard, almost felt, the boy's breath.

Then Walt hung up.

As St. John was leaving the house, the phone rang and he ran back to the living room to answer it.

"St. John, you're in." David's nasal drone.

"Just going out." How could he put David off?

"I'll join you." David knew St. John's habits.

"Well, I'm going to the shop to do some more work on the catalog."

"Suppose I drop in?"

David was asking . . . what was David asking, saying? He'd found a room near Columbia. He was telling St. John to write down the number of his new phone, a pay phone. David was saying he was sorry they couldn't. . . . Was anything the matter? David was asking.

"No," St. John heard himself reply.

David had hung up. Abruptly? No, he had said goodbye. Leaving the house, St. John knew he wanted to go stand outside the Roys' flat in Grace Court. Which floor?

He walked round to the Promenade, which ran parallel to Columbia Heights on the harbor side. The Promenade was relatively new—a long strip of concrete walk open to the greatest view in the world. St. John stopped to gaze over the iron fence at the lights across the river. The day's heavy heat was moving away, pressed gently by the evening air. A silent Colombian freighter in one of the slips below was lit at masthead, bow, and stern, and at the ports of several topside cabins. Across the river clear signs marked the Battery. (The familiar "WALL ROPE," near where the east end of Wall Street met the docks: a kind of *rope?*)

A trio paused near him. Two slim, neat men-boys in skintight denims and impeccable short-sleeved button-downs talked quietly with their companion, an older woman. "But Julia, my *dear,* you like *every*one."

When she turned, St. John saw it was David Brooke's mother. He knew her only slightly. Had she seen him? He passed on.

What had happened to him, then, that he wanted to go to Walt's apartment house and stare at his windows? But it was the thought of being the boy's father. And not so much *of the boy* either, but of being that other man.

A green beacon shone from the Seamen's Church Institute Building. He moved his eyes to the left, and he passed, as if there were no distances, from the Battery at the south tip of Manhattan, to the crowded lights of Jersey City near the opening of the other river he couldn't see, the Hudson River, Manhattan's west boundary. "No, of *course* Hudson wasn't Dutch," he'd said to David. "He was as English as I am."

To the left, and nearer, the pale stony green of the Statue. "A monument to your great dead," was *almost* what someone had said of her. How many steps in the Statue of Liberty? A hundred and sixty-one, according to David. How wide and high is the book she holds? According to David, forty-two high (same as her right arm is long), thirty-five wide (same as the diameter of her waist). And Fred Bartholdi sculpted her. In pieces.

What could stick, did. Now who said that?

St. John's head was full of words—pebbles. The absurd things he remembered! Like David saying, "We have no status unless we become aliens." David always seemed to be quoting.

The truth seemed to come in absurd packages—distant wordy formulas, implausible accidents. What the boy meant to him had sprung from a lugubrious caprice the boy would not again allow himself.

(Absurd forms. When St. John thought about it, David Brooke had got to be his friend through one of these distortions. One evening five years ago—at Monica Flower's—David had heard St. John tell off one of her guests and had adopted St. John, decided he was worth knowing.)

St. John heard a step near him; it sounded personal.

And then he heard Walt's voice. "I'm sorry I hung up." Walt stood with his hands in his pockets watching the harbor. St. John could think of nothing to say.

Walt spoke again. "I just thought you shouldn't have called. I told my mother."

"Everything?"

"She didn't want me to come out to see you, but I wanted to tell you I'm sorry about hanging up. I've never argued with her before. She's very upset. It scared me, but then I started feeling something different."

"Today you said I didn't really look like your father."

"You don't, really."

"So this was all a mistake."

"I don't look like him either. I look like my mother." Walt had become confident, gracious.

"It was a mistake."

They were silent for a minute. Then Walt said, "No, it's made me feel different. First I had to follow you; then I had to let you stop me; then I had to tell you things I'd never tell anyone—not even someone very close."

What about the moustache? St. John couldn't bring himself to ask.

"Then I had to be rude to you a couple of times; then I had to fight with my mother. I feel different than a month ago."

27

"You're young," St. John said. "The world's your oyster; you can be whatever you want."

"I can't be like my father. Tonight . . . I realized that he was my mother's husband."

"That's quite a discovery," St. John said, at once feeling that his slight irony was parrying plain truth.

Another silence. Down near the Navy Yard a fire-boat whistled.

"Can I come see you in the bookshop some time?"

"You needn't be polite, Walt."

Without looking at the boy, St. John turned away and moved on down the Promenade.

"Hey, Mr. St. John!" But Walt didn't follow.

There was Julia Brooke again. She certainly could wear slacks. In the flickering light through the young honey locusts she was coming back along the Promenade alone. She nodded to him.

Had William Roy actually had a moustache? If so, it would still be growing. Or would it? Or had he been cremated?

Now: go home or to the shop?

Julia Brooke had been at the soirée at Monica Flower's five years ago when he had been rude to that young man and then David had turned up and been delighted that St. John, whom he hadn't met, was telling somebody off. Remembering that November meeting at Iroquois five years ago, St. John couldn't see David except at the end. It had been the end of more than the evening. Slow-motion people, washed flesh, evening clothes. Julia Brooke patting some man's face, chaffing him, laughing at him out of large, dark, sharp, warm eyes.

Monica Flower hadn't been to blame. She'd been a mere active half-seen hostess. Like the Heights, the club had become less exclusive. But it had remained an institution, certified, as it were, by the formal invitations engraved by old Mulcahy in his creaky shop in Schermerhorn Street. And if it pleased Sally to be there and see the burghers of Brooklyn Heights all on one floor of a brick house on Willow Street, and listen to a young man—a member's son—evoke his two years at Oxford, and later hold a plate of Monica's chicken Newburg—then St. John was willing to hire a dress suit and wear it. He didn't blame Sally for wanting to be asked to join.

28

Of course, he had known some of the men. (Ian Harper, for instance, who occasionally came over from Wall Street to lunch with him in the shop.) In fact, he had thought he and Sally might have been asked, not because Sally played afternoon bridge with Monica at the Heights Casino, but rather because he, Peter, was English, and so was the evening's topic.

The young man had lectured—with slides!—and St. John had resisted muttering to Sally. Afterward he had talked to Ian Harper and two other men; he was explaining the art of fore-edge painting. Then Monica had brought that young Yankee Oxonian toward them. Had her slowness been apparent or real? Had she been deferring to St. John? He had been describing the fore-edge landscapes on certain early eighteenth-century books. ("Under the gilding they used to hide the picture; to see it you had to slant the pages; they say the gilding protected the color from the light.") He'd gone on to Edwards or Pall Mall and how brown monotone had given way to green, red, yellow, and, in 1790, blue. ("Then in the next century the young ladies ruined the art.") Thinking about it later, he decided that Monica and the young man had been waiting at his elbow for a minute or two before he let them in.

She had introduced St. John as a bookseller. (What had been the young man's name? Mrs. Fargo's son. Very tall. Instead of evening clothes he'd had on abrasive, greenish-brown tweeds, a fine-checked shirt with a spread collar, a brown Magdalen tie, and a waistcoat of amaranthine corduroy.) Between Hotchkiss and Yale, and Rhode Island in the summer, Tom Fargo barely knew the Heights.

He had peered sternly at St. John and had said, as St. John started to shake hands, "I must have a look at your stock."

Then St. John had felt a rush of rage—and the lucid green of Magdalen College lawns and the delicate, worn stone and all the other light-metered glimpses of Oxford held upon the fifty slides Fargo had shown, had seemed to St. John pure vandal theft. And the anecdotes . . . the timing. . . .

Being presented to young Fargo had seemed for an instant to put the two of them in St. John's shop—at one side, a table of books with spines facing up; at the other, a wall of dark shelves. In that moment of memory or foresight he had pictured Tom Fargo browsing superciliously and murmuring, as St. John had once heard a young man murmur in the shop, "I always judge a bookseller's prices by what he asks for the large paper edition of *The Seven Pillars*."

Yes, in that instant St. John had pictured them both alone in his shop. All the sneaky insouciance in young Fargo's lecture had formed one force that brought into St. John's mind a great blind memory—as if a toxin of dislike had drawn up a precious, dormant blood from far inside him. But that memory had remained blind for the instant before it subsided. And all St. John had been able to want was to humble young Fargo.

While Monica Flower smiled meaninglessly, Fargo had said, "I *must* have a look at your stock."

And St. John had answered, "Why *must* you have a look at my stock?"

"Why," Fargo had begun uncertainly, "why why why what a question! I suppose because it's so charming to hear that there's a genuine antiquarian bookseller, that is to say, among us. Well, that is, there are bookshops here—Womrath's and . . . but not—so I gather from my mother—not a shop like yours."

"Maybe you'll find it English."

"Let it be what it is. I must come round and have a chat."

Then St. John had burst. He had spoken quietly at first, then loudly enough to cause some of the talking around him to die down.

"Have a chat? Have a chat? As if I were that scout of yours at college, the old man you patronized by drinking a farewell pint with him? How close you felt to that lackey, how good you were to him! And how off-handedly you pass us your tidbits—the murderous pressure of the schools examinations—what did you say? 'More suicides at Oxford than at all the Ivy colleges put together?' And how *dare* you think you've absorbed England into your system? Congenial, cranky England, wise but a little silly—beloved, enduring!"

He had kept talking. He had stopped himself when he felt tempted to call Fargo on his Oxford accent—that patter of words and a couple of long-drawled syllables, a hop-skip-jump without the sprint. If that was put on, the condescension was not.

St. John had stopped himself, and had known Sally was watching and had heard. And he'd been distracted by the face on his right, the face of a young man who later introduced himself as David Brooke, and who had been smiling

30

conspiratorially, and who said, as St. John turned to him, "You were wonderful, absolutely wonderful. That phony made me sick."

And this had been the beginning of their friendship—or, more precisely, of David's conception of St. John's independence.

Poor Sally! That night, when they had got home and gone up to their bedroom and had reached that moment before getting undressed when one often felt strangely free and unmindful of the next day, she had stared into his face. She had taken his face in her hands and, not kissing him, had said, "You look marvelous in a dinner jacket." Poor Sally! In so many ways so nimble. He had known that in her compliment she was acknowledging that there probably wouldn't be any need for him to buy a dinner jacket. They might be asked to Iroquois again some time, but they weren't about to be asked to join.

And in fact, since then they had not been asked again, not even by Monica, though she saw Sally two or three times a week.

David had tabbed him. But St. John's behavior that night hadn't been all that typical. David took him for a rebel skeptic who thought the Heights a social cul-de-sac but was as happy living here as he thought he ought to be.

And Sally? She had borne his nastiness that night as the nastiness of a good, ordinary man.

Had that night made much difference? Young Fargo had never appeared at the shop. After that night hadn't Ian seemed to take a new tone with him—more distinct, not so blunt?

True, Ian had asked him to play squash at the Heights Casino. St. John had known Sally hoped he would go. Well, he had visited that second-floor court one Thursday afternoon as a spectator. That evening he'd told Sally he'd never be able to give Ian a game. Actually, St. John knew he could have picked it up; he was dead agile. But that Thursday afternoon Ian and the other man had seemed caught in a ghastly white chamber, chilly and exploding. And Ian, still lenient and civil and joking, had become also a red-haired giant crashing haunches with his foe. St. John hated games; he preferred walking—walking at night. He knew all these gentle streets and the sheltering grace of sycamores whose leaves the light from the street lamps turned pale olive.

He would walk these streets each night, and he would end on the Promenade.

VII

The hall clock chimed one as he came in. He couldn't tell Sally and Joan about the boy. Not because they were Americans. Not because he feared they might laugh at his wish to be someone else. But rather, because for all their careful interest, they wouldn't see he must be taken literally.

He had been enticed toward the shoes and scalp and skeleton and purposes and quirks of another man. He had for a few moments with the boy glimpsed his own odd willingness to be taken for someone else. And now he was living through a strange disappointment—that the identification had been wrong. (He knew he was letting a truth about himself hide in the fat of random thoughts. When he came right down to it, his thinking was mostly just a procession of separate parentheses.)

He wished David would drop in. But it was probably too late. What had David said on the phone tonight? St. John hadn't listened. Something about leaving the Heights, shaking the dust—going away if only to feel badly that he'd left.

Two years ago—it was late August and the St. Johns had just got home from England—he had told David his strange sensation about London—a pang, but a pang of indifference. It had been one evening here in this house—Sally at the movies with Monica, Joan doing something in her room. David had seemed to listen to St. John, and then had replied in that wordy, detached way of his. What had he said? "Seeing a person or place after many years, we're saddened if there's been a great change; yet if there *hasn't* been a change, we're also saddened. And the second sorrow is sharper than the first, for the unchanged takes us back the more surely."

Ten years from now maybe David wouldn't be so fluent.

St. John made himself a cup of instant coffee and went into the living room. Over the river in southern Manhattan, scattered oblongs of light marked the night labors of charwomen.

Where was the new Simenon translation he'd bought? There was a phrase in another Simenon somewhere that he wanted to find. He recalled its wisdom but not its point.

32

That book was in the shop—on sale—on the sale table from which David had pinched the green paperback. The Simenon was at the end of the table nearest his desk. *Le Président* —one of the few Simenons St. John had in French—not a mystery story. But what was it Simenon had said?

To go to the shop now, in the middle of the night, would be to risk running into David. Maybe the passage was just some of that fake wisdom Ian Harper had admired so much one day in the shop—some veteran regret smugly Gallic and highly exportable.

But St. John found himself at the front door, then on the steps outside, then in the empty street; found himself walking, walking on a whim, returning over the route he and Walt had taken and then—from the paper store to the bookshop—the route he himself had taken for so many years.

A policeman by a lamppost a block off watched him stop in the shop doorway. St. John had never installed an alarm.

Inside, he switched on his desk lamp. He found the book and fingered quickly through the last pages. He hovered over a phrase here and there, turned back, then again worked toward the end. He was close, very close.

Yes. This. In English it would go something like, "Everything derives from everything. Everything counts. Everything helps. Everything changes. There is no waste."

Well! The idea wasn't as close as he'd recalled. All he'd remembered of it had been what he'd *felt*. The passage had made him feel that his life had made sense. St. John leaned back in his swivel chair.

Had he ever been good at languages? But were those verses so bad he'd given Sally just before their marriage? He'd smuggled them out of the *Franciade*, the epic Ronsard never finished—two silent lovers likened to mutely standing trees.

He wanted those lines back. He wanted a number of things back.

He'd shown David another poem he'd written Sally—well, it was a translation. And David had sniffed out the French original and winced at St. John's phrasing. If only he could get back from David the knowledge of those lines, even the hour when he'd shown them to David. The sestet wasn't bad:

Then one twin life will each for each ensue.
Each in himself and in his dear will live.

33

Allow me, Love, to let my mind fly wild;

I am always sad—I live discreet—
And never can I bring myself content,
Unless I sometimes move outside of me.

And if Sally would give up *her* knowledge of the poem, too! St. John had passed the poem off as his own. He could have added, "After Louise Labé."

The present was like a geographical point surrounded by an expanding past. (He should write that down.)

A library of intentions stood around him. To translate the *Genealogies,* collect Ackerman, maybe be a linguist, go to university, really know something.

For one whole month at Highgate School he had skipped his French lessons. He'd been crazy about Italian, amazed at how easily he could read it. With no grammar he'd started on Leopardi. So in this immensity my thoughts drown and shipwreck is sweet to me in this sea. His French had suffered; he'd failed a test. Dry and dubious, his master had told him Italian grammar was harder than it looked; and after class the man had made him read some Dante aloud, and had then pointed out to Peter St. John that he hadn't the faintest idea of closed *o* and open *o.*

And what had made him squander half the night before one of his last history exams reading a book that was utterly irrelevant? That Victorian vicar's *Journal of Summer Time in the Country.* Willmott. A civilized man in the depths of Berkshire alone in his garden at night reading the Psalms by the "cool, green radiance" of glowworms—inching six of the most luminous down the page from verse to verse.

After his matric St. John had been enough of an English boy to accept the finality of failure. If you didn't make a university, you did something else. Yet he thought now that even then—trapped by his father's embarrassment—he had in some vague way disbelieved that failure. He had always understood that one day he would enter some distinguished life.

Linguist? Historian? What about a linguistic history of Brooklyn Heights? But did a man ever *really* want what he wasn't up to? When a man wanted that, wasn't he really wanting a false version of the real thing?

Two-fifteen. Sally and Joan comfortably asleep.

34

In Cromwell Avenue, three thousand miles east of here—exactly east?—his father would be at the kitchen table staring out the window as he sipped his first cup of tea and waited for the *Times* and the *Express*. (Alone, he had no one from whom to hide his secret sinful candies—sweets—hard and mildly melting in his cheek.)

St. John took up the Bouchet *Genealogies* and he saw the dim shape of his reflection on the calf board and he thought that after all he *would* catalog the Bouchet; and feeling that to get rid of the Bouchet would be like making a new start, St. John began to leaf through the fine thick paper, loving the substantial craft with which the gatherings had been brought together, and the masculine delicacy of the separate letters.

And as he heard a rapping on the front window and knew without looking that it was David, he felt the nearness of all the books in this shop—each of them scanned, and judged, and priced, each of them a shadow of his young designs.

the blue address book

"Was it necessary to stick us in such a small stateroom? It couldn't be much smaller." The assistant purser nods absently at David and turns away. His golden hair and his lean red neck are brilliant above his black uniform.

Returning to the counter he smiles at David: "Yes, as a matter of fact you and your wife indeed have the smallest stateroom in tourist class." The official precision of the last phrase makes a discomfort an affront.

"We reserved months ago. The steam pipes with those insulation jackets come just about to my nose when I'm lying in the upper berth."

The man shrugs—David feels they are all out at sea. "Perhaps you should not sleep in the upper berth."

David is appalled to find himself smiling at the man, who is also continuing to smile.

Again in the stateroom he sits down on the edge of the lower bunk and stares at the list of names. The voyage is into its second day—less and less time. Ontogeny recapitulates phylogeny; which was which?

David feels the ship's infinitesimal roll weight one buttock, then the other. What about stabilizers? Which direction is forward?

Here comes the voice and its companion-silence: words are suddenly clear as they pass David and Ellen's stateroom: "We couldn't find *scène à faire* in my German-English dictionary and I said, 'Hunt up a German-French dictionary, get the German for *scène à faire*, then—' and he interrupts me—he's always interrupting, slipping in something in the middle of what I'm saying, he's tricky but nice—says, 'What a crazy baby you are, maybe later I can find that German-French—' and I said, 'What do you mean *later?*' and then the steward came knocking with the lisp. . . ."

In the second manuscript David finds the two lines originally last in the first manuscript. But he can't use them in this second memory. He rewrites them in the margin of a random page of manuscript three.

St. John wasn't that alone. After "The Shadow" David knew that more people had to be embraced. Think how many faces move through one of our thoughts.

Which makes David—he and I are working well today—think of another of the origins of the project. One afternoon three years after he'd met St. John, David read some of an essay in a book he'd found in St. John's shop. Halfway through the essay, a large blond man entered—Italian—and started trying to persuade Peter to display Pelagian paperbacks. ("Because your pages are sewn in signatures they don't fall out; your binding doesn't split.") Thus distracted, David returned the essay to its shelf and, saying to himself, "I am a solipsist," left without saying goodbye to St. John.

The whim grew in his heart; the essay was right. The essay on solipsism was the only part of the book he read, and he read only half of the essay before, as it were, returning the essay to the book of which it was a part, just as, a second later, he restored the book to its shelf. But whereas he recalled the essay's title—"The Romantic Solipsist"—though not the title of the book, he recalled on the other hand the spot on the shelf where he'd found the book.

On a page of his red hard-cover notebook he wrote, "ESSAY: BOOK equals BOOK: WALDMAN'S."

That day—and later that night (his mother and father playing Scrabble with the Harpers)—the essay's idea seemed so obvious that it appeared to him not as an ingenious inference light years distant from some dim impulsive source but as a seminal fact that had caused all his insights. Of course, of course! The self was the only real object of knowledge, the only thing in fact known.

That night he walked the apartment transported by the idea's embracing rightness. His mother's baby Steinway waited in the living room, but his view of it had so altered it—if the piano in fact existed at all—that it was knowable only as a radiant device built and varnished in his soul; there it was—poised solid, richly brown, its music stand holding tilted a Bartok violin sonata his mother had endlessly played all afternoon, the empty, olive-tinted porcelain vase always on the asymmetrical octagonal piece of brown-and-gold brocaded silk from Hong Kong, where a cousin and her husband had lived for twenty-six years (till the early forties), he with Standard Oil, she writing letters in which she told her lost American friends and family the slow, limited histories of her numerous Chinese servants. David knew the latter only through tales this cousin now told twice a year at family dinners—continuously smoking, too phlegmatic to seem snooty, too amusing to be really boring in her nasal and protracted elegies. The piano and the brocaded silk—the vase Chinese, too—objects, David now thought, only in that they were origins of the ideas of them David collected. That night he looked at the piano and heard again the Bartok his mother had played that afternoon—working one run till she found the one small trouble (which she then played and played, down a third, thence down a fourth, up a half, repeat, until it had emerged so plain in her mind that she knew how now to hide it in the sharp, sad line of the total lyric).

I could not keep from David the consequences of what he had then prematurely embraced as true. "But where am *I*, if *they* don't exactly exist?" But then, approaching the piano, he found his mother's little blue address book lying on the top three keys, and seeing (so to speak) *in* the book (without touching it) the host of names so many of which he hardly knew, and knowing that his mother in a distracted moment (when?) had put the thing there, and knowing also that the book there on the piano corresponded to nothing already actual in his own self, he had to see that maybe the piano and his mother and his father were real, external objects and his own self merely a place furnished in part by *them*. And then: He heard his father's key in the lock, and moved quickly to the hallway arch, relieved, even happy.

Recalling the essay on solipsism and the short scornful ecstasy of knowing he himself *was*, he *was*, a solipsist, he recalls also the death—the universal, final separation—that came to him from the simple address book on the piano—recalls, too, the silly relief he felt as he watched the front door swing in, and then his momentary horror—horror!—at finding only Julia, only Julia—who called, "What's a seven-

38

letter word beginning with *m* and ending with *y*," and himself stuttering out, " 'Memory,' where's Dad?" and she saying "That's only six; he's having himself a walk on the Promenade," and David saying, " 'Maturity,' then," and she replying gaily, "That's eight, for God's sake."

Here now in the ship's smallest stateroom he recalls waking one day a week after, and wishing he'd read the other half of the essay on solipsism. At Waldman's he found the spot on the shelf where he'd found the book; but he'd forgotten its name; so that, as he thought about the half of the essay that he had read, the essay itself (whose title he knew but whose whereabouts he had lost, since he didn't know the title of the book that contained the essay) seemed a vivid brick in an insubstantial wall; or a deep black detail on a map whose other, surrounding lines are pale and faraway and permanent; or a few jet strokes of gouache laid onto a light pencil sketch. Mrs. Clovis was fond of telling the parable of the two houses, but she always got them mixed up— the castle on rock, the castle on sand—"One day a thunderquake shakes the rock and it crumbles; now *that's* a lesson." Though he never found the essay—well, didn't really look for it beyond asking St. John a question or two—the idea of solipsism helped to push him on into the project—to find out through actual projection if solipsism made sense.

Of course, once he started the project, he found local, proximate causes changing and changing his mind.

After "The Shadow" David had to project himself into a community. In his red hard-cover notebook he wrote, "TO DEFINE ONE PERSON BY PROJECTING ONESELF INTO A COMMUNITY OF PEOPLE SURROUNDING THAT PERSON." A community. For St. John wasn't so alone as "The Shadow" implied. Yet solipsism said one *was* alone. Anyway, David's self-projection into St. John's mind should have touched the daughter and the wife, and so many others who were part of his life—St. John's life. Yet David found data forming too plain a pattern: Joan, who had laughed Peter out of doing calisthenics; Joan making him wince when she innocently called him a real authority on crime stories; Sally, in the shop one day, telling that professor that Peter was a scholar and was translating Bouchet's *Genealogies*, and was a poet, too— she misquoted Peter's free rendering of the Labé; Hugh St.

John, querulously threatening that his diabetes would, as the doctor worried, lead to blindness and that when Peter at last came to see him again, he wouldn't be able to see Peter; St. John himself, one day speaking of Valentine Dyall and "The Man in Black" (broadcast all through the War), BBC's parallel to "The Shadow." "The Shadow," Lamont Cranston, wealthy young man-about-town, had brought home from the Orient a hypnotic power to cloud men's minds and thus be invisible. (What if your victims couldn't break out of it? They were OK, but where were *you?* Invisible! At the age of nine or ten David asked his father about the problem, and his father said, "He'd be a pretty lucky man . . . some of the time.") St. John was curious about Lamont Cranston, and though David could not include this in the memory, Lamont Cranston and Peter St. John suddenly began to walk around his mind. "Our old promises cast long shadows." Quote unquote Delacroix. David had to take out details that made the memory too schematic. Perhaps: impose *dis*order on one's memories.

The first time David and Ellen went out—that gray June—they sat in the garden behind that Hampstead pub and looked up at the outside plumbing crawling all over the brick wall, and David spoke knowingly of Valentine Dyall. And then Ellen kissed him.

She mustn't get away. On a ship you can't. But where is she? David turns in his chair and looks at the bunk. He sees, not me—for he can't—but Ellen's fresh clippings. That wasn't her own *Elle* she was cutting up yesterday; that was the ship's; her own *Elle* is on the closet shelf under a line-up of four pairs of shoes; these clippings are out of the ship's *Elle*. And then today she sneaked *Grazia* out of the library and started in on that. The steward mustn't see. David tucks the glossy clippings under Ellen's pillow, then looks out into the passage, left . . . right. . . .

Suddenly the thirteen- or fourteen-year-old boys are on him: "I think the man's a queer, he's always coming up telling about smuggling, and his hair looks dyed." "Yeah, but he's interesting." "Yeah." "Um-hum."

The man caught David and Ellen as they came out of second-sitting breakfast this second morning. "Well, isn't this a surprise!" To David the accent sounded a little Irish and just a tiny bit German today—like Colonel Abel's. The man wanted to do some serious walking with David and Ellen, and David said he had his manuscripts to see to, and Ellen challenged the man to chess, and the man no doubt quelled his irritation with the thought that the game would keep him in touch. What a nuisance!

Left . . . right . . . left: A woman comes out of a side passage, quickly crosses the main passage with her little boy, and takes him into the Ladies.

Left . . . right: The great bulking zoologist now breaks forth from his room by the men's toilet, swaying, embracing his jar. He pushes the toilet door open, stands with a foot on the threshold; but he isn't going in; he's looking ahead, but not as if at something distant; and David knows the zoologist is aware of being watched; very slowly the blond zoologist moves his head around toward David.

David pulls in.

David forces himself to sit at the stateroom table. With ceremonial apprehensiveness he slowly opens the East Lite Box-File, then raises the Lockspring.

In London the old man—or so David thinks—is waiting for the manuscripts.

The two lines of dialogue originally ending the first manuscript and yesterday removed to a random margin of the second, David now removes to the top margin of the first page of the third.

From the second manuscript he deletes "badge" and "cf." Another word or two or three resist, then pop out. David deletes "hi," deletes (sadly) "KLM."

II

A CABINET OF COINS

Mary Clovis

KODAK Hotel's not what it was; neither is the neighborhood, what with the Puerto Ricans. When I sit on my bench on the island in the middle of the Broadway-One Hundred and Tenth Street crossing and read my *Tribune* and try to get a little sun, I never know who's going to come sit down beside me. Ever since I lost my husband seven years ago I've taken care who I have anything to do with. 'T isn't easy for a lady my age. But more than the Puerto Ricans, and the Columbia students starting arguments all hours ouside the West End Bar, I'm sorry how Kodak Hotel's changed.

Call it a rooming house if you want. And I guess that's all it is now. But seven years ago you knew you were respected, you saw that people in the elevator were nice people, and even though the grand old apartments on the twelve floors of Kodak are broken into separate rooms, you felt you could leave a half-dozen large brown eggs in the community icebox and not miss two or three next morning. You could go to the bathroom and not find the sink stuck over with black bristles. Folks kept their radios down and you didn't wake in the middle of the night to hear someone in the kitchen yelling about Russia or . . . what was it? . . . Liechtenstein. Yes, and you didn't feel when you met someone in the hall just as you were opening your door that they wanted to look in your room to see how you'd fixed everything up.

I took Mr. Pennitt for a gentleman. Paid his rent each week at the office on the first floor, went to work at the hotel downtown where he's a bell-man. (Not a bellhop, a bell-man —as Mr. P. explains, a bell-man doesn't run around with valises, he stays in the lobby and often stands by the elevators.) Course I knew he overindulged in alcohol and didn't attend religious services, and now and then didn't get to his

42

job—you can't help knowing. But the main thing, he was courteous and tidy.

"Evening, Mrs. Clovis," he'd say, and burst out coughing—smoked terribly—and he'd mash his corned-beef hash into his little oven-proof casserole, seal it with wax paper and a rubber band, put it on his shelf of the icebox, and go back to his room.

He has Room Three by the bath, but his days may be numbered. I was—still am—in Number One right by the kitchen. In Room Two, on my left and just by the main door, was a nurse who worked at St. Luke's Hospital on Amsterdam Avenue. After her we had, until a year ago, another nurse. Down the hall it went: bathroom, Mr. Pennitt (Three), then in Four, Five, and Six three older women—secretaries—quiet as shadows. I scarcely saw them to say hello. They knew my times for using the bathroom, and I knew theirs. We were all private.

The changes seemed to begin with Terri, the new maid. Over one week she'll do two floors in the building. A very nice colored type. I wouldn't tell the management, but the truth is she never gives an honest clean, never gets the corners. I tell her just what I wish done in *my* room, so at least she does something for me. I've only had one thing against her: For lunch the day she comes she has hamburg fried with mustard, and the stench is something—so penetrating I have to plug the crack under my door—the keyhole, too. With her there's the *feeling* of uncleanliness more than anything you actually see. I *will* say she let me into most of the rooms one day to leave White Tower Daily Prayer Brochures; I hope to distribute Holy Bibles, too. (Mr. Pennitt won't let Terri touch his room, much less get into it; it's only lately we've guessed why.) Terri—well, she's so casual, the way she calls out *"Good"* morning, standing big and slow in my doorway like a personal acquaintance. Why on earth she goes to Miami every February I'll never know. Her boyfriend, who runs a funeral home in Harlem, sends her down for a month. And I bet he goes with her, though she says she goes alone. As Mr. Pennitt said, "Why does a Negro want to go to Florida? To get a tan?" "Coals to Newcastle," as Mr. P. said.

At first, Mr. P. felt as I did about the new people. "We keep to ourselves, Mrs. Clovis," he said, "and we've been at Kodak long enough to know the score, *n'est-ce pas?*" But then he got to talking with the new people; that was his mistake.

Of course, there was a business about his coin collection, too. One night not long ago I found him in the kitchen—his chair tilted, shoulders up against the wall, elbow on the table. He'd made a cup of Instant Sanka; been tippling in his room, I could smell it. And he'd been talking to himself; I'd thought he was with someone—David Brooke or that loon Morganstern—but in case he *was* alone, I rattled my doorknob before I came out. Mr. Pennitt didn't rise. His face was a grayish-tan and under that big blue light bulb the blood freckles over his cheeks had gone a goldy color. He looked up at me and said, "Mrs. Clovis, I didn't steal them coins."

"Which coins?" said I.

"The *coins*, the *coins*," he said. "That set of Christian Gobrechts that disappeared from the shop on Forty-fourth Street."

"Christian?" I asked. For how did he expect me to catch the little things he said? The man was tipsy.

"That 1836 silver dollar, and the rest," said Mr. P. "Christian Gobrecht, for Pete's sake, he prepared the dies."

I said, "I'm sure I don't know who that is, I just came in here to get a dish of vanilla ice cream,"

He laughed to himself—in that selfish way slightly inebriated people will do—and tried to sip his Sanka. His hand shook so much he spilled on his fly. (Mr. P. keeps a fine press in his trousers.) Well, he got down a quick sip or two, and it was hot, and he put down his cup and said a filthy word—to himself—and then he went "Heh, heh, heh," and looked at me in a certain way and said, "Mrs. Clovis—*Mary* —do I look like a thief in the night?"

And, not wishing to engage in a conversation with him when he was in that state, I said, quietly, "You're not yourself, Mr. Pennitt."

"Then who the hell am I?" he said. And then, as I left the kitchen, I heard him use that word again—but under his breath as if he was addressing himself.

I wanted to say, "Mr. P., you've changed since you began having to do with the new roomers." But if I'd been so frank with him—and in that condition—I'd have been untrue to my late husband.

A year ago Morganstern—Alonzo Morganstern—took Room Two, next to mine. First I worried about his dash-

44

hound Heinz running up and down our hall scratching his claws and barking—my! but a dash-hound can bark!—so it made me feel a stranger. I soon saw Heinz was nothing compared to his master.

Morganstern has a very big face and untidy red hair low on the forehead and way down wavy behind like Gorgeous George almost. Morganstern's tall and overweight. And his grin and his frown remind me of a nutcase I saw a photo of in the Post Office. But his voice! Always opera, all the operas that ever were. The second he's home in the afternoon that Victrola comes on, and he sings through his nose, German language operas I think, and says he's taking lessons for the fun of it. And he'll stop in the middle of a song, and yank open his door and holler something in German and say, "Sick 'em, Heinz!" and I'll hear that rush of scrabbling as that nasty little dash-hound charges down the hall. If a door's open he may stop and bark, the little rat, as if he thought he was a regular big dog—he *frowns* when he barks—but if a door's not open he'll just skid to a stop at the far end of the hall and turn himself around—if he isn't doing something *else!*—then come racing back, scratching the floor and breathing hard. (They're the most disgusting dog, *I* think. When Mr. Selbstein asked me if everything was all right, I asked him to prohibit animals, but he said, "I'm only the manager." Selbstein's Jewish, of course.)

But the worst thing about Morganstern, he's a Communist —admits it. He drives a foreign roadster, a sport car, and he's a Communist. I told Mr. Selbstein to get the police after him, but Selbstein said, "He pays his rent, he can be a Mongolian idiot." The horrid, horrid things Morganstern said I can hardly bear to repeat. The one time I almost went next door to tell him what I thought was when he shouted things about President Eisenhower. That dear man, such a normal, fine person: I think of him as General Eisenhower. He was too fine to get mixed up in politics. Morganstern called him names—just a name-caller, Morganstern is. But I controlled myself and didn't go next door to tell Morganstern what I thought of him for speaking so about Ike. A person like Morganstern should be shot. I wish I could just call up the precinct and make the police come take him away—with his dash-hound and his foreign car and his Victrola records. I got a look into his room one day when Terri was doing his bed, and he had a statue of a man's head on his dresser, and all over the floors were paint-roller trays with puddles of sticky paint. (He's always redoing his room, but it doesn't amount to much; squalid is what it is. Yes, squalid, that's the word Mr. Clovis would have used, and he had a knack for the right expression.)

Get Mr. Pennitt bickering with Morganstern, I almost expect a homicide. After Mr. P. got mixed up with Morganstern, Mr. P.'s life wasn't peaceful anymore. Once I said, quietly, to Mr. P., "Why not just leave that man alone, he's no good."

But Morganstern has said something to Mr. P. and keeps saying it. (I don't know what because I don't want to know.) And this something Morganstern has said gets under Mr. P.'s skin and he can never leave Morganstern alone. It has to do with the coins.

From the first, young David Brooke (Six) always took pity on Mr. Pennitt and talked to him. Mr. Pennitt brought out photos of when he worked in silent movies—there's one of him in a square-dance scene with white ducks and striped blazer—and David listened to him for hours. And except for Morganstern, who was always *at* Mr. P., David was the only one who got Mr. P. to tell about his coin collection. But I bet David never saw the inside of his room (Number Three).

David Brooke has changed, too. When he moved in, in about seven months ago, he was a quiet one. He studied, and I had him in for ice cream and Scotch shortbread, and he cooked lamb chops and baked potato, and when he went to class mornings he looked like he just stepped out of a band box. Then Morganstern took hold on him and lately David's in there all hours, and he even made so much noise himself one night in Morganstern's that my little Joey broke out singing even though he'd been put to bed under his cage-cover with a little extra snack of water and seed.

Now what do you know but David Brooke's got a girl in his room all hours. In the beginning he'd not have dreamed of it. But Morganstern influenced him.

I have a lovely room, but the apartment's really gone down. Finally I've had to put special signs on my little glass containers on my shelf of the icebox: "PLEASE DO NOT TOUCH —MARY CLOVIS." And do you know what Morganstern did? (I know he did it.) He took off my signs and put on his own, that said: "THERE IS NO SUCH THING AS PRIVATE PROPERTY."

I wish he'd pack and go. But what would we get then? And

anyway there's Room Four vacant. Who will come into Room Four? Why couldn't it stay empty? A blond man looked at it the other day, and Mr. Selbstein kept saying, "It's a real twelve-dollar room." *I* thought the man was more interested in the *rest* of the apartment. From the bathroom, where I was washing one of my surgical stockings, I heard him asking Mr. S. who lived in the other rooms. "Quiet people, respectable people," Mr. S. said, and I came out of the bathroom just after they passed down the hall toward the kitchen. The blond man had on a shiny, crinkled raincoat —he was very tall—and when he turned round to look at me his face seemed like a flash of dusky light in the dark hall. He nodded at me as I passed and I think he smiled, and just as I shut my door he said, "There are in all six rooms, are there not?" and sounded foreign—like a German who'd learned an English accent real well—like one of these double agents on the television. I'm glad he didn't rent Number Four. And anyway I'm sure he would have been happier somewhere else.

It's because of Morganstern that Mr. P. drinks more and more. I hear their voices. Then Mr. P. calls Morganstern a liar; then Morganstern says, "Sick 'em, Heinz," and that dirty dog tears out and barks at Mr. Pennitt, and next thing I know, Mr. P. has followed Morganstern into his room and they're yelling, and Morganstern turns on *Arabella*, and soon after, Mr. P. marches out and goes to *his* room, and an hour later he's muttering around the hall drunk.

Lately I haven't been able to help seeing the rent reminder they slip halfway under Mr. P.'s door in the morning. We all know he's behind on his rent. Someday they'll kick him out.

I stand in my room and look at my little glass animals on the dresser. I have a wallaby, a tigey tiger, a fawn, a giraffe, a weeny bear, and a pussy. I look at them all, and I say to myself, "Why can't people leave others alone?"

Now, in Room Number Five. . . .

James Judah Lafayette

J. J. Lafayette, a man who swings with the punches, as they say. That's me. J. J. Lafayette. "Where'd you get a name like that?" they ask me. "Lamentoff," I answer, "my father changed it to Lafayette." Most of the bums in Bunny's couldn't care less. But this Barnard College girl asks me, "Who ever heard of a Jewish bartender? Jews don't drink." That's what she learns up the street at college. Well, there's only one education a girl needs, and it isn't Homer. What does this Barnard girl bring into Bunny's? Homer's *The Odyssey*. She wants to loan me it. I say to her, "Give it or keep it, all or nothing." Then she tilts her head at me over her Black and White, and she says, "Jimmy, my boy, you have a sharp wit." She don't know I got a one hundred forty IQ. I ask her to tell me the story of *The Odyssey* and she gets all tied up like. "Exile and return," she says; "father and son and wife—symbolic figures." "Tell me the story," I say; "can't you tell the story?" Then she starts again, but some bum up the other end of the bar bangs his glass. When I come back I ask, "What's 'Odyssey' mean?" She looks thoughtful, and like she's trying hard: "Wanderings," she says, "wanderings, a journey."

We close at four, she wants to come home with me. I could have all the college girls I want. Someday I'll marry one and settle down in an apartment on Riverside Drive with a view of the cars on the West Side Highway and the roller coaster across the river in Palisades Park. But I'm on my own, like.

"What you want to live in a rooming house?" my mother says. "It's no life. You want to get married, you're twenty-five." What she really wants is me to live home.

She thinks I keep a harem up there in Kodak Hotel. But I just sleep there. In and out, in and out. Ten A.M. I'm up and out. I'm not back till after work the next morning at four-thirty. Close Bunny's, go down to Bickford's for hash and egg. Look over the regulars—chocolate drops for little boys and old men. The Barnard girl, I kid her along. She follows me to Bickford's, she wants to buy me breakfast. She gets fifty a week for the things she can't charge. But she don't buy *me* breakfast. Then we go back up toward Columbia University. She lives with her parents on the Drive. I say goodnight; she holds out her hand; I go; she comes too; I raise my hand to her; she wants it; I tell her she's ugly; she doesn't believe me but this time she stops like she don't know where to go. Before she knows it I'm into Kodak Hotel and she's just out there on the street.

I don't see much of the creeps who rent the other rooms

48

in my apartment. It's not really an apartment. Like, it's all private rooms with a bathroom and a kitch. Before I go to bed I check the icebox to see what's what. Mrs. Clovis eats a quart of French vanilla every day of her life—she's got purple hair like cotton candy. Luke Pennitt—he's a bum, he's at least sixty-five—he's got one shelf jammed with all these left-overs stuck in glass dishes. (One night I took off all the rubber bands, and I bet the icebox stank the next day.) A couple inches of corn beef hash like somebody's insides; black gravy with fat on top like paraffin over homemade jelly; soup, soup, soup—dishes of it! And all the same color. He buys chicken legs and backs at the cheap market downtown on Ninth Avenue. Then there's Alonzo—get that!—*Alonzo Morganstern*. He cooks on weekends only, when he can get one of his thirty-five-year-old girl friends to come do him a steak. All he keeps in the icebox is Tropicana Orange in a carton. That jerk he's got a sign on his carton that says, "COUNTERREVOLUTIONARIES HELP YOURSELVES." Then there's David Brooke. He comes from a good background, and he studies hard, probably has to. I grant you there are some other things about him. . . . He's always got something different in the icebox: a can of artichoke hearts, Stouffer's Spinach Soufflé, frozen black-eyed peas—plenty of vegetables.

I don't use the icebox, and I don't take other people's stuff. And I don't use the kitchen; after all, I don't want someone to come in and have a look at what I'm cooking. And, personally, I don't use the bathroom in the apartment either.

It's about five A.M., four-thirty, and I've closed Bunny's, had my hash and egg at Bickford's, come back up the street, ditched the Barnard girl, checked the family icebox; and I go on down the hall to my room. It's the next-to-last, Number Five.

I open my door without making a sound. I get undressed. Then: I listen in to Number Six. Sometimes David Brooke is padding up and down the floor, whispering to himself, making some sound he always makes. Sometimes he's talking in his sleep, complaining, calling names—and that's a story by itself. But lately he's talking to his girl friend. Get me, I couldn't care less. But I'm going to hear voices anyway, so I might as well hear them clear.

She's agreeing with him: "Of course you have to help

him, David. He needs someone to be interested in his coins, I suppose."

"No," says David, "it isn't only that. It's on principle, you see. Principle. I want to find out all I can about Old Luke before it's too late. I may leave here; he may die. The coins are all he cares for in the whole world, and I'm participating in his life by getting him to tell me. He's one poor little bastard with one thing in the world—surrounded by people who don't take the trouble to know what he is."

No kidding, that's what David says. He talks for a long time. I'm waiting for interruptions, you know. But there aren't any. David talks and the girl agrees. And then: I'm off. Into the arms of Morphia.

Next night same thing. Only she tries to get David onto personal matters—in other words, onto the bed. But he can't get off the subject of Pennitt, *that bum*. I'm in clean sheets; I left them for Terri to put on. (I never see her, I'm always out.) I'm like slipping down, down into that clean, cool feel of the new sheets, and I'm thinking about that soft dropped egg on the hash, and I'm listening to David and his girl. It's the best feeling in the world. I'm just about to go to sleep—I can either go or not go, one way or the other, it's up to me—and then the girl says something that makes me think I won't go just yet.

"I might have to move out," she says. She lives in another apartment three floors down. "I'm broke and I owe seven weeks' rent," she says.

"Why didn't you tell me?" says David.

"I didn't know you well enough."

There's a long silence. First I figured he's slapped one on her. But then she says, "Do you mind my kissing you?" And he doesn't say anything, and she says, "I couldn't help it."

Then something's making me sleep, and I don't hear nothing else.

The next night—well, it's after four-thirty A.M.—I listen in again. The girl is upset. "Do you actually care about old Pennitt's coins? And do you imagine he cares about you? He just wants someone to listen to him. He probably wants you to pity him and pay his back rent. And something else: He doesn't want you to *really* care about his coins."

"But," says David, "it's *your* back rent we were discussing. Selbstein will kick you out."

"I'd like to make him kick me out. He sits in that office

downstairs chewing peppermint Life Savers and scissoring out pretty pictures of New England from all the calendars he's had mailed to him, and all he wants to have to do with us is done through our mail cubby holes. Leave a letter, a message about a new rule of the building, a rent notice, yes; but when he ought to speak, he's so curt. He won't deal with us directly."

There's a pause; then David says, "He's isolated."

"No!" the girl cries out, "that's not what I mean. You turn it into something. All I mean is . . . I don't know what I mean. I want Selbstein . . . to come . . . to have to come up and *kick* me out."

"Well," says David, "I'm not going to give him the chance. If you need the money *I'll* pay the rent."

The girl starts laughing; then she's a little hysterical, like the hiccups but she don't have the hiccups.

"My hero," she hiccups, I think she may be crying a bit, and giggling. And then I think they're kissing. I must be polite in spite of my curiosity because every night at this point—when it looks like the plot is thickening—something in me sends me to sleep.

And also, I care what David does like I care what that Mrs. Clovis thinks when she looks in the street window of Bunny's in the morning. Or like I care what that Pennitt does with his time. A week ago I'm leaving the place to go down to Bunny's—I've got to shave and have a coffee and my usual English with peanut butter—and Pennitt must be on afternoons or maybe not working, but as I slip out of my room into the hall I see him up the other end bent over by Morganstern's door like he's slipping something under, and when he hears me come up the hall toward the front door—which is just by Morganstern's door—Pennitt straightens up fast and stares at me and says something I can't hear and lets out a little chuckle and sneaks off into the kitchen like he's got some of that nothing soup on the stove. But, see?—I couldn't care less what he's up to. He's a bellboy. At *his* age! Thinks he's going to hit the numbers for ten grand someday. My friend Aranho del Torto runs them in this area and he says Pennitt's played a quarter every weekday for years—never a three-digit, always just number eight. It hit for two-fifty in 1955, but Pennitt keeps playing it, keeps telling my friend del Torto every day, "The big payoff, ten grand, that's what I'm headed for." What's Pennitt want with ten grand? He's too old to go anywhere. In three months he'd drink himself out. You make what you are, you can't figure on luck. And the lucky ones are lucky anyway. I don't mean they got inside information; just that they're somebody already. Like that kid who goes to Columbia—he's got scratch in every pocket, what's he need with money? But he's got a girl in England—Oxford, England—he calls up every week to tell her what numbers to play on the soccer pools. He just fools around, he couldn't care less. Not even if he really hit; and that's English pounds! But he'll win, he's sure to. Pennitt's going to die with "Eight" on his lips. His last word will be eight. Thinks he'll make a mint!

I hear him in the kitchen talking to David Brooke. That's at four-thirty, five, when I get in. And there isn't a more boring man, believe me. Those nights I hear him in the kitchen I don't go check the icebox, I'm not getting involved. I know David gives old Pennitt a fifth of bourbon now and then. Maybe he likes Pennitt's conversation. But how can you listen to that sort of crap. It's all about coins—you might expect that from Pennitt. And I hear David going, "um-hum, um-hum," and when David starts to say something like, "Mr. Pennitt, what is the peculiar attraction of coins to the collector?" the old bum himself will go, "um-hum, um-hum" and then butt in with a long "Weeeeel" and "don't think I'm not in this for the money, the profit—oh, it's nice to know that the Old Testament shekels and talents were probably bars or rings of bullion, not real coins—but don't get the idea I'm not trying to buy cheap and sell dear, I'm reliable, see, I *deal* in coins, I'm no spendthrift fancier, I get behind on the rent because them bastards at the main desk where I work always stab me in the back and so I get docked a dollar here and there and never get the raise I need. Anyway I'm reliable, I'm *in* this coin business, see? I'm no eighteenth-century gentleman who can afford to keep a cabinet of coins for show-off and culture, I'm getting my capital gain all the time. Don't think I care about my 1652 Boston because the silver's beautiful—mind you I wouldn't have a cabinet of oak because the tannic acid would turn the silver coins black —and I don't care about my 1652 Boston because it has "NE" on the obverse and it was the earliest money in the American settlements; I care about how it goes up in value, I'm hard on this matter—don't ever get the idea I'm impractical."

And David, like he's scolding Pennitt, says, "Oh, Mr.

Pennitt I'm sure you do yourself an injustice, I bet you do value the historical associations." But Pennitt's interrupting him again telling about 1616 brass coins struck for the Sommers Islands down banana way—"hog money" they call it because it has a pig on the obverse—always Pennitt says obverse, reverse, this, that, showing off, like.

David's girl knows. Just a week ago I hear her saying, "Why do you give him whiskey? He's a sponge."

David says, "He needs an anesthetic, his life is poor, he barely has money for food and rent, and he likes a little drink, it helps him get out of himself and forget years of being small."

"It just helps him get *into* himself," the girl says—she has a habit of saying crazy things like that.

She's jealous, I know the type. David should play it cooler, he could turn her this way and that like he was dancing with her—but he doesn't know how to win by giving in. Unless he just couldn't care less about winning, maybe that's it. But I don't think he has a plan; you need a plan.

Well, the next night they're onto her rent again. David has given her money to pay it and he is telling her not to give it back, to call it a gift. Well, he's very cool about money, but he's not married to the girl, is he? But anyway she's saying she wishes she could pay it back; David says no it was his pleasure—*there's* a hell of a pleasure!

And then, soft and clear, she says, "I'd like to make a proposal." And laughs a little, but David breaks in and says no objections please, he gave her the cash and that's what he wanted to do. He says he never had a friendship like this with a girl, talking all night, free and easy, and she says, kind of hesitating, "Yes, I'm glad." And it seems to me they're kissing. And then I'm going down, down into an envelope of clean sheet, cool.

And next thing my alarm is jumping and cold spring sun is in the room, and I lie half alive looking at this hunting print the Barnard girl gave me—shiny horses and red coats moving past white fences. And I suddenly remember, and wonder what that proposal was going to be, and if David let her tell it. I don't hear no noise from the next room—David's, I mean, for the other side is empty, Room Four. Stillness in the apartment.

When I'm up and heading down the hall to the door, I see Pennitt—at first I *don't* see him—and he's standing just in the short hall that leads to the kitchen, and watching me. He's probably been poking notes under Morganstern's door, but me—I couldn't care less.

That night—well, it's next morning—I slip into the pad and again hear David and the girl. I've never seen her, but sometimes I see David in the hall and sometimes he'll drink a Budweiser at Bunny's and talk, and he wants to know how long this and where that and whether I like the neighborhood —very good background. Well, this night they're on the rent again, and David says, "Oh screw the rent, I wanted you to have the money, please don't think of paying it back."

Then she says, "Take *me* in payment." Well, I felt for a second that I was going to sleep, but I couldn't help hearing. Well, I been at this so long I know the difference between real silences and those fuzzy ones when something's being whispered or something important's being done. And this one was a real silence.

"What did you say?" David asks. He knows what she said; even I could hear.

She answers in a little different tone of voice, like. "Take *me* in payment."

"I don't understand," says David, and he gets the rest out quickly: "Or if I do understand you then I don't know you, but I know myself and the. . . ." He stops, and she giggles nervously. Nervously? I don't know.

I hear the bedsprings go; she must have sat down. (David's got his three-quarter fixed up like a couch so the room is like a living room rather than a bedroom. Got a big hairy black and white rug like a hide thrown over it. I looked in one morning Terri was cleaning. Terri's the maid; she . . . comes in and . . . she does the rooms.)

Now the bedsprings go again. Is David sitting down or is the girl getting up? Or was it David who sat down in the first place? It's crazy not knowing.

She says, "I upset you, for God's sake, *didn't* I?"

"Well, I upset myself."

"David."

A rustling, a stirring. "This business about the money. . . ."

"Forget the money," she says. Pause.

"No, I was upset because I . . . was nearly willing to take you up on this payment . . . business."

"Darling, take me up. I want you to."

I figured that at this point she's nosing around his face.

54

"You poor kid," he says.

"What are you talking about?"

"Feeling yourself in this position."

"I don't mind."

"I do."

"Why?"

"You don't have to sacrifice yourself because you borrowed or took money from me. What do you think I am?"

"I'm not what you call sacrificing myself." More bedsprings.

In a quiet, masterful voice, David says, "We'll forget about the money."

"I'd already forgotten," says she in a voice I can't quite figure.

"Why did you think I'd want you to prostitute yourself?"

"Christ," she says, "the word doesn't mean anything. I just wanted *you*. The rent's irrelevant."

"Um-hum," goes David.

"Oh this is too much talk for me," she says. "Good night!"

David doesn't say anything. His door opens and her footsteps come into the hall, stop while she closes the door quietly, then pass my door.

As I go off to sleep I wonder if that's the end. Naturally, I hope it isn't.

Of course, the girl was wrong to take the money. She confused things. I can see David's point of view. If you get involved, keep it simple. I'd handle her. In fact, some night I might call her up, maybe even knock on her door. She don't live in this apartment; she's been three flights down. Now there's a thought to go to sleep on.

My mother thinks I keep a harem. I'm better than that. I should live home? And hear my father all the time? Listen, he don't read Yiddish but he's got this book of translations, English. "So the Golden Peacock flew away," he's always saying.

> So the Golden Peacock flew away,
> East, to look for Yesterday.
> Trili-tra-la.
> She flew and flew, till in a hilly track
> She met an old Turk riding a white hack.

It's got no beat. But my father says, "So it's a translation, the beat is different, but you got the feeling, it's a beautiful translation." How does he know, he don't even know Yiddish. But he's always got this book.

> The Golden Peacock flew away,
> West, to look for Yesterday.
> Trili-tra-la.
> She met a woman in deep black clad,
> Who knelt at a grave, grief-stricken, sad.
> The Peacock now had nothing to say. ·
> There was no need to ask her, "Tell me pray . . ."
> This weeping woman at the edge of the way,
> Was the widow of Yesterday.

He should make a loud noise. Let him go back to Lithuania if it's so great.

I shouldn't think that, much less say it. But he's always looking at me and saying slowly, proudly, *"My son!"* and giving out with the poetry.

He don't even have Friday-night candles.

Terri

Well, I was amazed David Brooke—who Mrs. Clovis calls "Mr. Brooke" to me—should run into Franklin like that. Amazed David Brooke'd be *in* that after-hours club up off a Hundred and Forty-fourth street. But Franklin said David was with that Barnard girl, the one that's after Lafayette. What a bare room Lafayette has: hunting print, chair and table, not even a suitcase—"nary a Dicky bird," Franklin would say. Nothing to tell you about Lafayette, 'less you had an idea to *begin* with.

Why, I've hardly seen Lafayette to look at—that one Friday Selbstein requested that I do him a favor and help him out when the fourth-floor maid didn't come and he also asked me to first go in Pennitt's place and see a few things, and it was early (as I was to do a bit of shopping at Georg Jensen's Fifth Avenue for a pair of silver candlesticks Franklin said he absolutely had to have—they'll be mine I hope anyway when Mr. Franklin Benjamin and I do finally marry

—and so it was only just coming on to nine). Because I was curious I knocked at Lafayette's door—next to David Brooke's—and I hear a sheet rustle, then quiet, then a sharp slide in the sheet (I knew he's awake), then I knocked again, and I knew he must be on his elbow wondering—or could he have a girl, I thought—but then there'd have been a whisper. So he said, *"I'll* open it" and I got my passkey into his lock and heard him say, "No, wait" and a scampering cold barefoot on the floor—he hardly got a little rug to go over part of it—then he was pulling just as I was pushing, and then I see there's no girl, just a square fold of sheet (like he wanted to turn it back perfectly square as he got up) and Lafayette himself in a tartan dressing gown with nothing underneath. And I said, "Oh, I *do* know you after all, you the bartender at Bunny's," and he's almost very upset and keeps looking (upset) at the bed—Lafayette's very fresh-faced and tender-skinned with a mole over his upper lip and nice with a crew-cut and his big flapping eyelashes. "Oh," I said, "I was here and just wanted to introduce myself to Mr. Lafayette, who I never see when I come Wednesday," and he don't know what to do except mumble, "I'm usually up and out at ten," and I say, "Well ordinarily I'm not here till after ten, but don't tell Selbstein, though he probably knows," and I go on and then sort of die away because he's nodding quickly but lazily and he's got his shoulder against the edge of the door now and he's very easy, and there's a little way he has—he's jumpy but he's still easy because he was sleeping. He says, *"No . . .* no, no, no I mean, how about . . . I mean no come . . . come, come, come in are you going to do my room?" And I went in but didn't do his room. I felt better than I had felt in a long time and I learned something I'd forgotten, something I knew when my first husband who died so young was alive, something . . . something about waking up in the morning before you're really awake, and a little sunlight, and you're peaceful and kind of tired and kind of lively, it's only then that there's the special time. Only then.

I think I know Jimmy Lafayette a little now, even though after that morning he wasn't there when I arrived—and just as well—and of course I didn't start coming regular at that early hour on my regular day Wednesday—but once or twice or maybe three times I went in Bunny's and Jimmy was working hard and probably that Barnard girl was in his hair

—the one he told me about that funny Friday morning before Christmas.

Yes: The girl David Brooke was with the night Franklin
met him in the after-hours club, she must have known from
Jimmy where the club was, because bartenders know. Franklin said David seem like he and David was already introduced, he came and said hello to Franklin real nice, and
Franklin was much taken with David, and they talked.

"Well, what did you and David talk about?"

"Oh, all about you, darling."

Franklin smiles away at me: "All about *you*, pigeon
tabby cat."

"No, what?" I say with a little complaining in my voice.

But Franklin won't say or don't remember. But he often
ask me about David Brooke and even want to know his girl's
name—not the Barnard girl David's with that night, but the
other one, David's real girl. I only know the name because I
saw a letter on David's table, and course I don't know but
what that may be still a*no*ther girl—though I wouldn't guess
David wastes much time with the girls; he's serious and getting his degree in the post-graduate school. The letter only
said, "Dear Julia, I simply cannot continue coming to that
flat. There is too much separating us; by which I perhaps—
indeed, in a sense, undoubtedly—mean, there is too much
between us. Tell Ann she was sneaky to get me over on the
ruse that you and H. were off at an organ concert at Riverside Church. I have left the Heights. Love, David."

He's put papers all over his walls. He's got even a recipe
called L. P.'s Duck Soup: "Whittle carcass, then break and
stick in pot with celery leaves and ½ cup minced onion and
8 cups cold water. After a while melt some duck fat, slice
livers and heart, and fry. Eventually add to pot. After three
more hours add salt, pepper, ½ cup chopped turnip, 3 table-
spoons barley; eventually, take soup off stove, let cool, later
heat up. NB: Tell L. P. he might add ½ bay leaf and/or one
cup peeled tomatoes, plus, just before serving, a *soupçon*
fresh-grated nutmeg." Who ever heard of all this "eventually?" Well, that's a long soup.

Well, Franklin tells me all; he's a good conversationalist
and I do think he's right to be moral with me till his divorce
is final. Though I get to admiring his narrow trousers custom
made—fifteen inches—and his wrists, so slender—and the
stiff white spreadcollar he wears with his maroon silk shirt,

and great cowey eyes with heavy lashes. I want to touch him —and because he's so moral I put my hand inside his jacket and pretend to be going for his money where it's really his heart I want to feel there moving. And he's not sure what I'm doing and he'll say, "See, that's all a woman wants." So narrow in his pants and so fine a face—he's as light as me. And such a manicure, pearly fingers candysweet.

He tell me to give up Selbstein's, but I tell him I like that extra money.

Mrs. Clovis act like an old countess on the watch, and always fiddling with them silly glass animals and asking me how can I go to Gospel meeting where they play jazz piano for "I'm Gonna Walk, Walk, Walk All Over God's Heav'n." Well, the meetings is broadcast on the radio, that's what I tell Mrs. Clovis.

Who would live in a place like Kodak Hotel? Maybe a student like David Brooke—he's nice, always asking about the other roomers, what are their rooms like and have I ever talked to Mr. Pennitt. And he asks me about Jimmy Lafayette, and I'd wonder what he knew but he asks about *all* the roomers. One room's empty; one day I had to let a man into it, Number Four. Selbstein sent him up, he said; thought he might want to rent it; stayed there for quite a while till I went in to see and he was just standing staring out the window at the chimney on the other building. He didn't take that room. Who'd live in a run-down place like Kodak? The man who was looking at Four had heavy blond hair and one of them portable raincoats you fold up. Nice-looking type. But no doorman downstairs, and Selbstein in his yellow cardigan playing with that stopwatch that tells the day. And worst on David Brooke's floor is Pennitt, who never pays his rent and leaves an Iroquois Hotel card "DO NOT DISTURB" on his door, but I go in there anyway. Not to clean. How can you begin to do a rat's corner like Pennitt's.

That Thursday before Christmas I didn't see nothing but a few bottles and a bottle of Wildroot, and in the closet a big box and a big thing with a handle on it, some old no-good apparatus.

Selbstein kept telling me to look out for things in Pennitt's room, check it for out-of-the-way stuff, he never said what. Then this morning I'm not due to do that floor, but Selbstein says, "Have another look, have a look in his closet," so I do.

Well now I looked closer at the machine on the floor of

his closet. Like a nutcracker, only a huge one. No, not a nut-cracker, maybe a torture machine like what they show in the House of History at Coney Island. Pennitt's thing had a box-frame and a screw-rod coming down the middle, and a holder coming up, and on the tip of the holder was a little thumbnail of metal with some scratching on it. And you turn the screw with a great long metal rod kind of handle on top. That's all.

I told Selbstein, and he said yes, yes, yes, that's what the encyclopedia said.

One day I'll write a book about these people.

Abby Love

First I wanted to be with him, then to touch him, then for him to go all alert when he saw me appear. Then I wanted him to phone me, then to make me laugh, then to be intentionally impolite now and again. Then I began to want to embarrass him. And all this time—right from the start—I wanted him to make love to me.

I loved him; and the word does mean something to me and it doesn't to David, even though he goes out of his way to explain that it's gotten to be a cliché that the word has no meaning.

Why did I have to move toward David so indirectly? I'm sure he never guessed what I was up to. And now that he almost knows, he still hasn't the dimmest idea how like me it was to do as I did.

He thinks I never listened when he lectured me. But of *course* I know what he said. How many times hasn't he stood staring out his window, his back to me, explaining that what he knows about people is, as Rilke says, only what can be inferred from the disturbances they create in certain of his tissues? I know something about tissues! How often hasn't he taken up a book, let it fall open in his hands, then said, "Look, this guy has the very same idea—he wants to penetrate another consciousness but can't."

David thinks I never really saw him. Well: I've seen him bent toward his full-length mirror, tweezing out fuzzy hairs on his cheekbones and muttering, "What am I, some semi-erect primate?" How many nights—until they stopped using the advertisement—didn't I see him stop by Freedom Radio

Center to pose and act, and see himself on the TV that's fed by a camera at the back of the window display? *I* know him. And I loved that long silhouette of his, loved the contentious voice that always seemed to be on the verge of being tired.

And I not only heard and saw him. (I sound as thorough as David!) I also listened *with* him—for he's a listener—David is a certain kind of listener. Listened with him to Luke Pennitt.

David asked almost as many questions as he wanted to—like a radio interviewer who runs off a planned attack disguising his quickness, resisting his hurry—but old Pennitt kept saying what he wanted to say no matter what David asked. My goodness, what's the trouble with David? I want to make him forget, make him ease off, make him. Sometimes he seems *too* interested in Pennitt, too sincere; and always with Pennitt David makes mental and even real notes.

He tried to make Pennitt go chronologically, and would start out, "Now that was in 1924—you'd picked up a 1664 English crown with Charles I on it and a view of Oxford through the horse's legs and you thought you'd collect 'view' coins ... ?"

"No, for Christ's sake, I told you, I paid so much for that crown I didn't have enough cash for a Danzig view that turned up the next week, and I got sick of view coins—that is, most of them, notice, I say *most* of them, heh heh heh!"

"But what *did* you collect, in the end, I'm not clear about—"

"No, in 1929," said Pennitt—

"But," said David, "we were in nineteen—"

"In *1929*," said old Pennitt, "I'd given up animal coins—*there's* a swamp! Everyone's after them. You try to narrow it down; still you can't get a collection that's real special. I sold a South African springbok, a Fiji turtle, even my Saxony hen—mid-evil, y'know—and three Greeks—an Athenian owl, a dove from Sicyon, a turtle from Aegina—'course I'd been thinking of doing only turtle coins—"

"But I fail to see—" David broke through, as old Pennitt broke back, saying, "Then in '31 I was doing plants—Florentine rose tree, there's a pretty one, but the legends on plant coins—"

"Legends," remarked David earnestly.

"Legends? Yes, for Christ's sake, what d'you think I said?

61

Legends, inscriptions; 'course, they're abbreviated on the Greeks but—"

"Abbreviated legends!" David exclaimed, perhaps a little prematurely, imagining he had an idea, pounding his fist into his palm and looking sharply up at the ceiling where the drier displayed a pair of very baggy ski-pajama bottoms Morganstern had left there for a couple of weeks.

David's outbreak made old Pennitt speak kind of quietly—half pleased, half defiant: "Why, yes, yes, naturally." Then he went on, fast and mysterious. "In 1927 I started siege coins—someday I hoped to collect octagonal shillings of Pontefract, y'know."

"Um-hum," said David, "um-hum." And old Pennitt might stand up and stretch, and say, "But that's another story," or "That was before I got my big idea," or "I *started* collecting when I *stopped*—now figure *that* out."

He wouldn't mention rent while I was there. But catching David alone he would moan about how Selbstein was pressing him; and David would give old Pennitt a week's rent now and again, and would tell me how pathetic the old man was.

I can't get out of my head all that meaningless talk—David's with Pennitt—David saying, "Do you use Goddard's silver dip?" and Pennitt answering scornfully, "Never. Two reasons. The hydrogen sulfide gives me a headache and the dip cuts off the local tone." "The tone?" "The patina." "Can you fake it?" "In Sicily they use old coins for blanks, the forgers." "Because of electrolytic analysis?" "What?" "Electrolytic analysis." "How in Christ's name should I know?"

Pennitt would tire of David and give him a little grin and say confidingly, "Maybe you got some bourbon hidden away someplace."

David judged Pennitt too quickly. "Morganstern calls Mr. Pennitt avaricious. Isn't that ironic? Mr. Pennitt pretends he cares most about how his coins increase in value. But the truth is, he loves their solid historical facticity, loves the fact that each is a certain age—"

"*I* know what 'facticity' means," I'd interrupt—

"A certain age, each a concrete past. Each was *there then*."

With David's growing concern about Pennitt, our own trouble waxed.

Morganstern stabs at Pennitt, kids to hurt. His dislike of Pennitt is real, but his expression of it is light—or so *I* think—and he gets after Pennitt, predicting Selbstein's going to rifle Pennitt's room and lock him out for nonpayment of rent, and alleging Pennitt stole coins from a midtown dealer, and arguing terribly calmly that coin collecting is the last capitalist resort of small, stupid men who haven't made it.

Morganstern's dynamic; I must get him to give me a ride in his car someday; he calls it a souped-down Lotus, but David says it isn't a Lotus at all.

I'm not free. Two languages argue in my head: David's with Pennitt: "Henry VIII debased his coinage by adding alloys, didn't he?" "They all did it." "Not *all*, surely." "They did a lot of things. Overstrikes—" "Overstrikes?" "Sure, they stamp the type on a blank that's been used before as a coin. . . ."—versus *mine* with David: "You've added a chart for Room Four, but no one's in there." "As I wake up in the middle of the night and forget what my various charts and timetables for each of the roomers here are intended to arrive at, I say, with the famous Greek poet Fragment, 'I will make nothing better by crying, I will make nothing worse by giving myself what entertainment I can.' " "Oh David"—with apparent gaiety and casualness—"I must say I do love you." "That makes two of us. But in loving myself I'm loving you, too, since my you only exists as part of my mind. Shall we pop round the corner and have some beef and broccoli Cantonese?" "Nothing so fancy," say I, desperate but amused, and add, "Let's go Dutch." And David, preoccupied but (and perhaps because of it) rather dashing, dragging me by the hand toward the door, "I guess I love you, too. That is, when I don't think about it too hard." In such limited honesties David would successfully lose himself.

I, on the other hand, sought limited dishonesties in order to get David—who was my honest objective. Therefore I accepted my own indirectness. He did, of course, kiss me—good kisses, *my* lips, me. But constantly he would try to turn the scene toward his charts, his project—a project I never quite understood. Yet he worried over my rent—and I was glad to see him worry, though I was responsible for a lie. It was part of my plan that he should not merely be drawn into my life but that he should actually *pay* my rent. And, if the plan didn't work at first, pay it a second and a third time. Which he did.

But then he seemed to pass too quickly through the intimacy of paying my rent to a feeling that our status resembled that of cousins married by family arrangement. David's affairs of state—the roomers in that dark, sad, echoing tomb of an apartment—took him from me more and more.

Then I thought to almost reveal myself. Like some wild, wily, melancholy gamin, I offered my . . . my what? . . . as payment for the rent he'd stood me. Not "my body," quite apart from the fact that people don't use that expression that way anymore. Not "myself," because I never wished wholly to be "his." My *warmth*, perhaps—in exchange for his. Frankly he's a bit afraid of women—the closeness, the demand, the exchange of the fib that says, "I am beautiful and you are beautiful and so we make love as long as we possibly can each time—we go into each other." Yet *is* that what happens! God, before I knew David I never asked such exclamations. David isn't really afraid either, though that seems to contradict what I said. In a way he has too much courage to give himself to me.

Pennitt, Pennitt, Pennitt—Mattingly's *Roman Coins*. Yeoman's *Catalogue of Modern World Coins*, Askew's *Coinage of Roman Britain*, Brooke's *English Coins* (the last too technical for David, said Pennitt, who came into David's room only after repeated invitations and looked politely and noddingly at the few coin books David had recently bought).

"I suppose," David said (Monday evening of this week), "Charles I's reign makes one of the most absorbing studies in English numismatics. The Civil War, the king setting up mints where he had strongholds, Shrewsbury and Oxford—"

"Pieces were struck in silver," Pennitt broke in quietly.

"And the Tower mint having been commandeered by Parliament—"

"Oh . . . oh." (Pennitt's voice was startlingly soft, startlingly tired.) "Those Tower pieces are good, y'know. . . . But that Civil War . . . the coinage is so complicated. I worked with it off and on for years. I actually had to give up."

"Ah," from David, amply, comprehendingly, "why, in *fact?*"

"Too much," Pennitt muttered, and turned to leave the kitchen. "Just too much to deal with." But he wheeled about and seemed to have regained his spirit, and said, "But his father James had some good things—you'll always hear James' reign's dull for coins, but there're the silver pieces from 1604 have that legend *'Quae Deus Coniunxit Nemo Separet,'* Scotland and England, y'know. And for a while I looked round for shillings with his sixth head because they showed a Welsh plume above the shield."

"Um-hum, um-hum," from David, as Pennitt turned away again, tired, muttering, " 'f I had it to do over again I'd . . . ," and headed for his room. But he came back to the refrigerator, opened it, looked, closed it, then scuffed off.

Why did I then suddenly think of how fast David did things—how fantastically quickly he coordinated his performance at the stove when he was currying some kidneys and boiling rice and boiling black-eyed peas—or how fast he'd pull off his sweater, scratching it up his back, neatly skinning himself out of it, as if it had to be done rapidly because he had other, more important things to do?

He studies the charts and timetables on his wall: "MARY CLOVIS—sixty-seven; husband, compositor, deceased; prize possessions: seven glass animals; a strange brown mongrel bird called Joey; a one-hundred-twenty-five-piece set of old Danish breakfast crockery; a mid-Victorian Gossip chair (ca. 1860) (for nursing?) reupholstered soiled cherry, good example, according to Mr. Aranho del Torto, dealer (Broadway and—or, in actual fact, *near*—Seventy-first Street); an electric blanket, dark blue; a framed commendation from the acting executive secretary of the White Tower Gospel Society; a majolica doll of (according to the label) Martha Washington; two old, rather coprolitic bullets (mounted on a little block of pine) reputedly from the Battle of Gettysburg; a framed, blown-up copy of Wyeth's portrait of Eisenhower for *Time*," and so forth.

"Timetable of ABBY LOVE: Tuesdays and Fridays (except for vacations), New York School of Social Work; Mondays, Wednesdays, and Thursdays, field work at Jewish Guild for the Blind; for example, Friday: rise at eight, brew and drink a cup of Indian tea (Queen Anne's or English Breakfast, sent by Mr. Hugh St. John from Twining's in London), dress, brush teeth, neglect to wash face, stare at Selbstein downstairs, attend two lectures, study Italian word-list over lunch, rendezvous in Riverside Park with two favorite Schnauzers (small, dove-gray), attend seminar at N. Y. S. S. W., return to Kodak for afternoon coffee with D. Brooke (accompanied by chicken livers on toast or a very small, delicately soft jelly omelet done in her pseudo-early-American blue-and-

65

white enamel omelet pan), retire to room to read, take two or three neat whiskies at eight, join D. Brooke for dinner, retire for further study, join D. Brooke at midnight, walk to Canal Street (two hours), return by subway (two or three different lines if possible)"—and so forth. Can you make anything out of that? Same for the others, including Selbstein and Terri. Hearing that a young art student named Boswell Benson (who was a friend of Josie Wrenn, daughter of David's mother's cousin and wife) had taken a room on the floor below and wanted to meet David and say hello, David said, "One story trying to tell itself into another story."

Wednesday David and I had an enormous argument about political arguments, and then I told him I wanted to pay him back for the rent he paid for me, and we had a fight and I made him an IOU and I left. Thursday I didn't see him.

Alonzo Morganstern

I tell David Brooke that before I was a draftsman I had eighteen pro fights in the L. A. area. And he doesn't know what to say. I give Brooke all the openings—he can call me a fake, a jerk, a nut, a Red, a latent queer, a "patent fool" (what he called Boswell Benson), anything—but Brooke doesn't know what to say, he frowns and looks down at my second-hand oriental rug, and thinks he's trying to understand me. But he's so knotted up inside—outside, too! For I sense a ridge of rigid muscle around the base of his neck, he ought to dig it out and loosen up—so knotted that he can't keep a reasonably intellectual conversation under way. I press at him: "What do *you* know about Liechtenstein, Brooke? What do you know about the Marxist theory of money value?" And then he strains out a few words. He says, "Inheritance is the key; under communism you can't leave your son anything you've earned. You are what you are, and he is what he is. He can't depend on what *you* were. I mean. . . ." Then stops, glances at me, then away—like his mind is too sharp and full and his hesitation is my fault. Inheritance tax, that's what Brooke thinks Marxism is. Then he asks, "Which ought I to buy, an Olympia or a Hermes? I desire optimum lightness."

Let me tell you: I want to hear doors rattling open and

shoes marching around the hall, the icebox clicking shut, and me singing. I want to walk into our kitchen and challenge somebody and get answered back. But they look at me and smile and look away. I want them to say, "Look here, Morganstern, to what inadequacy in yourself do you ascribe your desire to attack me?" But how often do I get an answer back? *That's* what I *want!*

Not this Observing Others' Rights. That's just the little dodge to hide the big fear.

I think of Mary—she can't take it when I call her Mary—Mrs. Clovis in bed with flu: I just opened her door and looked in while her doctor was there, and she didn't even scream like a real person—she pursed her lips and then gasped. The covers were down; the doctor said, "Shut that door!" The big fear: Mary Clovis—with her round square sick-healthy rosy face that belongs in a Florida retirement commune—in bed with flu and being felt by the doctor, who has to press her abdomen to see if she has pain. What she feels then is what rules most people—most of the people in this apartment. They don't want to feel the touch. *That's* it!

Now I'm not going to say I'm only *kidding* Pennitt about his coin collection. Because there *is* something wrong with that hobby. But I don't mean all I say.

So he collects coins! That's pretty good. All right. But why the secrecy? Why *hide* the coins? I know why. They've got so close to Pennitt he's afraid showing them will be like showing himself—the little brown, stale secrets he's packed into that cell of his. I don't need that out-of-shape Columbia professor at the General Studies night class to tell me the psychoanalytic age has shown us we must force the secrets out.

No secrets. Open. Give. Manifest. Laugh at yourself. Laugh at thyself.

Hide-a-bed: That is one answer of the counterrevs, hide-a-this, hide-a-that, hide-away. But neither private property nor private horrors will be allowed in the world I plan. All will be. . . . Why, I've said this in California. (Actually I never had those nineteen fights, I said it just to coax David Brooke to come on after me.) I've said this in undertones to chance seatmates at the National Symphony in Baltimore; I've said this to a Texas state cop at Amarillo Airport, asking him why he really wanted those brims and that revolver —why uniforms? And I've said this to those long, nasty, small-assed, wonderful chicken farmers in overalls in down-state New Hampshire. (David ought to go to that country; he's not ready for the city yet, and the funny thing is he can't know this because he's lived all his helpless life here.) When you start admitting and stop hiding, then you ease up. So what if a psychotherapist has to help you—who cares how it gets done; but it must be done. I know.

My wife—and she did it to my three children, too—she was an early worm drawing that line beyond which you couldn't talk—or trying to draw the line. She'd say early in the morning as I was combing my hair or eating some fried eggs or getting off to my office in L. A., "Join one of these groups like A. D. A. but don't please be a Communist. You don't believe in it and it's dangerous."

I'd answer, "When I work on the guys in the office I'm not competing, I'm just living, doing something useful, stirring up a little ferment here and there, not worrying about getting ahead, just about why people say things to me and why I do or don't get a raise. The *why*, not the money itself. Because that's not the point as long as you have something to live on. And this is what ought to be—interplay in the office, a tussle, a little jet of hatred, *real* nastiness—but: publicity and humor."

My wife—she *was* my wife—would say, "You should have got all this out of your system at college, but of course you had to be original and not go to college."

"I wasn't being original," I answer (being open with her), "I was in the war, drawing submarines all day and night, and when I got out I wanted to just work and live and have a little interplay." My wife went to Mills College where she majored in music appreciation you might think. She married me partly because I didn't go to college; and she divorced me partly for the same reason—consistent. I had records of my tests and she saw them in my desk and got some creative idea from them—IQ tests, analysts' letters, grades from night school. There were reasons we broke, and I'm not afraid of them.

I'm always having to vacate places like Kodak Hotel. I been in five or ten of them up and down the nation. Well, *I'm* ready for the hasty, shitty little looks people give you down the hall, the shadowy hall, I'm ready to make something of all the energy there is in those looks, to draw everyone together; but I usually—I mean always—miss. Of course,

I meet good people. But something always comes up; someone is mad and moves to another apartment or rooming house; or someone moves in and upsets the equilibrium I've set up; or one person—a silent soldier wearing the stripes and chevrons the world gives you—spoils all the fellowship and interplay and gas the rest of us have worked up.

Heinz has been traveling with me for seven years now, sitting in the right bucket seat. I'll look over at him as we drive along, but he'll never give you that tilt-headed, raised-nose look of affection dogs give, he'll know I'm looking at him but he'll keep his eye on the road.

I'm always having to leave places. But here at Kodak I think we've worked something up. Seven months I've been here, and something's happening, at least with Brooke and Pennitt; and one of these days it'll happen with the old woman next door, the evangelist Clovis. (Husband had hardly any insurance; I like that.) I aim for a community. If Pennitt thinks I'm after him, well I am, but not in the way he thinks. So last month I heard of a theft of coins from somewhere midtown; I checked facts and began to talk about it around Pennitt, mentioning the theft, asking him if he had any Gobrechts. Said he didn't have a one; then admitted he once had had a couple; it's odd what you find out. Then I began to ask him what he thought, etc., and wasn't he at the Iroquois Hotel as a bellhop, Forty-fourth between Sixth and Fifth; and he might have had an eye on those coins for a long time, etc., etc., I needn't go into details. To my surprise he took me seriously and we've been having some problems; the hassle has been one of the better ones—complicated interplay—but Pennitt's drinking more than usual because of me, so last week—and actually last night, Tuesday—I got the talk into other fields.

What friends did he have, was he ever married, did he have a family, did he feel the world close to him? We got onto my philosophy of touching and, because he can't keep off his own subject, he said, "Touch? Well, I once came across a real honest-to-God touchpiece, a gold angel with a hole in it."

"So what?" I said.

"What do you mean, 'so what'? The king gave 'em out, gave them angels out when he touched sick people. Know what they were sick of?"

"VD," said I.

"Scrofula," says Pennitt. "The King's Evil. Divine Right of Kings, y'know."

"Scrofula's the same as VD," I said.

"No it isn't," said Pennitt.

"Yes it is," said I.

"Nope," said he.

"Yes," I said.

He takes me seriously. (Well, *that's* all right!) He knows his coins, I'll give him that. But I won't ease up on him.

"You pinch your coins and pet them to make them grow. You keep them in corners and touch them and hope they multiply, but there won't be any real multiplication in your life." (This is consistent with my philosophy of touching.)

Pennitt spits a lot of names at me. "What would you know about Visigothic trientes and French deniers and siege coins, hey? What do you know about anything? You never went to college and now you cut your classes at Columbia night school. *I* pinch coins?! *I* collect coins for money? Ha!" (He thinks he likes the sound, so he makes it again.) "Ha! In it for money my ass. That's what you know." Then his voice goes quiet, as if he thinks he's some kind of Shylock plotting in his underground office—*The Merchant of Venice,* Shakespeare wrote it before 1600—"No, not for money. . . ." (Gets up and has a look at the stove, where he's been boiling a soup all day—back and forth in and out of his room all day boiling duck soup out of bones he got from the hotel where he's a bellhop.) "No," he says, as if to himself, "not for money; but there's a secret about my collection and you'll never know it. I was going to tell you, but I've just decided not to."

"I'll get into that pack-rat room of yours someday, and I'll dig out your black money. You probably got it stuffed into your mattress."

He's screaming, suddenly he's screaming: "Mattress my ass! Keep my coins in a mattress! I got a *fifty-year-old cabinet!* You don't *buy* them today! You're a fraud, Morganstern, that's exactly what you happen to be!" (Fraud is a word he heard Brooke use.) "A fraud. And a Communist, a Commie!" He's shouting over his shoulder at me as he goes out.

I follow into the hall. He says, "I doubt if you're even a Communist. What meetings you go to? What organization you belong to? I bet you haven't got guts to be a Communist."

Mary Clovis's door opens behind me, and she says, "*Really*, Mr. Pennitt!"

Pennitt goes into his room, I hear him bustling around in there. I go into my room, leaving my door open as always. Heinz is lying on the bed watching. He'll get after Pennitt if I tell him to, but I know Heinz doesn't want to move. It's Saturday. I put on *Arabella*, the big soprano-contralto duet—"hanh hanh hanh hahhhhnh hanh hanh hanh hanh hanh hahhhhnh"—and I watch the hall. Brooke's door's opening at the end. But now I hear hissing—"Whish, whish, whish"—in the kitchen: Pennitt's soup. His door opens; I know he's standing there listening.

"Godammit!" he yaps not very loud. Then louder, "Godammit, my soup!"

"Your soup," I say.

Then he's running for the kitchen; he passes my door, slippers slapping. "Go*damm*it!" Then, from the kitchen that "whish" has turned into a "kaaaaaaaaa."

I follow him in; there's a frothy bubble overflowing the rim of the pot. "Kaaaaaaaa." The soup's mostly boiled over. Pennitt's been making that most of the day. Now it's boiled over. There's not much left.

Isn't it funny? Of course it's funny. "Why don't you plan things better?" I say. Pennitt's always saying he don't need a recipe, he plays it by ear.

Now he keeps his back to me, like he's protecting the remains of that duck soup. Doesn't even turn the burner down. "Shut that music off," he says. His back is to me, his long asinine ears hanging down, lobes purple.

Well it's his fault: he eats, drinks, and sleeps coins.

Thursday I was home early—pains. I had a Pan—so Brooke asks, "Pan? Pan?" I expect him to say, "That's the Polish for 'Mister': I said to him, "Pan African, Pan Am, *all*, the works"; pan-vasectomy is the "Pan" *I* had, because if you get your tubes tied off you can always untie them some other time, but I was committing myself to no more kids, so I had a pan-vasectomy done. Does it screw my love life? Not an ounce! It's true I don't like Pennitt keeping his door always closed, but also I don't like what I saw Thursday afternoon. It wasn't her day to clean, but I saw Terri just stepping over Pennitt's threshold into the hall. She saw I saw and she was going to speak but I shut my door on her. I wondered, "Should I tell Pennitt when he comes in?" I know he's owing

71

back rent; I heard him scoff at Selbstein, "Ah, who's going to know the difference in a thousand years?" And Selbstein was so surprised he didn't answer. So naturally, now—Thursday—I wondered about Terri. She wasn't even dressed for cleaning. I opened my door again. No Terri. I was about to take a shot at Pennitt's door with a coathanger. Then Brooke's door opened at the far end of the hall, and after we looked at each other for a couple of seconds we got talking and I forgot about Terri. Brooke came into my room. When I opened my briefcase he as usual got up quickly to come look into it.

Friday—this morning—David was tenser than usual, messier. And when I met him in the hall he cocked an eyebrow at me for a good morning. Then we had a little quick interplay about who'd press the button in the elevator, and Heinz gnawed at David's loafer and grumbled. On the way down David said to me, "Ever lend money to girls?"

"Brooke," I said—and I saw him ready to shy—"I never feel there's any continuity with you from one conversation to another. Yesterday afternoon in the hall we discussed your failure to keep to our weight-lifting plan, and I was forced to start calling you Chicken-Neck Brooke. Now you suddenly get onto something totally different. Learn logic. Think it out."

After a pause, and the elevator is passing the second floor, he says, scratching his cheek, "Oh, skip it."

On the way out we stop by the office to check the mail, even though it's too early. That Selbstein, with his kinky, wavy gray hair, can't stand to talk to me. He says to David, with a big sickening wink, "Well, you guys are going to lose your neighbor Pennitt today. I know he drinks and I know a couple of other things, and he talks about how long he lives here and says he knows the score." David's preoccupied with some note he's found in an unstamped envelope, and I'm just staring at Selbstein without saying a thing. Selbstein stops smiling, and suddenly he opens up his red ledger and acts really like some quiet psychotic and says to David, "I'll show him who got the scoreboard." Then he closes the book snap shut and works that grin over his face again and starts to say something but David says, "Yes," and shakes his head.

"I'm sending a man up to change Pennitt's lock. What am I going to do? Nonpayment of weekly rent!"

"Did Miss Love come out this morning?"

"Yeah, she pays her rent always Friday. Never missed a week."

"She pays . . . always?" David's solemn.

"Never missed. Say . . . you and her . . . ?" Selbstein is grinning.

At the outside door I said to David that I forgot the key to my car and Heinz and I went back to the elevator. Selbstein didn't look up when I went by the office.

FRIDAY AFTERNOON, LATE

You don't go *near* my room!

I run this house, you don't tell *me*.

I'll get the cops on you, you lousy bastard, I come home from work, what do I find?

The cop is coming. *I* got him.

Touch a thing in my room. I know the score, I been here eleven years.

You owe eight weeks' rent, seventy-two dollars. What's all the music?

I don't care if I owe seventy-two overstrikes, this is my place.

What's all the music? Turn it down!

Ha! He turned it up, Ha ha!

I'll get *him* out of here, too, that goddam Communist from California.

Get away from my door.

OK. *You* open it. *You* open it.

Not with you on my neck, you crum.

That music, turn it . . . !

Sick' em, Heinz!

Get 'em out of here, get 'em out of here, hey!—

Kick my dog!

Turn off the music!

Wait. I *will* turn it off! Here Heinz!

Go on, Pennitt, *try* your door.

And let *you* in?

No, come here, Heinz. All right, what's your problem, Selbstein?

I run this house.

You're lucky you didn't kick Heinz.

That piece of shit.

I had eighteen fights in L. A., I could smash you.

Look, he can't open his door, he can't open his door. What's the matter, Pennitt, bent your key?

You did something to my lock, you Jewish bastard, bastards every one.

I called the cop. He's going to have a look in your room.

You don't touch his room, Selbstein.

Nobody's going to touch my room!

Including *you*, you little crook. I know all about you. I got my information. I know what you're doing in there all these years. I know all about your coins. You little drunk, I know what to do with you.

What work do you do, you parasite? You take Pennitt's rent, you read seven newspapers a day, you drink cream soda and cut your calendar pictures, what are you Selbstein, you're a landlord, what right have you to take Pennitt's money when all you do is sit downstairs.

Comes the revolution, eh?

You're on the list, Selbstein, you're on the list. *You'll* go. You'll go first.

What's happened to my lock? My stuff's in there, everything I got. Let me in there.

Let him in, Selbstein, I'm telling you.

Mercy, what's going on here? Can't a lady be private? Mr. Selbstein, you must do something to keep the noise down.

Sick 'er, Heinz. No! OK, Heinz, come here.

That dirty, dirty little animal.

You'd walk a dog and when he stops look away like you think what he's doing is sick. They ought to curb *people!* Goodie poodie baby what's the too-doo boo-boo Heinzie Weinzie poodie poodle honey uzza Heinzie.

Dirty, dirty dog.

My lock! I swear I'll get the cops.

Police, trouble, reckless dogs, foul language—what's *become* of Kodak Hotel, Mr. Selbstein?

What am I going to do, I'm trying to get this bum out of here. You don't want someone living here not paying his rent.

Well, that's perfectly true, people should pay their rent promptly.

Oh God, Abby, we can't talk here.

I didn't really want to, you made me come.

Tell him, David! Tell him all the years I spent on my

74

coins. Tell him, he's going to take my room, I can't get in.

Selbstein?

Mr. Selbstein, my goodness, please—

Selbstein get out of here or I'll smash—

Abby, don't go, we're needed here, can't you—?

I know all about his coins, I called the cop.

You know all about squat.

I know you got a machine that *makes* coins. *Makes* coins, he *makes* coins.

Isn't that the limit, I always thought there was something strange—

Mary, I thought you were my friend.

Mr. Selbstein, let me just offer a word here, I've talked with Mr. Pennitt many times, and I know he's devoted to his coins, he's a real historian, and I want to help out if I can.

Seventy-two dollars he owes.

David, you're a booby, an absolute booby. And I'm going.

Brooke, you look at this rotten landlord and that's your solution. Go back to Columbia, Pennitt doesn't want your charity, you don't want to get in *touch* with people; you ward off, that's all you do—

Morganstern I've heard you for seven months and I think you're an unmitigated fraud. You say you take singing lessons and had nineteen fights in L. A. and belong to the Communist Party—

I never once said I *belonged*—

—and have this so-called philosophy of touching and tell us to get analyzed. But you can't sing and you're soft in the midsection and you don't really know Communism, I mean its significance, and you say "Where is Liechtenstein?" as if that—

Darling it's about time you talked like that to somebody—

And you're one big fraud, as far as I can see—what do you mean it's time I talked like this? Why should I *have* to talk like this to anyone?

Here! Officer!

You Selbstein?

The manager.

Which room?

This—

He changed my lock, my stuff—

Brooke, I'll bust you.

So what is it I'm going to find? I don't go into somebody's room just to—

Since when is this counterrevolutionary government considerate of anyone's home?

What is he, some kind of nut? Who's got the key?

Don't you touch my door—

You tell him, Pennitt—

Stop it, my stuff—

The maid told me all about what's in here.

Morganstern you said I stole them Gobrechts.

I never—

Well, my land, *I never!*

All right, then, Pennitt, you take care of *yourself* if I told about the Gobrechts.

No, Morganstern, Alonzo, don't go away, Jesus.

Open up, Selbstein.

That horrid Morganstern's turned his music on. It's just the limit.

My stuff—

OK, officer, I happen to know what we want's right in here.

There's nothing in my room, nothing at all. . . . You got no right . . . . No right even . . . looking.

Mercy, what a mess, Mr. P.

David, let's go to your room, these people have nothing to do with you.

What a mortal mess, and the stench!

All right, so he's got a machine that makes coins, but where is it, I'm on duty—Where you hide it, Pennitt, you little cheat, where you put it?

What? Isn't the—?

Your counterfeiting machine, where—?

It isn't a counterfeiting—

Ah, aha, so you do have one!

Everybody shut up, I want some names and then I'm not going to waste the city's time—

But officer, Terri the maid said—

Well, wouldn't you know! What with all that friendliness and the stench of mustard in the kitchen—

Knock it off!

Yeah, everybody should shut up, let the officer take names.

You too, lady. Lady! You just come here a second, don't go—

Mary Clovis her name is, Mrs.

I can't understand why *my* name—

Mary . . .

Mrs. Clovis. C-L-O-V-I-S.

But who took . . . ? Selbstein *you* took. . . . My stuff, it's gone, it's gone . . . gone.

You?

His name is Luke Pennitt. Double *t*. And I am Theodore Selbstein.

Officer, my name is David Brooke, and I'd like to testify to old Mr. Pennitt's—

Yeah, B-R-O-O-K.

E.

But they took my stuff.

What stuff? I told you, officer, he had a machine in here—

Mr. Pennitt, what is it that's missing?

My coins and my cabinet, my walnut cabinet, and . . . .

All I want is names. There isn't what you said was here, Selbstein, so I just want names, that's what I want, and no thanks for wasting Mayor Wagner's time and mine. Who's the nut that went back inside? And tell him turn that music—

Morganstern, his name is.

Yeah?

Selbstein stole my stuff.

Really, officer, I'd like to say that Mr. Pennitt has told me a number of times how long he's collected coins, and I can vouch for him.

That means a lot to me, buddy, I really care that you can vouch for him.

What about my rent?

You give him notice, if he don't go we kick him out, but that wasn't why you got me up here.

Anyway he can't get in. We changed the lock.

I know they took my stuff.

You want to make a complaint?

Where is it? My whole life! All those coins, not very many. . . .

See, officer, he did have the machine but he hid it.

Then who took it?

You see, officer, he *did have* it.

Telephone for Brooke.

77

Who is it; they say?

Peter something, I don't know.

I'll call back.

He's been using my house for a fake mint.

Yeah? Well, I don't see nothing against this Pennitt.

Mr. S. I *must* have *privacy*, and Morganstern won't keep his opera down, I'm doing my crossword.

I'll have you up in court, Selbstein . . . stealing my coins.

Morganstern! . . . Well, what do you know. Hey here he is, officer; turn your music down. He's a Red, officer. Admits it to everybody.

Officer this, officer that, you'll be calling *Heinz* a Marxist—

This guy is the real article, a real nut—

Don't listen to Selbstein, Pennitt, you can stay here as long as I say so.

Good luck, buddy, you got a great place here, if you have trouble collecting the rent that's another problem. This is wasting my time.

They pay you too much as it is.

What, are you funny?

What, is the law deserting the capitalist landlord?

There isn't anything under my bed, Selbstein, just gear.

More shit is what's under your bed.

Mr. Pennitt, let me give you ten dollars toward your rent.

What good is ten bucks when I lost my stuff?

Make you feel good, Brooke? Give him twenty, you'll feel ten times as good.

You're going out of this house, too, Morganstern.

Did you see if Miss Love went out to the elevator?

My stuff.

Mr. Selbstein, Mr. Pennitt wasn't hurting anyone, he's just trying to live.

You're a Communist, you had a Spic in here the other night, I saw her, *I* know.

All right, Selbstein—

You don't lay a hand—

Stop pushing, Selbstein, I gotta find my stuff. Let me back into the room.

Hitting him won't help, Alonzo, break it up.

All right, Brooke, let's have a bang-up, you and me, and what's this Alonzo bit?

Officer, this is my building.

The cop's gone, Selbstein. . . . Here! Here you go!

78

Lay a finger on me—

Let's have the key, Selbstein.

All right we'll talk about this.

I can't get into my room.

I had nineteen fights in L. A., Selbstein, now—

Hold—!

Godammit he hit Morganstern!

Alonzo, please.

Outa my way, Brooke, off my back. . . .

No, no, no you don't Morgan—

There, and don't forget I told you I had fights in L. A.

Aaaarghnnnh.

My goodness, Mr. Selbstein are you all right, mercy what's
happened?

Pennitt you come in here with me.

But my coins.

Come on in, we'll talk about it, have a little interplay.

I swear you and Pennitt are going. I'll get the cop, you hit
me, I hit you too.

Come in here, Pennitt!

Those two! Mercy!

They gotta go.

There's the music again, my land.

Let me in, it's me, *David*. We ought to talk about the
situation.

He's turned up the music and they're hollering at each
other in there. I told Mr. P. to have nothing to do with
Morganstern. I knew it would ruin his life.

But that isn't the point, Mrs. Clovis, we've all got to calm
down and talk and get to know each other for once.

Well, personally, I wouldn't want to know—

I'm going down to call the cops, he hit me.

I hate to say this, Mr. Selbstein, but I may have to move
to another floor, I don't get the same respect any more.
Listen to that opera music, and them yelling, it's simply
horrid. Inconsiderate, irreligious people. Godless perverts.

My gracious, David, what do you think *you're* doing?

I'm knocking on his door for Christ's sake, can't you see?

Well! No need to take the Lord's—

Morganstern! Pennitt!

Lord's—

Why the secrecy? I have to talk—

Lord's name—

Please, it's just me—
Lord's name in—
I have to speak to—
In vain. At least they turned off those dreadful operas.
All right, Brooke, what can anybody do for you?

{ Thank God they're here, every one, every single coin, none like 'em.

A little privacy is all a lady wants.

What's Mr. Pennitt got there?

Brooke, you've always got to know, don't you? But you never want to touch. Hey, Mary, don't go away, we'll have a party, you and me and Pennitt.

It was just that I wanted to help—

What did *you* ever do for him? This morning you were too full of your social worker girl friend so you didn't even hear Selbstein say he was going to get Pennitt out today, change the lock, what did you care, you knew Selbstein wouldn't attend to it himself, what were *you* ready to do. A very typical reactionary young quasi-intellectual tired reactionary, get straightened out, get yourself a good job, a decent apartment, and live like a man. I went in Pennitt's room this morning—all you need's a coathanger, crack *any* of these rooms—and I took out his coins, he only has a few, and his machine.

Shut up, that's all, Morganstern, no one's to know about—

What do *you* want, you looking for somebody? Haven't I seen you here before?

I am thinking of taking one of these rooms. Is it Number Four? Number Five will be empty tomorrow, I think the manager downstairs said just a minute ago, he looked a trifle excited—

Are you kidding?

Which is Four and which is Five?

Down the hall.

Thank you.

I'm David Brooke, surely I've seen you before.

Well, well, well, here's Mary again.

That's the man who saw the room the other day.

Mary, you're *with* us again.

I don't know *what* you *mean*.

Clovis, the evangelist!

Morganstern you are ungodly and sarcastic.

Very true.

A lady needs—

What does a lady need?

A little privacy. And good night!

I will go downstairs again and see Mr. Selbstein about the room; I think I like Five.

You can have mine, too, if you want it, Number Six.

Don't be bitter, Brooke.

And shut up about my coins and shut the door.

So Pennitt's been telling me he *makes* coins; he gave *up* collecting.

Shut the door. It's not true.

You just told me. He couldn't have a really good collection so he got hold of this old press—

Shut the door—

And he's got a pal who makes him a die once in a while and he screws them out and the coins he makes, nobody else has, and so he's got the only coin like it in the—

Shut the door—

Hear me, Brooke?

Shut the door, you stupid bastard, Morganstern—

Don't call me stupid, you little penny pincher. So you see, Brooke—*David Brooke*—you don't do nothing—anything— for anyone; in a pinch you aren't in touch and I advise you to move out—

Close that fucking door, Morganstern—

But one more thing, Brooke. I believe that in our various conversations you learned from me, you *learned*. So good night.

Please open!

(Shut up and pour yourself a drink, Pennitt.)

Please open!

(So long, Brooke. He thought he knew about me. Quasi-intellectual. Columbia. Let's have some music. But he didn't. PLARE PAY DEE AIEE DEE AIEE DEE PLARE PAY PEE DEE DEE AIEE.)

(Turn that opera down.)

Please let me in. OK, then! Oh, Mrs. Clovis?

(What?)

Mrs. Clovis, who was it phoned me tonight?

(I'm sure I don't know. I feel like the last run of shad, and I'm going to bed and I don't want any more. I don't want any more. I'm sure I wish I hadn't distributed Whaiee Towel Dayee Prerrr Broch this ratty apartment.)

81

Mrs. Clovis, can I just speak to you? . . . Morganstern! . . . Mr. Pennitt! What are you all doing? Mr. Pennitt I'd love to see. . . . Is it one of those old Mestrell Mill and Screw presses? I'd love to have a look at it. It must have cost. . . .

(All right, Morganstern, give that back, that's *mine*.)

I *know* about Mestrell.

(Go away, Brooke. Blow, Brooke, blow.)

blind john jones and the
ice-cream sculpture

If he hadn't shot off his mouth to Selbstein maybe Selbstein wouldn't have known about the coins. But Pennitt would have owed rent anyway. And Terri spied.

Or is this just another smug persuasion, self-persuasion? Poor smug Mary persuaded a part of her mind that she wanted privacy, when in fact a lawless need sent her heart secretly through wall after wall of that curiously dismembered flat, a reverse evangelism to bring the word of others to one's own hard-up self. Morganstern, too: breaching custom not by *means* of secrecy but to *attain* it. Abby the Indirect, Terri the Informer; J. J., who never let his left hand know what his right hand was doing. Muffled, mingled voices swirling about an impregnable egg of self.

A few minutes ago David told another lie to escape from the man in the captain's cap. The man can't stop talking about smugglers, Napoleonic cutters outstripping revenue ships, nocturnal mule trains waiting in Cornish coves. Is it only a matter of time before the man finds out which is David's stateroom?

David doesn't really understand the plan of the ship, but he can move from one part to another with a strange rapidity. The ship grows smaller day by day. Moving from one lounge or level to another, he is struck—"kaa-kaa, kaa-kaa"—by the lack of transitions. From library to purser's office (that insinuating blond fellow), from Mycenaean Room to men's toilet (that surly blond zoologist) there should be several things to note; but David hasn't seen them. First he was in one place; then he was in another. He forgets, when he is below, which way is forward and comes to doubt the relation of the barbershop to the stateroom, his and Ellen's dining room to the children's playroom, the bridge to the pool.

David, David, Sweet David: you've got the idea. You may play king if you want, so long as I, your precious, unpossessed *I*, remain your Richelieu, your perfect (absolute!) courtier—yeah, your ideaman, kid—*I*, so intimate with that which I've created that I seldom even think of myself as a kingmaker. Kingmaker in a richly ordered Scherzoid Holy Land. (Hide Ellen's clippings from *Queen* magazine; the steward may guess she stole it from the library.)

David pulls out his East Lite Box-File and puts it on the table. What has memory three to do with two and one? Should he return to two and make the relation of the Midas myth and the parable of the talents more plain? And falsify the facts?

Ellen.

Let her be, David. David is thinking entirely too much about Ellen.

But number three. That's the boy! Number three: That October when his sister Ann sent the baby home from England, he was in New Hampshire. He wanted to share with his mother what he was thinking; not by letting her into *his* mind but by entering hers (as if it were an apartment with furniture).

He had received a hasty letter from her and in her haste she had signed it "Julia." Abby had told Boswell Benson the address and Josie Wrenn had passed it on to Julia—to David's mother. Julia had heard from his friend Bobby Prynne that Bobby had put David on to a Dr. Bruder, and David tried to write her a stiff, quiet letter implying it wasn't her business. But after going next door to his kitchen to fill his Thermos with coffee, then returning to his desk, he decided he couldn't send the letter. And in the end, months later, he wrote "Cable." His mother wanted everyone to be well.

How insubstantial the causes! Each origin islanded and inadequate, at best (like each projection) part of an archipelago, at best "dustons" about a nuclear desire.

Yes. The blind man on the Heights, tall and scrawny, half-led by his sleek, subdued Labrador down Willow Street to Clark, over to the St. George Hotel for his daily Milky Way,

« P »

down to Pineapple, left (almost to Fulton) to the St. George
Playhouse (now defunct), where he'd talk to that eternal
friendly blonde in the box office finding out from her how
much sound track the new film had, then down to Orange,
left past Henry, Hicks, and Willow. And then David would
watch the blind man organize the final crossing (never *at*
the corner of Willow and Orange but always at the familiar
danger-point halfway between Willow Street and Columbia
Heights), and then at last cross the street, moving at a fast,
ungainly march (the dog against his right leg), cross to his
house. The blind man—known only as the blind man (though
John Jones was his name)—did several things well. He typed
Braille at dictation, his fingerbones seeming barely to move
on the few keys. Perhaps he was trying to pass himself off
(to readers who would never know him) as a person who
wasn't blind. Could he have managed without charitable
friends dictating to him and without the modest independent
income that enabled him to hire dictators? Twice—when
David was ten and then when David was home the Christmas before he finished Dartmouth—Julia asked Mr. Jones
over to perform, for he was, among many other things, an
expert ventriloquist. The first time had converted David:
next day he had bought a rubber-and-metal disc you placed
in your mouth. But unfortunately technique was needed too.
So David studied the *ABC's of Ventriloquism*. (And Halsey,
David's father, had to stand out in the hall—David in the
living room—and face in the right direction and see if little
David's sinister soprano was coming from the master bedroom.) (A Career in Ventriloquism for *You!* Rapid Ad-
vancement. See the World. Meet Interesting People. Free
Advanced Seminars—All Expenses Paid—"Ventriloquism as
Philosophy, and Philosophy as Ventriloquism!") The second
time Mr. Jones the blind man performed at Julia's bidding—
it was, of course, years later—he came to entertain half-a-
dozen hoodlets from P. S. 8 whom Julia had contracted to
patronize. And David stayed to watch, but forgot the boys'
poignantly slicked hair and their drab flannelette plaid shirts
and their interest in the remote, tolerant Labrador: Forgot
these things, because Mr. Jones made a mistake. It was in-

85

credible, a little insane: Doing an old Edgar Bergen routine
with a sort of Mortimer Snerd hayseed doll seated on his
thin thigh, Mr. Jones, David's personal "blind man," "the
blind man on the Heights," had—oh, *gradually!*—lost his
timing so his voice was no longer synchronized with that
doll's trap-mouth. The boys laughed—killed themselves, slipping down in their chairs, twisting toward each other—
laughed more at the deformed, leaning nods Mortimer gave
them, than at actual gags; but but but but the voice and that
wooden mouth! they weren't together! And David couldn't
stand it and left blind Mr. Jones alone in that living room
with the kids and Julia and Halsey. David did come back
for Julia's big sandwiches and the raspberry-and-pistachio
ice-cream sculpture of some unidentifiable cross between a
tree and a mountain; came back, too, to talk to Mr. Jones,
who didn't know David had gone out, and whose voice
croaked, and who smiled continuously, and who was the
only blind man David ever knew who, despite that royal distance, looked right into your eyes.

And David knew from that horrifying moment of "mechanical failure" that he must someday come back to that
childhood self now spinning deeper and deeper within him,
and project into someone else, project not his own voice but
himself—so his own voice would become that of the self
temporarily housing him.

Outside the stateroom the German steward is saying,
"Yeth, yeth, yethir, I fill pee hoppy to, yeth. Oh . . . you
thed mith? . . . oh yeth, mith . . . no, ath I thed thir I fill
pee—"

And the familiar voice interrupting: "I know which is his
stateroom but I don't want to disturb him. Just give him this
note when you see him." Smuggler-man! No, no, no, no, no!
Always somebody getting in the way.

David, hear this: The girl and her silent girl friend are
coming by, stopping: "And he said, 'Listen, I found a
German-Italian dictionary, took it out of the ship's library,
now if we can find a French-Italian'—he says '*Aiee*-talian'—
'then we just get *scène à faire* into Italian, consult the
German-Italian to ascertain the German, then use your—'

but I interrupted and said, 'You didn't really find a German-Italian dictionary—' and he came right back at me, 'Baby, baby, baby' real soft—and I mean tremendously cornily, if you know what I mean, *he* never went to Mr. Harvard's college—and he sat down on the berth and gave me one of those fantastically open grins and reached for me, and I said, 'You're a huge fake,' and he said. . . ." A door closes and the voice vanishes.

From a page of the third memory David removes that phrase of his mother's and rescrawls it in the top margin of a random page of memory five.

Check notes for two, David.

Dutifully he does. See, old chap? Seeeeeeeeeeee?

The Frenchman (cf. Bouchet, Simenon, Clovis) Eloye Mestrelle (also known as Mastrelle or Meustrelle—Menstrelle?—David scans his handwriting to see how he habitually forms *n* and *u*—Menstrelle or Meustrelle?) in 1561 introduced (as it were, David, "imported"!) into England the process of coining by mill and screw. This process improved over the simple hammer and anvil but met with little favor from mint authorities and few coins were struck by mill and screw after 1572 until it was generally adopted after the Restoration. Place flan between puncheons. Turn bar of press. An impression is at once made.

But, thinks David, *"Who made Pennitt's dies?"*

Forget it, buddy.

He gets up.

OK, David, *have* a break. But do not forget this is the third week—I mean, the third *day*—out, and the old man in London is waiting. *OK, have* a break.

David looks into the passage. Again—no, Davey, don't please feel sleepy, it isn't sandman time yet—again the thirteen- or fourteen-year-old boys come down the passage from the direction of the zoologist's stateroom: "You mean he's just going, to look?" "He's an engineer—the German guys on the job don't like getting an American in—" "I thought your dad was Irish." "He *was*, but he came to the United States when he was a kid, and we've lived in New Rochelle ever since." "Whadda ya mean, *we?*" "I mean my mother and my father—I mean, after he married her—that

was before I was even *thought* of." "So why's he got to go
to Germany?" "The authorities want an American expert—
so they're sort of sneaking him in as an exchange observer.
He wants to look into the English Channel, too: they're
deepening it to improve communications—" "Who?" "*I*
don't know. But mainly we're going to Germany." "What's
your dad going to do?" "There's this city on the Rhine River
near the North Sea, it's sinking down." "Cut it out." "No
stuff, it *is*." "So what's your dad going to do, observe it?"
"Yeah. And help them with his know-how." "To keep it
from sinking?" "No. To help them sink it." "Cut it out!"
"No bull." "Cut it out."

Where did the Mill and Screw get Mestrelle? Got him
hanged, if it was, as most authorities think, Mestrelle.
Accused of forgery. People suspicious of his importing,
sneaking in the new method, Frenchy.

Back inside the stateroom David hears behind him the
whisper of something coming through the message-slot. Oh,
no doubt from that man in the captain's cap. He never had
given David his card. Here, on a sheet of ship's stationery—
a stiff not very endearing gray Basildon bond—were the
words, "Our conversation about smuggling was very interesting. May we continue it in the Scrabble Room before
Second Cinema? I have something to show you, a true collector's item."

God! Go away! (Better meet him, D.)

Julia's letter that October forced on him her own share
in the project, her compartment in the night train of memories rushing in his mind. In that letter she had said, "How
could you know what I want for you?" Oh, those lonely,
fiery gill edges of the engines on her Icelandic turboprop!

In "Cable" he needed a distance—an invisible but palpable
pillow to buffer away everything palpable.

David deletes "No" at the beginning of the fourth para-
graph of page one. From another page he deletes S.P.Q.R.
(Small Profits Quick Returns), Halsey's familiar cautionary
remark. But, to take the words away from his father. . . !
The memory remains exact, though. "Get a grip on yourself," J. J. Lafayette had said one night to the Barnard girl.
"That's the only way."

Imagine Julia *before* she got the address from Josie. That was part of his plan.

Simplify. Forget the denizens of Kodak. Get one person. Set the voice back in its shadowy flesh.

III

CABLE

JULIA Brooke holds the cablegram away, as if she has to to look at it. Her seven-week-old granddaughter lies at this moment high over the Atlantic. The fingertips of Julia's left hand feel chalky on the cable's crisp paper. They are cracked from pressing the strings of her violin.

The cable tells all but the flight number:

> BABY ARRIVES IDLEWILD 1:55 P.M. SATURDAY
> MANY THANKS LOVE ANN AND DAN

Why hasn't the cable come sooner? They might have paid her the courtesy. Ann is too sensitive to be thoughtful, too busy telling about the strangled arpeggios of a Humphrey Searle sonata. (Julia flew Icelandic last year.) But why does the cable seem so important? Ann's airletter two weeks ago said they were sending little Julie back from London. Yet these transoceanic words stuck on stiff paper hit Julia like a large black headline.

"I've enough to do without this," she finds herself thinking. "I'm sixty, though a young sixty, untired, complete. Well, almost complete. But what the devil should I feel about my minute granddaughter being delivered to me like this? Why does it seem so strange, the movement of little Julie from them to me, while they sightsee in London and I move around this living room?" Julia stands alone in the apartment in Brooklyn Heights.

Isn't the flight riskier for a baby than for an adult? Julia sees Julie deep in the bassinet, floating free of fusilage, sleeping on, as the torn sea takes her and hides her. Once, at Race Point Lifeboat Station on Cape Cod, Julia watched her son David star in a Coast Guard Visitors' Day exhibition. Yet he was just another sailor, as, in chambray shirt

90

and nonregulation bell-bottom dungarees, he was drawn fifty yards down the air in a mock-rescue by breeches buoy. A little brass-barrelled cannon made a hollow bang, and suddenly before her eyes an arced, then drooping, line hung over the crossbeam of a fake mast that stood in hard ground. Then David was scrambling up the ladder of the mast, fiddling with blocks. And finally, his long, helpless legs dangling through the holes in a bulky canvas bucket, he was hauled serious and self-conscious from the top of the fake mast to a pathetic mock-safety on the red, dusty earth near the baby cannon.

Julia gazes blindly at the cable.

Her husband Halsey hates cables, trans-Atlantic calls, unannounced arrivals. Especially hates surprise encounters in public, prefaced by "It's Halsey Brooke—hello, Halsey!" Words burst from behind before he can see who it is. He says that at sixty-five he meets enough melodrama in the papers and in the simple things that happen: friends suddenly showing their age; Julia taking a remark in a way he hasn't meant; David expounding his passion for stationery, speaking facetiously but low and rather madly about his wish to own a stationery store—files, folders, Chile Bond (rag content, cockle finish . . .).

Today—Saturday—Halsey is in Chicago checking his branch office. Right now—a nonflier—he must be preparing to board the Manhattan Limited. He won't expect Julia to take the subway from Brooklyn Heights to Penn Station tomorrow to meet him. If he isn't arriving tomorrow morning at Penn Station, if he's staying on at the Pick Congress on Michigan Avenue, he won't wire her. Won't phone. He'll write special delivery. That's Halsey. To him, Western Union spells hysteria. Yet he's not afraid exactly. He isn't difficult —not like David—and he isn't sluggish or even very nervous. He just has a deep, steady apprehensiveness. It isn't the H-bomb; he says he can't conceive of New York falling, can't conceive of nuclear lightning or nuclear rain. Perhaps it's death he's afraid of. Halsey would have made a good, dour doctor, smelling faintly of Lysol and his own strong, male skin.

Medical school was Julia's faint ambition once. But only an ambition. Ambition is a kind of forgetting, David used to say.

Like Halsey, David hates telegrams. But David has difficult reasons. Or so he says. More than telegrams he hates the way he says people rely on connections—lines they see among themselves, cords, wires, stays, guys . . . fibrovascular, fibroid.

David. Is in New Hampshire. He didn't take that lovely big sweater she had given him. Ten months ago a card came postmarked Portsmouth showing wide slopes of bronze foliage on Mount Chocorua. The brevity of David's message chilled her hands and made her blush. Someone else might have wept. But how much can you write on a postcard? David said he had dug in near a SAC base on a dead-end dirt road that reached through woods till it broke down and the woods took over. David made the woods sound like an old car. David is—or was—living in a trailer.

Julia drops her hand, letting the cable hang by her thigh; she gazes out a living room window across the East River at the gray towers, the far fortress of lower Manhattan. And she recalls the last time David was here in this apartment in Brooklyn Heights. Eighteen months ago. She hears him lecturing her. Take away eighteen, was he twenty-nine then? It was his last night. He was, as he said, going north; he called Brooklyn Heights a gentle tomb, and she told him she thought he'd done the entombing. That night, Halsey was in Chicago. Sarah Fearon—she was then Sarah Davidson—phoned, and Julia said of course come over with Quincey. But she knew she wasn't asking them over to say hello and goodbye to David. The four of them talked in the living room. But then David faded away from them, and suddenly Julia realized that he had moved from the living room to the dining room and then around through the kitchen and hall to his own room. He had gone back to his packing. At eleven she told Sarah and Quincey she must help David pack, and they left, and David sulked at her and then lectured her.

"Why did you ask your cronies in, my last night? You didn't especially care that they saw me again."

But since he didn't understand, she couldn't tell him that she feared his presence, especially this last night; and she couldn't face him with his own truth—that he was just as glad Quincey and Sarah had come. But Julia and David found their talk bending into abstraction. She said—it was by then midnight—"Sarah prefers the lower Manhattan skyline at night, but I like it in daylight, especially in the morning, it's like the models in the General Motors Futurama at

92

the '39-'40 World's Fair." David listened to her call the skyline a rank of organ pipes—an open-air organ too big for a church to be built round it. And David, as he got out his pajamas, lectured her: "That skyline is just a skyline. Don't talk to me about organ pipes. You might just as well call that skyline a graph, and you could make it show anything you wanted. I listen to you play me a Bartok folk song on your violin, and I think of the bridge your strings cross—as if they were the bridge. It's all fiddle—" David let himself smile at the unintended pun—"don't you see? These connections are just a form of subjective anesthesia. They keep us from seeing something else."

Julia chaffed him, he seemed content to be called incoherent and dogmatic. He never did say what seeing all these connections *kept* one from seeing. For some reason she didn't ask him. Why?

What David said was too obvious to need saying but too queer to be understood.

Had he picked up from his college friend Bobby Prynne the little epitaph he spoke to her that day? "Mother, I have the will to fail." She came back at him brightly: "Do you swallow this nonsense that failure is the only appropriate act today in America?" But David simply said, "*Yes*, as a matter of fact."

At thirty-one David holds tight to a very young face—trim, chubby cheeks and an untouched mouth, small and calm. One of Halsey's business memos might call David's face neither firmed up nor finalized. At thirty-one David can't be expected to write her often. But living alone in a trailer? And living on what? She wouldn't think of asking Halsey to offer David a job. Halsey and David know the offer exists unmentioned.

Is she gloomy, or what is she? She doesn't know.

Here she stands, alone in her living room, facing a fine fall Saturday. She is a mere sixty. Meeting little Julie at Idlewild ought to be like becoming a grandmother all over again. It seems impossible Julie should be only seven weeks old. Julia is in a way glad that Ann and Dan can be rash. They booked tickets long after Ann got pregnant. Less than a month after Julie was born they three flew to London. Now they've realized their mistake. They've arranged to fly their seven-week-old bundle back—not to Washington, where their apartment is, but here to hers on Brooklyn Heights—well, to Idlewild.

Meanwhile, for their long-joked-about honeymoon, Ann and Dan are joining a charter flight to Tel Aviv. Ann wrote that their moment of truth enveloped them that first London Sunday, "grit flying in the sunny wind." They had searched out Petticoat Lane Market. Dan was carrying the bassinet. Without warning, as they pushed through the packed street past stalls of old shoes and cheap crockery and kosher salami, they found themselves marching in the middle of a famous little band. "You won't believe it, Mother, but they're called The Happy Wanderers." They were playing "Love You in the Morning, Love You in the Evening." It reminded Ann of the Salvation Army on Central Park South. Then and there they knew they must dispose of little Julie.

Julia looks at the cable.

Bobby Prynne, David's old Dartmouth friend, is back in New York, has been phoning her all week. He says not to worry about David. But Bobby doesn't really care. By Monday, Bobby's wife Connie will have spent the final fortnight of their wrecked marriage studying churches in Mexico City. She has been waiting for the divorce decree. Bobby says she seems to be cataloging all those churches. Each day she airmails him one or two maledictory memoranda on law, love, and money. Her letters describe didactic portals and lacey eighteenth-century façades. Bobby says, "Connie thinks she's still in college, but still she knows that *she*—the girl she's been living with all her life—is unquestionably getting a divorce." Bobby works himself up. "This long-distance spectacle pleases me."

Halsey lunched Bobby at the Downtown Athletic Club Monday, before Halsey caught the Chicago train. He called Julia to say goodbye. He said: "Bobby Prynne's OK. He's not a little college genius any more. He's ruined, like the rest of us. He's kind of gruesome. I admire him. At lunch he was nauseated, frowned a lot, ordered a Miller's, drank a couple of mouthfuls, then nearly spit up into his plate of oyster stew." Bobby has been selling floorings for Johnson Cork out of Chicago. He's thinking of moving back to New York.

In Halsey's wing chair Julia finds the soiled oblong of one of last night's late tabloids. It is folded to pages six and seven. Six has a shot of a half-blanketed girl nude down one side, face pallid but made up as if with blood and dirt. Did the photographer turn back the blanket to get more flesh? The girl is dead. Half reading, Julia looks down the column under the photo.

But now the phone goes off. The dead girl holds her, and Julia feels far away from the metal voice in the receiver. Bobby Prynne is calling for the fifth time this week. Between tense self-interruptions he extends the hope that he and she can revive their romance. "You know you still like me," he says, with a special color in the word "like." She tells him she's sixty years old. She tries to split her mind so she can receive the words of the news story and still attend to Bobby's nervous drone. She fails to manage either. If only she could find a way to kid him as she used to, then she could now yield up that faintly illicit sympathy for which he once came to her. When he and David were in Hanover years ago, Bobby used to send her prose poems: all about a small sloop, spray, sun, and speed in Sunday races on the Sound near Riverside, Connecticut; scudding clouds and some lean girl he crewed for; his sudden desire to veer off the race course out to sea. The newspaper story drags at Julia's mind, as if somebody in the room is tossing questions to be relayed to the person she's talking to on the phone. Julia is uttering perfunctory phrases. Bobby's tone, jabbing across the city, for a moment sounds the prenegotiation menace of a blackmailer. He is saying he knows she can't wait to see him. His humor isn't even proper self-pity. At last, when Bobby Prynne orders her to hold on while he lights a fag, she stops him, asks him to supper, and, intentionally bumping his rhythm by interrupting herself with a breathy pause, finishes, "Until seven, then, Bobby, goodbye." His sounds recede and die as she returns the beige receiver to its rest. Her other hand holds the newspaper, and she returns to the incredible tale of the poor destroyed girl.

But now another break. Julia hasn't been alone in the apartment. Josie Wrenn waits under the arch between the living room and hall. Her new brown-suede jacket shows its unbrushed patchwork of textures even more than when it is buttoned up. She is grooming it to look seedy, but she can't easily mess its surface and its style. It is tailored, aloof, genuine, and in fact—though Julia would not tell her so—it suits a girl of Josie's background. She watches Julia half over and half through the narrow strip-sunglasses she has left just above the tip of her nose, so that Julia thinks she must appear

95

two-toned to Josie's bifocal view. A darkish skin and careful non-use of cosmetics give Josie a nice natural mask, appealing and nameless.

"May I not come back till after dinner?"

Julia wonders if Josie has seen the picture in the paper.

"Come for dinner with your friend," says Julia. "Or not; whatever you want. I'll have Mr. and Mrs. Fearon, and a college friend of David's, that young man on the phone the other night, Robert Prynne. And don't worry about dishes and serving." Josie slides the glasses all the way on. "Josie, your mother will have a strange impression of me if she hears how much I make you help."

"I haven't got dishpan hands," says Josie. "Also, I don't write home."

Josie is the child of Julia's California cousin and his wife. The latter writes Julia two or three times a year: long tributes to Emmett Fox and Mental Science, and reports of certain vibrations that have recently told her of a peculiar connection she and Julia enjoy. She says Julia is under new stresses. Josie's mother claims to have conquered appendicitis through constructive thinking. Josie resisted, and then fought, a theatrically well-spoken tutor with whom she and her brother had studied at the parents' Hereford ranch in the Santa Ynez Valley. Then she went to a school near San Francisco. Finally, after letters and a dialogue of wordy telegrams, she got leave to go east to finish herself at Cooper Union rather than dawdle four more months at school and four more years at a suitable college like Mills. Her disappointed parents understand she will live with Halsey and Julia. By running the vacuum cleaner and dishwasher, by passing deviled eggs at cocktail parties, she will pretend to be keeping herself.

Now, with the chance of a free night, Josie speaks without conviction: "But you'll want me to take care of the little girl."

"No. She's all mine."

"Then I think we'll stay in Manhattan. We might go to a party."

Julia feels suddenly that her no-questions-asked policy with this girl has become a bit arch. But it is necessary to the pose of freedom and power that binds Josie to her. Still, Julia would like to know who the boy is and where they are going. In jeans, Josie's hips are a bit pointy.

To hold her, Julia is about to wave the newspaper and ask if she's seen the photograph. But instead Julia sits down by the phone. And at that moment she sees that it must have been Josie who bought the paper. She must have read it in the subway riding home from the Art Students League.

Josie says, "You're looking puzzled, Julia. I never saw such a vague look."

"Well, it's such a beautiful day," Julia answers. Julia has never objected to Josie's calling her by her first name, though lately it has made Julia feel she has no other name. Josie deals her parents the same camaraderie. Or isn't it really imprecision?

Josie stares a moment more. Julia thinks, "Perhaps she's just gazing past me through the window toward Governor's Island." No, they've changed the island's name. To what? Well, it's the same island. Now Josie is on her way out. Her ankle boots whisper down the hall carpet. Julia wonders why she wanted to keep her here. Not for entertainment exactly.

This morning Julia's mind seems to have worked apart. Two branches seem stretched in the same direction, though how far from each other she can't tell. Josie has gone: Julia hears the elevator, an organic purpose radiating its groan through all the public and private life of the building, over cosy funereal carpets and into bright kitchens.

She gets back down to the article. A seventeen-year-old student, apparently suffering from shock to her central nervous system, has died after taking an overdose of benzedrine, "at a party almost certainly given by, and unquestionably attended by, drug addicts." The writer gives the official "re-construction"—what a proud word, "reconstruction": discovering her to be dead, her companions must have stripped her, lined on fresh eyeshadow, rouged her mouth and cheeks, and arranged her on her parents' stoop. (The parents live some blocks east of the Village; the girl has been—had been? —without an address for eighteen months.)

Standing here, watched by her furniture, Julia pictures what happened. (Does her pity for the parents miss the point? Still, her fantasies can only stage what she knows; her fantasies are honest, if perhaps inexact.) The milkman, not the parents, discovers the naked girl on the steps, doesn't know what to do. A policeman comes; it's too early in the season for cops to wear those great tough overcoats, so . . . what can the milkman and the cop throw over the girl? The

97

milkman is now scared. (Though awe can stiffen one to face horror, it's more difficult to look at an *undressed* female corpse.) The milkman bickers with the cop. The milkman feels he can't stay while the cop goes around the corner to the call box. The milkman says he must deliver his milk. The noise . . . the noise at last tugs the parents out of that deep, deep dawn sleep; mother first, father second. But what next? Julia wonders. (Julia flew Icelandic last year.)

She has to stop. Her visual imagination cuts off, as if she's lost power in one part of her brain. The day is turning out strange. The minutes flying at her like arrows seem aimed at another target far behind her. She is in danger, but she is irrelevant.

Through the morning, thinking of the benzedrine case, she remains at this edge of revelation. When the mother and father came down to the door, then what? To Julia this question remains unfinished business. What exactly was the scene? The mother alone? The father alone? The paper doesn't say. Julia feels that her curiosity is both scandalous and sympathetic.

Facing a crowded day and wondering about the poor parents of the poor girl, Julia feels herself withdraw from her waiting schedule. She has to order food for tonight.

She'll order food for six, in case Josie and her friend join the party. Julia doesn't think the old Fearons will like Bobby Prynne. It was terribly clever of Quincey and Sarah Fearon to find each other. Widower and widow, seventy-six and seventy-one, they were married in a little church in lower Manhattan on a hot August afternoon two months ago.

Before Julia meets Baring-Gould for lunch, she has to buy a telescope at Belz Opticians for Halsey's sixty-sixth birthday. She ought to go to Schirmer's to buy the Handel sonata she wants to learn. But she hasn't time today. She thinks of the strands that hold her life in place, join her to her family and her friends. She thinks that what happens today will be linked in some curious way with the case of the poor dead girl.

On schedule, Julia rings her friend the butcher at the supermarket. He takes the grocery order too. He will see that her things aren't delivered till after three-thirty, which will give her time to get back from Idlewild. She sees the butcher wiping his hands before he takes the receiver at the other end of the line, imagines him thinking that phrase David brought home from enlisted-man's talk: "She's a good head." The butcher's cleaver and Ann's cable come together in her mind with the newspaper story.

On schedule, she leaves the apartment. The self-service elevator is unmanned. Jay must be out having coffee or placing a bet. He's an inefficient elevator man, but he fixes TV sets at cut rates. And he's good to the children in the building: he picks up their skate keys outside on the sidewalk, finds their scarves on the low hedge. So nobody reports his absences. He has told her a new man will take over the afternoon-evening shift from old Robinson.

Walking to the subway she tries to lament the changes that have come to Brooklyn Heights. Houses and people have disappeared. The Heights has become smart in a new way. Once snooty and remote, now it's a terribly OK place to live. Halsey doesn't care. He has his windows on the harbor: that's all he wants. He likes to talk baseball with Mr. Pascoli, who has had a narrow little fruit-and-vegetable store on Hicks Street for thirty-five years. He likes to talk stamps with the son of his old barber on Clark Street; the father died on the IRT on a Monday in 1950; he had been fishing for flounder in Sheepshead Bay the day before and had taken a horrible sunburn on his legs; he collapsed on his way to work. He was seventy; his son carries on.

On schedule, Julia finds Belz Opticians. She has decided not to buy a quasi-antique, but Belz doesn't sell that kind of thing anyway. Halsey won't care whether or not his telescope looks like the one in the decorator's window on Fifty-seventh. He just wants the thing to work. A modicum of power. The young salesman agrees—power. He fusses with a tripod and seems to forget Julia. Unmasked, she quickly explains that her husband wants a telescope at the living room window—not for effect but to get closer looks at the harbor, the tugs, the helicopters, the Seamen's Church Institute Building. Julia is told by an older salesman they'll deliver the telescope Monday morning. Halsey will by then, she hopes, be back in his office, back from Chicago. His new telescope is just a rather fat white cylinder, disappointing.

She hears Halsey grousing about the decline of night-train service. By now, he will be brooding at his window in the Manhattan Limited. Unless he's changed plans.

On schedule Julia meets Baring-Gould. His long hands

with their fans of sticklike searchlight fingers gently pencil the air in front of his couch in the waiting area near the street door of Stouffer's. He'll never marry. His immense blond head rolls up when she comes in, and he rises heavily. He's beginning to lose control of his torso. Too many carbohydrates, too many long lunches. Is he forty-five or forty-six? He kisses her, remarking on how little make-up she wears, to which she replies that she wears a lot of make-up, for she needs to. (She can afford to say that to him.)

For a minute—it's most unlike him—he talks shop. Usually he seems unattached to any job, usually he talks about anything but his job. But now he is explaining . . . Edie Echo, a twenty-one-inch doll you talk to, an endless twenty-second tape records anything you say . . . talk into either ear, a kid can arrange a conversation with Edie by spacing the recorded words properly. B-G designs the occasional soft, stuffed toy—Dodo the Winter-Goose—B-G does the embroidery himself, cross-stitch, French knots, and under Dodo's eyes two irrelevant beauty marks, pear scallops done in neat Broderie Anglaise—but more and more B-G prefers mechanical tricks like this Edie. B-G does a lot of photography; he calls his apartment a studio. Julia has been there twice in ten years.

At lunch they laugh; he makes her laugh. He touches her wrist and pretends to be planning love: When can she visit the studio again? Can she come to Bernstein? Would she like an enameled pillbox he found on Lexington? Halsey must see the studio one day—B-G makes Halsey seem the object of a conspiracy of condescension shared only by B-G and Julia. B-G's talk is like steady, fast touch-typing. He wants to know if she is going to wear a disguise to the airport, and if the diamonds will be in the baby's blankets or taped to its toes. (Julia flew Icelandic last year.) She feels the traffic of inescapable but incomprehensible conversation about them. B-G's long quivering smile hints, hints. Bobby Prynne's menacing irony over the phone returns to her ears; he seems more vivid than B-G, as if she were farsighted—as if the near were veiled, the distant distinct. Maybe she's *getting* farsighted. B-G has just told her she's a bore today; he has just kissed her cheekbone.

All her life she has disliked arriving early for planes, trains, buses, or ships. People who always give themselves thirty minutes leeway at Grand Central or the Port Authority Terminal, an hour or even longer at the Hoboken pier of Holland-America, seem pitiable. Without its usual comfort, this notion comes to her again as her cab, with its brand-new rattles, rushes and brakes and cuts out of Manhattan onto the rapid expressways of Queens.

Julia flew Icelandic last year. If Halsey had come to England with her, they would have sailed home. She was alone, like little Julie. She flew Icelandic because it seemed quaint. But they stopped in Reykjavik at midnight, and all she could see of the island was a huge map in a corridor of the terminal building—a glacier in the middle, fjords on the fringes; she would have sent H. some postcard views of that high, sunny cascade, but she thought they would be an anticlimax, for she would be home before the mail.

The cab driver is talking. As if without warning, she is having to pay him; they have reached the curb in front of the international arrivals building, and she is for the first time aware they have met almost no traffic for most of the trip. Saturday, too.

"You're half an hour early," the young man tells her, handing back sixty cents. She now sees he must be Puerto Rican. Or Cuban. Or South American. His skin passes strong and shiny and tender over the bones. "They want you to be ahead of time anyway," he adds with a wink. She's twice his age. Leaning toward him, her knees and feet together, the tapered skirt of her red-tweed suit drawn neat across her thighs, she believes in her own gracefulness, feels it wind endlessly through the tunnels of her body. She tips him and answers that she is not taking the plane, she is meeting someone.

Standing tall on the sidewalk as the cab edges past her to the rank, she pushes on dark glasses against the October sun. Taken unprepared for an early arrival at the airport and for the cabby's announcement of the time, she stands gazing over at the new TWA terminal, at the sloping spaces of the new concrete wings that roof this much-publicized structure.

She has time, she'll have a look. She walks toward the ominous bird of a building, passes a dozen airline lounges: Scandinavia, French, Argentine, Lufthansa. . . . She crosses toward TWA. On the island in front, she examines the bulky, fluent concrete wings, she feels the curves. Frank Lloyd Wright? No. Saarinen? Maybe.

She moves to step into the road—she wants to have a look at the inside—Ann says it's always moving, the inside, the angling curves that follow and retreat. But Julia is compelled to stop. Not a lumbago twinge; she hasn't slipped off into that region of injected pain that now and then Halsey knows. She has felt, not a touch of pain, but a touch as of some electric eye gone wrong—which instead of opening a door paralyzes its violator as if he is a single frame of a movie reel. Though she is early, she feels she must get moving: but she is held.

And, granddaughter or no granddaughter, the outside of the air terminal and the man on the roof must be looked at. He is smiling at her, then looking quickly down at something by his feet, then back at her. As he lounges there, on one canted wing of the roof, a pale float of nimbus cloud passing slowly across high and far behind him makes his position seem perilous and his easy slouch a reckless risk. For this moment, studying him, she sees an aerial stunt man standing in the sky; it seems that his nerve is simply his absorption in his own skill. Again he contemplates whatever it is at his feet. Then he grins hopefully at her, and she feels herself arrested—lovely red shoulders level, one foot beyond the other, not close enough to make a diva's concert stance nor far enough apart to make a pace. She feels weakened and silly. She submits to an unhealthy separation between herself and that fat-faced pretty workman up on the wing of the roof.

She can't respond as she did the night coming home from the theatre on the IRT. Mr. St. John, a neighbor on the Heights, whom they hardly knew and had met by chance on the drafty, social platform at Forty-second Street, sat down beside Julia as the car ground and lurched off into the darkness leading to Thirty-fourth. Then he began loudly to pretend deafness. At first not understanding, Halsey, who sat opposite them across the aisle, then grasped what for him was an appalling mischief. And in the stony stillness of the train's delays at Chambers Street and then at Wall, St. John's explosive "What say? What? What?" to Julia, shook Halsey, who tried to cover up with a knowing smirk. They had never met St. John formally, and haven't met him since the subway act. Enjoying Halsey's discomfort then, she thought, "I married him for his naked shoulders, not his humor." But at the same time she knew his malaise wasn't public embarrassment, not that at all. Nor was he thinking that the rumors about St. John were true—the rumors that St. John, oppressed by the increasing number of cars parked on the Heights, was himself the mysterious tire-slasher. What upset Halsey was his own fear that the imitation was often the real thing. Deafness. You kept coming across deafness of one kind or another.

Now Julia must respond to this character on the Idlewild roof, yet she cannot. Bobby Prynne's voice returns: "I just have to be with you, and as soon as possible. I guess I want to talk—but that isn't really it. I never could communicate with that son of yours. I prefer you."

Then Julia's moment of immobility ends. But she must return to International Arrivals. And events take over. Julia can't understand. The people, the plane, the baby, the steward—and a strangely neuter stewardess—drift vaguely in the remembered eye of that pretty man on the roof.

Then, just after meeting the plane, examining the baby, commending the stewardess who has been in charge of the baby and the steward who has been in charge of the stewardess, Julia finds herself gripped, stopped.

This time it is a sad man, but that isn't the point. Her mind splits again, between the watching man and her lagging irritation that it isn't convenient to carry little Julie in her arms.

No, the man won't stop looking through the window of the waiting room. And the point is: It is Halsey. Yet Halsey is due at Penn Station tomorrow morning—Sunday morning —and Halsey doesn't fly, simply will not. But grimly from under his brown fedora, Halsey is having a depressed, faintly alarmed look at her. This time the motion comes from her, though she goes on feeling petrified. The man won't move. She offers a smile. She waves her left hand. As soon as the boarders ahead of him curl through their gate and door and march toward the plane—whichever plane it is—Halsey will have to move. There are travelers in line behind him.

Now a dark-blue uniform addresses her: "Madam, did you forget something in the plane?" An airline employee wouldn't say "Lady." She likes "Lady." "Lady, I don't know, I just don't know." "Lady, your guess is as good as mine." "Lady, please, your turn will come, just stand in line."

"Madam," this fellow had said, "did you forget something in the plane?"

"I wasn't in the plane," she replies. (She flew Icelandic last year.)

"Well, you shouldn't be out on the strip. I thought you were on the London flight." (To or from?) "You shouldn't be mixing with these inbound passengers until they pass customs." The padded, platformlike shoulders bear small gold insignia, something winged, ready to fly off.

She asks, "Well, how did I get out here?"

Deciding the question is too much, and suggesting she follow the other passengers, he darts away from her importantly, falling away, shouldering off like a banking plane.

Her eyes don't follow him. Where is Halsey? The Halsey man and his comrades are headed toward the plane. There he is. It isn't he. But it *was* he, it was Halsey.

What has happened to her today? A second change of life? She is Julia Brooke, a powerful person, beloved, dressed in a red-tweed suit.

She doesn't have to declare the baby, or the stacks of diapers that come with the baby. A customs clerk gives her a self-conscious twinkle and says, "Looks like the airplane has replaced the stork."

On the way home little Julia remains to her a stage doll, whose authenticity exists for her, the loving grandmother, no more than such play-props may cause emotion on either side of the footlights.

She leaves the cab at Pierrepont and Pierrepont Place, then walks the block to Montague Terrace. She passes the buried site of the old garden, where proper children were licensed on certain dowagerly terms to play, and where now twelve neat stories of ice-cream brick fill the air. She walks where the toy span of Penny Bridge once hovered over Montague Street Hill. David raced his sled down this hill long before the planners created the Promenade, long before they filled up the incline (like kids joining one triangular block to another). Julia reaches her building, and a man pulls back the iron-latticed, glass-paned door into her lobby, and she passes through. He trails her into the elevator, which he then lifts, slowly, to the fifth floor. They meet each other's eyes, dimly and amiably acknowledging the fact that he is the new elevator man, indisputably warden of the lobby, keeper of the shaft. He has the authority of an alien's aloofness. But also, he's quietly anxious to please her.

At her door she notes her impulse to ring, then puts down the bassinet, unlocks the door, hoists the bassinet, and steps into her hall. Didn't she leave a light on? It isn't on now. Hasn't she taken the freshly sealed envelopes from the top of the great chest? They lie there still. And hasn't she shut the living-room windows? From this end of the hall, she sees that one window is raised about a foot—one of four living-room windows that, with two in the dining room and three in the study, give dour Halsey what he's always wanted: a prospect of the harbor. For years he longed for an apartment with a view just like this. Now, what Julia has felt unclearly but with a nagging certainty, she feels again: She believes that somewhere in the apartment someone real is standing quietly, identifying her sounds there in the hall. "This is my day for hallucination," she thinks hopefully. She wonders if she ought to stay.

But her bold-treading tour of the five main rooms, and the shadowy kitchen, and then at last the maid's room—where Josie chooses to sleep, because of its private entry—seems to prove only the emptiness of the flat. Yet the silence stiffens. She can't even hear the usual shouts of the Puerto Rican boys playing lazy Saturday afternoon soccer on the hushed, echoing piers. Twenty-five years ago Halsey took Sunday walks on those piers with David.

She must wake little Julie—for company. The child has seemed drugged. Who is waiting in the apartment? Why won't the child wake? On her side asleep, Julie seems a papier-mâché object. She can't be taken seriously. A papier-mâché memento of something real, but not the real thing itself. Indeed as unreal as this other presence in the flat is real.

Little Julie wakes gently. Julia frees her of her sweater, dress, and diapers. Julie's backside is chafed red. Now, washing and swathing and pinning and feeding the creature fail to free the house of this presence. Julia almost asks out loud, "Who is it?" But she doesn't want to speak to this unseen presence. She is vaguely shocked that she feels so little fear. Ah, what a peculiar baby, stoically inquisitive, a human, supple, and not quite yielding body, firm, dignified, discreet, too young to know her grandmother. An angel face? Only a crude angel. The child's silence seems a response to this unseen third person in the apartment. Is little Julie in league with him? *Him?*

Leaving the baby in the borrowed crib in the guest room, Julia goes quickly to the other bedroom and takes off her suit and her dark-blue Ferragamo shoes and her stockings, ties her orange gown about her, and, against all custom, lies down to try to sleep. But the suspicion that someone remains in the apartment remains in her mind. You can cover just so much territory, she thinks. You can't keep everything before you: You're a victim of sequence. There are so many doors, a thief could elude a searcher and slip back to rooms already checked. In a former, smaller flat David used to play such ingenious hide-and-seek with Mrs. Bine, the elderly baby sitter, that one day she told Julia she couldn't come again unless David would agree not to scare her. Julia gets up, looks at the baby again, then prepares what she promises herself will be a long stewing bath. And she still feels the presence. Perhaps—and the unreasonable idea startles her—it is someone unbalanced, like Bobby Prynne.

Lying warm, she submits to the stirring waters of the tub. She wonders why she wants to quell the pleasure. At the same time she sees all her activities—the total of her life, or as sour Bobby Prynne might say, her commitments—assume the filtered pastel she now sees as she gazes at ceiling and walls through filaments of steam. No telephone here. Not even a mauve wall phone to match the ceiling. She is alone. Her abdomen relaxes, it seems released. In the heat the fibers of her calves loosen. Her body tries to reweave itself. Can she be tired? It seems impossible. In case the baby cries out for her, she has left the door open. Her hands won't float. How many hours will it take her buoyancy to turn to bloat?

She imagines herself taking shape under soft chemicals in B-G's darkroom. She regrets not having gone to medical school. But her wish was never strong enough. For years she's attended operations. But that is one thing. The young novelist she's heard in a colloquium has proclaimed that writers must refer to scapula not shoulder blade, clavicle not collar bone. That is another thing. It isn't for that that she sits in a dark observation room to watch through a kind of skylight as masked actors twelve feet below her perform a thyroidectomy: a woman's neck gently peeled; the thoroughness, apparently casual and hence inhuman and removed; the talk, heard through the intercom; the pauses; the one red animal ditch in the loneliness of the sheeted patient. Julia goes because she can pretend to be a medical student; also because she is obsessed with the probing and the softness and toughness of human insides. Often she has gone with the young son of Dr. Falco, their friend, who makes the boy see operations every other Saturday. At that age she spent Saturday afternoon at the pictures, where she could dread the climax of the latest installment of *The Clutching Hand*. Today's thrillers bring a corrupt actuality the old ones never had. *Psycho*. Hitchcock's famous shower curtain rustles through her mind. What is the right language for Halsey's rheumatic heart? Rheumatic fever is an arteritis—which is an inflammation that undermines small blood vessels—which causes lesions that appear in connective tissues—which affects many organs. But Dr. Falco says the various manifestations often appear unrelated to one another. Looking along her body she wonders if death obliterates one's sex as well as one's life. Rheumatic fever licks the joints but bites the heart.

She has to escape the rectangle of warmth. (She flew Icelandic last year.) Elbows up, she levers herself out of the bath, her body's lift defeating the faint suck as the water holds on. You don't feel wet until you get out of the bath. There is plenty of time. This has been true all day. Perhaps preparing dinner and caring for little Julie will help rid her of this sense that someone is in the apartment with her. How can she not love the baby? She doesn't love the baby. The baby exists in another room. Julia wants the time to pass quickly. People live below her and above her. She has taken the trouble to know them. But she feels closer to the imaginary companion who stalks her here. But now she is looking forward to Bobby Prynne. He has something to tell her. About David? No, about himself as usual. Bobby.

Quincey and Sarah Fearon come at six-thirty. Talking fast and cheerfully, they pass into the guest room to admire the baby. They ask Julia almost in unison why she has let Ann and Dan impose so. Julia takes their query as quizzical, replying that her granddaughter has now seen England and has no need to study it further.

Quincey and Sarah are flying to Mexico for a February vacation, and even four months early they seem to be pre-

107

paring to go. Julia senses that it is not so much a trip out of the country—for Quincey's rare-wood business has drawn him to Chile and Uganda—as the sweet risk of a honeymoon. Except for weekends in Putnam County they haven't been away together since their wedding.

Julia moves them into the living room. Quincey and Sarah have straight backs and full, pretty, white hair. Settling them, stuffing two fruity old fashioneds for them, she feels surrounded by their desire not to bore her. They depend on her for company once a week; this need distances them from her, puts them at a different point on the graph. Or *do* they really depend on her?

They can talk about almost anything; they do it well. Reflex leads them to retell anecdotes bequeathed them by their children or grandchildren—Sarah's eldest granddaughter being introduced to one of the Kennedys at a ski lodge; Quincey's grandson hectoring ban-the-bomb picketers who were slowly sleepwalking back and forth opposite the new embassy in Grosvenor Square. But when the Fearons speak of Brooklyn Heights and of the life they are now pursuing, it is with a calmer authority.

Quincey begins, and then finds himself committed to, a discussion of Ian Harper. The Harpers' three-story wooden house, delicate Federal, has been demolished to make room for a ten-story cube. Ian calls his hobby a joke: He builds Lilliputian furniture. Ian makes, and sometimes gives away to a few of his friends on the Heights, relics of a smaller society he imagines: early Georgian highboys, exquisitely scaled down in real walnut and fitted with sliding drawers and brass handles; Queen Anne card tables with ball-and-claw feet; fanatically decorated press-cupboards; Regency chairs with lyre-shaped splats. In the apartment to which he and his wife have been relegated, Ian has a maid's room for his little lathe. Just a month ago, in honor of Ann's baby, he gave Julia a two-inch grandmother clock veneered with a mock-marquetry of seaweed. Speaking of Ian and that house, now destroyed, Quincey turns inward—his syllables whistle and his voice is slow; and over his second drink he wanders into a mute moment when he obviously feels he has let melancholy get tedious.

Sarah, who wants to preserve traditional Brooklyn Heights, works for the Community Conservation and Improvement Council. She seems to have grown more happily

108

enthusiastic as her public letters and reports have made less and less impact. Long ago—it seems long ago—she railed at the extension of the Belt Parkway, and then in a pamphlet she prophesied the "predatory buzz of strange motors patrolling our borders." How long would it be, she publicly asked, till the predators took in the cinch? Look at Cadmon Plaza! It's going to spread; they moved Henry Ward Beecher a hundred and fifty yards away from Borough Hall Court House—Greek Revival, they'll get that, too—but when they get to the Bowen house they won't move it, they'll just take it apart and throw it away—perfect Gothic Revival, those sashes that look like casements, those cast-iron railings. And what about those lovely chevron patterns in the spandrels on that other Gothic house on Willow Place? "Why must we advertise our history? Why must the Long Island Historical Society put up a plaque on that house on Willow Street to show where the Underground Railroad had its tunnel?" Sarah always ends by asking how long the young New Orleans poet lived here before he published that fifteen-thousand-word eulogy on the charm of Brooklyn Heights: three months! three months!

Now Julia is aware of being the speaker. She hears herself saying, "Why not accept these changes, put up with them? A city is for people, many people. We can't blame the birth rate. Or maybe, you know, that's *all* we can blame." A twelve-story, balconied apartment house has grown up on the ground of that famous old lady's one-and-a-half-acre garden; the garden had been restricted to children under five and their mothers. Years ago Julia was visited by the presidential spinster, who satisfied herself that the Brookes were well-spoken. She sat at the window on the third floor of her brownstone across the street from the garden and kept her binoculars on the sill. David moulded crumbly sand towers with his pail. The afternoon the mounted policeman paused to look in over the hedge, David had loaned his pail to a little boy he was playing with in the sandbox, and when David called to Julia, "The policeman's going to jump his horse right in here," the little boy pulled up the leg of his shorts and relieved himself first into the sand, then into David's pail, and the old lady pushed up her window and cried, "Stop that child!" Julia gave up the key to the garden when Ann reached five.

The Fearons sit watching Julia. She knows they are

hungry. Bobby Prynne hasn't come. The three of them mustn't wait.

As she and Sarah carry in the soup, she sees, from the dining room, how Quincey pauses to stare at the news photo on the desk. He doesn't lean forward, doesn't touch it. Before leaving this morning, Julia clipped it. As they sit down, the old Fearons in concert begin asking about Halsey. Julia knows they have never understood his abruptness, his skeptical eyes. The Fearons are being polite. Do *they* pity *her?* There are three for dinner. Julia hoped for six.

But as they are finishing the ice cream, Bobby Prynne does come. His smile is bilious and remote when she opens the door. He has on an old—probably Brooks Brothers—topcoat with the raincoat side out. Julia brings him into the dining room and Quincey and Sarah look him over. He lets Quincey get up to shake hands. To Quincey and Sarah his status is suspect, his person consistent with their suspicion. Having seen him in bathing trunks, Julia knows that his trousers keep their crease because his legs are too slight to challenge the form imposed on the cloth. Freckles and a dull lemony dusk in the pigment wash his worn cheeks one or two shades darker. Always atilt, his big narrow head takes his body with it. His head is so big that at first you don't notice the heavy, strong, straight hair—sharp mahogany auburn. Seated, he asks what surprise Julia has wrapped inside the luke-warm veal birds she puts on his plate. Materializing there in her apartment, Bobby seems to Julia for a moment to embody an invitation to her from the Fearons to join them. She thinks, their average age is seventy-three and a half.

Bobby concedes nothing, and long before the Fearons nod and chatter their way down the hall and out the front door, Bobby has pressed them unkindly, foolishly. Julia and Quincey have faltered into silence as Bobby has tried to confuse Sarah.

"No, you've got it wrong," he explains, smiling helpfully. "The missile gap isn't how far behind you are in the production of missiles; it's how great a gap in *minutes* there is between the firing and the hit. You're right that it's better to have a small missile gap. But you're wrong about what the missile gap basically is. You don't have to read *Scientific American* to know about this sort of thing."

What talk there is keeps returning to Bobby, though he

objects to this. Finally he says since they insist on getting into his private life, he'll give them a shot-by-shot account of the last loving battles he's fought with Connie. Though the awkward discontinuity of the conversation makes time seem to part stiffly and slowly as they push through the evening, still it is midnight when the Fearons vow they must go. Bobby declines when they offer to walk him to the subway.

When Julia returns from seeing them down the hall, Bobby brings his drink over and joins her on the couch. Now he starts, accusingly: "I thought they'd never leave. All right, I like people, it amazes me how much I like them, they notice me, and I make them notice themselves. But I still thought your friends the Fearons would never go."

Julia won't oblige him with a real rebuke. But with a conscious struggle for a tone she hardly conceives of, she says, "Holy Moses, they *are* my *friends*. I love them. I know why you dislike them: because they're Republicans, because they try to be sparklingly well-informed—"

"And because he wears a Tam O'Shanter when he marches over the Brooklyn Bridge every morning to that office he's officially retired from."

"Do you blame Mr. Fearon for being alive?"

"Yes. I blame him for being a certain kind of alive. And why isn't he tormented with anger that he can't be a husband to her?"

"Perhaps he can be." She feels her arch smile stick on her face.

"You *are* frivolous. You are, after all. You have to defend yourself, and so you start fooling with me. Look: I cannot stand being laughed at, why should I make out I can? My little impossible wife was always suspicious of you, even after meeting you just a couple of times. That's one thing she never was with me. Isn't that a howl? With all she knew about me she was never suspicious. She believed me when I told her I thought there was a God and when I said I didn't want children in the 1960's."

Bobby is getting maudlin. And he is shaking his empty glass at her.

"When she flew to Mexico, Connie wouldn't kiss me good-bye at the airport. We were late and the plane was ready, and to get her onto the strip I was going to pick the gatelock, but a man came. I would have picked the lock. As a lover I'm vicious and quick. Connie wouldn't kiss me. She did stop and give me a seamy little sermon. She said I didn't want to be connected to anyone. God, I love her homilies. Connie was direct. She hates a lot of my best qualities. She doesn't pretend. Do you know something? It's OK for marriages to bust up. It isn't the end of the world." Bobby Prynne scratches a callus on his thumb-tip. His sulking mouth seems to say to her: "Well?"

Something must now be said by her.

"But accepting divorce shouldn't be merely permission to leave off wondering why your marriage failed."

Bobby laughs that old man's "heh-heh" through the nose. "I guess the only ethic is to know what you're doing and why you're doing it."

Julia stands up as Bobby pats the outside of her thigh.

"And what if your reasons for doing something are wrong? Does knowing what they are make them less wrong?"

He runs his look up and down her figure. "You aren't worth my time," Bobby says quietly. "You're just like your solemn son David. Just a smug moralist posing as a fallible, warm-hearted heroine. You and David don't believe in disaster. Your whole family, except for your husband, doesn't believe in disaster. He's amazing. I really got through to him. With fifty thousand a year and a couple of Edward Hoppers on his walls, still he's practically disaffiliated. He's one of the most beautifully grim characters I know. He's ready for disaster. I think he suspects there aren't any marriages or sons or daughters. I'll have another drink, please." Bobby offers his glass.

Rather than throw him out, Julia brings him the news photo from the desk. "Isn't this a disaster?"

Bobby is down on one elbow. He's worked half an arm under a couch cushion. "Isn't it?" she demands.

"No."

"Have you seen this picture?"

"I've read all about it." He moves his tumbler at her. "Here."

Julia finds she is afraid to stand on her rights as hostess and elder. She begins, "This girl. . . ."

"With the kissable lips." In the photo the girl's rouge is black.

"*You're* responsible for this sort of thing. What do you

112

know about how many Puerto Ricans live in one room on Joralemon Street or off Cathedral Parkway? You've been out of New York, and trying to spoil your marriage, and perfect your sneer. Look at this picture. What did her parents think when they opened the door?"

Bobby seems to wake up. "How do I know what they thought? I don't try to know. Maybe the girl found out what it was all about. Maybe she had her vision and then her body gave up. You're trying to goose everybody and make them healthy. And you want to participate. In her life, in David's, in . . . that little baby's in the guest room—" Bobby halts himself with a few of his tenor cackles. "And you think it would be nice to be responsible for this little art student who took too many bennies. There's a nice rhyme."

Julia feels surer now. "I *am* partly responsible"—and then, as if she has known the girl in the picture—"but she wouldn't listen."

Bobby speaks less haltingly. "You've got it exactly wrong." His ploy of rhetoric, Julia thinks. He proceeds: "I have to show you how it's all connected. That girl is listening, she's looking at you, like an old statue with bulging, blank eyeballs. She's not saying you're responsible for her but that you're responsible for yourself, what you've done to yourself." He exhales, part sigh, part groan. He is on the edge of amusement. "Make me another drink."

"But my dear man, even assuming she has something to tell me, do you think I need to be told I'm my own fault? And *fur*thermore. . . ." She puts an old dame's stage hauteur on the "fur," hoping she can set off an interruption from him. But raising his elbows and planting his fists in the cushions, Bobby Prynne crutches himself several inches closer. Then he places his arm above her shoulders on the sofa-back. He is waiting, concerned.

"Furthermore," she goes on, driving her words before her, "it's hopelessly confusing to hear such contradictions from such a well-educated young man. You'd better decide whether this girl in the photograph was done in by me or by someone else or by herself."

"Don't be so earnest," Bobby says, now apparently again exhausted. "Stop trying to con me." He is not exactly drunk. What is he? The words come automatically into her mind's voice: "He's disturbed, sick." Somehow she has said them to herself in order to dismiss their possible relevance to Bobby.

Now she must humble him some way. He is close to her face. Discomfit him.

Tired breath blows up from his stomach. He leans. And now gently kisses her neck. His breath spreads over the skin. The breath is a presence. But his dry mouth was merely another surface.

He is leaning toward her again. She still doesn't turn. *She* con *him?* Perhaps. He doesn't kiss her neck, doesn't kiss her. Then he leans back. She looks. And he is embarrassed. But then the shy give-away comes from the young man: "No woman is old," Bobby says, seeming to shun her as he stares across the room. She sees him being noble. He's not in love with sixty-year-olds. He's being noble, trying to speak some transcendental honesty that will be true but polite. He's not looking at her. She has humbled him, and he her. No, he isn't really drunk.

Trying to recapture the scene, he sardonically says, "The great earth mother has to have a child once in a while to keep her status. You're one of these night creatures who indulge in parthenogenesis. They procreate all by themselves." The long word and its explanation blunt the barb.

The evening is over. This skinny man's face gives off a pasty distance; his large face no longer looms; it has sunk sallow into the final frame of a news photograph.

"Please go, Bobby. And if I see you again, good. Why don't you write David? He's all by himself. He lives in a trailer. Of course, you know that. He has a real mailbox."

"That's a start," Bobby mumbles. She must get him away, away.

"And he's thinking of driving to the Canadian Rockies next summer—or so he wrote Ann."

"He can tour the early-morning dewline, or whatever they call it, the air-force boys, he can do that, for all I care." To her surprise, Bobby jerks off the couch onto his knees and then rises swiftly and strides uncertainly out of the living room under the arch into the hall.

"Take your coat," she calls.

She hears his softened tread press over the carpet, then the brush of cloth and buttons over a hard surface, then, after a moment, cloth and buttons hitting the hard surface. The chest. She does not hear the front door open or close.

Why bother to check? Has he flopped down? But she scarcely considers this. Bobby is essentially a subversive—in the broadest sense. Perhaps now Bobby is through with her. He once preferred her talk to David's.

Has Bobby left the flat? Slowly she moves to the hall, then through it to the open doorway of the guest room.

She stays on the hall side of the threshold. Bobby lies stomach down across one of the guest beds, his floating body aimed away from the door. The baby is silent.

Bobby murmurs, "Didn't wake kid up. . . . Dead to th' world." At her right, outside in the hall, his coat half-covers the chest.

Julia wheels the crib to her own bedroom, hers and Halsey's. In the kitchen she removes the dinner dishes from the machine, buffs off the smudges, puts everything in its place. She pours boiling water through the inverted cone of coffee she has spooned into the filter in the top half of the Chemex hourglass flask. Josie feels milk is bad for the complexion; coffee late at night helps Josie sleep. Julia, pouring the water through the fresh grounds, sights down her bent arm—her bow arm, where violinist's sinews and tendons have kept the flesh from beginning to swing, as the underpart of Sarah's arm does when she reaches for an hors d'oeuvre. But Julia hasn't played in three weeks—must get on with some sonatas, must play some quartets, must take a few lessons.

In the bathroom she dribbles skin-freshener into her hand from a flowered bottle, French porcelain she bought on the main floor of Liberty's last year just before she flew home from London. She has mixed it herself: three ounces rosewater, two ounces witch hazel, half an ounce of glycerine, one teaspoon Twenty Mule Team Borax. (She flew Icelandic last year.) She rubs her face and hands. Then she stoppers the flask and goes for her bed. One night years ago she infuriated David, who was discussing Shakespeare's will—she said, "He left his wife the second-best bed, because that's where they had all their fun."

For a minute or two, or three, or four, the strands of her tired spirit lie drawn between fear and fatigue. On waking she will always stretch her long arms gloriously out from the bed, then down stiff over her body. How often at that physical moment has she visualized the lives—the moving bodies, the eyes—of all the people whose lives are her life?

But now they seem different people: some traveling away, some traveling toward her—but all discreet. B-G, Ann, Dan, Connie Prynne, Bobby, Josie, Halsey—trickling diminutives —David.

She believes—for the first time in her life?—that she is no more than herself. This strong, intricate bundle under an electric blanket. A phrase blinks on at one front of her mind —a phrase, yes, from one of David's college books—a very sad and rather clever and distinctly cynical book: "devoid of secret dimensions." That is how she feels.

She has left a note for Josie. Instructions about the baby. Remarks about Bobby.

The alarm is set for seven. Why bother to meet Halsey? Well, the alarm is set. She'll go to Thirty-fourth Street: so easy on the West Side subway.

She hears a key. Now, vaguely, she registers the sounds of Josie and her friend. Gasps of whispered giggling. Julia hears her distant mind breathing words. She flew Icelandic last year. In the hotel before she left London, she heard on the radio an old voice singing that gentle, corny old thing, "Love Is Like a Violin," and when they refueled at Gander she was impatient to leave the great new waiting room but had to stand for several minutes near the guard who stood by the stopped escalator ready to start it again when he got the word.

She has only six hours. Monday, Tuesday, Wednesday, Thursday, Friday, Saturday. So many strands.

David is saying, "Cable-length is a hundred fathoms."

Down or up?

The half-conceived thought on which she is drawn into sleep—that she has but six hours—becomes another half-conceived thought as, at seven, she reaches for the alarm button. The clang of the clock cuts through the pillow of her sleep, and she is aware of waking up gratefully. This is her thought. But what does she in fact feel when she feels grateful?

Now she is moving; she has time to worry the riddle of her gratitude. But though she has time, she feels rushed. She drinks her coffee too fast. Why grateful? There will be sun today. Josie's door off the kitchen is closed. Would Josie dare?

116

From the front hall she views Bobby Prynne. During the night he has turned onto his back.

Now she is clicking along the Promenade on her almost direct route to the Clark Street IRT. Lower Manhattan looms near her: the great stone organ pipes stand up into the Sabbath cold. She turns up a cement ramp onto Clark Street, skims the last rapid blocks to the St. George Hotel building. A bale of Sunday papers waits on the pavement; funnies on top, like wrapping.

Julia just catches the elevator. As a child David would stand under the "Beware of Pickpockets" sign, archly inspecting his companions to right and left. Bobby Prynne would rather pick the pockets.

Julia barely catches the closing door of a Seventh Avenue, then strains past into the car. Gratuitously the door opens again. Then it slides and rattles shut, sounding an old logic that, as she sits down, brings back a lifetime on Brooklyn Heights. Of course she accepts the architects and civil engineers and immigrants. Quincey's melancholy bores her. But —bearably, and in the used, mortal comfort of the IRT car with its two long rows of facing seats—she knows what she saw last night. She saw that her accepting appetite will not save her. In the car there is only one other person, the conductor. And he is at one end, actually straddling the gap below which this car and the next one back are coupled. Julia gazes at the ads above the windows opposite her.

In Penn Station she waits by Halsey's gate for thirty minutes. She doesn't leave the gate. As they pass her, she examines the straying, serious travelers. The high mausoleum echoes dully. And then at last, a little late, Halsey Brooke labors forth frowning, and is astonished to be met.

reflex therapy,
or what bruder didn't say

Alone: He sleeps: He dreams. (But not perchance!)

I furnish David, of course, with a fairly wide selection of dreams. In this dream David doubles: One of him has the experience of the dream; the other David interprets it. The experiencer comes on down a lane (the lane is like a room) and, half knowing that the form ahead sitting in the tall American ladder-back chair is Halsey, his father, this first David approaches apprehensively, fearing a shock. Halsey's head hangs down as if dead (scalp cleanly visible along that old-fashioned middle-part line in the pepper-and-salt), but the open eyes seem intent on his lap, and this strained bend of the neck, though it has the attitude, lacks the final slackness death would give. As *this* David goes up, Halsey rolls his head up wearily and stares at David with a warm, puzzled, slight raising of eyebrows. David keeps his face turned toward Halsey as Halsey watches him stroll by—David's head pivoting, yet seeming (like a golfer's during backswing) to be motionless. Nary a word does Halsey say, and at last David, to keep his own head from twisting off, has to seem to let his father stare him down, has to pivot head round forward, for he's coming to a town. Now the other David (like one of those stage narrators playwrights stick in just by the wings to comment on and connect the bits of drama the playwright shouldn't have *needed* a narrator for) calls out with icy enunciation, "Symbiotically speaking, David doesn't want to lose his head!" Then I run the encounter through again. And again David A approaches and passes and Halsey looks up and watches, and this time David B calls, "The son's guilt in the presence of the father." The third run-through, David B calls out, "The father has been evicted in his shawl; the son is the new tenant." Fourth: "Afraid Halsey won't look up; afraid Halsey will." Fifth:

"Afraid I've come too late for Dad, too early for the door."
Sixth: "Cf. Kafka's diaries on the pros and cons of marrying." Seventh: "Because this is the age of explanation, explanations have become useless parodies." But the eighth time
through, slackness has entered the body, has stricken the
neck, and Halsey doesn't look up; and as David A stops to
weep, David B starts singing slowly, spasmodically, "HARK
the HERald ANgels SIing, GLORY TOOO the NEWborn KING." So
that, half-weeping, David is forced infernally to move by
jerksteps forward, forward, forward, toward the door that
leads to the town that leads to the city. . . . I wake David up!

In the age of explanation a veritable chaos of elucidation
is possible. These exact memories must be themselves. So
David couldn't include that other bit in three about the rest
of the Coast Guard Visitors' Day Exhibition—too suggestive.
With a fid he had set out to part strands in a line in order
to do a sample splice, but the smooth, hard wooden fid had
slipped because he had gone at the job too quickly (hoping
to seem efficient), and it had taken a whole lot of fumbling
and holding and spreading and straining to get a couple of
new strands into the hole made by the fid. Once he looked up
and saw his mother had been diverted by something off on
a bluff overlooking the beach; but his father stared seriously
on at the exhibition.

It'll be tea-time before David knows it, and he's got to
get on to four. So what if the causes behind the project are
insubstantial: Their very insubstantiality is a key to the
grandeur of the project. Remember the man who built on
sand: I speak as much to the reader as to my David.

The junior-year-abroad voice appears in David's hearing,
talking apparently to its companion-silence: "And with his
hand on me like that he tells about the wise men who followed the star—*you* know, it's in the Bible somewhere—and
they came to the stable and as he crossed the threshold one
of the wise men tripped and—"

Dr. Bruder didn't seem naturally a humorist, but his reactions the second time David went to him seemed farcical.
Yet, as it happened, they had their uses; and David was glad
there had been no couch, no absurd couch on which could
occur the parody of a rape. When David entered the brown-

and-mauve office (with polished wood floors and good oriental rugs scattered somehow austerely), Bruder had yawned
and stood up, and then watched, and then turned to the
window overlooking Lexington. His wide, shaggy, sandy
head and great hunching shoulders made David think of a
moron.

And as before, David started telling stories about himself:
how he held the longest, dearest, most lethal grudges out of
which nonetheless he could never bear to exact vengeance;
how he'd forgotten how to hit a forehand, his wrist seemed
to grow suddenly self-conscious on impact and twist back
and forward, sending the ball *way* the hell out or bouncing
it over the net like a Ping-Pong serve; how he'd forgotten
how to spell, and would sit staring incredulously at *was* and
is; how since the age of six or seven he'd had this dream
about an amber-lit, careering West Side IRT car making the
run under the river between Clark and Wall and back again,
and David was the car and throughout this run his hands
and cheeks and shoulders were being abraded by gentle,
fibrous, pulpy tissue (he slowed down and couldn't resist
telling Bruder his own interpretation of the dream).

Then Bruder said, "What do you want of me?"

And without answering, David passed on to more information: how he would be devastated if his mother died (to
which Bruder answered ditto); how he was forever dismay-
ing people who took him for a good listener only to find out
his "um-hum, um-hum" served as mere tokens of attention
and that he hadn't heard a word. Bruder came back from
the window.

"Maybe some reflex therapy in a few months. *Maybe,* I
said." And looking hard at David, he said, "Jeepers, you're
a bore!" (The *o*'s and *r*'s were Pa. or Jersey.) "Look, you
don't want me. Anyway, not yet." Suddenly Bruder began
to look like somebody David had known long ago or for a
long time.

"But," said David, "that isn't quite all you've got to say."

"Don't go to another doctor."

"But the very fact I've come to you—"

"The ontological verification that you need therapy? Now
I'm God?" Bruder turned again to the window.

"I want to talk. And furthermore you mixed up needing you and believing you."

"Yes, well, you can't just talk; you've got to find someone to talk *to*."

"That's why I came here," said David.

"No it isn't. Said the mirror to the man."

"No tricks for Christ's sake. You're supposed to dope out *my* riddles!"

"Maybe reflex therapy after a while."

"After a *while!* Like some kind of afterlife! Tell me *something!*"

"Not now. Stand by."

"Surely this isn't standard procedure."

"There *is* no standard procedure. There is no s.p."

"How come you have an abbreviation for it if it doesn't exist?"

"I'm not going to help you and I want you not to go to another doctor."

"If you had a long waiting list. . . ."

"I have. And you were pushed right to the top of it. You have influential friends. But right now you can't use me."

"What shall I do?" David felt Bruder was playing him carefully; yet maybe Bruder wasn't thinking very hard about anything.

"Find out why you came to me."

"Think?"

"Yes, think."

"What about?"

"Maybe . . . some of your friends?"

"What . . . ?"

"Hunh?"

"What about them?"

"Just . . . ."

"Get straight . . . ?"

"In your mind . . . ."

"What they're like?"

"Crazy!"

"What?"

"Good."

"And sort of project . . . ?"

"A sort of project?"

"No: Sort of project. The verb . . . ."

"Um-hum, um-hum."

"And you won't take me?"

". . . a sort of treatment."

David felt he had created the course of this interview by some remote control from his own pulses, a control *he* had no control over. (And I feel almost obliged to inform the reader that in a sense David's surmise was right.) What good was it, thought David, to end up finding that what was being elicited from you was your own idea? Yet neither Bruder nor he had seemed the pusher in that odd exchange—but rather, someone else—or some*thing* else, something *so close*. Moronic as Bruder had looked, he had a growth of hair David had always wanted: blond, sun-bleached hair, shagged over a sun-brown face still asleep or half-asleep on faraway sands.

David was in any case sure that Bobby Prynne had put him on to Bruder. That part hadn't arisen mysteriously from inside. A few minutes after this second interview, David phoned Bobby. But as David was about to complain about Bruder, he contained himself. Bobby would say, "You're sick but not sick enough." Or, "You mustn't have understood what he wanted you to do." (Bobby had the knack of always getting the better.) Instead—for a second forgetting Bruder's little prescription, as one might forget dreams—or had it *been* in fact Bruder who had made the suggestion?—David said to Bobby, "I've decided to work it out for myself."

Afterward, did Julia pry? Or did Bobby, in order to disturb a situation, phone her and say, "I recommended . . . ."? For she knew.

Outside the stateroom, voices—glimmering faces:

"What iss your field?" The scientist with the jars.

"Anything undercover!" The smuggler-man.

"Ha! That is very good! *I* am in two fields at once. I am a microbiologist and a general marine zoologist. This trip has afforded me opportunity to conduct seven-day experiment. Requires constant watching. I am not at liberty to explain project."

"Yes, well I do a bit of the old research too. Do you happen to know where this young chap—I say you have a most remarkable resemblance to me, didn't it—?

"Yes. I felt it a piece of unattached evidence, that is to say, evidence for which the use iss not yet forthcoming, eh?"

"Young chap name of Brooke, y'know. 'merican."

"Oho! Ho ho! Guess which one of dese! Ho ho! Guess which!"

"Oh I'll find him yet, heh heh."

"Guess which iss hiss sdaderoom, ho ho! *I* know. *I* know."

Hide Ellen's clipping from that stolen *Harper's Bazaar.*

Always forgetting: The two lines of dialogue removed on the first day from the end of the first manuscript, transferred the second day to a random margin of the second, filed the third day at the top of the third, David now moves to a random page of the fifth memory.

Oh he had said, hadn't he, to Bruder, that several memories, seminal recollections, reverberative reminiscences, fructifying retrospec—"Get on with it," Bruder had said—lay in his mind like islands, unattached to one another. And then Bruder had said in a highly suggestive tone, "Don't try to connect them; you'll never manage it. The causes exist, but most of them we just can't know." And the glow in those sky-blue eyes had told David unequivocally that Bruder was urging him to do just the opposite: to work out the connections.

David: Four. Yes, good. No, leave the screwdriver alone; get on with the memory. Little to alter, surely. But wait: I see changes here that I never authorized. Of course I suppose my modesty makes me forget how ingenious this David of mine is. Here is an important explanation, which the reader may take or leave as he will: At first David and I—leave the screwdriver alone, David—at first we seemed to disagree about Duke Amerchrome. This was in fact in my opinion in a sense to some degree the first difference we had had, though I hesitate to generalize. (Mind you, generalizations are always in some sense true.) David, let us say, saw—no, *wished* to see—in Duke a huge, born image of midcentury America. And ere long I knew that my own view of Amerchrome as a mere monster of ego wouldn't prevail. Of course David—ingenious bastard that I have made him—saw something fascinating (whether or not it was the truth), and in admiring compromise (you may take that ambiguity in its fullest sense) I let David work this idea out: that Duke

123

Amerchrome held, in his turning, pressurous self, the full parodic significance of the land he lived in—lived *off*. My difference with David isn't evident in this ingenious chronicle (*vide seq.*), for in a sense there never was a difference. Since David is my invention, how *could* there be a difference between us? I have made him—if you'll pardon the phrase—in my own image. Let me, discreetly, say this: All along David and I had felt for Duke Amerchrome what is here shown.

And did David go West, as his mother imagined he would? Yes, he did: For he wished to visit the bowling alley where Alonzo Morganstern had been working when he met his wife. And did David find Alonzo or his wife? No: David studied the operation of the "curtain," which upon being hit by the ball activates the "table" that houses the respot cells and pin cups; he studied the way in which the "table" drops down, the respot cells pick up any pins left standing on the deck; he studied the way in which, after the "table" returns to its original position, the "sweep" lowers and pushes fallen pins into the pit; studied how after the second ball the respot cells don't pick up any pins; studied the pin-wheel that takes fallen pins to the distributor, which drops them into pin cups.

This screwdriver. All right, David, *look* at it if you must. Homer Boulos got it for Duke, who gave it to Mary Amerchrome, his young wife, who in turn gave it to Michael Amerchrome, from whom David pinched it. It is a "seven-level" screwdriver, so-called by electronic technicians, who use this plastic-handled tool with the two-and-a-half-inch blade for so many purposes—chipping, hammering, as a low-voltage shorting bar, prying—that they rely on it constantly.

Ellen's hand on the stateroom door-handle: David pockets the screwdriver.

David carefully removes *u, v, w, x, y, z*, and *a* (one of each) from Michael Amerchrome's special alphabet soup for teenage ulcers.

IV

AN AMERICAN HERO, OR THE LAST DAYS OF DUKE, MARY, AND ME

WAKING, I found myself far above by body, which I imagined still swam in pieces somewhere below. The sound that woke me was the clear little drill of Duke's electric toothbrush. Duke, my father. His Broxodent: for hard-to-reach surfaces, front, back, behind; sixty strokes a second. My disembodied eyes saw on the bedtable my worn dictionary. Fattened by years of use, it displayed along its lengthwise edge my name in graphite capitals: "MICHAEL AMERCHROME." I thought I could hear Duke's hum above the toothbrush. I slept again faintly bilious but content that it was April.

Minutes later I felt Prokofiev's Classical Symphony under me: Duke downstairs grunting out his six-thirty asthma exercises. As I merged again with sleep I remembered that it was Monday and that at the end of the week I'd be eighteen.

At eight-thirty I sat at the long chestnut table near the kitchen door of our beamed living room. Up my legs came the clean starch of my narrow khakis, and round the slope of my neck the collar of my fresh white Oxford. I was mourning over my coffee, which Mary says is bad for my dyspepsia. Mary was talking to herself in the kitchen. Duke was now upstairs. I heard a toilet flow, then Duke singing: "Night and day, you are the one . . . day and night, night and day." Somewhere above, he shouted, "Mary, today phone Herb about delivering loam and grass seed . . . ." Then his voice became indistinct; perhaps he'd poked into a closet. "Godda ginna flower bed bevoid a bulldozer move heaven earth"—he often gave orders from a distance, and Mary often ignored them.

Now, shouting and singing, Duke burst onto the bare New England boards of the second-floor hall. I heard Mary murmur, "My God what a racket, he has entirely too much personality." At the landing Duke called out, "Why is everything so damned quiet?" Then his barking holler became a chant, and suddenly he cantered downstairs singing, with a melodic dip on the last liturgic syllable, "Here I come, ready or no-ot." Then, as I looked back toward his sounds, he appeared. There Duke stood, at the hall threshold, grinning like a horse, one eye half closed in arch suspicion.

He'd changed from the tired violet tights in which he did his calisthenics; now he wore a maroon suede jacket and a black shirt and a limp string tie. While I watched over my shoulder, he grabbed his flash camera from the top of his desk and cried, "Hold it!" and popped his picture before I could shy away.

"What's the good of that?" Mary asked. She had come to the kitchen door.

Then she retired, as Duke said, "Michael's face looked absolutely void. I can't bear to see that kind of darkness on a face."

Now, coughing, Duke made for the table, and insisted on shaking my hand.

"Michael, begin the week right, come in with me today; take in a class or two. It might corrupt you."

I didn't answer. Keep quiet, as someone says in my quotation book, and people will think you're intelligent. I would add, Keep quiet and people may not trust you. But there was honesty in my silence this Monday morning, for I had nothing to say. Still, didn't I feel doubt throb outward in me and work toward my waiting voice? I thought, Why does Duke force me to question everything about him? Why must I be mean?

Duke took two long steps to the Magnavox, dropped on an LP of F. D. R.'s speeches, and came back to the table. He lifted one grasshopper leg over his chairback and slid smoothly in to eat. Why did he have to sit down that way?

Mary muttered sweetly in the kitchen, "Oh, there it is. How can I be so stupid?" Then she scuffed to another part of the kitchen, and I heard her sigh and say, "I hope this is going to work, with everything in it"—which was followed by the drone of the Waring Blender moaning into action.

Duke breakfasted on yogurt, wheat germ, crusts of local

126

honey, figs, raisins, and a cup of hot water and lemon juice. His gray, woolly head bobbed above his bowl as he mumbled his health mash and jabbered at me. Behind him, F. D. R.'s Fala speech moved on suavely, and Duke lectured me. His wide, thin, jittery shoulders rode to and fro, and he seemed to have forgotten F. D. R.

"Ma' a' orpha'," he said through a full mouth. I'd heard these words for years. "Man's an orphan" was what he'd said. He sipped from the smoking cup of lemon and water. "Don't inquire into your past," he said. Then he spoke very fast: "Not because you might hate it but because this way you won't be tempted to turn into what your past might tell you you are."

Duke climaxed his meal with a concoction Mary brought him: a stiff shake of oranges, carrot shreds, celery, unpasteurized milk, raw eggs, and pitted prunes. Between gulps he went on: "You might find I'd been a murderer or a monk, or that your grandparents had been president, or that all your uncles—if you have any—were acrobats or accountants. The point is, make what you are."

Now Duke happens to be a noted historian. For a long time I'd assumed he was entitled to strange ideas about the past. But recently I'd begun to wonder what he'd been up to before—and even for some time after—I came along. And on this Monday I couldn't help seeing luminous slivers of the past in those honey crusts, couldn't help hearing crunches of the past from his munching mouth. And as the past swam in bits toward me, the future filtered back through my Monday morning. And as Duke talked on, I saw the word Monday break up, and between each letter come—but in reverse order—a letter for each of the five succeeding days of the week. And helplessly—for it seems that my mind works this way—I saw these ciphers breed a sentence: My Sense Of Far, Near, Time, Distance, Wandered Across The Years.

I knew Duke had married at sixteen, and had therefore been booted from Trinity College (Hartford). He'd married again during the war, when he was a government cryptoanalyst in Chicago. Unless I was a bastard, Duke's second wife must have been my mother. I knew that Mary, the third Mrs. Duke Amerchrome, was my stepmother. Mary is thirty-five, Duke fifty-four. Their marriage has been childless.

I don't recall anything that happened before I was about

six. From then on, or at least till Duke married Mary when I was eleven, I knew only nurses and housekeepers. They lived on casual—there I go; well, casual—terms with Duke. In my mind they were always girls with families. Duke would say, "Diana's sister has two little chipmunks like you, Michael," or "Helen has to go home for Christmas."

Even when I was six, and Duke referred to his parental self in the third person, he was "Duke" to me. "Duke won't be too late tonight, Michael. Helen will read you *The Iliad*." (Where is that tall picture book now? I didn't know what Duke meant, calling it "abridged," but I didn't dare ask him. I liked Hector better than great-kneed Achilles or hairy Agamemnon. Graceful Hector—what could he do but run away from speeding Achilles?)

The pictures in my *Iliad* and my *Famous Bible Tales* reassured me, for I lived in a world of words. Duke had created this world. It was a live, whirling field of circuiting syllables crossing and recrossing their hues and denotations until in the coiling, popping arcs of their grounded and ungrounded attractions these words became an expanding family more real than the things my dictionary said they referred to. Sir Humphry Davy had not merely brought into contact two carbons and a voltaic pile (the electric battery): indeed, said Duke, the "arc light" thus created was also Noah's ark after Noah, Shem, Ham, Japhet, *et al.* left it; and, as Duke said, "more crucially" this arc light was a spectral fourth son of Noah's and God's imagination who remained inside the empty ark, a luminous bow radiating invisible arrows. This arc of light was in fact the holy force of fusion and confusion both feeding the Noahic Covenant—multiplication, government, "one language-one speech"—and, in the Babel judgment, seeding among men the differences that both part men and make them collide. Noah had been told to make the ark of gopher wood; this, Duke ecstatically urged, was God's pun for "Go far." Duke would ask, "And what did Sam Morse say by electricity in the spring of 1843? What was the electromagnetic word he keyed from Baltimore to the nation's capital? Unh? Unh? Unh? It was, 'What hath God wrought'—both question and affirmation, the two always both separate and one."

"Michael," I'd say to myself, "even if your brain is a hot transformer out of control, imagine you *can* control it—and go slow, go slow."

I knew the names of some of Duke's friends in those earlier days. But I seldom met these men and women. In my head, like a catechetical dream I'll never be quizzed on, I have a list of our addresses over the years and of Duke's jobs. Yes, slowly now: teacher, fund-raiser, political speech-writer, journalist, curator, even—in a documentary on world federalism—actor, director, and film cutter. But of these chapters I know only the titles. For instance, I never saw the film he made, for he got nervous about it when it came out, and the more I asked, the more he insisted I not see it; he said his moving image on the screen made him feel dead. I believed that if I had shown no interest in the film, acted as if it didn't exist, Duke would have pressed me to see it. But honesty wouldn't have let me experiment like that. I couldn't compromise my nature.

The spring I turned eleven, Duke suddenly announced we were leaving the small college in southern California where he'd been teaching for two years. The month we spent at a dude ranch in Williams, Arizona, that summer was one of the few periods during which we gave much time to each other. By day Duke browned his body on the patio and tried to learn the guitar; and I learned to ride. Yes, on a round-bellied white mare I would trot among the western pines tutored by an old friend of Duke. This was Billy Tell, an elderly painter whose bald head was fringed by a long fall of orange hair. I would bump along and, beside me on an eager bay quarter horse, Billy would laugh at me and yell at me to stick by grip instead of balance. "You've as little talent for this as your pop," said Billy one afternoon. And I replied, "He could be a cowboy if he wanted; he could be anything he wanted." At dinner our last last night I referred to Duke as "my father." Billy started to say something, but Duke broke in with a loud "No!" and clamped a hard hand on the table edge. *"Duke to you!"* he said to me. Then he relaxed, as Billy started to kid him, and Duke added, " 'Daddy-o,' yes, but not 'father.' "

Late that night, as he and I took a walk round the swimming pool of that ranch, then round a putting green, then down behind the learner's corral, he recurred to his pet theme:

"With no real knowledge of where you came from, you're a free agent. Freedom and appetite I wish you. All men are orphans."

Then he got onto the signatures of things, which I then thought—and in a sense still think—must be a phrase to do with handwriting. But I kept figuring an answer to what he'd said about orphans.

Dimly feeling the import of my answer, I finally said, "I don't even know you're my father."

"You never know such a thing," he said. "Oh, go ahead and check. With a little postage and wit, you can dream up a dossier of pseudo-facts on where you were born, who your grandparents were, what kind of childhood I had, etcetera."

Hell, Duke's a famous historian. But even then, when I was a brooding eleven, these words he spoke seemed a slippery credo for an apostle of the past. Still, the idea drew me. If I had no past, I had nothing to be ashamed of. At eleven, and indeed until we came to New Hampshire when I was sixteen, it never occurred to me to ask a couple of simple questions. Did my past extend only up to that time—around my sixth year—at which my present memory opens? And second, what is the time from then till now?

But when at last these questions formed in my big idle mind, I had become another person—a suspicious son—and though I dared, I no longer wanted, to ask Duke the answers. An answer came to me those six days that second April in New England, the week with which this tale has begun.

It was what the University students called BERP week—Boys' Economic Recovery Program week. (How Duke loves abbreviations: SAC, UNESCO, ASCAP, VIP, NAACP, AAUP, CORE: "Hieratics of a complicated age," he calls them.) Spurred by tradition, the girls BERP the men—i.e., they ask them out and stand them beer, pizza, movies, dance-hall tickets, even gas. But you can read "Ego" for "Economic," and one fraternity sticks a six-foot thermometer into its lawn to register day by day, as for a charity drive, the rising mercury of BERP's received by its brothers.

Duke thought a fifty-four-year-old professor neither too old nor too reverend to be BERP'd; so, though he turned down several girls, he accepted a Monday date. Monday morning Mary was speaking less as my stepmother than as his wife, when she told him he'd become a sinister man, almost a potent idea held in her imagination. She told him she couldn't get away from him but couldn't get close to him.

"What's happened to our relationship?" she asked him. "But," she added, "if you have to fill up every evening of the

130

week, that's what you have to do. I'm past thwarting you."

But he replied she never had thwarted him. And as she went back to the kitchen to refill my coffee cup, he got up from the table and stopped her with a predatory, ambushing, overbearingly long kiss. Then he put her at arm's length, his huge hands on her slight shoulders, and said, "Go about thy work, woman." And she gently, oh so gently, slapped his face, and laughed; but when she tried to slap again, she got only his back, for he had turned away.

When Duke scooted in late in the afternoon, or gunned off early in the morning, he always looked alone. His Volkswagen, which he vowed to launch as a boat one day, capsuled him from us; in fact its smug motor, before he cut it or as he started it and revved it, seemed to grow a bubble round him. The bubble was like one of those twentieth-century windows. We could see him but he couldn't see us. Mary or I might watch him from the door, maybe call—but he wouldn't notice.

Monday of BERP week he hustled home for a four-thirty swim before he picked up Sue Gardiner, a student who was going to "take" him out to The Rodeo in Blue Bridge, twelve miles away. From the stony bank Mary and I played catch with him while he kicked and lunged about in the bay. I undershot him, and the rubber ball, refusing to skim, wedged back a brief drift of water. On our splintery dock he had stationed the Zenith with its aerial run up. Aimed out into the bay, the violet orchestrations from Luxembourg seemed sharpened and closeted by the wide air. The scene recalled our first visit to this woodland house in New Hampshire.

Something Strauss, something from a waxed, glassy ballroom had been coming from her Blaupunkt FM as Miss Greave, the real-estate agent, had ushered us away from her ranch wagon. She had clicked off the ignition and put the radio on battery, and far away the Strauss resumed, untouchable.

Duke had been drawn from the East-West Fund for World Federalism (Chicago) to a chair at a young university in New Hampshire. I'd been included in this preliminary trip east; Duke had already come once for an interview; Mary had planned our final move for two months later, mid-August.

Doris Greave's imported FM gave a kind of accompaniment as she led us toward the great cocoa-colored lodge and its corner of bay shore. Perhaps she simply liked using her equipment. I think she was in dark competition with old Mr. MacAdam, an agent in town; she had wired and written Duke describing the house.

As she led us past the magisterial red pine that rose slowly out of the center of a circular plot, Duke took Mary's hand. Fifty-odd whitewashed stones braceleted the hard-packed earth. It held the pine as on a dish—gave it a second size, the scale of Mary's Japanese gardens, distant and delicately old in their deep trays. Duke reached his right arm across Mary's way and round behind her spine. Then—with me at one point of the circle, Miss Greave at another—Duke danced poor enthusiastic Mary round the tree, puffing out a limerick half under his breath about Orion and the Pleiades and Taurus the Bull; then he ended hastily with the "Waltz Me Around Again, Willy" chorus—all of this to the Strauss tune that trailed us from the car. Then he shook his head and laughed, and said, "I used to dance a lot with a gal I had centuries ago."

Miss Greave allowed houses and clients to sell themselves. She is a long, large-eyed operator in her late thirties; she skis, hunts, golfs, skin-dives, and boats. It seemed to me that day that in her orange-and-mustard checked suit she carried a certain military loveliness in her stride and in her olympic calm. She gave off a Yankee humbleness, and she seemed less afraid of not pleasing than proud of a balm that traveled with her. I had felt it fill her ranch wagon as she drove us four meandering miles down the Philips Point Road.

Grave and willing, Miss Greave watched Duke waltz with Mary. Professorial strangeness, she may have guessed. (Duke calls "strange" the great mid-twentieth-century cliché.)

Once inside the house, Mary vanished, I politely explored, and Duke jabbed at Miss Greave. "We'll stick a moose head over the mantle, and in the kitchen a deer's ass over a spinning wheel—and we'll install press cupboards, churns, a harmonium, and a larder of S. S. Pierce Indian Pudding. That should tickle the hooples around here, eh Miss Greave?" Duke thought he was taking New England in a warm sardonic embrace. When he passed through to the screened porch on the bay front and then out to the grass bank with its mossy pocks of granite—and never a scuff or creak or tread or little cry from Mary, wherever she was in the house

—Miss Greave kept easy and passive and amused.

"There's clay in the flower beds, but you can grow most anything," she said.

"Clay for pottery, ceramics," Duke said.

"Yes, somewhere around here, I should think," replied Miss Greave.

"I'll put Mary to pot," he said. "I want her to garden, too."

"You might have to shingle that roof," Miss Greave said, pointing to the garage. She turned her big, high, tan cheeks at Duke, then extended her arm toward the bay. "Better not swim there," she said. "The sewage may not stink, but its all through the water."

Duke took in a slow bulging breath. "I could take my asthma exercises out here," he said. "Of course, I shouldn't live at sea level, and the fact is that on general principles, *entre nous,* Miss Greave, we won't stay in New Hampshire more than two or three years. But here, here it's salt, it's a salty bay, the sea's just over that far shore beyond the SAC base. This bay"—he hushed his raw bass—"is a *salty* bay." Miss Greave's FM played on.

Duke was still adoring salt our second spring in New Hampshire. Monday night of BERP week he crackled in our drive about eleven, trailed by another car. I heard girls' collective laughter as Duke led them in toward the house; I knew immediately that there'd been one of Duke's shifts, and I was willing to bet that the mysterious, absurd, unfortunate Sue Gardiner (whom I'd never met) wasn't with him. Yes, Duke said, when I met him downstairs, Sue had left The Rodeo early in a friend's car; she'd been tired. Three new girls had nabbed him, and he'd invited them back.

"I wanted to meet this Sue," I said. And this sent the girls into giggles.

One of them, speaking to me, but seeming to address her chums, said, "She doesn't think Duke is God any more." Then the three of them recited in hilarious unison, "Duke is dead, God is dead, some crass ghost will come instead," and went off again into titters.

"Let's change the subject," said Duke, pretending to be anything but proud of the incident the girls were alluding to. One morning a year before, Sue Gardiner had shown the stress of her studies and her devotion to Duke by lapsing into delusions that landed her in the state hospital in Concord for three months. Duke had kept aloof from the case. I assumed he had accepted a Monday BERP from Sue this year just to show her he understood she was showing him she'd recovered. She had re-enrolled in February and was now taking one of Duke's courses.

Duke did now force the talk away from Sue, and we opened some beer, and a blonde named Linda somehow maneuvered the conversation so that she could quote a long passage from *Catcher in the Rye*. She, like her friends, wore an olivey sheath printed with neat little motifs and topped by a button-down collar. Starting with something about "leave my cabin and come back," she went on to end with

but he couldn't write any movies in my cabin . . . . I'd have this rule that nobody could do anything phoney when they visited me. If anybody tried to do anything phoney they couldn't stay.

Linda kept nodding vigorously as Duke thrilled her by saying, "In America we lose our innocence too soon. It's the fraudulence of the cheery 'Hi,' the assault ad men make on you, our self-absorption in our rich man's guilt."

But then he puzzled the girls. "Still I love billboards for their honest vulgarity: That leaping Buick shoots up into the picture like a Chris-Craft coming up over a grossly near horizon. Or take the Leaning Tower of Pizza outside Boston. That'll last a thousand years; the imitation improves on the real thing; tragic hilarity is what it possesses."

"By itself or in your mind?" I broke out.

"It *is* part of my mind," he replied, addressing no one, just looking off toward a portrait of him that hung over the living room telephone. "Because," he went on, "my mind is America. And my blood is pumped into me from all the filling stations on this continent."

"No wonder you gas so much," I said, and the girls—his consorts and his acolettes—saw they could safely laugh, and laughed against me.

"Michael," said Duke, "you're jealous."

"Listen," I said, "I'm mad that you leave Mary and sail off with these scrubbed virgins at your age."

I had to stop. I was spoiling Duke's Monday BERP. And I was imputing dishonesty.

"At my age?" said Duke. "Nobody knows how old *I* am. But ask these kids how they enjoy me."

"I wouldn't dare," I answered. "If your fans want you to act like a myth, go to it."

"I will, I will," he said, murmuringly, and then let off a crescendo of stage laughter.

Well, I went back to my room, where with lights out I'd been listening to the Mozart quintet Mary'd bought for the clarinet line.

Chamber music lets instruments sing singly, or so it seemed to me. Yet as I played the first movement again and again and heard the perfect tune released by the violin and then returned by the clarinet translated into a skeptical minor, the clarinet seemed less and less a solo voice. It seemed to me that its violet solitude was audible only as one part of the game of offerings and acceptances, advents and farewells, sudden louder agreements, dominants, and final weaves.

And where was Mary at this point? She had exhausted herself in little pecking jobs all day long, and hadn't finished any of them. At nine she had come to my room to kiss me goodnight. Her pink-and-mauve-striped nightshirt hung just to her kneecaps, and her fragility made her seem taller than five-four. On my threshold against the doorway of light from the hall, she had waited for me to come and hug her. With a turned-down smile, she had said, "I took a powder." Which was her innocent, New Yorkey reference to Seconal. She was well away by the time Duke came home with the three students.

After I marched up to my room, he drew them out to the water. He was singing them his folk song about Aunt Rhody's husband, Pa, who bred golden geese. Watching from my window, I heard him mute his grinding voice. A mackerel sky broke the moon's light, but I could see enough. Duke spoke: "The night is different from the day, did you ever think of that? Blessings on this bay." He held his arms outstretched toward the water. "Salt sea cures my meat. Always wanted to buy on salt water. Listen, if I can run out as soon as I get up, and douche myself in salt water—no matter how cold it is, or cold the air—I'm safe. My spiracles and pores receive the sacrament of salt. No kidding. The salt goes in and in and in." He paused. "And what happens then?" Even from my angle, Duke stood tall above his listeners. "Why, out comes whatever venom is in me. I don't mean germs. I'm talking about all the corruption your work builds in you." He chuckled genially, apologetically.

"I mean, that *my* work builds in *me*. Yes, this bay is a veritable saline solution."

Nervously but impersonally, the girls exhaled that special dim wail that hints at gentle, sophisticated, internal amusement.

"Seals swim in here from the Atlantic. There's a bounty, and I'd shoot them if I were a hunter—though I love them. But I'm a hunter of ideas. And sometimes, up to my armpits at seven in the morning, lingering in the salt, I see a seal out there in the middle, his dark puss whiskering toward me just above the wave. I yell at him so hard my voice rings back from the far shore near the air base. And that seal watches. Yes, we're both taking the salt into our systems. We both know how it is. Then again I let him have it—a salty bellow they listen to clear round the bay, maybe beyond the hill on the far side, maybe as far as where the SAC base runways begin.

Duke stilled his voice and honed its arch tone: "Hunters hear me and cock their guns!" His audience stirred, and gave up an eager laugh. He went on: "I can't faze that seal, can't stare or scare him down. Finally, I go under—swim maybe twenty-five yards. When I come up, he's gone." (Duke never swam twenty-five yards under water in his life.)

About a half hour later I watched him kiss the girls and see them into their car. Then he stripped. And then, humming hard, he waded out into the silvery shallows, knifing his arms through the glimmering water. At last, he fell back and lay. And I felt out of place, and felt, somehow, watched; so I left my post and went to bed.

But I couldn't sleep. In my poor stomach the acids worked, and as if there were some connection between my thought and my digestion, my insomnia fed on a mix of Duke's speech to the girls and a violent undersea vision of my tender stomach. Little telelabels flicked on and off identifying things in that bathyspheric world; gastric juice from the walls of my stomach met bits of the sole fillet Mary had broiled me for supper; hydrochloric acid dissolved the salts; pepsin changed the shreds of fish meat into proteoses; Duke's commanding voice appeared as a stick of ruby light with words taped across it saying, "Release the pylorus," and this ring of muscle eased open and a jet of chyme, the thin soup to which my food had been reduced, sped into my duodenum, and Duke's voice appeared again, saying,

"Check out jejunum, ileum, appendix, and colon." I saw an air bubble disengage from the floor of my stomach and rise and veer out of sight up into my esophagus; and as I belched, feeling a small, quick antiperistalsis work a dim taint of nausea upward, I passed into sleep.

Tuesday morning Duke left earlier than usual, and so I couldn't tell him what I'd seen inside me. Breakfasting on coffee, stewed figs, and a pale poached egg, I thought of Duke's speed, his race, his constant attempt to beat his own schedule; and I momentarily (and passively) faced the thought that if he dropped dead in class today or had a cerebral hemorrhage in the VW, I wouldn't be able to tell him my strange gastric vision.

For years Duke had run such executive and shifty schedules, I'd come to wonder how thorough his life could be. "You have to find your own world," he'd say, grinning evilly as if he'd just made a joke. At home he gave Mary and me what he called freedom. He felt that the economics of the hearth should tend toward laissez faire. He'd not meddle with Mary—she could cook for us, or *he* would cook, she could darn his socks or damn them, type his manuscripts or play the clarinet, do everything or do nothing. "Find the laws of your own development," he said. Of course, because he didn't interfere with Mary, he had more time for his own work. But this theory made some sense to me.

For the two years since I'd graduated from high school in Chicago, Duke had sponsored my sloth. He might have been trying to inspire me when he said, "Many men never locate their own truth. They're scared to wager a few of their glistening years finding out." He failed to see I didn't feel I was *wagering* those years. I didn't feel there were any risks to take. I didn't think I was losing anything.

At first he assigned me books. For example, an old physical geology text. Holding this out to me at arm's length as if it were a ceremonial gift, Duke said one morning, "Study synclines and meanders, and see how our world is a body. Study faulting; it'll shrink the landscape for you, make you feel near it. Then you'll think of time, and the landscape will appall you." He gave me Spengler to read, and Toynbee, and *The City of God*. "Most books should be read at no more than two sittings." He told me the great historians were the men who'd seen the whole thing in the light of single key laws. He urged me to worry more about the keys

137

than about the wild medley of pseudofacts. "The only way to understand anything," he said, "is to begin with a general conclusion about what you'll find. Honest tendentiousness."

Later Duke left my education alone. *"You* must choose the books, only *you,"* he said. "Your knowledge must organize itself from within you."

He did spare me a tutorial here and there. But history was difficult with Duke, for he saw allegories everywhere. We couldn't drive to Boston on an ordinary trip to the Record Shack without Duke declaiming the omnipresence of the journey motif. "Life is a journey," he would say as he passed a massive diesel truck on Route One (and then cut in ahead too soon so that the truckdriver honked in helpless anger). "Life is a journey, a pilgrimage," Duke would continue. To which Mary, if she were with us, might answer, "Life is a drag." Then, as if to show she'd been kidding, she'd lean to kiss his long cheek, but he'd counterploy, "A drag race!"

Just before he married Mary—when I was in New York with them—he took me out to New Jersey to go over the ground of the Battle of Monmouth. And at the spot where Molly Pitcher's well was supposed to have been—there along the Pennsylvania Railroad tracks between Freehold and Englishtown—he delivered a winding meditation on a line out of Chaucer: "Now up, now doun, lyk boket in a welle." "There you are," said Duke; "life can be imagined as a vertical alternation or oscillation between pulls downward and upward; down went Molly's bucket, up came the water that she risked her life to bring to the rebels; the American fortunes were like that bucket, and there would have been no 'up' without a 'down,' no clear triumph without the personal immersion in the dark depths of revolution's well. Take Dante. Justice and Mercy. Good old J and M. Examine the movements through Hell, Purgatory, and Paradise; only through the downward quest can one find—indeed qualify for—the upward way." Then Duke worked into circles and the spiral of history. But I did manage to get him to tell more about Molly. He admitted we were standing at what was only *advertised* as Molly Pitcher's well; admitted, also, that she'd been identified as Molly Maban, Molly Hanna, Molly Hayes, and Molly McCauley; and that the husband she had followed as his camp moved and whose place she probably had taken at a cannon after he was killed, may not have been her husband but just a boyfriend. " 'Lie

138

there my darling while I revenge ye,' " Duke quoted. Yet he confessed that other more formal sayings had been ascribed to Molly, and he quoted these to me, assuring me, with a frightful sort of uncharacteristic seriousness, that evidence existed verifying all of them.

The old sexton we met in Tennent Church blinked at Duke's "Now up, now doun," and tried to take Duke down when Duke said that the bloodstains on the pews where Washington's wounded had lain, were touched up every year for the tourists.

"Them's the same as always," the old man said, "what's your proof?"

But he only fell into further pique and uncertainty when Duke said he was glad they did touch up the bloodstains, for thus history was being saved. "Saved!" he cried, shaking his index finger at the old man.

But this incident wasn't typical of my education. My studies were mostly solitary. And the further I read, the more thinly I felt I was spreading myself.

More and more, I turned to my dictionary, as if it were that "easy reading" that always lies a bit too near the hand of the scholar. Indeed, I *read* my *American College Dictionary* (A Random House Book). There's hardly a word in it that isn't underlined. I know the definition of about 125,000 words. When asked, I can even reproduce many of the drawings: for example, "triskelion," that lonely figure of three legs or arms joined at one imprisoning center; or "tesserae," unfairly easy to draw, for instead of creating a mosaic out of pieces, all you do is draw your shape and then throw over it a cross-hatch of lines, the resulting cell-like pieces being, of course, the tesserae.

Duke calls reference books the core of any decent library. But the only reference work he owns—except for *Who's Who in America*—is an *Encyclopedia Americana* he got free for endorsing it. Actually I own more books than Duke. He'd rather use libraries and travel light.

By the time we came to New Hampshire I had assembled two gay wallfuls of books, most of them paperbacks. However, a year ago my reading slowed down. There seemed to be too much. After reading Revelations, I had begun the Old Testament; but I bogged down in Genesis 5: After Seth came Enos, who begat Cainan, who begat Mahalaleel, who begat Jared, who begat Enoch—and they all lived well beyond

139

normal expectancy. I would go to my books now and then and slip them into new color sequences. Mary, who had been a textile designer, would look at my shelves and call out the technical color names: *Shakespeare*, geranium; *The Story of Engineering*, light burnt sienna; *Christopher Wren*, lemon; *The Art of Plain Talk*, by Rudolph Flesch (the book I hate most out of those I've read), Irish Nile green; *James Morris' Venice*, cobalt blue; *A Casebook on the Beat*, mood indigo; *The New Astronomy* (A Scientific American Book), spectrum violet. Then Mary would teach me to compare tonal values by squinting at the colors till I could hardly see them. I gave up reading because I was paralyzed by quantity. Also, I discovered that Palomar watchers see the Andromeda nebula as it looked two million light years ago. So the glimmering oval I thought I saw through my thirty-one-power homemade reflector telescope might not be there at all. (One light year; 5 quadrillion 880 trillion miles.) As if this weren't sufficiently defeating, there came an added crusher: The remotest nebula you can get a spectrogram of isn't just satisfied to be far away—twenty-four million light years; it's flying off from us at thirty-five thousand miles per second! What about *that!*

I forewent serious reading, but I gave my imagination a kick. In what I then identified as my less innocent moods, I'd fancy Duke one of those pedagogical con men you read about now and again in *Time*. Somehow you have to admire these wandering scholars who fake, or apparently fake, their way into professorships. Preceded by forged credentials and now soberly flanneled and clever-eyed, the aspirant comes. He smokes Winstons with the dean, is sniffed and sounded by potential colleagues (menacing and menaced). Soon he's in. Soon his pupils bless his personality, his gags, his taut classroom silences, his interesting exams, his human force. And—do you know? he *is* good.

I had sat in on Duke's classes and had heard him wake up his fans preaching Bakunin or Berdayev at eight A.M. And as he had felt for and found his phrases, I had shared that communal shock he could set off that may or may not send a pupil to the stacks but always for that high, dilating moment makes him think he can see so much more than he does—or ever will. I had heard Duke cry, "Genius is the ability to counterattack nightmare," and seen the hands that pinched the ballpoints jerk into action. And I knew Duke's

140

grand laments. One night when we were living in Chicago, he drove back late from a cash lecture at Carbondale and proclaimed sadly that he'd come from southern Illinois, where the last Indians chew tobacco spiced with coal dust.

He was always in the classroom, you might say. And in the actual classroom he was always in a kind of marketplace. When he took up what he called his Socracutor technique, you now and then wondered if, sequential as his steady questions were, their demands were uninventive rather than luminous, quick but not alive. And when he walked and rushed his cross-examination into that final cul-de-sac where you were supposed to discover for yourself a great meaning, you felt both that nothing had been answered and that Duke had been trying merely to surround you with an atmosphere of electric and seditious quest.

I must, in all honesty, say that the facts of Duke's debut in New Hampshire had been simple and public. He sported like a royal train a bibliography of short books and long articles on a variety of subjects: the Battle of Ticonderoga (one of his special fields, he says); advertising art (in which he says he takes a tragic joy); John Dewey's hobbies; Hobbes and the great chain of being; *The Bay Psalm Book* (Cambridge, Mass., 1640); communism and modern dance; Kant and Camus; Christian fascism—many more. He had had two hundred copies privately printed of the final section of a novel he had never finished; he claimed that the first part would have shown that the whole book was about world federalism; he titled the fragment *Noah's Fourth Son*. Duke's range is famous, but reviews of his books—or so I hear, for I never read his reviews (or his books, for that matter)—have been restrained. Duke quoted me one proudly: "With this new book the versatile Professor Amerchrome has kept his amateur status intact." Duke said this was what he wanted, for it was better to know something about everything than to know all about something. "Be what Pascal calls the *honnête homme,*" Duke would say; "but *honnête* doesn't really mean 'honest,' you know," he'd add, with that coy smile which I could never answer with the question it seemed to invite.

On his New Hampshire appointment, *The Blue Bridge Chronicle* and *The Mohawk Listener* ran a story released by David Brooke, our neighbor, who writes for the university news bureau: Dr. Roland—"Duke," I'd have added—Amerchrome, distinguished cultural historian, had been named Ercole Fortuna Professor of Humanistic Sciences. (This was the first endowed chair at this new university.) Quoted as deeply approving the chair's title, Duke explained that he had tried in his own "humble and flamboyant way to demonstrate the crucial connections among the major fields of human inquiry." Brooke reported that Duke would be affiliated with no department, be responsible only to the president.

Against the latter's wishes, Duke set out to teach four courses: The History of Science; Colonial America; Teaching Machines, Language Labs, and the Pupil's Awareness (live on closed-circuit TV the first year, taped the second); and The Open Society and the Philosophy of the Road. But when would he *think*? Well, by our second spring, Mary had stopped asking that question. Friday of BERP week he would deliver his second annual Fortuna lecture. Monday Mary told him he'd pull a big enough audience without her.

Tuesday of BERP week Mary was even busier than usual. Of course, she seldom finished what she started. One day it was gilding pine cones, the next practicing her light-brown clarinet as if she were a faltering herald. Another day she'd be passing her frail arms over the knitting machine Duke had brought her from New York. This Tuesday it was papering a room.

"It might rain today," said Mary. "That's what I told Duke. But he said 'Look at the sun I ordered for today.' So maybe he knows. Rain wouldn't be good for the wallpaper."

When we lived in Chicago Duke had surprised Mary with six rolls of William Morris wallpaper. He'd been sent on a study-tour of England by the Splinter Forum for World Federalism. He'd contrived to fly the paper home from London without having to pay excess weight charges or duty. Printed by Sanderson from the original Morris blocks, it had cost Duke over a hundred dollars. Yes, Vine 45 was just what Mary wanted: night indigos and jungle greens and purples, dream-bound leaves on searching python creepers—precariously a design.

Mary would roll back one of the cylinders far enough to see the print repeat. When I had asked to help, and then when Duke had told her to get a professional in, Mary had only answered that she wouldn't let anyone else touch the paper—it was Duke's present to her. But in Chicago she could never bring herself to attack a wall. The six rolls came to New England with us.

Tuesday of BERP week Mary asked me to bring up the stepladder. Then, in three scuffing descents from the attic, she transferred the Morris paper to the guest room. She knelt on one of the beds, looked oriental in the tender neat tuck of her lean limbs as she bent to ponder a magazine article on wallpapering. Its title: "Homework for Husbands." She had to be alone, she said. So I left her.

The phone rang once during the day: Sue Gardiner, to say she must see Duke but couldn't find him, couldn't find him.

In the afternoon Mary raced our other VW, a microbus, into town to buy plastic sheeting and paste and a knife she didn't need and a soft clothes brush she also didn't need. She was back just before Duke came home for his dip.

Cradling her up in his arms, he cried, "World, I give thee my all-American wife, daughter, sister, mother—my petal, my pine needle, my syllogism." And then he kissed her fine, long, drooping nose and her short straight raven hair while she lay in his arms, indignant and taken. Oh, then he rumbled and guffawed, said it was about time Mary stuck up that fruity wallpaper, then titillated himself by saying it was about time Mary's project got off the ground.

Just as she had, twenty times before, so Tuesday afternoon, as Duke held her, Mary turned on herself and announced to him—not to me—that the Morris vine was the test, the pivot.

"Before I married you, I was almost making it," she said. Her New York accent slid into her words especially when she elegized that time during which she had designed furnishing fabrics for a friend's Forty-second Street studio.

Our neighbor up the Point Road, that sneak David Brooke, told me Mary's accent could be Lower East Side, Bronx, Far Rockaway, or even lower Myrtle Avenue in Brooklyn. But to me it was the voice in that secret apartment by Riverside Park—two and a half dusky chambers strewn with floor cushions, complicated by brocaded screens, haunted by tray gardens and tubular parchment lampshades on ceiling pulleys. That September day I first met her, Duke was off high in the hives of Manhattan; he was, he said, having a look at I. B. M. and exhorting them to go into teaching machines. Mary received me in lemon velvet slacks

143

and a Persian-blue button-down shirt (the tails out).

Her telephone was ringing as she opened the door, and she at first said, "Oh, hello, I just have to go answer. . . ." But then, after momentarily fading back into that dark hall, she returned to me, and said, with a nervy chuckle, "Let it ring, Michael," and took me quickly around the neck and gave my cheek a long but somehow light kiss, and then looked into my face and asked, "It *is* Michael, isn't it?"

To me her accent—the air breathed by the meanings of her words—means Riverside Park. Means languid, chattering private school kids my age who lounged around and slapped a fuzzless tennis ball back and forth into casual but significant squares chalked on the pavement. Her accent goes with those few perfect walks we took, following her mad-eyed Weimaraner puppy up to the statue of Kossuth and back. (We left that dog in Oregon.) We had our secrets, Mary and I: Once, for example, she found me a hair-straightener on Lexington Avenue who tried twice to unkink my dull brown hair.

But more than our secrets or her words, I hear her accent: the nasal New York vowels opened into their component sounds—so seemingly sloppy in their precision next to the level sounds of farmers at the livestock fair Duke had once taken me to in the Salad Bowl of southern California. I hear Mary nagging a feather-fingered salesman at De Pinna's: "His trousers should show a little sock; they shouldn't break over his instep." How subtle his self-abasement, as this funereal host wrinkled his brow and brushed his talons down the cloth once more. He pretended to condescend to what (as I pointed out outside to Mary) he archly overimplied was Mary's too-smart taste.

When we were free of the store, wandering down Fifth Avenue, and I was taking the salesman apart, Mary chided me in her little girl's whine: "Don't be so hostile and complex." And she took my arm—she twenty-eight, I eleven—and made me feel unerring and piratical.

I stood up for Duke at their civil wedding four days later. A month afterward we were off to Texas, where Duke would be visiting curator of the Sam Houston Museum.

Gradually Mary stopped sending designs to New York. From time to time she'd show me how the blue in her gums was fading; she wasn't sucking a paint brush anymore. From Texas to California (my third stop there) to Oregon to

144

Chicago, Mary transported a gathering family of objects that seemed to spring from her nerves. First, wood-carving knives with removable guillotine-slanted blades; then the caramel-colored clarinet—a marvelously metalled mystery you felt you could just pick up and play; then a book-binding kit with which she planned to make two plastic-morocco collections of the off-prints of Duke's articles. Duke urged Mary to sculpt or paint, but she said she had never been an artist and wasn't going to start now. She'd give art a miss.

Billy Tell had done a five-by-five portrait of Duke, and Mary set out to frame it. God, what a likeness! Part ad, part poem, redolent of Presley, WBZ's loud and musical and scary news reports (every half hour), motivational research, Chagall. Above the tall, rutted rectangle of face, a helmet of violet Brillo hair glittered like a halo of mail; round the margins of the canvas swam the tiny shrapnel of Duke's universe—a Shell sign (lighted and, in my opinion, revolving), indigo headlines tilted and falling, an orange towel waiting in midair like the Superman capes I used to fly around in at Gaviota Beach near Santa Barbara; a low-cantled roping saddle atop a leather-covered gymnast's sidehorse; a white-swathed bride posing on a sky-blue Thunderbird fender; a Louisville Slugger sandwiched in a hot-dog roll. Also there was a jukebox whose music appeared in a cartoon balloon that contained a log cabin (up from whose chimney grew a green nuclear mushroom); in the lower right corner of the canvas Abraham Lincoln in a snowy toga that revealed knobby knees gripped the shoulder blades of two bleeding slaves who flanked him.

Mary had decided on a simple deep frame. She had bought a square, two saws, a miter box, and a workbench fitted with two vises. Her sawing style was vigorous and two-handed—risky for the blade. She actually finished the frame. But since she knew her right angles weren't exact, Duke's wordy breakers of praise numbed her small pride in what she'd done. Duke knew what she meant when she called her wallpapering project a test case.

So absorbed was she in her plans Tuesday that she forgot she'd asked a guest for dinner. So she had to open three tins of kippered herring and three jars of ravioli and sauce. "American ingeniousness," Duke announced, patting her behind.

The kippers were appreciated by our guest, a young Oxford historian named Harry Tindall. He lives down the Point Road with David Brooke. In vain Duke had several times asked Harry Tindall to dinner. Finally, this quick, towering, skeletal Englishman had been trapped by Mary. She hates the phone. When she had called Tindall, her little halts and nervous embarkations humbled him to pity her and say yes to her invitation.

Well, after dinner Mary disappeared upstairs, presumably to look at her wallpaper.

Duke started in on history.

"We historians share the epistemological crucifixion with all the other poor blokes. We're just first-person narrators."

Tindall, his long flint face pale but for the cherry speckle on the cheek bone, suddenly bulged his eyes at Duke—in despair or scorn, I think—and then used savage hesitations to say, "Yes . . . uh, yyyyes . . . I quite . . . seeeee."

But Duke turned his eloquence into a new channel when they argued method. Historiography, he said, was scientific fiction.

"At least you don't call it *science* fiction," returned Tindall. He said that apart from prospects of other Edens and other apples, maybe on Venus or Mars, he thought science fiction solemn irreverence.

But Duke seemed quickly to dam Harry up, and began to ladle out a spiel I felt I'd heard before.

"Say you case a bookshop in Revere, Mass. You find an early copy of Cotton Mather's *Manuductio ad Ministerium* and stick in it some fossiley papers Richard Mather used as first-draft scratch sheets for *The Bay Psalm Book*. (Excuse my hobbyhorse.) You check at Harvard. You do a piece proving Dick *wrote The Bay Psalm Book* and in his revising drew on Joe Blow over in England. You suggest that each time he relied on Joe rather than his own ear, he gave in to a paler phrasing. But now: How can you know Richard Mather wasn't revising someone else's translations? You've combed diaries, run handwriting tests, even ciphered the name of somebody's mistress—your science still turns into fiction before you're through. Your fluency's just vapor."

Tindall cut in: "But in print you qualify your claims."

Duke fed a thrill into his voice: "But you don't want anyone to take the qualifications seriously, and you don't take them so yourself."

146

I heard Mary scuffing slowly downstairs, whistling the end of Brahms' First Symphony.

Duke gave his face a solemn, smiling, open look, as he finished. "You live a paradox. The best you can do is embrace it, eat it like a seven-course sacrament. The paradox is like the finite radio-telescope finding the heavens to be an infinite four-dimensional saddle, expanding in all directions."

"I know nothing about science, but why do you say 'paradox'?" said Tindall, looking at his watch. "Oh, it's half ten."

But Mary now flew gradually into the room, pausing by the desk and then the butterfly table, loath to interrupt. Her hands and arms were full of black cards, compasses, greaseproof paper, tracing paper, glue, and a rainbow of cellophanes. She began to speak: together we were going to make home mosaics, an old *House Beautiful* told how, Harry Tindall could take his mosaic home tonight and mount it in a window. When a few of her cellophanes slipped away from her and floated to the floor, Tindall picked them up. Then he checked his watch. But now he seemed to start acting, seemed to transform himself. With an arch bustle of elbows and some delighted crowing—which made me hunch my shoulders and absolutely stopped Mary and made her shyly calm—Tindall arrayed tools and materials and spread out at the huge table near the south wall of our old woody living room. He said he was trying to reproduce the east window of his Oxford college chapel. And Duke, without a hint of his usual double meanings, suddenly murmured, "Isn't *this* the family group!"

We watched Harry work. His at first pretended but then intent interest in Mary's mosaics seemed worthwhile. "I need indigo and orange," he said, looking over the cellophanes, "orange and indigo." And I resolved that Duke should not wheel us violently away from this simple moment. Yet simultaneously I felt that somehow Duke's behavior had caused this firm Englishman to do what he did.

Wednesday morning of BERP week David Brooke, Tindall's housemate, came sniffing. He often visited Mary. I knew he encouraged her to feel forlorn. Peering at the music, he would sit down at the baby grand and accompany her clarinet études. Or he and Mary would compare conductors, Mary defending Bernstein and bewailing her exile from New York. David would allude to a chronicle he was writing of

147

Tindall's adventures in New Hampshire. But he never gave us details. He'd squint, and say softly and slowly, "We none of us know each other. It's the problem of knowledge—the problem of history and personality."

Me he patronized. And when Mary was out of the room, he pumped me. Wednesday she wanted to be left alone with her wallpaper, and David sank into an armchair in the living room. He looks about twenty-eight. I think he's keen on Mary. He's always sucking in his big bubble cheeks and scratching his flaky forehead. Has wide, strong, yellowish teeth and long loose legs. As Duke would say, he verbalizes easily. Yet David doesn't really know how to talk to you. Either he butts in and speaks for ten minutes straight—intense and blind and using phrases like "Of course, ultimately," "complex awareness," "in fact in my opinion." Or he doesn't come back at you at all, just gives you "um-hum, um-hum" after each of your sentences and sometimes in the middle.

Wednesday he was curious about what I wrote in my diary —I call it my nocturnal. When I would speak, he'd edge to the side, as if trying to get out of my line of sight. I'd gradually follow him round. This morning, small talk took us about a hundred and eighty degrees around. Then he stopped trying to get behind me.

"Do you record the secrets of this peculiar household?"

"No," I answered, "I'm keeping them from myself."

"I sometimes feel there's no center here, no dry land."

"Like a houseboat?"

"But then, your remarkable father . . . ."

"How do you know he's my father?"

"True, he doesn't act like one."

"Why do you care?"

"I just want to find things out."

"Do you object to Duke?"

"I'm impartial," David said, staring at the ceiling. He was going to give me one of his labored interpretations. "I'm a snooper. That's my disease. It's sheer egotism, for when I find out about a person I find all I've done is come face to face with a thick mirror. But at least I end by looking at myself. Take your father. He seems to want to be a mystery. Never takes one view without adopting its opposite. 'Government originates from the people; but let the people be taught that they are not able to govern themselves.' That, he passes

148

off as his own. I heard it from a student, checked with Harry Tindall, who said Jeremy Belknap, a New Hampshire clergyman, said it. One of your Dad's students—who incidentally thinks your Dad's a kind of god—says your Dad reverses himself all the time. Monday he'll tell a class that inertia and nausea are the only proper responses to our society, a society dying of lies and impersonality. Wednesday he'll tell the same class that we must love and devour our land, from the corn-on-the-cob Chaplin has to eat in a barber chair in *Modern Times*, to the passion of the Moral Rearmament boys and the John Birchers; that like new Romans we must eat everything on the plate and then tickle it up out of our stomachs, then eat again. Your father's students are so crazy about his style and his commitment they feel they must plunge into the sea of what he says and somehow live in it, be nourished by it."

"What's your point?" I asked.

"That Professor Amerchrome is either a genius or a mad fool or a fake."

"He's more man than you'll ever think of being," I said.

"That, my friend, is true."

"You don't understand Duke," I said.

"No," David replied, "but I will." And he paused on the way out our front door to say, "If you want to talk about this some more, you know where you can reach me."

"I've got a good reach," I retorted.

I went upstairs and lay down with my April horoscope. Mary looked in at noon and told me I was wasting my life.

"You lie there thinking how blue you are, or how yellow. Do something. Even be a bastard. You can't live like this forever."

Well, then I tried to go on with a one-thousand-page novel I was reading, but, as usual for the past few months, I got caught in one of the author's closet observations. I call them that because they close me into their suggestions, and before I know it my suspicions of the author are so many and shifting that I'm cut off from the book and have to stop reading. Does that sound normal? Well, this time he'd said

Giorgio examined his nails, not, as men do, fingers in against the palms, but rather in the manner of women, the whole long irregular oval of the back of the hand beautiful and banked.

Well, I read this and I wondered, first, if the author was right, and, second, if he wasn't setting up pretty tight rules for those who might wish to belong to the American stud club. So there I was, flat on my back, having read only a dozen sentences and stopped already.

Duke turned up at one. A committee meeting hadn't come off. It was his first defeat in a week that, all in all, turned out rather badly for him. It was as if the committee members had cut his class. He'd reserved a room in the huge, hangar-like Union a young architect had recently swollen out of the ravine behind Mill Street. Duke seemed to run ten or twelve committees. I knew he loved using the Union, arranging working lunches. But Wednesday no one turned up. He'd come home to tell Mary all about it. I heard him in the hall saying there were two kinds of people: the floaters and the marchers.

Finding me on my bed when he bowed and tilted that kinky-haired gray head in past my half-open door to stare at me, he whispered harshly, "Thinking? Thinking?" Then he gently closed my door.

I heard Mary tell Duke in the hall, "Analysis, he needs analysis, I know it, you know it."

To which Duke, rather too loudly, replied, "He's read Horney and Fromm and he can do better analyzing himself. He's aware, he has awareness. Now he's got to embrace."

They passed into their room, and distance and doors filtered their words to a bumpy mechanical hum. Then they came through the hall again, Duke nagging Mary about grass seed. "You've got time for those toy gardens on the window sills but not for my land outside the house."

I went downstairs forty-five minutes later. Duke was snapping up the last raw carrots and walnuts and cauliflower buds of his lunch. I declined his invitation to join him at the Misses Greave's that night. Then, with a hissing, strangely fussy complaint about three aged members of that truant committee, he was off, bound for his university office.

A few minutes later, Sue Gardiner phoned again, and I spoke to her.

"I have to see your father," she called into her instrument as if she thought my ear was plugged.

I liked her voice, though not its volume. I had never seen

her. To provoke her I said, "Well, why don't you go find him?"

"I've missed him," she answered ambiguously. "He's never in his office. He's probably drinking coffee with students in the Union; he's not in his—" and here her tone turned ironic—"his special 'Do Not Disturb' hideaway in the library."

Duke had lectured his classes on the true meaning intended by the patriotic endower of the new library, in the pedimental motto, "THE TRUTH IS EVERYWHERE THE SAME." Duke called it fascism. Yet the library had served him well: Because he headed the library committee and, as well, occupied the Fortuna chair, he had wangled a kind of isolation study, the envy of his colleagues (so he said). It came complete with an electric typewriter, a dictaphone, a Mexican rug with, as he said, venereal symbolism all over its pattern, a tiny refrigerator, and two monster deliciosas spiralling their leathery, ovate leaves up barky spruce poles. To certain students Duke gave away keys that fitted the door of this study. This gesture came from his conviction that a university should be a community of scholars. I didn't know what to say to Sue.

"Better call him here later. What did you want?"

"It's personal. Isn't it always personal with your father? I mean that in a nasty way, but probably you didn't catch on."

"Can I help?"

"I never heard of anything so idiotic," she replied. "You haven't even begun college." Then hurriedly she started another sentence with "Oh why did I—" but I crashed my receiver down.

Duke would be home for supper, then off to the Greave sisters'. From the turn of Sue Gardiner's voice, I felt she was after more trouble. She didn't call at suppertime, and I forgot to pass Duke the message. He had changed his plans for that afternoon, he said rather darkly. Instead, he had spent it with the president.

I heard few disputes now about our real-estate agent Doris Greave and her sister. The latter was the notorious aviatrix Deirdre, who flew a yellow, singleprop Cessna up and down the coast streaming blue banners that might advertise HONEST ABE'S LIVE ANIMAL FARM or BEAULIEU FOR STATE SENATOR. There were no disputes now, because Mary had

151

had a vision. From one of the bimonthly evenings of the Greave sisters' Humanities Club—at which Duke presided—Mary had brought home a vision. She relied on it whenever Greave Wednesday took the last little slack out of a week that was already getting away from her. The vision? Duke haranguing when he was pretending to be a mere moderator. The vision? Eleven women—including four wives from the SAC base—submitting to Duke's foaming formulas. Mary quoted these to me: " 'It is only through the solitary orgasm that we connect, only through supermarket aisles that we pass to the American soul, only through Elvis that we shake through to the true Mozart, only through mountain motels and the oil-depletion allowance that we find the knowledge of our home, only through being rootless that we find the one deep American root, only through failing courses that we locate true scholarship, only through time see life, only through corruption be innocent.'

"After this," said Mary, "they had coffee and glazed crullers." The one husband, a Mr. Homer Boulos, had approached Duke calmly and asked if marriage was the way to solitude.

So, without jealousy, Mary could forego the Greave sisters' Humanities Club. Noncommittally she would decline each time Duke invited her to come along. She could smile at Duke's hollered greetings when Doris and Deirdre came generating past our shore some nights in their twenty-foot power boat.

Well, Wednesday of BERP week Duke was delivered to our dock around eleven-thirty. Doris and Dierdre moved off into the bay before I could make it down to see the goings on. As Duke stepped cautiously along the rickety dock, he was talking to himself—or so it seemed. Perhaps he thought I'd be near enough to listen. Stepping off the boards onto grass, he shot his light up at me.

"Michael, Michael," he groaned, "sometimes I think my life and self and mission make a harmony only because I'm such a big stomach of a person that I can give strange bedfellows room to swim around inside me. In terms of emotion and thought and taste and quantity, I'm a goatish Dispos-All. David Brooke joined the little women tonight. It appears that the alumni magazine will print a profile in depth that will tell about me and my rackets."

"But," I said, "you don't think what you do is a racket."

"It is, in a way," he murmured, as if he were considering the idea for the first time. "*I'm* a racket."

As he neared the screened porch, he put an arm around my shoulders.

"You can counterattack nightmare two ways. You can blinker yourself and simplify. Or you can bless the whole teeming, tipping world and devour it. But maybe only God does the second. And for God the world may not be a nightmare. How's that? The world as God's nightmare."

(Was Duke saying the world *was* or was *not* God's nightmare?)

I ducked away from his arm. He'd been leaning on me. I could smell the Greave sisters' Newburyport rum on his breath.

I said, "Now you're telling me that all your talk about embracing is no good. What *am* I meant to do?"

"Pity me. Pity is the feeling that arrests the mind in the presence of whatever is grave and constant in human sufferings and unites it with the human sufferer. Even scorn me, Michael. But anyway, notice me."

I doubted the tremble in his voice as he said, "When you teach people day in day out, you get close to yourself." No, I didn't believe Duke. I suddenly didn't. Yet worse, I felt my stomach oils curdling, and I could only think of what Duke had made of me: a suspicious son.

Back and forth the length of the living room—reaching up to slap a beam, bending down to claw fingerfuls of macadamia nuts—Duke talked to Mary about the strange evening.

"That one husband who always comes—of course, they *all* always come—Homer Boulos, *you* know. He wanted to know how I could defend socialism and capitalism, subscribe to both."

"How *can* you?" Mary asked. She was lying on the big couch with her eyes closed.

"Why? Because both are necessary. And the only life is in accepting both. Only by taking both into our systems do we embrace the time. I told him we must seek profits but at the same time must feel our guilt at *wanting* to take profits. And we had to work for paternalistic government at the same time we resisted and loathed it. I told him I was trying to be fully American. He said I hadn't decided whether I *was* an American. Which is also true, but I didn't tell him so. He said there was a limit to how many paradoxes you could live with.

And suddenly, with David Brooke busy in a corner taking notes, I felt every person there in the room was unsure about me."

Mary stirred, raised her knees. "But no one can speak really well to an audience unless he's a little afraid of losing it."

"And at coffee," Duke continued, unaware of her shifting body on the couch, "the questions were—what shall I say?—polite."

Again Mary drawled languid nervous words at him: "You expect too much. Those people—ugh!—you expect too much. All they want is a little free knowledge. They think they want to discuss. But they want to be fondled."

"Well, they don't want anything after tonight. I sensed this, and told Doris I wouldn't be coming much more this spring, if at all. I told her I have to finish my book."

"What book?" Mary asked.

"History. Imaginary history. I don't know. It's planned, not started. Takes the form of a will, or several drafts of a will, in which the legator changes as he goes along, first switching legatees and bequests, then reducing his bequests until finally he leaves—well, you'll see."

"That doesn't sound like history to me," I said. It seemed Duke was addressing only Mary.

"I got the idea from Harry Tindall, a real case he wrote up. I'm elaborating on it. But it *is history*."

Mary rose. "I'm going to bed. This is too complex." I watched the parts of her limbs operate smoothly as she lounged toward the door.

And I followed her. Duke was saying, "Having proved that I *can* accomplish too much, I'm going to prove I *can* do *less*."

He had told me not to bother reading his books and articles. Why had I consented? And without having read his work, had I the right to find now something dreadfully thin in what he claimed to be about to start? I resented, not the possibility Duke might be less than a great man, but my own obligation to suspect him. What kind of a world is it in which you have to be suspicious of your father? I said to myself that I half suspected Duke didn't really exist—that he was the product of a concatenation of sounds that for years and years had swirled round me fed from a source I could never see, that he was the product of the liturgy of hearsay, that he was the reputation implicit in his name, that the public world had conspired to assemble him before my eyes but that there was no Duke. However, this thinking sounded too much like Duke's enigmas, so I abandoned it. Yet, wishing only to be honest and loyal, I found myself compelled to corruption—filial treason, general nausea.

When Duke told his classes what he breakfasted on, was he posing as a prophet? Was his morning asthma therapy in actual fact meant to keep his muscles toned up? Did he believe what he said about the bay salt? Did he care that Mary took Seconal some nights he came home late? Did he believe what he told Harry Tindall, that history-writing was just fiction? (*Just fiction: just:* the meanings joined and bred.) If history-writing was just fiction, how could Duke go on? *Go on:* Actors said that, did that. Did Duke really know anything about Cotton Mather? Was there something wrong in Duke's palship with Doris and Deirdre Greave? When he embraced opposite points of view, was he acting, was he honest?

As Mary left the living room, Duke called to her to come back. By then I was up; and as I reached the threshold he called to me too: "Michael, I'm not finished."

At the foot of the stairs in the hall I looked up. Slouching up the stairs, lean dark Mary seemed to ride slowly, slowly along the rail. Duke turned on the radio in the living room, as I started up the steps. The American Airlines Show from Boston: The theme made you see yourself on a transcontinental night flight, your trench coat stowed above, a stewardess appearing in the carpeted aisle with your brandy in a tiny carafe, pilots breaking strongly through thin air, the navigator taking absolute clean LORAN fixes.

In the upstairs hall, Mary turned to me. She opened her thin arms for my goodnight. At my touch, her little ribs seemed to locate the structure of my hands.

"Night, Mike."

I held her, I held her. My breathing was broken by the rise of a belch bubble which I almost squelched.

She heard my breathing catch. "Mike? Mike? What's the matter?"

All I could answer was, "Well, Duke . . . ."

Thinking she guessed what I meant—and that the catch in my breathing was nervous sorrow—she then said, "Yes, I know. He doesn't seem to help you. He's so involved with the whole world."

I hugged Mary harder. I pulled back my head to kiss her cheek. I had always thought her small, extended breasts unreal—not false, just unreal. But against me they were objects; they were tender and strong.

Now Mary was patting my back just below my neck—patting slowly, rhythmically. "Try not to be too upset," she said. Somehow her words didn't carry enough conviction.

I kissed her again, the corner of her mouth.. Her body seemed within my scope, protectible, understandable.

Then—the music behind him—we heard Duke's tread, and then his feet on the stairs.

I went to my room. Duke and Mary talked for several minutes. Then he went downstairs and turned off the music. Then he came up again.

I didn't sleep for a long time. Lay on my back, palms under my head, and imagined camping out with Mary. But most, I hated how Duke forced me against him. Made me doubt and even indict him. Mary had put fresh sheets on my bed. My thinking seemed to go faster, but actually I was slowing down. "Yelow, blue, blue, yellow": Mary's words repeated on me. "Yellow, blue, blue, yellow." It must have been when I began to see stars seeding my dark ceiling that I fell asleep.

Thursday morning I started awake when a faraway jet blew its sound barrier and rattled my window panes. My clock said ten. I was aware of laughter—Duke's hacking, attacking guffaw, and over it Mary's trill. Since he was on tape Thursday morning, he didn't have to appear in person till two.

What had Mary served me for supper last night? I tried to recall, for I felt inside me my customary morning gas.

Duke tramped by my door and cracked loudly down the stairs. Then the front door banging shut sent a concussion through the house. A minute later, I heard Duke's VW rev and then drone off out the drive.

I was out of bed in a moment, standing erect in my green ski pajamas. Yes, Mary and Duke had been laughing, but doubtless at Mary's wallpapering—Duke derisively, Mary with gentle, genuine simplicity. What was that nebular hypothesis about the creation of the earth: *nebular hypothesis.*

156

I thought, "Of my nebulous self, a solid must gather. To move, to do, to show."

Not to *say*. For words were like a mortal dust a vacuum cleaner could never suck up nor splashed water ever lay. I must move—preserve myself from the contamination of Duke's theatrics and from the impurity of having to judge him a fraud. To act as a man—to be pure.

Barefoot I walked to the guest room. Mary knelt under the arch of the stepladder. Why she hadn't moved it so as to have elbow room to smooth on the last inches of a strip of Vine 45, I didn't know. Why she had pasted her first two strips so far apart I didn't know either.

She glanced at me through the ladder rungs, and said abruptly, "Get dressed please, Michael." She seemed to have forgotten last night's embrace.

I padded to the ladder, and she finished pressing on the strip. Sunlight lit the Morris vine, which wound on and on, remote and indestructible, from unit to unit of the dark design. There was a long strip along the baseboard, another strip five feet above it running along under the molding. I supposed that Duke had derided the apparent planlessness of this beginning.

"Mary," I said seriously, "Duke was laughing at you, wasn't he? He thought you were stupid to put the first two strips so far apart."

"Get dressed," she said flatly. Then, like a dancer withdrawing from an imagined narrow space, she rose backward holding her arms sensuously in front of her. She turned to me, and we were very close.

I said, "I think it's a fine way to begin a wall. This way you get a sense of what the wall will look like. And Duke laughed, *didn't* he? And that's why you're mooning about."

"You're the mooner around here," she said.

I held her shoulders and pulled her to me.

"Oh, Mike, you're such a baby."

I felt something in my stomach pulse. I kissed Mary but caught just her cheek as she turned her face.

"I love you so much, Mary."

"That's nice," she said. "Now get dressed. And brush your teeth."

I kissed her neck slowly, but then she put her fists in my stomach and pushed. "You're the worst kind of messy innocent. Leave me to my wallpaper and go do something of your own." I stepped back toward one of the guest beds, and tried to pull Mary with me. However, she ducked under my right arm and went smoothly to the window. On the sill were a sheet of notes and a pot of paste. She was cautiously silent.

"So you put me down," I said, simultaneously wondering if I meant present tense or past.

"If you're going to be sick," she said, without turning around to me, "be real sick. Be a nut."

"But I want you and I want to help you." I felt the old elastic of my pajama bottoms low over my abdomen.

She turned now. And, arms akimbo, she said with neutrality and naturalness, "So rape me."

Then she looked rather uncertainly at me—perhaps because she wondered if I'd now think her vulgar. Then she looked at my pajama pants, and said, "It's hard to be much in pajamas. You've got to be naked or dressed."

Hearing a car in the drive, I said to Mary, "Didn't I make it clear what I want?"

She smiled dearly and came to me and kissed me lightly on the lips, and turned back to her wallpaper, chuckling and saying, "No, lambie, you didn't. And I love you for it."

As I blindly crossed the threshold, she called, "Close the door."

The car wasn't Duke. It was David Brooke.

I opened the front door to him.

"Ah," he said, "lounging pajamas." He sidled into the hall, threw a sharp glance up the stairs, then looked at my pajamas again.

Cannily, he squinted at me and said, "I watched your Dad perform at the Greaves' last night."

I didn't answer him.

"Mind if I go see Mary? I just want to say hello."

"She's working," I said. "Doesn't want to be distracted."

"I'm just going to make love to her," he said drily.

I knew David was facetious, but as he ascended the stairs, I thought to protect Mary. Perhaps Duke knew how David looked at Mary, how his voice gathered an intimate fervor when he reminded Mary of New York. In her weakened state of loneliness, she might suddenly decide to kiss him, to start arranging meetings with him when Duke was away. I couldn't leave them alone. I was protecting them all—especially Mary, but Duke too. Maybe Duke couldn't stop moving restlessly about the landscape. At least, if at last he did choose to spend more time with Mary, he wouldn't by that time have been cuckolded. Slowly I started up the stairs. I heard the guest room door open, and Mary say, "Oh God, hello"—then the door closed.

But why was I going after David? And I in my pajamas. Why on earth?

Back in the living room I now stared down at one of Mary's Japanese gardens, green on its sunny sill. Its two delicate bridges recalled Mary's hard skeletal hands. Its two hill-mounds of moss recalled the way Mary tilted her dark head as she touched at tiny parts of her creation. Minute ground pines and cycad ferns prickled and softened the contours, and I recalled Mary's bemused study of her minuscule landscape. Duke would say over her shoulder, "That's a poor imitation of a lycopodium." And without saying anything, Mary would twist round toward him and smile at him with a kind of amorous scorn, and then lean against him supple and nestling. Now I visualized her hips in a tightly wound kimono (all flowers and sheer silk). And I knew I wouldn't trail David after all.

Protect Mary? Protect Duke? Aha! The family honor? No. My sole impulses were my greenhorn's lust and my fermenting envy. Overwhelmed by the knowledge of this, I settled into a soft armchair and thought of the inescapable corruption that surrounds this sad world.

Or was it simply that I was proud to have seen through myself?

But now the door upstairs slammed, and I heard a tread that must be David.

A moment later he passed so nonchalantly and genially into the living room, he seemed for a second to be my host and to have been keeping me waiting.

"What a foul mood that girl's in," he said.

"Why should you think 'that girl' wants to see you?"

"I *know* she wants to see me. But she's distracted. She told me I ought to be out hunting news."

"It's true," I said.

"Well, you find news in odd places. Mary said your Dad was meeting with the commencement committee tonight. Since they've *finished* their meetings, this must mean that something's gone wrong. My guess is that at the moment

159

they'll have to get a new commencement speaker. So you see, news may be anywhere."

"If I were Duke," I said, "and they needed a commencement speaker, I'd propose myself."

"He'd do it," said David. "He's capable of almost anything."

"His life proves it," I said.

"Proof," murmured David. "Proof."

We hesitated to speak; then, as if challenged by me, David, as I began to say, "Duke is—" broke through my voice quickly: "His life proves that if you keep moving fast enough, people will fall for your act. Your Dad knew this when he was teaching at a certain college some years ago."

"Name it."

"Yes," said David meditatively. "Well, you know its name. Seven years ago. Yes, a few months after your father put out his popular analysis of the 1777 Battle of Ticonderoga. A colleague at his college queried one of your father's sources, queried it in a note printed prominently in a national historical review. Your father quickly answered, promising a detailed explanation in print. The source at issue was a letter from one of Burgoyne's grenadiers; it had gotten through to a friend of his in Captain Murray's army in the south; the grenadier claimed to have overheard Burgoyne talking in his tent one night on Sugar Loaf Hill just before the British moved into Fort Ticonderoga; Burgoyne, according to this grenadier, knew he could cut rapidly down to Albany if he'd only forego his European methods and travel light with only his auxiliaries, a few light guns, and the cream of his regulars; but, feeling that in the end the war wasn't viable for the British, he decided to proceed with his full force, believing that his inevitable defeat—whether at Saratoga or someplace else—would stand in history as a symbolic instance of the old order's inability to adapt itself to new problems, and feeling, as your father says in his book, that he, General Burgoyne, 'must act out his role as an instrument in the American revelation.' The California colleague queried the source, the very existence of the letter. Your father replied that he was preparing a full answer. But he wasn't. He was planning to get off the faculty where he was in constant close contact with this man who questioned his work. Your father was in fact arranging to be appointed Curator of the Sam Houston Museum. It was crystal clear

160

what he was doing. But only crystal clear if you had all the facts."

"Which you now do have," I said.

"Which I now do have," said David. "That is, the important or relevant ones. By pulling strings your father contrived this new appointment, immediately announced to the president that he felt his further researches into the American mind necessitated his acceptance of the offer, kept the change secret till after commencement, then removed himself and you to New York State, where one newspaper carried the story that Professor Roland Amerchrome had 'come home' to Ticonderoga to work on an appendix for a new edition of his study of the battle."

"Well, tell Duke, not me," I said, rising. "Because his past is his own business. And what are you hunting? Truth? If you go so far, don't you have to keep going and show the full truth?"

"You're sounding like your father."

"Behind every fraud—"

"Yes, I know what's coming. I've heard Duke say this."

"Behind every fraud—if this is a fraud—there's an honesty." I was trying to word my fright and fury away into the warm late-morning April air. Pretending to be interrupted by a slight belch, but in fact interrupted by my awareness that I suddenly had nothing to say, I said, "Don't—"

"Then," said David Brooke triumphantly, "your father spent the summer at Ticonderoga, or nearby, and—"

"No, don't!" I cried, and moved forward dangerously, pretending I was about to fall on David Brooke there in his armchair. And he, not understanding the effect my pajamas were having on me, rolled out of the chair, putting it between us.

"Then," said David, his voice alive and stalking, "your father sent to the sacred journal in question a remarkable report on what had happened to that priceless letter—dare I call it a document that existed only in your father's mind?"

I took Duke's lacrosse stick from the hearth-stand that had been meant for tongs and a fire shovel. I moved uncertainly toward David, cocking the stick with my right hand as fulcrum.

But as he backed and I padded tentatively toward him, and we exchanged low threats, we were too absorbed to hear Mary descending the stairs. And David now reached the door just as she did. He backed into her, and she hugged him and drawled sarcastically, "Guess who, guess who?" and I snapped the lacrosse stick forward a few times as if I were warming up.

"Look," said Mary, "I didn't mean to put you down like that upstairs. I was so involved, you know. I'm committed to this wallpaper. Frankly I don't know what I'm doing. Look, David, come for supper tonight, eh?"

His grin politely fixed, David nodded and accepted, and without a look at me murmured goodbye and made it into the hall and out the front door. Mary had invited that betraying bastard, that factious ferret, to supper. It would be the last supper *I'd* ever take with him.

"That silly boy," said Mary, half to herself. "He was hurt that we had Harry Tindall to dinner Tuesday without him."

I didn't answer but went up the stairs in three-step barefoot hops. All I knew was that I was going to my room.

Ticonderoga! The place between two lakes, the Iroquois precisely called it. What did David know? When I was eleven Duke and I spent—or *I* spent—a summer—that summer David spoke of—on Lake George. To study parts of the terrain of the "great Ticonderoga affair" (as Duke called it), we took a cottage near the lake's north tip. He wanted to be within striking distance of Crown Point and Ticonderoga but far enough away from the imitation of John Hancock's house that the historical association used for its archives, so that he would feel he was making a fresh nonpartisan approach to his subject. Then he put me in a boys' camp a few miles up from Bolton's Landing, and for three weeks or so I and my fellow campers, pausing among the trees like a troop of natives, would watch wonderingly as he skied by in the afternoons. But then he left the area. He phoned me the last week of July to say he had to go to the New York Public Library; and I didn't hear from him again until the end of August. By then he had been introduced to Mary, and he summoned me to New York to spend a couple of months at the Algonquin.

Shouldn't all this have been part of David's history? But if David told the truth, the part of my past he revealed must, by Duke's reasoning, push me away from the clear ground of choice. Wouldn't this story force me into a deeper suspicion of Duke? Perhaps make me want to be the kind of historian Duke perhaps wasn't? Make me break with him publicly? Make me change my name? Cornered by your past, you make of yourself what your past tells you you are: *sic*, Duke's thesis. Yet I kept telling myself all afternoon that David's mean story meant little to what I might want to make of my life. If Duke had done what David said, then Duke had done what he had done, and that was that. If Duke was perhaps a somewhat suspect scholar, what mattered that to me? My mind grew woolly. No doubt David's motives colored his snide inquiries, but, as Duke said, history-writing is a game, the more personal the more profound. As I made my way—or was drawn—into the "buts" and "howevers" of how right David and Duke were, and how free I was, I felt compelled to turn away to something simple and present.

So I spent a methodical, terribly cautious and slow afternoon repeating an experiment I'd learned from Duke. Over my window I hung a blanket through which I had cut a tiny hole. Beyond the blanket—and well below the level of the hole—I stationed a flint-glass prism where the sun's needling path through the blanket hole would hit it. Beyond the prism I draped a bedsheet over two chairs. Then I examined the Newtonian spectrum of primaries into which my glistening arklet translated its fuel of light. Violet, indigo, blue, green, yellow, orange, red—they were all there, regular as measured time.

And yet—do you know?—I didn't believe in what I had done. The inevitability of those silent colors in my dark afternoon room merged with my sense of how easy it would be to erase them—merged also with my memory of Duke's lecture words one afternoon in Oregon—or was it Chicago or California or Arizona: "As a nineteenth-century Frenchman (whose name escapes me) said, 'All cosmological theories eventually turn into untenable hypotheses'; you may without fear of being far wrong advance to the darker conclusion that all scientific findings are momentary myths, greater or lesser as they remain apparently tenable for a longer or shorter time." I heard Mary pass on her way downstairs. I imagined—for I could not in fact perceive (though maybe in a sense I could see)—the refracting particles that stood in the submarine air between me and the seven primary colors, and I wondered what the colors truly were. Once Duke had slyly said that optics—"opt-ics"—was the science of choice. As I imagined these apparently invisible motes fouling my sight and even being breathed in and (in altered form) exhaled by my strangely autonomous body, I began to weep. And I began to shake, as if some drop of air or water must bump its way up out of me so I'd be free and clean and clear. I hated each sob. The spasms forced on me a rhythm I couldn't control—a great twitch. But now—for I stood just above the prism—my tears found its twinkling slopes. And suddenly I became fascinated by the effect of this salt water—made by my ducts but also by the agency of the air about me—upon the seven colors locked in their sequence on my bedsheet. And I hardly noticed that my spasms disappeared.

When Duke drove in at five, I was sitting on the ground near the house watching Mary try to rake up pine needles. He got out of the VW and walked toward us slowly.

"I saw the president today. He says I've rubbed people the wrong way. He says he received a document last week that pretends to be a petition requesting my censure. Fifty signatures, all faculty. They say I've snuck onto too many committees, that I've had no business trying to reorganize the curriculum, that my courses overlap courses in various departments; and then they say at the end that my general behavior is not consistent with the dignity of the Fortuna chair. They attack my use of language labs."

Mary seemed to be on the point of making her usual ironic and apparently unsympathetic comment; she never seemed to feel Duke was in danger. But now, in a neutral, rather nervous tone, she asked, "What about language labs?"

"It's simple. I don't think it's been done before. I simply have all my students sometime during the term make a tape in which they evaluate themselves, say whatever comes into their heads—a sort of confession, a self-orientation. I tell them they must get acclimated to an age of publicity and analysis, and must never be afraid to let the world know what's truly inside them."

"What makes you think you get the truth?" asked Mary.

"I get *a* truth."

"And are we going to be kicked out of here?" I asked.

Duke didn't answer; Mary went to him and hugged him. But he broke away, for he'd had another idea. "I know: We'll give a monster commencement party out here. We'll ask everyone. And between now and then we'll put up parody billboards all along the driveway. Maybe they'll give my priestly colleagues a notion of what I'm up to."

"Why? Why? Why?" Mary wailed.

"Someone," said Duke, "has to be a full tragicomic instrument of the times."

"You're all theory," Mary said. "Not natural."

But Duke went on: "Yes. A billboard at this end of the driveway, and a set of signs along the drive. I can see it now: Number one: 'For paradox, proverb, and last-minute fun'; Number two: 'For prophecies, commotion, wit by the ton'; Number three: 'For the balm of revelation and a little bit of jive'; Number four: 'For chaos that makes you glad to be alive'; and at last, as pilgrims make the last turn, they will see my billboard: my face framed in a teardrop medallion ringed with stars containing small profiles of me—and occupying the major space, these high words: 'AMERCHROME IS ALWAYS HOME IN PERSON OR IN SPIRIT.' "

"You better hope they're pilgrims and not vigilantes," I said. "But what's your point of view?"

Duke tilted his head at me as if he thought I was crazy. Then he seemed to explode in loud bursts of words: "That that that that one can, you can only act through contradiction; act effectively: that is, I say 'Who will blow my horn if I don't blow it myself?' On the other hand I say, 'If I am a man, I am a fool, and lest I appear to hide my folly I must act like a fool.' " He laughted scornfully and desperately at me: "Michael, it's too obvious to need to be said. Greatness, folly. The two—" for a moment Duke seemed to be mumbling—"the two blended, demonstrated, interdependent." He started to use his hands—those long hairy spiders—but as he swung a palm out to his side, he suddenly was startled—i.e., in my *opinion*—to find he had nothing to say to accompany the hands or for the hands to accompany.

I sensed that the moment's momentum was mine. I said, "But why be more foolish than you need to be?"

And Duke said, quietly, "I need to be this foolish to prove my grandeur." And he hazarded an apparently cool smile.

"You don't believe you're a fool," I said.

"Stop it," said Mary. And then, frowning at me, she said, "Duke does know he's a fool."

Then she took Duke's hand and they walked away toward the house. As clearly as I had known anything this week, I knew that her sadness was saying, "The real trouble is that with people at all perceptive Duke's act doesn't come off."

David Brooke was back at six. Though Duke had in any case to leave at six-thirty, still David's appearance seemed to push him. Duke flicked on the radio, then turned if off, and as he and David pursued a slow conversation, Duke seemed to be looking for things to do around the living room so that he wouldn't have to sit down. As Duke straightened his copies of *Time* on the desk, David spoke on carefully.

"This is an odd meeting tonight, isn't it? I mean, the committee finished its work last month."

"Committees are never quite dead," said Duke, and went to the liquor table.

"What has been your function?" asked David, interviewer-style.

"My function?" said Duke musing. Then he emerged from his little tenseness and in fact bawled brutally, "To provide ideas and then act on them." Then abruptly, as if his sudden abruptness with David had unmasked an awkward defensiveness, he took up a bottle and said, "A little Muscadet, David?"

As Duke gave us wine, David kept looking at me nervously, no doubt fearing I might raise the question of Ticonderoga. Duke went to the dinner table and tore off a piece of half-sliced garlic bread from the warm loaf Mary had brought in.

"Look," she said, "are you eating with us or not?"

"You know I'm not," said Duke.

"You're messing up my table."

"Mary," said David, "are you developing a tummy? You seem plumper. You're not pregnant, are you?"

"If I am," said Mary, "it was an immaculate conception."

"Why say that, why say that?" said Duke fussily. He sounded lame. David muttered, "Immaculate conception isn't virgin birth."

Duke put a Jimmy Giuffre record on the turntable. But then, as if he'd changed his mind, he said, "Well, I'm going now." And tossing off his wine and stuffing the rest of his bread into his wide mouth, he took his flashlight from the mantel and left.

"Let him huff and puff," said Mary. She lighted two of the lime-colored candles Duke had brought her from New York, then switched off the dining room lamps.

In candlelight, as we three sat down, I felt my identity

as stepson vanish. Mary and David started to discuss Jimmy Giuffre; "The Sheepherder" had come on, and David was explaining its homeophonic basis.

"Once I took a few weeks of a course in electronic music at the New School," he said, as if explaining how he knew about Giuffre.

The Giuffre music, independent dialogue overheard as if seen through an old thick green bottle, seemed to be Duke, the memory or presence of him.

David was saying, "There are real simple things in this that you don't hear for a long time. Textures? Patterns? A pattern of disconnection that holds all the currents in the same pool."

Now I rose, almost unwillingly. "God," I said, "I can't stand phonies and I can't . . . I can't stand people who are smarter than I am." And taking my plate of spinach soufflé and cold ham, I walked out on Mary and David.

Halfway up the stairs, I heard Mary say, "Baby!"

Was Mary betraying Duke?

Half an hour later, if only to watch over Mary, I went to the stairhead to listen. I hated to snoop, but I had to make sure David wasn't misleading Mary. Yet I heard no mention of Ticonderoga or me. By now the Giuffre had gone off, and David's words reached me almost as if theatrically projected.

For he went on about Tom Sawyer and Huck Finn being the two faces of the American character—something about the square romantic and the impulsive empiricist. Then he seemed to come closer to Mary.

"How you and Duke can stand this . . . milieu, I don't know. I reconnoitre fraternity row and hear 'Say Wonderful Words to Me' gushing from a loudspeaker in a window and see the Bermuda-shorted animals with their flat-top haircuts playing their flying-saucer games and sitting around with petrified muscle-bound grins, and then I walk into the main stem and see clean Olympic girls coming out of Dante's Sandwich Shop gobbling heroes, and then I stop transfixed at the curb as the Outing Club's Happy Wagon sails slowly by, blaring its announcement of the Moonshiner's Ball and the Senior Class Island-in-the-Sun Goat Roast and Home-Brew Picnic at Winnepesauki, and then I stare at two broad-brimmed state troopers all in green eating ice cream under a lamppost and they stare back two for one and keep staring. Mary, you're out here in the woods but surely you feel the air. And you hear the SAC bombers guarding you all the time. The university and the air base—debasement and imprisonment. That's what we have here."

"I have Duke," Mary said, so quietly I barely heard her.

"And he has his audience."

"No," said Mary. "That isn't *so* true. If he knew I'd do anything in the world for him our relationship could break in two. But he's an odd, odd man, and we stay close because he imagines I can resist him. Distance ties us together."

"But what kind of life is it?"

After a moment Mary said, "Duke's a man."

Still later, from my doorway, I heard David say goodnight and heard that missed breath of active silence in which they were almost certainly exchanging a kiss. Then Mary's soft ironic city sympathy said, "I'll pray for you."

And still later, when I was in bed, I woke in the presence of Duke. That is, I knew he was at the door looking at me, knew the fact simultaneously as I passed into consciousness—so that I was able to keep my eyes shut. I heard his slight wheezing and felt his face, as it were, upon me. And I suspected that if I opened my eyes and acknowledged him he'd become again that certain Duke who never dared say ordinary things to me. And so, as he watched me, I could fancy he watched *over* me. And then—for my eyelids were tense and the crack of light had widened—I turned away from him as if my body had asserted its need for rest.

Returning to sleep I heard Duke faraway say to Mary, "There's a lot of support for the faculty petition. Maybe there'll be more after tonight. When they talked about who to ask to speak at commencement, I suggested myself, gave them a list of my regular topics with a list of prices. But old Marcus Black—you know, the physics professor with the English accent—asked me if I wasn't just using the university to publicize myself. I went in with the spirit of his sarcasm and answered that of course I wanted publicity. If I didn't blow my horn, who would? At least I was a doer, which was more than I could say for the insecure sinecure floaters on the faculty who never publish, and who always ridicule ambition. But then Black got the rest on his side, and they simply started to ignore me. Oh, but I'm tired of being an academic gypsy; I think I'll stay put and fight these people. I've given a lot of creativity to this place."

There was silence for a few minutes. Then I heard Mary

say—and it was the last thing I heard before I dropped back to sleep—"Hold me."

Friday Mary's clarinet could be heard from time to time upstairs. I gathered she was working on the wallpaper, then taking a few minutes out to have a practice, then returning to the wallpaper. When I looked in on her once, she was sitting on a bed poring over a Green Stamp catalog. She blinked at me and said, "We have fifty books of stamps, and I think we ought to cash in for something, but they offer so many . . . so much . . . I don't know what to pick." I don't think she even added one strip of Vine 45 the whole day. We had a quiet supper, she and I, and she asked me what I'd accomplished, and I said, "Nothing, as usual," and she shook her head as if she were tired.

At ten to eight I was in my seat in the auditorium waiting for Duke to appear. His Second Annual Fortuna Lecture had been advertised all over town on posters that listed his topic as "The End of History."

I sat near a door at the left side. Several rows in front of me sat our neighbors, David in profile talking insistently at the side of Tindall's head, Tindall setting and winding his watch. Then a few people near the stage started clapping, I heard a healthy baritone behind me say, "This'll be a whale of a lecture," and Duke came slowly out of the wings, smiling and nodding, then shaking clasped hands beside his head as if he were a prize fighter calmly set to retain his title. A dimming of the audience lights brought out the brightness of those that lit the stage; grinning, Duke waited and waited and waited, his large, dark, warty eyelids half lowered in kindly quizzical ease. Then he called, "This will be to some extent an audience participation lecture." He showed his teeth in a long grin. "I want to bring out the animal in you. I will take up that point later."

Now, as he reached under his lectern, he seemed to pull far away from me. "What have I here?" he asked, producing a small wooden box. "It's got a lot of stuff in it." He pulled out a gold trinket. "Here's a Phi Beta Kappa Key. What's it worth? What am I bid?" Laughter. Then, when it died, one short guffaw. "But it doesn't fit any door, does it? It opens a lock but not a door. It'll get you a job with IBM, ICBM, AT&T, NAM, Unilever, Anaconda Copper, or the State Department." Now Duke went faster and spoke more and more harshly and yellingly. "ICI, NBC, USIS—" he began to bang the lectern, and with his last fast phrase— "AA, AAA, ASPCA, ASCAP, and E equals MC squared" —he drew a glad howl of partisan laughter that passed into applause. "But I'll take that point up later," he said, turning grave.

David Brooke had bent forward, already recording Duke's remarks. Next to me, a Negro girl wearing glasses scribbled away into her notebook. In the row just in front of mine, but off to my right, a creature in a navy blue sort of smock and with long yellow hair that hung down into my row offered Duke a face that to me in profile seemed a model of piety, lucid lust, and womanly pity for male greatness— all these approvals wrought or cancelled out into holy, profound, and perhaps imbecilic repose.

"They say you kids haven't a philosophy." Duke's words produced a clear silence in the auditorium. "They—the rejectors at home and in Europe—they say you are just programed, mass-manufactured machines fed on mathematical mediocrity; they say you are getting cleverer and cleverer in your colleges all over this country, better and better able to do the jobs America has for you. And this that they say is half true. But only half. And you, our America, *will* do what you *must* do. And if one half, the machine half, the clean, conditioned half drives you one way, the other half is a drive within you that is your own. It is a will, a long, dark river of autonomy and appetite. And this other half is a private untouchable voice that says, 'I want, I want, I want.' "

Duke, from his high stage, had them begging. "Now, the first half, the robot, the clean scalp, the reserved, predictable white-hearted brave, merely responds to the great American broadcast. But certain rejectors at home and abroad—they shall be nameless—cry at you, 'Conformity! Conformity!' and turn away. They spurn you, because when you graduate you will go to business school and then to an insurance job in a glassy new building along Route One Twenty-Eight; they spurn you because you will go to grad school and become teachers teaching classes in which the only decent pupils are the ones who want to go on to become teachers like you and then teach classes in which the only decent pupils, the only ones that are being *reached*, are the pupils who are going on to become teachers, who—" and Duke pretended to be continuing with this circular gag, but the laughs

170

and cheers came, and he was enabled to make his transition the entertainer's proper jump from successful impact.

"But this other half that looks yearningly at me when I lecture—looks yearningly at me even when I'm on TV and can't actually see you—this half wants to know; this half wants to know all there is to know; this half wants to agree with the rejectors and say, 'No, America at midcentury is a stinking whirlpool of materialism, a hum of statistics, an actual-size model landscape with toy trains and toy cars and jerky mechanical automated men operating the switches and signals along the tracks, and cement rotaries made like perfect puzzles over and under which move perfect bright automobiles as if tracked and moved by subterranean transformers; a cityscape, a web of gray urban cancers that widen till they join each other in one vast twenty-first-century necropolis.' Yes, this other, wanting half, wants to know all there is to know but is in danger of being influenced by the rejectors so that it will say, 'No, no, no, advertisement is vulgar, cities are death, conformity bypasses the short circuits that are the only, the painful path man can take toward creation.' All nations shalt thou teach. But this other, wanting half in you, in most young Americans, knows that the rejectors are wrong. Knows that somehow we must embrace what we and our nation are, must let ourselves be trapped at the same time that we want, want, want. OK then, where do we go from here?"

A bald man who sat near Brooke and Tindall now got up and walked stiffly to the left exit. As he passed me, his cold blue eyes were staring blindly ahead of him and his mouth was grimly pursed. Duke paused to watch him. Then he looked hopefully around the audience.

"Well, one way is through opposition, struggle, dialectic." He paused again, and a benevolent, crafty smile came over his face. "Do you hear what's in my mind? Do you hear?"

And a murmur of "Yes," rose dimly from his audience. "Yes, yes, yes."

"I feel some questions."

"Questions," echoed back to him from some of his students who had seen this routine before.

"I hear some questions."

"Questions."

"Who wants the questions?"

"Questions, questions."

171

Harry Tindall had leaned forward, head bent down. I felt myself clutched into the beating heart of the audience. A tall man, doubtless a professor, rose and walked up the aisle and passed me as he went for the exit.

Rhythmically, Duke called, "Who wants the questions?"

"Questions, questions."

"Where's the man?"

"Oh where's the man?" called Duke.

"Where's the man?"

"Do I see a hand?" Duke called.

Hands went up all over the room.

"Yes, *you*," said Duke, pointing toward the right side. "You, you are the man."

A short, muscular fellow in a blue T-shirt stood up. He looked proudly around him, and said loudly, "It's time for the old Socracutor technique." Applause rose round him and spread to the whole auditorium as he worked his way out into the aisle and walked to the stage. His eyes were on Duke as he mounted the steps.

"Look," said Duke, "look where the crew-cut beast rises from the listening sea and creeps to the shore, evolving in his fertile brain plans to supplant him who calls him."

Duke shook the fellow's hand. "Your name?"

"Bobo Paramus," the fellow said sheepishly, with a glance at the audience. And from the audience a muted cry of facetious love echoed the name: "Bobo, Bobo."

David Brooke's right shoulder was shaking as he rapidly transcribed what he saw and heard. When he paused and looked around and behind him, his eyes caught mine and he winked unsmilingly.

"What have you been meditating?" Duke asked loudly.

Bobo paused, and then, with an uncertain grin, replied, "The squirrel running round the tree trunk and the philosopher walking round the tree?"

"No, no," called a few members of his (or Duke's) claque.

"The ends of education?" said Bobo.

"No, no," called the audience.

"Freedom of the will?" said Bobo uncertainly.

"No, no," called the audience.

Then Duke said, "The idea of history," and the audience quietened.

"Bobo," said Duke, "you've been inquiring how the historian arrives at his vision."

"Yes," said Bobo agreeably.

"Who *is* the historian?" Duke asked.

"He who recaptures the past?" replied Bobo unsurely, sticking a hand in a trouser pocket.

"But what is the past?"

"It is what happened."

"But, when?"

"Earlier than now," said Bobo.

"But when is '*now*'?"

Bobo paused, and stole a look at the audience. Somebody in one of the front rows said something.

"No coaching from the audience," said Duke benignly.

"The past is everything that is not the future or the present," said Bobo Paramus.

"What is the present?"

Bobo paused again, scratching his jaw. Then, as if suddenly recalling an old answer, he said, "The present is the momentary crystallization of act, materializing mysteriously from the dark future and, like the Anglo-Saxon sparrow, on the point of passing into the past."

"Quite so," said Duke, above a ripple of cheers. "Which means that as soon as I say, 'which means that,' the words whizz out of one darkness into another."

After a pause, Bobo said—apparently in order to say something—"Well, yes, if you want to put it that way."

"Then," said Duke, "the historian deals with the past. And his material is increasing constantly at an enormous speed?"

"Yes, sir."

"But what do you call his material?"

"Facts," said Bobo quickly.

"But what is a fact?"

"Something that has happened."

"Can you give me an example?"

"Lincoln's Gettysburg Address."

"What do those three words refer to? Something like '18 Pickett's Drive'?" (Duke got his laugh.)

"No. They mean that Lincoln made a speech at Gettysburg."

"Wrote it?"

"Yes."

"How do you know?"

"Testimony," said Bobo. "Drafts in Lincoln's own hand. Reports from eyewitnesses."

"How do we know a speechwriter didn't write the address?"

"We don't," said Bobo happily. "But we think that—"

"Yes! We *think* that Lincoln wrote the speech. Well, give me another example of a fact."

Bobo looked at the audience. His gaze stopped at one point, and he seemed for a moment to be daydreaming. He turned back to Duke.

With a certain calm pride, Bobo said, "The will of Horatio Sinclair, Walpole, New Hampshire, 1857."

I saw Tindall come erect in his seat. He had been hunched forward, head down, as if embarrassment had laid a physical burden on his shoulders, but now he was paying attention. Rigid attention.

"Who was Horatio Sinclair?" Duke asked.

"A scholar," said Bobo. "A scholar who . . . was . . . going to . . . leave his books to . . . for a library. But . . . couldn't make up his mind . . . how . . . to make conditions"—Bobo shook his head, smiling proudly, humbly—"or something."

"Yes, very good," said Duke. "Now, if we know anything about these plans of Sinclair's, on what is our knowledge founded?"

"On the manuscripts. The will. *You* know, the *will*."

"One will?"

"Several."

"Do we know in what order the wills were made?"

"Sure, some are dated."

"Some aren't?

"Yes."

"So if the historian is to draw conclusions about the kind of man Sinclair was and what he meant to do with his vast library, and if no records exist telling what other people thought about him or telling us about this man's life, then we have to go on the various versions of the will. Is that right?"

"Yeah," said Bobo.

"Well, then, are we dealing with facts, Bobo?"

After a longer pause, Bobo gave Duke what looked like a truculent smile. Then he said, "Yes, we *are* dealing with facts."

Duke's line was on top of Bobo's answer even before Bobo finished. "But who knows who wrote those versions of the will? Who knows what caprices or accidents interfered with the man's real intentions as he wrote out his bequests?"

"At least we have the documents," said Bobo nervously.

"But who wrote them and when? This is something we can't finally know."

Bobo frowned at the audience, then said rather edgily to Duke, "Well, we *have* the documents and we can study them. They're interesting." He smiled, feeling he'd got his teeth into something, yet, I think, feeling a bit apprehensive and even bored. "And the documents *are* past, are part of the past," said Bobo; "you can't deny that. And you can't deny that the documents are facts."

Duke was making his *impatient* sounds: "Unh? unh? unh? unh? Yes, well, then, who is the historian, Bobo, and what is the nature of his work?" The question had come too soon, hadn't been forced.

Bobo thought, while Duke made his quick sounds: "Unh? unh? unh? unh?"

"Well," Bobo said—and the auditorium was breathless— "You can't trust him unless . . . unless. . . ." Bobo was confused.

Harry Tindall started to rise, but David Brooke turned to him and put a restraining hand on his arm.

"Well," said Bobo, "the historian is writing a sort of fiction."

As he finished this answer—an answer that sounded strangely mechanical—the audience clapped and cheered raggedly. And Bobo raised his clasped hands like a prize fighter.

Then Duke said, "Opposition, struggle, these are the tools we need, to get at truth, or what we imagine is truth. Thank you, Bobo."

"Thank *you*," said Bobo. "Learning was never so much fun." And, holding his meaty shoulders stiff and straight as if he were balancing books on them, he descended the steps and returned to his seat.

Duke continued: "But if the historian is only imagining what may have happened, should he therefore give up his profession and seek certainties?" The audience began to stir. Somehow it seemed Duke had demonstrated his Socracutor technique too early in the show.

My gaze wandered, and Duke's long sentences reached my brain only as fragments. "So it may ultimately be that . . .

parody . . . the historian . . . can be honest only if . . . let him embrace modern awareness of the limitations of inquiry . . . let him do what will both embody his insights and allow him to be reasonably truthful . . . let him write imaginary history . . . or let him . . . and you . . . Americans . . . How do you act in an age of fraud, imitation, counterfeit . . . in which the Taj Mahal is parodied unconsciously in the design of a new motel . . . in which there are more people writing up their experience than there is experience to go around . . . in which . . . yes . . . . I ask and ask again . . . what is to be done? And I give you the answer whether you wish to do business with ideas or with die castings . . . in . . . or in . . . . The answer is to embrace our world. To find gaiety and tragedy in the confusing juxtapositions of items in news broadcasts, to accept your second and third cars, realizing that if you cannot fashion a Thoreauvian simplicity, you can be a significant embodiment of the age's absorption of the individual. But parody . . . hello, America . . . calling all cars . . . Paul Revere . . . by embracing that which embraces you . . . being careless and exploratory in your quest for knowledge . . . letting yourself be drugged by the world's fair of verbal ambiguities in which we live, yet at the same time being *aware, aware, aware,* and intensifying your victimization by the age you live in and, more, by the nation you live in, thus can you, as Spinoza says, preserve yourselves, be conscious of the trap you can never slip and the part you can never doff . . ."

Harry Tindall seemed alert in a different way. He wasn't so rigid, but his head was tilted back a bit, and his figure seemed braced. David Brooke's right shoulder kept shaking.

Duke's words tore at me and I couldn't understand him and I felt mortally embarrassed. It was only my fear of being noticed that kept me from fleeing.

"And who is to say . . . ?" His sentences seemed to grow long. "Yes, who is to say . . . that the City of God shall not find incarnation in a city of man of which parodists a hundred years ago couldn't have dreamed?"

Less and less, Duke seemed to be addressing the audience. "To embrace the age is to act. But to be happy with TV commercials while simultaneously hating them: isn't this being dishonest? No! For today there is too much against us. So we try to digest the lonely and the lovely and the monstrous of our American age. Accept the mass proliferation of all

176

colors of salesmanship. Yet scoff at it simultaneously. Write and publish our autobiographies while simultaneously scoffing at self-advertisement. But to embrace is to be embraced. So do we risk losing our wills? Yes, of course. But the key is to embrace and at the same moment reject; love as we scorn, choose to be both conscious and unconscious parodies of our age and thus both body it forth and stay half free of it. America is your body and you cannot deny it."

Now, pounding the lectern, Duke uttered single words: "Whitman, Willkie, Spinoza, Belknap, Dante, the Mosaic design, Joy, Parody." He held the welling enthusiasm of his audience until he couldn't hold it back any longer. And then, with the word "You!" he smashed the bubbling vessel and applause exploded and gushed and spread and ran like the marvelous reassuring sound of a garment factory in its rhythm of steady, useful, mad, powerful creation.

Duke was receiving backstage. In the crowd I kept close to David Brooke, who might drive me home. Harry Tindall, released by Duke's final shot and the first rattle of claps, had walked quickly to the left exit. By now he'd be driving out of the parking lot. In the lobby David told me Tindall had murmured that Duke was a cap-and-gown beatnik. David didn't agree, but said his own opinion wouldn't matter in the news release he was going off to write. He said he was suddenly sorry he'd told me Tindall's opinion. Then he added that saying you were sorry didn't do any good. "And in any case your father simply exists, a bit larger than life—like Harry Tindall."

I absolutely hungered for simple words, words of one meaning. Was David exonerating Duke, accepting him for his flamboyance? Or was David tossing me the cliché in order to cloak his real belief?

People brushed me against David. With many words he strove to stare through me to the definition of what he meant. I walked away from him. He was citing his pal Tindall as if Tindall were Samuel Johnson.

If only Mary were here! To hold my arm, drive me home, direct her blinking dark eyes shyly past me as she listened to my urgent talk. If I'd pressed, would she have let me help her tonight? Let me roll back the cinematic stills of Vine 45, mix paste, hold her ladder as she stretched?

On the small plaza outside the auditorium the crowd

spread. I drifted into a clear strip of sidewalk to my right. At the corner of the building I met a new crowd of students surging along from a side entrance. I pressed through their mass and found myself at some steps.

It now dawned on me that I'd simply wait for Duke and hope that if he wasn't going home he'd take me with him wherever he was going.

For quite a while I stood alone.

Then suddenly, as if I hadn't been listening carefully enough to hear it stop, the heavy mumble inside wasn't there any more. And wondering which exit Duke had taken, if indeed he had left the building, I saw a girl push out the door and come slowly down the steps.

"Michael Amerchrome," she said, approaching.

"How do you know me?" I asked.

"Through your father," she said. And then darkly in my recollection I knew her voice. "I've seen you driving with him."

"Sue Gardiner," I said.

She seemed to forget to stop smiling, so at first I thought her simple-minded. She it was who a year before had lapsed into delusions that Duke was God and that Duke was dead. This week I had thought of her from time to time, dimly fancying that she could say something that in the depths of bad digestion, self-hatred, and filial nausea I needed to know.

No. I now saw her smile wasn't stupid. It was fixed on her face by an anxious bright curiosity, some secret joke.

"I'm late," she said, still smiling. "I tried to speak to your father, but—"

"*I* wasn't waiting for you," I said.

She raised her eyebrows and the smile disappeared. "Who said you were?"

I tried again. "Where is he? The noise has stopped in there."

"I know where he's gone, if you want to find him."

"No. I'm going home."

"Duke's gone to College Wood with the forestry kids."

"Where's College Wood? I mean, which of the woods is it?"

"There's only one forest right near the campus. You must know that."

"Well, I guess I'll get on home."

"Driving?"

"No. I do a lot of walking."

"Four miles is a long walk."

There seemed nothing more to say, but Sue remained solidly before me; she didn't turn to go. Her plumpness disconcerted me. Compared to Mary's figure, hers carried a good deal of surplus—a puffiness at her waist, a fullness in her arms, a slight fleshiness below her cheek bones. Her face was large and soft, and her short, abundant light hair wasn't very well combed.

"You look like your father, you know."

"What do you mean? He's another type entirely."

"No," she said. "It's ridiculous, but . . ." and then she laughed. "You have his kinky hair and his roostery neck and his active Adam's apple and the big bony Indian nose all narrow till it gets to your nostrils. Your nostrils are a little splayed, like his. It's very funny, the resemblance."

"Well, I don't know what you're laughing about. Say, aren't you the Sue Gardiner who cracked up last spring?"

"You know damn well I am," she said. "Only I'm not sure I cracked up. It's not worth talking about."

"Will you walk down to the end of town? Then I'll go on out the Point Road home."

We turned up the walk along the side of the auditorium, and came out on the little plaza, and walked toward a string of buildings now rose-yellow and shadowy in the streetlights.

"I wanted to get my tape back tonight," said Sue. "You've heard about these tapes? They're self-evaluations. I don't know what Duke wants them for. When I got backstage, there was Duke talking to a gang of students, and the president was grinning and nodding, and telling Duke his talk'd been provocative. And I couldn't stand to ask Duke right then. He'd have had to go up to his office anyway to get the tape. And anyway he might not have given it to me. So I finally left. You can't tell what he'll do with those tapes. Last year he took a little piece some boy wrote about his parents' divorce and had it printed in the university paper. Then he persuaded the boy this had been a healthy thing for him, being open and public and committing himself and saying the hell with everybody else, why be afraid to tell the truth about yourself. So maybe he wants to publish the tapes."

"Why did you want yours back?"

"Oh, some idea I had about keeping myself a secret. I

179

probably got it from Duke—one of the sparks he says he tries to throw off. 'Don't give anything away,' he always says, 'act it out.' "

Walking toward the new Memorial Union, we passed the brick physics building, with its U. S. Government generator truck stationed at one end.

We passed chemistry, geology, social sciences, history, modern languages, English; we passed arts (with its long carpentry annex where Mary had made a flounder-shaped breadboard); then we passed the minareted administration building—relic of an early twentieth-century cow college. We passed a bookstore, isolated from the small shopping area the other end of town. Now darkened, the bookstore's window caught some of the distant illumination of a streetlamp, and the titles of the books seemed ghostly warnings and clues. There was a small poster in one corner, picturing Duke, advertising his lecture and a few of his books.

We descended Memorial Ravine, its carefully watered green now a dusky blue touched by a faint yellowy sheen thrown from the fluorescent lamps. Bulldozers had made the ravine, and it was the site of the Memorial Union, which itself was now floodlit and almost deserted. Pausing at the cement bank of the new moat, I saw how it meandered round the great structure, guarding it with a cleverly asymmetrical loop. This enormous humped shed seemed to be trying to thrust itself up out of the ravine floor.

"It's new," I said, "and it's very sad. But it's there and it's usable."

"Are you trying to impress me?" said Sue.

"It's a parody of a quonset hut."

"*Thank* you, Duke," she said. "Do you know you walk here as if you were seeing the university for the first time."

I couldn't answer, not because what she said was true (which it more or less was), but because its truth seemed terribly moving.

We walked away, past the fresh-planted saplings and on up the other side of the ravine.

"We aren't going in my direction, are we?" I asked.

"No," she said.

We walked a long way, and finally we found a dirt road. On the right a wooded hillside rose gently; we entered the woods. Presently we heard singing and, somehow apart from

180

it, a banjo—fussy, accurate, and in its fine steel flow sedate and lonely. Soon we perceived shoulders and heads and the fringed bloom of a fire; and then, when we came near enough to see the yellow wink of faces and hear words, we stopped among the trees and I leaned against a rough pine trunk and Sue leaned into me.

Duke's back was to us, and his head swayed with the song. Someone near the fire called, "Duke, some more clams?" But Duke raised a finger, for the man who was singing had gone into the last verse of his song:

> When I first came to this land
> I was not a wealthy man.
> So I got myself a son,
> And I did what I could.
>
> And I called my shack "Break my back," and I called
>   my cow "No milk now," and I called my duck, "Out
>   of luck," and I called my wife "Run for your life,"
>   and I called my son, "My work's done."
> But the land was sweet and good
> And I did what I could.

Sue whispered to me, "You should hear what Duke says about folk songs in class. He sings them to us, but then he says the whole bit's been corrupted. I don't think he really believes anything either way."

I kissed her, but only caught her cheek as she broke away to watch.

The singer had headed into "I Was Born About a Thousand Years Ago," and he had the crowd with him—Duke and his fighting bass, too. Then, when they ran out of words, Duke took over and sang modern additions:

> I was sitting there with Socrates one day
> When that ship from Delos came on down the bay.
> I said, "What's to drink Old Socks?"
> He said "Hemlock on the rocks."
> So we clinked our jugs and sang out Happy Day.
>
> I was the archetypal Yankee go-o-getter;
> Among the Puritans there was no better.
> I indulged in vice and sin

With that cutie Hester Prynne;
Yes I helped her win a major scarlet letter.

But several students had begun to talk loudly, and Duke stopped, and we heard him groan and laugh and ask someone to refill his paper cup from the keg. But nobody seemed to hear him. Then he called to a boy with a guitar, "Hey, if you got a capo I can—" but a girl started a whiny rendition of "Lush Life" and the guitar picked her up with a march of syncopated ninths. There was a lot of talking, and a lot of walking back and forth around the fire.

Then, as the group bawled out "Irene, Good Night," Duke rose stiffly and made his way over legs and feet, and slipped away from the fire and the students; and we saw his shape vanish as he went down the hill to the dirt road where cars were parked. Below us, as he now switched on his lights, we saw part of the path they made. After a few moments he passed below us, and as he made a rise, his tail-lights were briefly visible.

Then we were walking again, walking back toward town. When we reached Memorial Ravine, Sue said we would go to the library to Duke's hideaway.

"Do you expect to find Duke there?" I asked.

"No, I want to look for my tape."

Approaching the library with Sue, I said, "How come your shoulders roll up and down like that? It looks funny."

"It isn't very beautiful is it?"

"No."

"You're not very diplomatic."

"I hate not telling the truth. No, I mean—"

"You poor shit," she said. "Well, then, I'll have to tell you the full truth about my shoulders." She was being ironic. "I carried a trombone to school from about ten to sixteen. I can't help walking this way. I guess I roll."

But I only half heard her, for I was searching the lyrics of the songs we had heard the fireside group singing. I felt there had been in those words some special meaning for me.

Sue had the two necessary keys—one to the side door of the library, because she was an honors student doing independent research; the other, to Duke's office itself—he'd given it to her the year before.

As we crossed the dark reference deck, Sue's sandals slapped the marble floor and my sneakers felt neat and powerful. Lamps outside cast the tables and desks and file cabinets and magazine racks into a spectral streamlined terrain. We were being watched by knowledge, ignored by knowledge.

On the third floor we passed through the history stacks to get to Duke's office.

"This is where your father has his midnight conferences," said Sue, scratching the door as she probed for the lock. Then we were inside.

When Sue turned on a fluorescent lamp on the desk, I felt Duke in the room. Pale-armed faces gazed up at me from the Mexican rug. From a table by the window, the cloudy mirror of a TV screen reflected the lower half of me. Duke's refrigerator stood by a couch, which had been upholstered in a cheap, modern blue-and-yellow weave. On a table a row of books he had written stood guarded by two white plaster cherubs joyfully clashing cymbals that seemed growths on their little hands. In the far left corner—always growing—the monster deliciosas spiralled up their slender spruce trunks.

"Here they are," Sue said, bending down behind Duke's desk. "All the tapes in a carton."

"You can't take those," I said.

"I think you're right," she said, coming round toward me. "But I also don't think you know what the hell you're talking about."

"It's simple," I said. "They're his property. And since I couldn't rat on you I'd be in an impossible position. I'd have to be straight with Duke *and* you at the same time."

Why she did it, I didn't really know at the time—but she came to me and pressed her cheek against my shoulder and clutched me, chuckling all the time. "Oh," said Sue hoarsely, laughing, "you're wonderful. You're sad."

Then she stood away, smiling, shaking her head. "Your reasons are no good. One night a year or so ago we were up at the lake, four of us—and one of the two boys, the one who had the car—his parents' car—was all bent out of shape and couldn't drive home. I didn't have a license—neither did the other girl. Neither did the boy I was with. But he could drive, he knew how. But he wouldn't drive. And do you know why? He said it was because he'd promised his parents he'd never drive alone until he got his license. I could drive a little, but he wouldn't let me. So we waited six hours till the other boy got unbent and then we drove back, and I and my girl friend got disciplinary pro. It didn't matter, really. My date didn't like me. He was a blind date, and when he first saw me I could tell he was suddenly forcing himself to keep looking at me with interest. I saw that first impulse to look at something else. Anyway, his reason for not driving was stupidity, not honesty. Not even fear. Just pomposity. And that's why you don't want me to take back the tape."

"This is my father's office," I said.

"He'd laugh to hear you say that. He's given away fifteen or twenty keys to this room."

"Why did you bring me up here?"

"Why did you come? You're so passive."

"I was being . . . friendly."

"Oh Jesus, try again, will you!" She stared at me, very calm. "OK, you were lonely."

We were half-sitting on the end of Duke's desk. I worried about the light escaping between the slats of the Venetian blinds.

She spoke again. "I probably thought it would satisfy me to take the tape back while you were with me. Make you an accessory. But that doesn't make sense."

"What's on this great tape?"

As she began to explain, my eye was caught by the titles of Duke's books on the table across the room. I could just make them out. Was I getting nearsighted? I picked Sue up in midsentence.

"—ideas all over the place, flickering on and off, never developed. For weeks in class I watched him thrash his arms and then sit down and park his feet on the desk top and stare at the class for ten minutes without a word, and then say, 'I don't know what I mean, but I know I'm right.' I wanted to reach out and have him reach out to me and just simply tell me what I was supposed to learn. They used to say he gave the same lectures in all four of his courses, but that may have been a joke. Famous teachers often have a lot of enemies."

"So my father's a big hoax; I know that."

"No!" cried Sue, "that isn't true." Then more quietly she said, "However *I* may feel, that's not the truth. He does set off discussions; every night the dorms are full of discussions he's set off. He says, all he wants is to start a little intellectual ferment. He got me to feel that to be great a man has to let his full inner confusion speak. Duke's certainly confusing. He's hard to take notes from because of his long periodic sentences. I used to frown at him in class—an all-purpose frown I could use to show doubt, or understanding, or devotion. I didn't want him to think I was either hung up on him or convinced he was a fake. I got so I thought about *him* and *me,* not the subject he was teaching. They say Duke 'opens doors,' but I'm not always sure."

Sue was trying to sail around the main point. "What about the tape?" I asked.

"One day in class he said, 'Each of you wants to be a passive believer in me, and each of you has his true distortion of me.' Then it was something about the teacher as God. He said, 'I'm a parody of God for some of you. But why think a parody is a distortion of the real thing. Today, maybe parody *is* the real thing.' Then he was on something else, but I kept thinking about the God idea."

Sue began to walk about the room, slowly, deliberatively, alone. Her story approached its point. She'd had a conference with Duke just before an hour test the preceding April. (Here? In this room, with Duke at the desk, in the chair I had my back to?) She had asked him if on the test he might ask them to write on the *lives* of men like Samuel Sewall and the Mathers. And Duke had replied that she could write on *anything,* whether connected to the course or not; and then he had grinned his evil grin and offered her a Hershey bar. "It was like when he made us give *ourselves* our grades at the end of the first term. He said the grade we gave ourselves would be the grade he'd put into the book." Sue had tried to study for the hour test; she had gotten down to it that afternoon—a Friday. But she kept remembering the word "anything," and after an hour or two she had stopped studying and had just sat. "I didn't even read my notes." And she sat idle all Friday night and all day Saturday, and all Saturday night. "But now my idea. . . ." now her idea of being in some strange communion with Duke got translated into something else. She thought of his bare shins above his white athletic socks, she thought of his broad yellow buck teeth grinning when he'd made a joke no one got. "And in a moment of simplicity Saturday night, I said to myself, 'The truth is, I just want to be hugged by him, I want him to make love to me. Why kid yourself?' "

Yes, all her ideas—which were mostly his—had gotten mixed up with his skin and with . . . "with the big, pitty pores in his nose, and his hippy grace when he'd wheel toward the

185

blackboard to write 'federal theology.' " And the disappearance of his ideas into his flesh and of all his assignments into the word "anything" had made her think . . . "think, or feel, or think it would be exciting to think, that Duke was . . . no, it's silly, I tell myself I'm beyond all this stuff now. . . ." that Duke was dead and at the same time that Duke was—had been?—God . . . "boredom and loneliness and wordiness, it all made me put words down on paper, 'He has died into the flesh, He is—was God.' "

The Sunday morning of that mad, desultory weekend, she had started to say aloud, "Duke is dead, God is dead, some crass ghost will come instead." But a very clear voice inside her kept saying, "No, this is an act, you're only playing at being crazy. You're really in control." But then she got taken to the health center and she kept saying her jingle about Duke, but kept it up partly because she hoped Duke would come and visit "me and say something warm. But he never came. And then, when they took me . . ." to the state hospital in Concord she wondered if maybe being willing to keep *up* the act *made* her *in fact* insane. "See what I mean? Maybe the very *desire* to keep it up was cuckoo, even though I had this clear knowledge inside me that it was an act. If they'd tried to give me shock treatment, I'd have stopped the act, I know I would have . . . ," but then again she wasn't sure, for if the act was real. . . . I saw Duke sitting in the garage designing his parody signs for the driveway, heard him telling Tindall one had to be an instrument and being told by Tindall that Tindall was suspicious of musical metaphors. . . . "I mean," Sue was saying, "you don't keep on acting crazy if it gets you kicked out of college and upsets your parents. I was a parody of an insane person, but I *did keep acting.*" Sue turned on me that smile of inward discovery that isn't meant to be received by anyone outside the smiler. "Then it all passed, and I came back here. I'd found out Duke wasn't God and wasn't a fraud; I'd found out he was a man; and even if he's kind of an oaf, he's funny."

She had cornered him in the booth at The Rodeo Monday and had started asking him why he used these teaching gimmicks . . . "taped self-evaluations, using class time to divide the class up into committees—little clusters of us that would work out reports on one aspect of the week's subject, other gimmicks . . . ," and she had asked him sharp questions, which he had answered only with a guffaw. He'd gone off to students in another booth, and she had left, had driven home with someone else.

Sue was close to me, peering at my face; she was talking quietly. I was grateful she was still talking, for I had nothing to say that I thought would be true.

"When I made my tape, like the other kids, I told him all about my act. That I had half-suspected I didn't think he was really superhuman or dead, and that I just wanted. . . ." Her dress, blue and yellow, her voice stern—asking me now a question.

"What?"

"Sometimes just a bull-thrower?"

"Yes."

"Then I wanted to get the tape back because I thought there was still the mystery of last April tying us together, Duke and me, and then I thought that after all maybe it wasn't the truth I'd told him, and then I said to myself, 'He's just my teacher and he gave us an assignment,' and now I'm just coolly curious about him. And I don't care if he listens to that tape or not. Why get ulcers over all this. At least there's the truth in that tape that my breakdown was a mix-up of play-acting and helplessness and the two can't be separated. . . ."

She wasn't talking anymore, she was waiting for me to speak. But instead of saying something, I was hearing certain of her phrases repeating in my mind—I didn't recall hearing them at the time she'd spoken them—"made me take myself less seriously, that's something."

She was looking at me quizzically. "You do look like Duke." And she giggled.

And then she said, "I gotta go back. I'm not even signed out at the dorm. I'll have to crawl in."

I reached for her shoulders, but she backed away and chuckled. "Nix," she said. Then she got serious. "It's just that you didn't listen very carefully to what I said, and now you think it would be nice to have a slap and tickle in your father's office with one of his students."

"Slap and tickle!" I cried.

"No, even now I didn't say exactly what I wanted to say. It was the way you looked at me, and the way you weren't really listening to my long spiel tonight. I can't say any more than . . . well, I'm not interested."

"But you've got to tell me, what's wrong with me, I just reached out—"

"Why the *hell* do I have to?" she cried bitterly. Then she smiled again and looked down at the rug. "Now we're going." She put the key to the office on Duke's desk. "What do I want with that silly thing?"

Near her dorm she said, "I'll probably settle down someday and write the Great American Cookbook."

When we stopped at her walk, I tried to kiss her, but she pushed me away and shook hands. "If I were writing in your yearbook, I'd write 'Here's good luck to a guy who really needs it.' Good night, Michael Amerchrome."

"Good night," I said, thinking the "Michael Amerchrome" was kind of affected.

I hiked home. It was all of four miles, but the crisp temperate night air seemed to purify my insides. Sue would say, "Purity, what crap!"

Well, my stomach felt better than it had for a long time.

But Saturday I was no clearer in my mind about what I should do. Yet for the first time I found myself assuming I *should* do something. I thought I'd phone Sue, but then I thought—as if from the sour puddles in my stomach—of that key lying on Duke's desk and of her new indifference toward Duke; and I thought of all Duke's students—years and years of them—shuffling out of his classrooms and passing into the world, and remembering him in a way that was strangely like forgetting him. I thought I must reach inward not outward.

When I came down to breakfast, Duke was on the phone and Mary was outside hosing the flower beds. My stomach was sour—but not from the scrambled eggs Mary had given me last night at supper; rather, from simple emptiness. As if he were trying to watch the person he was talking to, Duke kept his large almond eyes slanted right and down into the lower drum of the receiver. "You're all a herd of cattle! And it's my own goddam fault for making learning too goddam attractive! I put too much creativity into my teaching and look what I get—" I heard the student laughing loudly at his end—"cattle and creeping things and beasts of the earth!" cried Duke. Then the student was saying something; then Duke went on: "No, you'll have to find that out for yourself. . . . Think I'm going to do your research for you? . . . Yes, the androgynous Adam, seminal, very seminal, a rich topic.

. . . No, I'm the teacher, you're the student! . . . Yes. Footnotes, bibliography, the works. . . . Well, you might try Migne's *Patrologia*." Duke hung up abruptly.

Almost as he hung up, the phone rang again. It was the president. The board of trustees was meeting Saturday afternoon. "Well," said Duke, "I don't actually know which press will undertake to publish it. LSU, OUP, UC, CP, S and S, I can't tell at this date. . . . Yes, sir. . . . Well, if you want to show them something, I can give you an offprint of an article that came out in December. December and April seem to be my months, but I just don't happen to have any monographs in the press at the moment. It's because what I'm working on is so long. You know, as one of those boys, I think Tertullian, said, *'nunquam Ecclesia reformabitur.'* . . . Yes, sir, well, it's hard to translate. . . . Thank you, thank you. . . . Yes, goodbye." He hung up, and sighed. Then he said, half to me, "That young bastard does all the little things right. He just said he believed in me. I've got him where I want him—in the presidency."

"Why don't you tell him the truth," I said, without conviction.

But the phone went again. Doris Greave now. And during this conversation, Mary wandered in from outside. She had her work gloves on. She went to a window sill, stared at one of her tray gardens, then took up her Green Stamp catalog and sat down at the table where I was having coffee. "No, of course she won't," Duke was saying. "Yes, well, I'll get Michael to come. . . . OK Doris, Roger and out," he said and hung up.

"Doris and Deirdre want to take me deep-sea fishing, Michael; I told them you'd come, eh?"

"I got things to do," I said.

"Like Mary," he said drily. "No, you come on with us. You might learn something."

I thought of the driving, sunny boat, pitching southwestward, and Duke in the cockpit forward, yelling at the sisters and drinking Ballantine Ale and holding casual dominion over them and me.

"No," I said. "Maybe I'll help Mary here."

"Look," said Mary, holding the catalog up over her head. Half kidding, she tried to interest Duke in what the stamps were worth. "What'll we get? How about two sleeping bags or a stove for camping out?"

But Mary knew Duke knew she was tired of not getting on with her wallpaper. And he refused to joke in her way—wouldn't, just to be nice, find something outlandish in the catalog and say, "That's the very thing!" Instead, he released a long baritone belch—probably artificial—and said, "Trade your stamps in for the services of a professional wall-paperer."

Without a word she left the room and went quickly upstairs.

"That got her," said Duke. "I got her last night, too."

I couldn't speak. Had Duke said what he knew would spur Mary? Or did he just mean to be mean. Could I do anything to ease Mary's marriage? What were my true motives in *wanting* to help? Any judgment or action I took was bound to involve me in self-interest, meddling, even betrayal. And loyalty, honesty, and a pure, clean, straight freshness are what I put my money on.

I'd expected Duke to keep on about the fishing expedition. But he went upstairs and changed to his old paint-spattered khakis, and when he returned he had on a wise and ridiculous fisherman's cap with a long, black bill. (He was always appearing in articles of clothing I hadn't known he had.)

We stared at each other, and Duke saluted unsmilingly.

I said, "You don't know anything about deep-sea fishing."

"Aha!" he said quietly. *"Don't* I?" And then, magically—or perhaps because I misgauged the moment during which I took a last sip of coffee—he wasn't there. He'd vanished from the living room, where I was having my breakfast; I heard the front door close softly, and I listened to the perfect motor of his VW strike the air, then fade away.

Well, in the afternoon—a time when our house always seemed bigger—I met Mary in the upstairs hall. She had decided to go to the Green Stamp store—subnamed the Blue Bridge Trading Post.

On our way we stopped in our own town to buy provisions. Mary's disjointed gabbling had melted into an eager simple gaiety. "Duke's right, you know," she said; "the supermarket *is* beautiful."

She kept the stamps with her; they half filled her Mexican straw basket.

In the store a woman I didn't know—which isn't saying very much—looked hard at Mary. Looked hard and then smiled hard. Doubtless Mary's jeans interested her most, but it was Mary's sandalled and unstockinged feet that she mentioned.

"My goodness, aren't your feet cold, and it isn't even May yet?"

"They don't feel a thing," said Mary.

"Well," said the woman, a brownish, stringy, frontier-type in a denim skirt, "well, I worry about you." And she threw Mary a violent grin and turned away.

Quietly, Mary said to me, "She may be a faculty wife. She may admire Duke's salary. Maybe I met her at the University Folk Club." This group Mary had gone to just once; on her blouse they had pinned a plastic-sheathed card saying, "AMERCHROME, FORTUNA CHAIR." Asked to give at a later meeting a talk on her "hobby" (for they'd heard she did textiles), Mary had gently declined, privately swearing she would never again be seen at the club. Now, staring after the tanned woman who had seemed so solicitous about her feet, Mary said, "I don't think I know her." Then she dropped her straw basket into the metal cart, and said, as I started to wheel it along, "I don't know what I want; what do we want?"

Seeing several shoppers ahead of me, I felt suddenly a fine, sure flow from my brain through my hands to the four wheels of the cart—it's the front wheels you have to sense, for they pivot. Leaving Mary behind me, I launched the cart into the crowded aisle. Lightly I brushed one woman; then, slickly missing a head-on collision with a stack of Heinz cartons, I angled into a small passage between the cartons and another woman, and slipped through it, faintly recognizing that I'd expected my increased speed to get me through more easily; now I saw before me a cart full of cut-rate Chicken of the Sea tuna and all-purpose insecticide bombs, and almost instinctively I chose the right-hand alley; then, raising my back (fixed) wheels off the floor, I shifted my stern left then right and slid neatly through the narrow passage; an employee who was slowly filling a cart with a phone order saw me as he prepared to enter the passage that I was navigating and, alarmed and wary, took the other lane. And then, I had reached the far end of the store.

In another aisle I found Mary examining a case full of plastic bags; in each bag grew a small, branching Venus fly trap nestled in vermiculae; Mary was reading the instruc-

191

tions. As we passed along the aisle, we hesitated at several stages: We looked at the pickles, the Jersey lettuce, all the Swiss soups dehydrated in their envelopes, the plastic lemons and limes with their fuselike valve-spouts. And then we came to the bread shelves.

These stood at the far end of the store under a giant mirror-eye tilted to give a store-length view from the cash counters. Two little boys were looking at the boxes of doughnuts; a large, aged woman was handling sandwich loaves; a narrow-trousered man with a rooster tie (antique locomotives) took a stick of French—or is it Italian?—bread and a pack of crumpets, and stood reading a contest offer printed on the wrapper of a long jelly-roll.

As Mary gazed at the wallful of breads, her hand moved slowly, unconsciously, to her straw basket in the cart. "Oh, Michael," she whispered, "something's happening." And then very quietly, yet squeakily and coyly, "Whee, am I dizzy, Michael? Please, am I dizzy?"

"What is it?" I asked, placing my hand over hers on the strap of her straw basket.

"Oh it sounds stupid," she said. "All the wonderful doughnuts and honey-breads and coffee rings and English muffins. It seems stupid, but I seem to see them multiplying: yellow and blue and green and red and blue and white."

The boys, the man, and the woman were watching Mary.

"Michael, I have to do something, this is so lovely." I became aware of the canned music the supermarket hoped would lull its patrons through their ears just as the vista of package colors would lull them through their eyes. "Wonderful, wonderful Copenhagen . . . ." the city where, according to Duke, Americans feel most at home when they go to Europe. Mary was saying, "The breads are . . . no, that's impossible! The bread shelves are telling me to—" then she rolled the cart toward the people. "Here," she said, pulling out a handful of Green Stamp books, and offering them to the old woman. "Have these."

"No!" said the woman. "*I'm* not taking them books."

But Mary dropped the books into the woman's cart, and then gave her a dozen more.

Then she moved toward the man, who started to back away, keeping his cart between himself and Mary.

"You, too," said Mary.

"Yes?" said the man, trying to grin.

"Here," said Mary, and scooped from her basket into his cart perhaps a dozen or more of the fat books.

He looked as if he were about to say, "You shouldn't," and as if he desired only to be a couple of aisles away from Mary. But instead, he frowned and smiled—I guess he was trying to show too many feelings or moods at the same time, for it didn't come off. He was trying to be smooth, calmly surprised. The two boys pressed Mary for the rest of the books, which she gave gladly.

Somehow we got back to the checkout counters and through and out of the market.

In the car Mary said, "That's simpler now, isn't it. We don't have to go to Blue Bridge. We've given away our stamps."

She whistled "Copenhagen" all the way home, and twice when I began a conversation she didn't respond. When we arrived she went straight up to the guest room.

Duke knows everything that goes on. I wasn't surprised that by late afternoon he'd already heard of Mary's performance in the market. Yet, if he knew of her sudden need to unload the Green Stamps, did he know of the silly, real revelation that had impelled her? At the moment when she had felt the breads multiplying and had conceived a passion to *give,* I had failed to speak, failed to find the good, pure word that would show her I saw the meaning of her wish. But perhaps I had felt that the lovely trouble that hypnotized her should remain hers alone.

All through supper Duke quizzed Mary. He seemed to think she had been insincere in what she had done. "But did you honestly think the bread shelves were speaking to you?"

"In a sense," said Mary. "Look, can I explain a thing like this? It was like forgetting to think. All I know is, I saw coffee rings, brown-and-serve rolls, red-white-and-blue-wrapped sandwich loaves; and at the same time that I felt stopped, I also felt I had to give all I had. Those Green Stamps had to be . . . spread, published, I don't know. Can't you see? Anadama, Tip Top, Pepperidge Farm—they were all too great to touch. I had to respond."

"I'm dubious," said Duke. "It sounds like you were trying to—"

"Well, I bet I get it from you!" cried Mary.

"So you admit your act was an imitation of mine." Duke laughed rather defensively. He'd said too much, and he knew it.

Mary put her fingers over her eyes and smiled. Duke pursued her. "Fifty books' worth? Don't you believe in the Green Stamp redemption plan?" He seemed really put out, scornful.

By now we'd moved into the main part of the living room. We'd had supper late, and the brass ship's clock next to a window said ten.

Mary began to weep quietly, shaking her head and chuckling a little. Duke turned to me and said, "Now we've done it."

"I haven't done a thing," I answered. Did Duke refuse to guess that he had disheveled her mind? "Duke, you haven't the sense to see that Mary's half nuts because of your . . ."— I felt for the words—"your arrivals and departures." (I barely registered Mary's low, uninterrupting words: "Oh, Christ, do *you* have to talk like that, too?") "She feels you're insincere. She sees a bag of grass seed by the front door and five untouched rolls of wallpaper in the guest room; the phone man brings a new red instrument for the kitchen; you subscribe to three new magazines, and they arrive; you post a week's creative schedule on the bulletin board in the hall; you tell Mary next week you'll be in New York meeting world feds, you tell her to get up a dinner for the governor of New Hampshire. The freedom you give her is to leave her alone most of the time."

"You're telling the truth," said Duke. "But the truth-teller—"

"No!" cried Mary.

"—is a kind of instrument unable—"

"NO!"

"—fully to understand the—"

"No!"

"—truth he tells. In a sense—"

"Shut it off!" cried Mary. "Father, son, what did I get into?"

"No, wait," said Duke. "I'm in the same boat, Michael. Now you've just told a lot of truth. But you don't see how it applies. For example you're really putting onto Mary your own problems. You're a really eloquent expression of your

194

own selfishness. You're a romantic solipsist. Unh? unh?" Then, to himself, he muttered, "Santayana."

"Well, you've made me what I am," I said. "I've been . . . I've been . . . ."

"Conditioned?" said Mary, and laughed quietly as she dried her eyes with a great red bandana.

"Yes," I said, "conditioned."

"OK," said Duke, "you've been conditioned, turned out." He made slight groaning noises, as if at a private thought. "But not just by me."

"Conditioned is what I've been," I muttered.

"That's what you had to learn for yourself," said Duke with a hint of querulousness and plaintiveness in his voice. Then he was droning dully, old-manish: "That's what I wanted to ensure you learned by yourself. You can only learn something really well by believing at first that its *opposite* was—"

"No! No!" shouted Mary. "More words. They're true. But they're words. Oh, my God, my God!" And she rushed from the room and we heard her pattering upstairs.

"Where *are* you!" I shouted at Duke. "God, I want only to be honest and clean and straight."

"That's not very original," said Duke. " 'And hence no force, however great, can draw a cord, however fine, into a horizontal line which shall be absolutely straight.' That came out of a physics book." He had amused himself.

"If you're not here in person, are you in your books? I'm afraid to read your sacred books. I don't think you're in them either."

"To write a book is to try to be a person one never in real life actually is."

"I can't *depend* on you. I don't *know* you."

"But why in heaven's name should you know me?" Duke asked.

"You've failed me."

"Why? Because I don't make life easier for you to digest?"

"I don't know these words."

Duke moved toward the door. I heard Mary's feet above. With a strange, unearthly coyness, Duke said, "At least half of what I say, I believe."

"If you're so shifty," I said, "why don't I want to find out certain things? Where was I born, who were your family, what did your fans think of you in California and Texas and

Arizona and Chicago and New York and London? Why don't I read your books? It's not because you told me not to. You force me to go around suspecting you, suspecting everything you say; but then somehow I don't want to go further than suspicion. You're making me a phony."

Duke spoke oratorically, but his tone was distant and amused: "If we say we have not sinned, we make him a liar, and his word is not in us."

"You're not honest with me."

"I'm not an honest man."

"No one says that sincerely."

"I'm a performer," said Duke. "A live embodiment. But an embodiment of what?" He turned and walked through the door into the hall, and a moment later I heard the front door open and close.

I followed him out into the moonlight. He walked faster, then stopped near the whitewashed stones ringing the red pine. I came to him.

"Your book on Ticonderoga was a fraud. I bet most of your other work is, too." I had hardly known I was speaking. I wanted to suck back the words, for they were based only on hearsay.

Now, sadly, Duke said, as if he had known my mind, "Hearsay is so often true."

And hating his knowledge of my mind, I felt about me only my body, my body—one and simple.

Then my right fist hooked out by itself, glancing off Duke's left temple.

He didn't laugh, but put down his flashlight and just went to work. I put my flashlight down inside the white stones that ringed the plot where the red pine stood; and as I was raising up again, Duke caught me over my right eyebrow. I managed to stand, but Duke gave me now a sickening slide-jab that seemed to start under my ribs and cut me in two. After this—ever so slowly, I thought—Duke seemed to put his left in my mouth, twisting his fist as it contacted.

I was down—then up on an elbow.

He may have been surprised I didn't get up and come on.

He wheeled, picked up his flashlight, and strode to the shore of the salt bay. "Mary, Mary," my thought bleated, "come out here and take me in your arms."

"Come join the seals," Duke called, as if he'd forgotten

196

our fight and wanted to play. Yes, the salt did keep him powerful and humorous.

Now Duke took off his clothes. Then listening for a time, he stood ready in the moonlight that he faced. Then, for a moment, he turned back to me and stared, silhouetted there with the silver-blue light behind him.

At that instant I recognized that for some time the bay air had carried the digging beat of a motor. Now, it was heavy and near.

And now I saw a boat close inshore, just a dark purpose on the water. As Duke turned around to see, he was hit and surrounded and clothed by an electric eye of white. Then the motor's drill cut out and, to the faint descant of her sister's "Hallelujah!" (for it must have been her sister), Doris Greave shouted, "Dr. Amerchrome, is that the real you?"

A lot of hoarse giggling came after, and Duke put on his shorts.

Then he was wading toward the boat; I followed to the bank. But now I heard a motor start behind me. When I turned, I saw the microbus back out of the garage. Mary had darkened the house. Now the Greaves started their engine and when I called "Mary!" to Duke, he didn't hear. When I looked back again, Mary's tail-lights were bobbing away out the drive. The Greaves cut their spot. Their voices came to me dimly—frantic-sounding over the roar.

By the time I reached my room, the engine had been gunned several times, but the boat was still there. I had forgotten my flashlight, but I couldn't force myself to go outside again. Nor could I bring myself to switch on any lights.

In the kitchen I found a bayberry candle and lit it. When I reached my room, the Greaves' engine had trailed off across the bay. For a long time I looked out my window at the bay and the moon. Duke's clothes made a small heap near the edge of the water.

At the door of Duke and Mary's room, I stood in the dark holding my candle. I stood at the gate of Eden—but on which side was the garden? Somehow I imagined that a creature—Mary, Duke, David Brooke, Harry Tindall—might see the light from either side of the threshold and come toward me. Living through this night of intemperance, I felt it was my fault I was alone. Can you believe that? I felt it was my fault I was alone.

Duke wasn't home by morning. It was my birthday. I couldn't bear to open Mary's mauve note, folded in half and pinned to her pillow.

Our house was empty in a new way—free of the agitations that had made it live.

I went through a bowl of wheat germ and honey. I administered to myself a dose of grapefruit sections, then sloshed the remains around in my dish watching the pale yellow tadpole buds make shadows on the bottom. I had forgotten to clean the can opener before opening the grapefruit. I found three Fig Newtons Mary had left by the sink. I put them in the cookie jar. I kept hoping to hear Mary scuffing about the kitchen. So early in the day she was dreamily efficient. She mused, and served Duke's breakfast. He might be humming Puccini or Victor Herbert while he spooned up yogurt, and sometimes Mary would hum from the kitchen so that she and Duke contrived a vague duet.

I found myself phoning David Brooke. Could he drive me to the bus station in Blue Bridge? Yes, he'd be delighted.

On the way I almost said to David, "Duke has ruined my life and Mary's; he cares only for some phony vision he has." But something silenced me. David pried delicately, but his cautious mildness didn't fool me. He wanted to know why Duke or Mary couldn't have driven me to Blue Bridge. He wanted to know how long I'd be staying in New York. Would I try going to college?

"Perhaps Mary will join you for a week or two or three. I'm sure she'd love to take a holiday in New York."

"She'd rather be with Duke," I said, realizing as I said what I thought would irk him and put him off, that what I'd said was probably true.

After we passed Blue Bridge Bowladrome and the first long, lonely porches on the outskirts of town, I wasn't really with David. We passed the bus stop, passed the new motel, passed lawns and square frame houses. ("Homes," they are called.) Finally we stopped at Stern's Market. This is a replica of an old-time general store; it stays open Sunday until one-thirty in the afternoon; Mary likes the gentle Eastern European fellow from the Bronx who runs it.

"Just another forgery, another imitation," said David looking at the big porch and the great pickle barrel and the sign that said "EVERYTHING FROM PRALINES TO OVERALLS."

"So what," I said. "It's a nice place."

After I cashed a forty-dollar check, David drove me back past the houses and the motel to the bus stop.

"Let me hear," he said. "I'm always interested. Oh, I'll pop over tonight and tell your parents I gave you a ride." He seemed tired, downcast.

"No," I said, "don't do that."

"Sure? Why not?"

"Rather you didn't."

"Oho!"

But he was only acting intrigued. He seemed tired.

"What's the matter with you?" I asked.

"I'm just now tired by what I imagine your life to have been. I feel as if I could put it into words someday. To hold it. Preserve it. And maybe I will put it into words."

"Goodbye," I said. "You don't care about me, but at least you *know* you don't."

"But if I do put your life into words," David continued, "I'll always have the worming fear that it happened to me and not to you."

"So long," I said, and got out.

"Oh, wait a sec. I've meant to give you this." He handed a manila envelope out from the back seat. "It's an account of your father's career as . . . a maker of history, you might say."

Then after a flickering smile that may have been David's attempt to cover his shame, he put a hand on my arm and said, "No, I'm sorry, I won't give it to you."

"It's a piece of fiction, isn't it?" I said.

Which seemed to decide David. "Then take it and read it sometime." And he put the envelope in my lap. "You won't believe me, but this is the only copy I have. I'm not going to print it."

Instead of asking him if he wanted a medal, I said a friendly goodbye. "Don't go yet," he said nervously, as I moved away from his car. I stopped, but I couldn't think of anything to say to him. I felt terribly close to him, terribly *like* him.

And so ended the six last days of Mary, Duke, and me. Pitching and rolling down the great highways to New York, I forgot the envelope. It lay under my raincoat in the luggage rack. And there I left it, when I left the bus. Heaven knows where it is now. Maybe it will be published someday. But if it demands answers from Duke, he'll have them.

Right after my exodus, I wrote Duke and Mary I'd taken a room in a Manhattan YMCA. Those first few days I walked up and down Fourth Avenue looking at second-hand bookshops. I met two girls from Cooper Union in an Automat. I believed I was casing New York, judging it. But then, beset by noise and sticky-footed on the vast map of human streets, I decided not to persist in being my own spiritual mayor—and instead elected to let the city run me.

Some ten days after I arrived, I found a letter from Duke waiting for me at the Y one night. I went up to my room, intending to read the letter. But when I got there I found I was afraid to open it. I thought that if I opened the envelope, Duke's words would rise out like a genie and laugh at me. What was my honesty worth, when I now said to myself that I couldn't stand being laughed at? I left the letter on my bedtable and left the room and left the Y. And suddenly I was running.

I ran for blocks, ran round clusters of people at street corners, spurted past long, lighted store windows, until I found myself at Forty-second Street and Broadway. I thought I would take a subway uptown, and I went down the stairs and made for the turnstiles. But then I stopped, and somebody pushed me away from the entrance to a turnstile. I stopped because I suddenly realized I really wanted to know what Duke had said in the letter.

And so I turned around and walked for the stairs. But before I reached the stairs—the stairs out to the northwest corner of Broadway and Forty-second—I passed through a fascinating underground complex of cluttered stands. I was vaguely aware of pop music. For sale were newspapers, paperbacks, jumbo hot dogs, papaya juice, jiffy-booth snapshots (four for a quarter), and pistol games under glass. A couple of signs advertised "KING KORN STAMPS." Adrift in the passage stood a stubby old man in a greasy white apron. People veered by him as they raced for the stairs. Hard light cast upon his baggy face a gray-gold sheen. He was smiling, puzzled.

Eyes sharply aimed—but not at anything near him—he seemed to be considering the song some loudspeaker poured round us. A very young tenor was crying through the electronic glucose of an organ:

> Tell me, Tel-Star, where can she be,
> Tel-Star, Tel-Star, show her to me.
> Tell her, tell her, I'm so alone,
> Tel-Star, guide her home.

I felt like saying, "That music is full of clichéd thirds, its melody is meaningless, do you know anything about Tel-Star, do you know that Tel-Star Two may have a far more elliptical orbit, thus making it visible?" But that old man, that silly old man liked the music.

In a dream of waking, I walked past the old man, made the stairs, passed the all-night movies, and made my way to my Y. In my room I opened Duke's letter.

Tomorrow I'd move out of that denatured room—away from its buffed, dented linoleum, its clean hospital threat. I must be downtown, where I'd be attending classes in July.

By the Bible on my bedtable the management had left a notice of the next bimonthly Fellowship Lecture; under a reference to Matthew 7:1, big black letters asked, "DO WE DARE JUDGE OTHERS?" Thinking of Duke's slick, groping, sad harangues at the Greave sisters' club and thinking that I'd never bothered to go with him there to hear those harangues, I answered the big black question: "Yes—but you have to judge rightly."

I'd hate not to be judged at all.

In his letter Duke said he hoped the Y made me feel independent. He went on, as follows:

> You waltzed out on your birthday. When I got out to Doris and Deirdre's boat, I wasn't quite over my head and I stood there in the water having a drink with them. Eventually we took a ride, and ran out of gas, and slept till almost noon. And then, lest I embarrass them, I swam a mile home; and then I found you gone.

I *bet* Duke swam a mile!

I felt good and tired, so I lay down in the sun near the old pine and had a powerful rest.

Mary's back. She's finished papering the guest room.

Have you felt that cutting out doesn't amount to much—
I mean, leaving home doesn't amount to much—when
you're nineteen years old?

But *Duke,* I'm only *eighteen!*

We miss you. We have a birthday present for you.
Where shall we send it? Do you need money? You must.
And don't be falsely proud about taking it from me.
It was yours in the first place.

Is your digestion bad? Cinnamon toast might help,
for cinnamon is a well-known carminative. Was it an
Old Testament medicine man or was it I, years ago, who
said: "Cinnamon Rains Eupepsia And Turns Inflow
Outward Noisily."

You, Michael, are the young man from the country;
however, you're going to the city not to be corrupted
but to find what you were before you went.

With acrostics, acronyms, anagrams, and theories, Duke
continues to fight back.

What he said about the Greaves mattered little to me.
True or not, a small truth either way.

Mary loves Duke.

Digging into the old Sam Houston Museum stationery,
Duke's ball-point script slanted both ways—high and graven
and quick. A lonely P.S. said: "Do you still quest after my
past? You'll never know about me what—in what has been
your frame of reference—you think you want to know. But
console thyself, thou wouldst not seek me if thou hadst
not found me."* In no matter what island of allusion Duke
may hope to-lose and leave me, I remain his faithful failure.

I close this account neatly. I watched Duke's and Mary's
naivetés seem to break their marriage, until, sorry I'd lost
my innocence by peeping through theirs, I saw that the core
of their marriage had been mine as well. I had been married
with them. And this discovery meant that those six April
days had been first as well as last days.

After reading Duke's letter, I threw up my window and
leaned way out. To my right, through thickening mist and
fog, I saw an all-night cafeteria. Ah! At midnight or at two-

*The reader will recognize that unconsciously Duke had raided Pascal.

thirty A.M. or at four—to have buttermilk and a double egg-burger with relish, mustard, catsup, and Worcestershire!

Peering left toward the Hudson, I could see less and less. I began to take great calisthenic gasps of the condensing New York air. Near me, to my left, I could see the lovely red of two fuzzy lanterns marking a shoal of street the city had been tearing up.

Then I was feeling rain. I couldn't tell just when these crystal pills began to break upon my head or my turned cheek. Slowly the rain increased.

I stayed at the sill much of the night.

Since then, though at first it seemed—as, I think, it usually does—too late to be so wise, the idea of recapturing what I had fancied was my innocence has attracted me not at all. Innocence bores me stiff. As for the past, to find mine would be as laborious and defeating as to count sixty strokes of Duke's electric toothbrush in order to mark time. But without being able to count the strokes—and of course you can't count them because a Broxodent makes just a steady buzz—I can still understand what that little expensive gadget *is*. And as I watch my present acts instantly become past, I recall that the most vital kind of past *is* visible to me—my own human self-interest, and bravery, and kindness.

Scanning Duke's ingenious acronym (*vide supra*) and musing over what I've written, I find that my six days parody the six days of creation. Have I, then, unwittingly forged a form for what I recall of those six days? Or was—is—the form just naturally there?

Now that I see plainly what happened during those six days, I'm thinking of destroying these synoptic notes. Why should I publish them? I guess I'll send one of the four carbons to David, for "in a sense" (as David would say), this document is history.

« b »

suicide in a camel's-hair coat

Davey old Crock, that wasn't so bad, was it? Given the basal
hone, the honest accuracy of the fundaments on which
rest our chronobserevelations, why *not* use the voice of
Michael? And why *not* make him leave sooner than he—
you might say—actually did? He had to blow his Eden someday, didn't he? But don't touch up four any more. One
change I wonder about—turning yourself into a bore who
pretended not to understand Duke: an alteration in our
original master plan. But of course I see that the decision
was a creative and therefore unanalyzable one—you (or
rather, we) saw it as a counterpoint to Michael's newborn
awareness. Yes? Adam old and new? Unh? Unh? Oh, the
New Testament myths are threaded through with an almost
embarrassing adroitness and discernment and orientation.
Now that I think of it, it *was* of *course* in the first master
plan that we decided to speak through Michael; you felt
nearer him. Did I object to that change? I objected, in the
sense that the change seemed a move away from strict
order and of course I didn't want such a move; yet also, I
didn't object, for you are merely a projection of mine, you
are my creation, and all your flexibility is due to the charis-
matic, proteochameleonic juices ever in and of me. Indeed,
why *not* march under Michael's device—a canny-eyed lamb
couchant on the altar of an ego pretending to be halved by
the magician's old pearl-handled Persian surgical saw.

David isn't paying attention. He forgets himself; he interrupts my thoughts so that I, far humbler than he, now
and then imagine that it is *I* who interrupt *him*. Well, listen
to him: lovely chap: bright! "But was it Duke or Michael
I was projecting into? And Mary! Mary. This found *you, too*.
It was my only means of touching you."

« C »

Time to get on: Number five's waiting. So's the old man in London.

David, as he watches the Ping-Pong game aft on the boat deck, tries not to think of another, particularly painful origin of the project. But he cannot help thinking. But the man in the captain's cap has caught him again. David has been waiting for two honeymooners to lose interest in the slow, reaching, piddling game they are giggling over. They hold their paddles in the old-fashioned way, like pens or spoons, handle up, head down. A small boy, with whom by tacit agreement David assumes he will play, has begun to call out the score. As it nears twenty-one, the groom begins to glance with blank menace at the boy—and also at David, with whom he associates the boy. But now the man in the captain's cap has turned up at David's side.

God! He must be fifty; the gold-umber tone of his face is so finely, cosmetically graded from cheekbone to chin-point, the health so startling, that the man's youth succeeds only in certifying his age.

"Those cutters outstripped any revenue ship." The voice not so English today—almost Cape Ann-ish.

An interminable rally is in slow progress; the players, fallen silent, seem moronically engrossed.

"Little fishing village in Cornwall you'll learn all you want about the smugglers; take the early train from Paddington, change at Liskeard. Have my card." David takes it, as the man goes on about man traps and mule trains and the slow-sailing cutters the revenue agents had to use after the Napoleonic Wars (though not for too long after).

The Ping-Pong rally appears to have reached a climax.

A village where . . . "skin divers go out every afternoon for sea urchins, sell the shells, y'know. Now *there's* a smuggler—a sea urchin! Tries to sneak his life through from one day to the next by hiding in the shell that he—"

"Rather far-fetched, aren't you?" mutters David.

"Twenty-one!" the small boy explodes, going after the delicate, free ball, as the honeymooners bang their paddles down on the table and rush into a laughing embrace.

"Spines all over the shells, brown, green, mauve—"

"I know," says David, who doesn't. "Just a sec," he calls to the boy and, holding up an index finger to the smuggler-man as if to say the same thing, he walks to the port passage and heads down it.

That fifth origin brushes near him as he walks.

Think back—David wants to think back, back, back: Michael. After Michael took an overdose of Seçonal—a severe overdose—Duke came to see him in the hospital. Why *Brooklyn* Hospital? Why. . . ? Duke had been lecturing that weekend at Mills College near San Francisco, and so of course Mary got to Michael's bedside before Duke did. Duke came humbly, and demurred when the nurse (with not quite enough lightness) said wasn't Mikey a naughty troublemaker; and Duke was frankly incensed to find the hospital hadn't given Michael the telegram wiring a hundred dollars (for a young resident feared that any communication from Duke might disturb Michael further)—and then, standing awkwardly by Michael's bedside, Duke handed Michael the paperback he'd brought as a gift (*Existentialism from Dostoevsky to Sartre*), but as he did so Duke realized it was the wrong thing to bring, and so dumbly and greatly did he feel this that he failed to see that Michael perceived the embarrassment—and also failed to see that Michael was delighted and moved to see his father recognize, then try to hide the recognition, that this book was a stupid book to bring. Then Duke lost himself in staccato inquiries about whether Michael got enough raw root vegetables.

To include this annex of memory four would have been as madly disorderly as to deal at greater length with. . . . Was that the smuggler-man who peeked from a men's as David went by? It couldn't be. . . . Where was Duke now? Between what two points? Conferring by four- and five-way phone hook-up with professors in Puerto Rico, New Brunswick, Leeds, and Tucson? And . . . has a tiny new experimental walkie-talkie (with a fine potentiometer to regulate the amplitude of any incoming audio signals, should there be any) replaced the compact, transistor-sized dictaphone (a 101 Fi-Cord with replaceable twenty-minute tape) he so often addressed when traveling his beloved subways during those sudden overnight flying pleasure trips to New York?

Ellen's in the stateroom cutting out two fashion photographs she has found in the ship's copy of *Poland*. I have to restrain David's impulse to fool with Ellen, have to make him know letting go like that will only make Ellen depend on him for sociopsychic sustenance, and next thing he'll find himself obliged to fill her, give her transfusions of mirth to keep her alive. I alone know how Ellen acts as a disturbing influence on David. (And what disturbs that kid disturbs yours truly!) Just listen:

"Well, then, *let* me read them." "Why *haven't* you ever read them?" "You never asked me to." Why need she read these exact memories David and I have? "Did you hear what I said, David? You never *asked* me to read your bloody memoirs." "*You* should have asked. How could I force them on you?" "Because you're proud of them." "Then take this first two or three." "*Three* I'll take; I'll take as many as I can." "Look, you don't really read very fast. . . ." She takes one, two, three, reaches for four (typical!). "Just take three." She roots under four, sees the first page of five: "Who's Harry Tindall? Oh I know—the Englishman I barely met and you told me once or—" "Take the three, and stop snooping, you're the worst snooper." "Hold it!" She squeezes out a line of lanolin and salves David's wind-burned mouth. He tries to talk while she does it; and they start smiling. (Ugh!)

She goes away; she won't read those manuscripts; she'll just play chess in an after lounge with the boy she plays with.

David remembers the afternoon of—wants not to. And instead he takes from the breast pocket of his khaki shirt the little seven-level screwdriver he took from Michael Amerchrome: Plastic handle insulates, so seven-level may be used as low-voltage shorting bar, though the metal pen-(pocket-) clip on the handle's side makes you wonder; large enough for a firm grip; light enough to be used as a mallet on delicate components; small diameter of shank permits its use as a probe in confined places or as a chisel to scrape away corrosion between narrow-printed circuit channels; when magnetized, the small shank can retrieve metal parts that fall into restricted spots. . . . David remembers again the fifth origin, the afternoon of January 18—that date clearer than the year—yes, what year *was* it?

He was fifteen and a half, quick on the uptake, a lanky adolescent who walked—he knew it of himself even then— in a leaning style that made it difficult for the onlooker to say whether David had rhythm or not. (Ah, where is that Afghan hound who, at a noble, lonely trot—and, in foul weather, shod in red plastic bootlets—led his master along Eighth to MacDougal at twilight?) And as David came to the corner of Willow and Clark, somehow silent and, for that minute, unoccupied, he was aware of something way above him, something (in a way) huge.

And he looked up. And there, by one of the front parapets of the Towers Hotel, stood, or lounged, a man, far away but intensely, darkly clear in a camel's-hair overcoat, and with the most understanding eyes in the world (in those days, when asked, David would say, "I've got 20-15, that is, I can see normally plus an unusual degree of farsightedness") and David stopped. He knew he had seen accurately; the man was watching him; furthermore, no one was around—and because of this, David could hardly believe the slow simple movement the man now made. Yes, with one foot stepping onto a low cement wall (the last boundary—seven, eight, nine stories up), and then swinging the other up after, but never touching it to the cement wall, simply swinging it through, as if, watching David—seven, eight, nine (?) stories below—he was showing him how to kick through, no, dance a strange simple step, yes, dance "through"—and as the moving foot swung on like a pendulum, swung out, out, why the man pushed gently with his standing foot, never screaming or calling, never taking his eyes off young fifteen-and-a-half-year-old David Brooke with the normal vision plus a degree of farsightedness; and David, turning round, then, to face up Willow Street, turning in fact away from the silently falling man, saw with utter clarity that somehow he should have been able to enter the man's mind and tell him to live—to live. And David walked: pace after pace up Willow, with the first gathering shouts behind him, up away from the man—a man who had in fact sharply lessened the distance between himself and David. Had projected himself gracefully. And David: "I might have entered his mind and changed it." "Nothing that night. Julia mentioned it. No one knew the man. David said nothing. Project.

The junior-year-abroad voice runs more up-and-down today, more eager but less sure, less firm; and it and its companion-silence stay in one spot, near the door of David's stateroom: "Well! It's more fun than bridge with Mo and Joe. Honestly, if they call each other Dad any more I'll sweep-the-cards-off-the-*ta*ble. You might think they were playing double solitaire and just using us as . . . as . . . my God! as *voyeurs!* But Igor really gives, and I couldn't care less if he ever finds out what a *scène à faire* is, I just think I wasted bags of time not sacking in with him the first few days."

David strikes out "deaf" from a page of five, then "B.C." Finding that remark of his mother's on a random margin in five, he transfers it to a page of seven, then erases it from five.

Get away. Must get away. But *David,* you've work to do; binding work—the task of gathering these memories.

OK, go; but don't be long. (Naturally I want David to ring the changes from time to time.)

The giant zoologist watches from his stateroom doorway. He doesn't take his eyes away—heavy yellow brows. As David goes toward him—toward the men's—David hears from a stateroom a guitar and some voices and the smuggler-man's—is it? it has a cider-bloom-sweet depth—chorus—God! not *that!*

> Follow the drinkin' gourd,
> Follow the drinkin' gourd,
> For the old man is awaitin'
> For to carry you to freedom
> If you follow the dri-ink-in' gourd.
> Well the river bank makes a mighty good road,
> The dead trees will show you the way.
> On the left foot, peg foot, travellin' on
> Follow the dri-ink-in' gourd.

V

ANGLO-AMERICAN CHRONICLE

I am a snooper, with access to many sources of information. Therefore I knew Harry Tindall when I first saw him in mid-September. I knew he was a young Oxford historian who had recently arrived in New York aboard the *Mauretania,* that lovely antique aunt of the Cunard fleet. I knew he had ridden the New York, New Haven, and Hartford to Boston, transferred from South to North Station, and thence had come to New Hampshire on the poor old B and M.

In my car outside Emma's Coffee Shoppe I was tormenting myself with that day's issue of the *Mohawk Listener,* a county daily that features Christian-Republican editorials and a weekly page of letters to the editor. Over the top of my *Listener* I saw tall Tindall come marching down the sidewalk with two aluminum suitcases. A band of beanied freshmen stopped talking as he passed. Though the air was mild, he had the hood of his scanty duffel coat up. The bones of his cheeks and nose parted a path before him. Small mouth, long wedge of jaw. He looked a simple, destined Hillary heading for the foothills of some Everest. He had in fact come from the B and M flag-stop. After he passed Emma's, I watched in my mirror as he strode heavy-heeled toward the far end of town.

A week later I noted an anonymous letter in the *Listener.* Printed as part of the editorial strip, it reported that a "Britisher," the new addition to the university history department, had identified himself, in more or less private conversation, as a Socialist. Three days after that a Mrs. Molly Hume answered the letter. She argued that the *Listener*'s justified reaction to recent political trends at the university should be waived in Professor Tindall's case. The university and the state, she pointed out, were "indeed fortunate" some of their "young people" would be exposed to the "genteel re-finements" embodied in "the British tradition." Moreover, Professor Tindall's politics could hardly be expected to enter "the classroom situation."

In October I made further entries in what was developing into a terse Anglo-American Chronicle of Harry Tindall's career in New England. By then, as I'll explain, he and I had become housemates. October 5, I recorded that he had built makeshift insulation into one wall of our living room, and had begun to read *The Scarlet Letter*, announcing his rate as five pages a night. October 20 seven huge canvas sacks arrived from Oxford, and I helped avidly to unpack Tindall's library, which ranged from the final elegance of the Claren-don Press dark-blue buckram (charged at Blackwell's) to the faded, brown-framed Penguin Shaws he'd splurged on at his hometown stationer's years before. Also on the twen-tieth he reached page 80 of *The Scarlet Letter*. On the twenty-fifth of October, coerced by the dean, Tindall entered and won the faculty wood-chopping contest. On the twenty-ninth, in response to a pupil's anxious query, Harry ex-plained that the alpha, beta, gamma, and *nil satis* of the grading scale he used had nothing to do with numerical percents—he simply could not give a quantitative mark to an examination essay.

But I broke off my chronicle. Its bareness seemed foreign —in the deepest sense of "strange." It recalled Christmas Greetings Dell and Bill Craddock had sent me four years running. They wrote racy travel guides for a New York firm, and seemed to their relatives and to me—perhaps even to themselves—to be spending a lifetime abroad. Their printed message comprised a sequence of entries for forty high spots of the year just past. I believed that beneath the coy straight-face of their messages they were—perhaps sub-consciously—trying to imply that in spite of their rootless-ness they carried their "home" with them. These messages featured the three- or four-fold echo of items like "Dell de-cides Athens isn't her spiritual home," or "Bill argues with the Swiss Guards at the Vatican"—running gags, or, if you will, refrains. Reviewing the first naked facts of my Anglo-American Chronicle, I felt that it, too, contrived to miss the truth. To preserve and remember Harry Tindall, I needed a more human method. I must be able to get ahead of my tale, and behind it. I was as fearful of rigid systems as I was obsessed with my English friend.

At the time he came to New Hampshire I had been camping for eight months in a secondhand trailer near town. I had bought it from a commanding Egyptian who called himself Jesus Shane. For years he had been selling tackle and bait to vacationers on the northern hook of Cape Cod who stand on the summer beaches grimly and peacefully casting for stripers. He is in a longer trailer now (but no doubt his pronunciation remains unreconstructed—"Gape God"). The trailer he sold me had had silver sides, but in the parking lot at "Shane's Point" they had been glazed and cut by sandy, salty winds.

At the time Tindall came I had a job writing news releases for the university information bureau. It is a new university and sets great store by publicity. Since my active vocabulary is noticeably richer than my superior's, he confined his editorial strictures on my frankly baroque style by and large to laborious ironies designed to appear to hide a fundamentally benign hint that he and I were ultimately "in this together." Though sparing the blue pencil—in his case a silver automatic loaded with red, mauve, olive, orange, and black—he murmured one morning without looking at me, "I'm sorry the new Hotel Administration Ph.D. program is too American for you." And once, when I reported the proposal to give Styles Bridges an honorary degree, and referred to that senator's "total legislative and ideological *oeuvre,*" my superior, with a costive smile but without looking at me, said, "You know what we do to guys who import foreign words into the language . . . ?"

Weekends I was trying to make sense of more than a thousand papers in the west room of the main house of the Oakes estate, Indian Farm. The estate is reached by the Philips Point Road, along which occurred some of the most terrible collisions of the war which that tragic King Philip waged in the 1670's against Puritan colonists. The Oakes have two hundred acres—woods and bumpy pasture sloping to the shore of New Bay. Across the bay a piney ridge partially secludes a vast SAC base. At almost any hour of the day or night you may see a bomber lift slowly above those trees.

Andrew Oakes alone represented the family on the estate. An uncle and two female cousins lived in New York City, a score more relatives all over the eastern and western states. Andrew accepted me as a vagrant chronicler whose seedy researches gave proof of the Oakes family's distinction and its past. But I would have given up trying to sew together two century's worth of events and relationships, had I not been under the spell of one of the old Oakes, a nineteenth-century senator. Yet Harry Tindall's activities seemed even more problematical, especially after I came to know him well.

The second week of term I called at Tindall's office in the history department to beg a page on Oxford for the alumni magazine, my other job. Obliquely I alluded to the Oakes annals, and the locked closet I knew was full of fat stamp albums, and the dusty butterfly tables in the main salon, and the battery of pewter that made the dining room look like an armory. A student interrupted us, but before I left Tindall to her, he and I agreed to spend Saturday at Indian Farm. Andrew Oakes' great-great uncle had so named the estate before the Civil War, when it had covered half Philips Point.

On our arrival Saturday I unlocked the boxes of family papers to show them to Harry, and he quizzed me about my method. He made me feel like one of his students. No doubt he was severe with them. Still, as I later learned, they enjoyed him, called him "guv-nah." His accent they took to be both typical Oxford and typical English.

To Andrew Oakes, with whom we dined that first Saturday, Harry appeared English in a different way. At forty Andrew could recall two years he and his older brother had lived at a snug public school in Sussex, the holidays in Lausanne and Paris with their parents and cousins, the first-class Georgian in South Audley Street where they had twice stayed with a young friend whose London consisted of tea at the Victoria and Albert and matinees in the West End. Unwittingly, Harry brought Andrew a general and now genial memory of cold classrooms, brutal pedagogic humor, beans on limp toast, and the impossible ethic of soccer waged in the mud and, at Andrew's school, without substitutes.

After veal and Quiche Lorraine came the ritual of the salad. "Everyone in the Oakes clan can toss a salad," Andrew said. Later he and Tindall and I returned to the television room for coffee and more Scotch. On the top of the set Andrew's mail lay strewn. I knew he stored the bulk of his

213

post in the box at the head of the serpentine driveway. Every two weeks he would transfer the collection to the place where it now awaited him. And there most of it would stay for as much as two months—*Gourmet* magazine, electric bills, circulars from Sweaterville, U.S.A., duplicate or even triplicate ads from a maker of unwrinkleable trousers, and, of course, requests from the local office to install a bigger box to hold the volume of mail. Tiny envelopes on a chair or table were evidence that Andrew sifted the weekly take for invitations.

But Harry Tindall may not have noticed Andrew's mail. For in the afternoon I had shown Harry the summer house half-hidden among trees a hundred yards behind the main house. I suspect that all afternoon and evening Harry was imagining what he could make that summer house look like. In any case, that night he suggested to Andrew and to me that Andrew rent it to us. Why should curiosity have so overwhelmed me that I accepted the proposal—as did Andrew—even though I hardly knew Harry Tindall?

Andrew asked us to come to lunch the next day—when the sun, as he said, was "over the yardarm"—and discuss rent, heat, electricity, paint, everything to do with how to live in that summer house. Andrew and his wife had lived there until she died. She had died in fact three weeks after his father. Several chests of clothes had drawn the cold, slow mold of five years' desertion, but Andrew had moved most of the personal effects to the main house. Begun as a studio-retreat, the summer place had grown. Bedrooms, bathroom, kitchen, living room, "heating plant" (as Harry hopefully classed the drafty place where the oil heater was), attic, storage space—the house had extended itself at random through the woods like some subtle zigzag telescope. Moved by his love for this chaotic structure, Andrew's hard-headed descriptions of its kinks and crannies rambled on for hours. Shoulders forward, Andrew prowled, padded, rather than walked or strolled. His narrow, peering face, tan all year, completed a small, alert body.

Late-evening bombers were leaving the SAC base, aiming low over us, when Andrew at last stopped talking. He stopped, apparently because he had run out of information. But in the first instant of his pause, he contemplated Harry as if Harry were a well-mannered but dangerous inquisitor. I believe Andrew had suddenly wondered why he'd been so ready to rent the house.

"Have you keys?" asked Harry.

"You won't need a key," answered Andrew. "You're part of the estate. There's a ghost in your attic and in winter, squirrels. But you won't be able to keep them out of this house any more easily than you'll be able to get them to come down into your living quarters." This cryptic defense came from a sardonically solemn face, and Andrew must have been amused at the humoring solemnity with which Harry chose to receive it.

When we managed to see Andrew, those weekends he stayed home, he gave us permission to make the changes we had already made. We might cut elm and locust and pine and birch where we found them; we might walk anywhere on the estate. He would prefer us not to try to get into the chapel down toward the bay in one corner of the pasture. It had remained closed in Andrew's lifetime, and, as I knew myself, his grandfather's will had ordered it left alone.

To us it seemed impossible that Andrew should remember where each picture frame and spare tire and book and blanket had been left, as if in readiness for a scavenger hunt, in the long barn and in its loft and, next to the barn, in the string of rooms tacked together to make a second summer house.

Just before Christmas, that first year, our young postman, in his white Renault, steered and skidded in from the main road over the snow to bring Harry two packages from Currington. That day, in what appeared to be a sudden mania to release words and communicate the truth, this postman insisted that the Oakes had no idea of what and where their possessions were. "Andy runs his power saw with plain gas and when it breaks down, instead of fixing it and while he's at it finding out how to fuel it, he goes off and buys another, leaves the dead one in the barn, then hardly uses the new saw from one spring to the next. Financial suicide I call it. There's a circular saw sits in the barn behind two desks, and he doesn't even know it's there. I've worked for him. Ever since the chicken house—one of their experiments—burned down ten years ago with twenty-five hundred chicks inside and two firemen and the town cop standing by hoping the wind off the bay wouldn't blow sparks over onto the roof of the main house—ever since that day, nothing's happened on this place."

But if another truth crackled through his cosy informa-

215

tion, he was wrong about how much Andrew knew. He knew that there were seven children in the little eighteenth-century graveyard cloistered as if among a gathering of protective parents, far down the pasture in a group of elms and pines. He knew the dates of their births, their ages at death; and, with a rum sour in his hand, he could recite the frightening epitaphs with an actor's inward preparation:

Rebecca Joan Edwards. Born April the 8th in the year 1799.
Died March the 20th in the year 1803.
He that hath no children, knoweth not what is love.

A sunbeam in a winter's day, is all the proud and mighty have
Between the cradle and the grave.
Never strong, never sad,
Always suffering, always glad
Of Thy blessings in her heart.
Thou hast called. She must depart.

Andrew knew that there were two parts of a copy of a fifteenth-century triptych in our attic; that there was a sword inscribed *Christus vincit, Christus regnat, Christus imperat* (words that shocked Harry's voice into falsetto, for they might bear, he said upon the question of the so-called two bodies of the medieval king). Andrew knew there were iron bedframes, knapsacks, backgammon sets, several hundred inch-square tiles abandoned from a time when he and his brother had made mosaic tabletops.

In the barn, near the other summer house, Harry found the slabs and partitions of a monumental desk—not one of the two the postman had mentioned—and with Andrew's jeep we transferred them to our house, where Harry assembled them in his room. One Sunday soon after, when he joined us for lunch, and politely inspected our newly painted rooms, admiring and joshing our work, Andrew paused over the huge desk and asked Harry how he'd discovered one of the drawers, he knew it had been left under two milk cans: and he told us it had belonged to the peculiar ancestor I'd been investigating, the senator whose Lincoln signature, reputedly obtained just before the president departed for the Ford's Theatre and by some reports Lincoln's last official signature, now hung framed in the west room of the main house. And of course, as he said, Andrew didn't mind our taking the desk. He did think he might put locks on the barn and the unused summer house just in case. He would lend us the key when we needed it. Of course, we were welcome to make use of what we found, there or, obviously, in the attic here. He would appreciate it if we would tell him.

Several of his things became so certainly and, as it were, invisibly parts of our house that now my memories move, room by room, in a silent cinematic chronology past objects I know so well I cannot see them. For instance, the trestle table in the kitchen: Andrew and his brother had hammered it up out of unfinished pine one weekend; it had been designed, so far as it had a design, for the kitchen of this very house, and, many of his last bachelor evenings, Andrew had served on it—to Lee, his fiancée, and to three cronies—French ragouts, cuts of moussaka, versions of local lobster. Lee had preferred a simple Swedish table for this dining half of the kitchen, and Andrew had obliged her by removing the trestle table to the barn. Harry and I returned it to its home, and from its top he furiously scraped a hard surface of grease. We never moved furniture once it was in place. We transferred what we thought we needed out of the barn or attic, and into the square and round holes of which I am sure Harry imagined our rooms were composed. We hauled a daybed, internally injured and hence unopenable, and we threw over its back a brilliant Greek blanket. We moved in three tatty straight chairs; a bulky, indomitably stylish Chesterfield; a chipped mahogany cabinet for my recordings; and, against Harry's wishes, a leather elephant, stuffed solid and surprised, three feet long and two feet high.

I forget the order in which, during the first weeks of our residence, we moved these possessions of Andrew Oakes, though it seems to me that we did the moving in the late afternoons. One raw twilight in November, Harry had driven Andrew's jeep to the barn, backed it to the high, ill-fitting doors. Somewhere the buzz of a jet, private as the distant sound of a neighbor's chain saw, cut off as the plane passed into another acoustical world. Minutes later I followed Harry, tramping over Andrew's main lawn, gripping the flashlight we would need. Halfway there, with part of the driveway between me and the barn, where Harry could be heard knocking about, I noticed Andrew's station wagon. He had come home early, and in the darkening twilight, he had stopped parallel with the barn to observe his busy ten-

217

ants. His motor idled; dashboard lights dimly suggested his head; I believe he was looking toward the barn—as he thought, toward Harry and me. For several moments I felt the three of us paralyzed in our separation, until from a window of the barn, but without seeing Andrew's car in the dusk and perhaps without even looking from the window, Harry hallooed my name so that his appeal echoed all about me, as if aimed everywhere save where I was. The echo fell. I started walking again. Andrew, I think without seeing me, drove on round to the garage, ending his unannounced watch. More clumping from the barn. Harry searching. Then, less sharply, my name again. I pressed the flashlight button, firing the beam ahead of me; then I released the button and with my thumb rubbed the switch forward, lighting my path again; and authority answered from the black barn: "Ah, good, you've brought the torch!"

Then, navigating under five cartons of what I discovered to be discarded Oakes stationery, Harry emerged in the side doorway, where the jeep waited. Now Andrew was forty yards behind me in the thickening darkness. I heard his feet on the granite flags that led up to his front door. Harry had stamped back into the barn.

For Christmas, this first year, Harry proved he could write legibly by devising, complete with corner filigree and fake foxing, a pseudoparchment facsimile of a medieval "extent." With the gift—intended of course, for Andrew—went the explanation (typed by me) that the "extent" of a manorial estate listed rights and lands—usually with details of tenants' obligations and next to each item its annual value to the lord, whether in rents and services from tenants' lands or in profits from lands the lord farmed himself. At the bottom, in spidery script, and high jargon, Harry noted that he and I were expected to thresh seven and a half bushels of wheat for the festivities on St. Andrew's Day and Midsummer.

His essay for the alumni magazine on the English tutorial system won Harry a dinner invitation from the president of the university. "American Gothic" he called the president and his wife, their faces "spectacled rectangles of unequivocal Kansas health." They introduced him as "our young Briton"; they had been briefed by someone (and, indeed, they announced to their other guests) that Harry had "published."

His first spring, pressed by Marcus Black's wife, Harry

gave a talk on bibliophilia to the Mayflower Club. Spurned by the conspiratorial band of female members, Marcus sat on the hall stairs clucking and chuckling at Harry's quips about Moroccan goats in the sixteenth century and predatory American collectors in the twentieth. Also, that first spring, Harry chaperoned a masquerade at a fraternity and, costumed as an English laborer—holey corduroys tied with string over the knobs of his knees—he guarded the beer kegs all evening. For audience he had a gang of coeds, among them a pirate, a peasant, Martha Washington, a trapeze artist, and a cigarette. The last of these was encased up to the neck in a white cardboard cylinder and peered through a tan headpiece labelled "Micronite Filter." To those girls that night, he was simply and totally English, as he gulped from a paper cup and bawled to them that, compared to good bitter, there was so much air in American lager that a pint of it would hardly wet a chunk of Kentish flint.

Still, my impression is that he generally kept his rule to go into town only to teach and to attend services at Trinity Church. Partly self-induced the first weeks by his desire to seem almost parodically English, his vogue eventually waned. This was after he had come close to telling those who watched and sought him that in fact he was on his own, had independently picked this appointment rather than three years with superior students in Nigeria, and would not regard himself as some species of emissary or exchange scholar. At first he found himself beset by a beaming circle of Anglophiles: a real estate agent nostalgic for the Eighth Air Force and the early forties; the grinning, bewildered head of athletics at the high school, whose pride in his English wife checked his quiet terror that he might be too stupid to give proper support to her campaign as leading young hostess in town; a contractor's widow, Anna Mary Benson, who loaned Harry ten issues of *Britain Today*, gave two dinners and a "Sunday-night supper" to honor him and to show her slides and, between praising the shepherd's pie at the Ivanhoe Hotel—which Harry knew was near the British Museum—all but embraced him with joyful demands for information about London which Harry was quite unable to satisfy. "My forebears were all cutpurses and smugglers," he told her. His hairy tweeds, his bangs (combed specially for evenings out), his boulder-like brogues, were too English for words, a dozen admirers said. It was natural that Harry feared for his work, not to mention his identity—and re-treated.

From a student Harry borrowed rough-bottomed skis, old bindings, and sticky old boots. Certain secret afternoons in January—the first year or the second?—as I looked far down the pasture I could see Harry's featherweight parka fresh from the factory outlet crawling red and miniature over the waves of white. He was calmly disgruntled when I followed him down one day. He had brought an instruction booklet with him. On a short, steep hill behind the chapel, Harry tried to learn turns, tried to make himself lean downhill rather than up, and somehow refused to let himself turn correctly. When it was simply straight down, he managed, efficiently, inexorably, wings out, long face pink and stiff in the oval window of his hood. He never put himself in the hands of a teacher, at least not a skiing teacher.

Night after night, and so many afternoons, he fixed himself at his desk. The stillness of our separate labors, a stillness that snaked from his room into mine via the bathroom and hall, tied us together in live friendship. Then the creak and scrape of his chair moving back would print the image of Tindall on the card or page before me, and his voice, as he got up to stretch, would say, "Ring the changes, ring the changes."

Each fortnight, on a sheet of his Oxford college stationery, Harry listed fourteen people to whom he would write. Having finished his daily airletter—"a fact in every sentence" —he would ink out the appropriate name. As he said, he had not got a first at Oxford. "You and I are both good second-class men," he told me generously. But he never let his mystique about "first-class men" work like fog into the cabinet of his mind where he kept his plan to recoup all losses, obscure the curse of a respectable second, and one day re-enter his holy city on better terms. He wrote to his old tutor, and he wrote to three friends who had stayed on at Oxford as graduate students; he wrote to his college bookbinder, and to the high-church clergyman who had taken part in his conversion and with whom, on several tours, he had studied the gray cathedral fabrics of Salisbury and Durham and York. The answering letters he arranged in the middle left-hand drawer of his desk, insisting he was a pack-rat historian who would some day throw away his clothes to make room for correspondence.

"A middle-aged crank with a tidy mind, I am." At twenty-six he envisioned himself an unwashed eighty, tottering down a library aisle, checking references as if counting decades of a rosary, and happily vague about his nine or ten children, whose names he mixed up or forgot. Is it possible that Harry disappeared into the past and the future, as, living in the same house with him, I set out to fix him with the eye of understanding?

I see circular black-rimmed glasses and his eyes behind them, as he looks round at me when I interrupt his work. For a moment the eyes pop at me, floating alone out of the darkness of his person—headlights of the man my friend against whom I fight as helplessly as he is himself. The instant is over: ears grow beyond the eyes; a forehead rises high, the nasal escarpment drops into form above the jutting ledge of chin. The pieces, miraculously, fit. He will now say, "Ring the changes, always ring the changes," for he always says this. And after he answers my question he will put pad in book, book in shelf, new pad and book before him.

At the end of his first year in New England, Harry Tindall, quite against my advice, mailed his great stubby brogues back to the shoe company's central office in Piccadilly to be repaired. He had bought them a week before sailing, even though a London friend, as they made their way down the Strand, had preached him a sermon about Italian shoes and Englishmen abroad. Each Thursday evening, that first year, Harry would put a record on my turntable—as a rule, Mozart horn concerti, for the sake of certain associations they had for him—and sit by his fire cleaning his brogues. He would rub them and buff them, not with the fine, bemused eye of a man who has nothing else to do, but sternly, thoroughly, so that, though they may not have been able to reflect his face, they came back at him bright brown, neither light nor dark. Over the record player, across the room from him, hung my print of Wyeth's eagle, whose wings embrace the aerial view as he stares far down upon a farm. "Too clever by half," said Harry. "The artist is there watching over the bird's shoulder. The gimmick is shocking to no purpose." Above the fireplace Harry had hung a water color of deer grazing in the park of his Oxford college; the lower fourth of the surface presented a calendar for the year 1883. Our house, in the Philips Point Woods, five miles from town, was for him a luxurious novelty; and he settled in, happy with his books, with the birch stump he sat on by the hearth, with the shoes in his hands or on his feet. If, when he first came to America, he planned to send the shoes back to England in a year's time, he planned—or hoped—to send himself back after two years.

He spoke as an exile, but he planted himself among us and he worked. Whether searching medieval liturgy for still more proof of what he and his Oxford tutor thought of as the two bodies of a king, or proclaiming the chronicle of the Great Rebellion to his pupils at our university, where he taught history, he turned himself always, as he said, to "the next thing."

If he'd had greatness thrust upon him ahead of his schedule, he'd have thrust it back. He said he was too young to write his first full-dress study: Why leave oneself wide open? Why commit academic suicide? He would scatter short shots when he was absolutely on top of a subject: three pages on early uses of the word "Elizabethan"; four pages about certain ambiguous mottoes on thirteenth-century French coins; six pages on an independent library for medieval studies projected a century ago by a rich gentleman of Walpole, New Hampshire. In this essay a true Tindallian image climaxed Harry's argument—he was, of course, speculating from documents, not reporting a visit to a real room in Walpole:

> Admitted to this gentleman-scholar's workroom, we can see in his revisions the chips and shavings left from an intense but finally unfinished effort to define the conditions of his bequest. His own intentions remain dim. Most of his manuscripts and printed books eventually passed into and out of the hands of Goodspeed, the Boston dealer.

But if "chips and shavings" suggest carpentry rather than a scholar's dedication, they are actually an implicit compliment paid by Harry to his chosen world.

Like motes of dust filling the sunlight in a room, the events of our friendship hang in my memory. No doubt they form a chronology in Harry's mind. I see him at Anna Mary Benson's annual spring soirée, revealed suddenly to her

222

guests standing tall in profile behind a flocked, eighteenth-century screen, head crowned with a tea cosy, face leering down on a little woman who is herself just visible above the screen's edge. I think of him snoring on the sands of an island in Casco Bay one September morn, his exploring feet out beyond the flap of an ancient pup tent and visible to our host and hostess and me as we wade back from our early dip. Or I see him armed with the "Hoover" (as he persisted in calling it) tracking bugs and cobwebs over the ceiling as far as the cord will reach. Through a window I see him just before snow-time, passing among the pines about our house, slashing down snarls of thicket, searching for slender bones of branch and even elbows of twig, which he will build up into little crisscross forts of kindling before he brings them into the outer storage room (which he calls the "barbecue" because of its old open fireplace).

A putterer, Wanda Woodrow called him. Hunched on our crumbling brick steps, she would applaud Harry as he mowed the diseased, bumpy lawn that he planned to make into a perfect trapezoid. He hacked the rooty flower beds or pounced on rusty clusters of pine needles, while Wanda, indecipherable she hoped, spoke at him endlessly out of her remote dream.

"And what do you hope to do with this sick grass and these mongrel bushes and years of marine clay?"

"I'll make a domestic wood," Harry answered, joking but not joking, "with a clear patch of England round the house."

She never helped Harry, not even when he was cataloging his library or, with a droll stack of complexly punched cards, refiling his notes. "A kiss, is it really closer than conversation?" she asked him from her chair across the living room by the phonograph. "Do we judge people by what they say or by the noises they make?"

To goad her, Harry answered, "The kiss is an invention; conversation is natural. Therefore, I prefer a kiss."

She told him she was waiting for him to fulfill her and that if he managed this feat he'd discover a new psychic potency in himself. To this he replied that maybe that time had come, for he knew she would back away and pretend to spoof her own solemnity. She had many opinions about love-making.

For him, as he explained to me, her charm lay in what he thought her weakness. "This is always true of charm," he went on. "How whimsical and pompous she is, and still a fine girl." It seemed to me, eavesdropping uneasily sometimes from the hall, that his charm for her rose up in his more and more tenderly masked intolerance of *her* charm. Whether because she felt I truly knew her, or because she felt I ignored her, she disliked me. "You think I'm making an experiment with this English Charlie, don't you?" she asked, tossing in a trace of Harry's slang. "No," I replied. "I think he's experimenting with you. He thinks you're a type, and maybe you are." Another time she objected to my face: "Nothing has happened to it. It hasn't given way anywhere. You have a kind of perverted dignity."

Uninvited, Wanda walked through our door the middle of March, Harry's second year at the university and three months before he was to return to England—for good, he hoped. She was carrying two records of the Jimmy Giuffre Trio and a small Vuillard scene, which she soon began to discuss, more or less by herself. (A lecturer had shown her that the bureau in the painting had no knobs, and this had set off in her spasms of perception about the solitary woman in the foreground.) Now, she had finally come to him. Harry had been aware of her for many months.

Wanda was practically hipless, but she had gentle, narrow shoulders. Five-ten, striding, bony, blonde, she jostled the students at the university. And it was officially understood around campus that she lived in the leaning, magnificent steepled barn a few miles out, with a crew of bearded potters loosely allied to the art department. I was unable to get access to her file in the dean's office, but I knew she was enrolled as a special, nondegree student. Thursday afternoons she sat in the lacrosse stands to see the brave new boys, would-be air-force officers, marching in their blue ROTC suits. And she heckled them, calling many by name. Improbably, three of her dearest friends were neat, trimcheeked girls studying occupational therapy while they watched for husbands.

A long time after the events and moments recorded here, I learned that Wanda had rather publicly vowed to "get the Englishman," which sounded not at all ambiguous to her audience. Tindall had known her as a notorious Viking-Amazon, class-pedant in the one course she had taken from him, and the author of a fully but fictionally documented term paper penned across fifty sheets in rapid, careful capitals: it was entitled, "Reflections on the Scaffold: A Study of the Last Words and Final Behavior of Certain English Royalists Just Before They Were Beheaded: 1644–1649." On the title page she had crossed out the words, "YOU SEE WHAT MIGHT HAPPEN TO YOU."

She kept most of her own story to herself, and so Harry knew little of her home in northern New Hampshire, her mother's childhood home, to which the woman and her daughter had turned after Wanda's father had been discarded. Of the town, drab and spectacular in the first foothills of the Presidential Range, Wanda was proud and afraid; and she offered no anecdotes.

Her mother had followed her father along the pointless route of air-force bases where he seemed never to be stationed for more than a year. "Eventually he was noncommissioned officer in charge of education," Wanda said bleakly. "At least that's what he said he was. He made out lists for bulletin boards."

Louisiana to New York to Ohio to California to Georgia—a billet for Athens had died on a superior's desk—wherever they went they had found living together delicately unnerving, inconvenient. This had had nothing to do with prefab coops or the professional transiency. Wanda grew into a sense not so much of their displacement as of their lack of desire. Harry said he didn't know what she meant by "desire." Wanda shook her head. Her father seemed weirdly anonymous in her vivid pictures of him: his apprehensive face, shaved and dead when he left in the morning; at night drinking steadily, a bit flabby in a turquoise shirt worn outside his trousers, moving his hands somehow mechanically by means of his heavy, hairless white arms, he would tell his tales of what had happened from month to month of the year he had worked as a salesman for a Rochester brewery: "What was that man's name, I can't just recall, it doesn't matter." He would complete his shapeless stories, but somewhere in the middle he would lose interest in details. He would say he was sorry he'd never learned anything about the brewery business.

They had seldom received mail. With that vagueness that can sometimes be so precise, Wanda told us that wherever they had gone they had failed to leave impressions. Wanda would say to Harry: "I'd like to take you to all those states we passed through. It would be like seeing them for the first time." One day, after saying something like this, she started to polka round the living room squeezing herself as if she feared her self would get away, singing, "I love everything and everybody—all, all, all." But Harry broke up her dance with his serene, honed rightness: "That's too easy to say. It's an escape. Love everybody—except in the Christian sense —and you love nobody."

Harry said he wanted to take her to Oxford, but his energy was all for Oxford, not Wanda. He had adopted Oxford.

"Why should I tell her about Currington?" he asked me. "It just complicates my thinking. It isn't really my home."

When he grew old enough to feel anything further from him than his mother's dusty garden plot and the packed house where she nourished his father and her widowed, defeated sister, and all the children of the two marriages, he had discovered that he lived in a north-country town. At school he had learned that Currington was fixed at the mouth of a valuable river, and that Currington's markets, and its iron, and the coal mined nearby under the sea, made it almost as important as Carlisle. Harry's father, a fiercely uninformed Tory, had drained out most of his years, like many of Harry's people, at the steel works.

A shaggy young master led Harry and his classmates through Currington Hall, trying to give them some of his conviction as he lectured on and on about the great Rowen family, whose home it was, on a hill above the river. Sir Christopher Rowen had—as the school text put it—"entertained" Mary Queen of Scots here at the start of her long imprisonment; Harry Tindall found several of her letters in a calf octavo at the local library, among them an ornately worded message to Elizabeth begging money and clothes. Near the dockyards, in St. Michael's Church, lay Sir Thomas Rowen and his wife, Katherine, massively commemorated atop their tombs by sleeping effigies—he in full rocky armor, head pillowed by helmet, she in an outsized square headdress and a mantle clasped at her breast by a rose. Both of them held hearts, and as Harry's teacher pointed out at length, two symbolic dogs held the lady's hem where it hung over the marble. Alone, or with Jaro, his Czech friend, Harry had taken the gray street, as if it were a river, from St. Michael's down to the docks. "From the castle walls a man may see/The mountains far away," Harry quoted. From the docks one could take a long look across the Firth at the Scottish hills. The town itself sat indifferently rooted among dark marshy flats. Harry's caution grew with the years into what now seems to have been the born historian's willingness to wait for evidence. But before he was very old he sensed the truth about his town. And marching home at night—perhaps pausing in a fantasy of professional football to kick up a sphere of crumpled gutter paper, trying to keep it in the air, he felt almost trampled by the evidence he saw and foresaw: the ranks of uniform, exhausted back-to-backs waiting for him along the Victorian streets. He was even more determined when he came to America than when he first went to Oxford.

It still seems to me that Harry's life did not mingle with Marcus Black's or with that of anyone else at the university, except Wanda and me; and she and I, in our own styles, remained foreigners on the campus. Four times Harry excused himself from dinner at the Blacks' house—always regretting that he found himself in the last part of one stage of his work. He came home for lunch. Like Marcus, he never joined the ingrown gossip of the faculty dining room. He never went near the office of Marcus in the new physics building, but he talked to Marcus in the library or when Marcus peddled out to Indian Farm to see him.

For Marcus, a large old musing man, Harry was the bearer of tidings, a kind of fellow-countryman from a country Marcus had hardly known. From England, where his family had stopped en route from India to Canada, he had only what he referred to as a spiritual passport, representing a citizenship as unofficial as his citizenship in India, where he had been born, and in Canada, where he had been raised among Methodists.

Harry's digging in the tough beds about our house called up out of the dry bell of Marcus's voice, "Fair seed-time had my soul, and I grew up,/Fostered alike by Beauty and by Fear." He imagined that Harry's cuckoos were his cuckoos (or Delius's), Harry's autumn that of Keats. When he said, one day that second spring, that Harry came from the murmuring heart of England, his vatic syllables clutched his feelings, cushioning them with resonance and mock-heroics. This act Wanda laughed at, even as she loved Marcus's eyes of the lightest blue lurking steady and yet absent, deep under white bushy brows, even as she knew that Marcus was more than half serious.

To me Harry would say, sternly, "Dear Marcus: He doesn't take a sabbatical; he's only vaguely intrigued with the nuclear reactor (and he won't be in charge of it much longer); he says he wants to paint; but he doesn't paint; he doesn't make the great surrealist film he says will immortalize Indian Farm; he doesn't see that ability cannot exist apart from its embodiment in work."

It was difficult to defend Marcus, not because I didn't believe in him, but because, in my slow words, his notion of being human, educated, sane, sounded distressingly like the cliché of the "well-rounded individual." How could I explain to Harry, Marcus's loathing for specialists? And how could I explain to him how Marcus imagined himself marching across lunar deserts planting a saint's staff in the sands? That was a project worth carrying out, but how could I describe it to Harry? Marcus's small, perky nose, together with that steep descent from the peak of his bald, bumpy skull to the back of his collar, struck me as the wrong advertisement for the stoic humanism Marcus preached. How could I tell Harry these things? I was lord privy observer without a phrenologist-king to report to.

Despite Harry's regimen these two years, he occasionally seemed to enter—to discover himself penetrating—Marcus's life. Harry compiled five pages of notes on the family saga of William Thornton,* an early nineteenth-century painter whom Marcus collected and on whom he promised himself to write a monograph someday. In my own Oakes files, Harry had come upon clues to the wanderings of Thornton and the girl, Rose, a daughter so haunted by her vagrant father that she left her fiancé and her mother and for years accompanied her father as he ostensibly pursued the trade of journeyman artist. One weekend in southern Maine, Harry found further information in a small public library: Rose Thornton's father was reputed to have left a brief will bequeathing his daughter his reputation, the only thing he had to leave her, and, as he was said to have put it, "like most of our possessions, not truly ours in the first place." The

---

*Not to be confused with the William Thornton who built the main unit of the Capitol in Washington, at least up to (if not including) the octagonal base of the dome's peristyle.

apocryphal story of the bequest reported that when he contracted to paint a picture in someone's house he demanded one unusual condition: absolute privacy. If the picture was to be a portrait, his easel must be set up in an adjoining room just inside the door, the subject in the other room, presumably close to the doorway. Only thus could he pose as the author of work that, in fact, his daughter had done. Harry gave these revelations to Marcus, to do with as he pleased. Marcus responded with a set of pencil portraits of Harry, none of which pleased Marcus, though he gave them to Harry as a remembrance. Privately, Marcus told me this Thornton material wouldn't do—it wasn't what he had in mind for his own monograph. It had nothing to do with the poetry of Thornton's—or his daughter's—work.

There were, of course, collisions between Harry and those who briefly touched his life. But the collisions were hardly fatal.

"No neurotics for me," said Harry one night after a session with a New York cousin of Andrew's.

He had asked us to help entertain her the Saturday of her weekend at Indian Farm. Before eleven, he had left us to her, departing for his customary late walk in the lower pasture. Almost without transition she had brought forth for us, especially for Harry, her religious malaise. She had been drinking too fast.

"If he was the son of God and all, why did Christ call out, 'Father, Father, why hast thou forsaken me'?"

"You mean, 'My God, my God,'" said Harry politely. "That is the fourth of the seven cries from the cross; it fulfills and underlines Christ's manhood."

"Well, what about the second?" our guest went on. "What about the second? 'Today shall I be with you in Paradise.' That wasn't true."

"It's meant figuratively," said Harry.

She had drunk too much. Her exophthalmic eyes, threatening to bulge from their sockets, glistened with tears that somehow would not fall. She had fought Harry. She wanted to be touched.

"I want it to be true, don't you see?"

"And indeed it is true," Harry patiently replied.

"But it can't be true—and it can't, because I want it to be," she cried.

"Then believe because it's impossible. That's the point, I

229

would argue," he said with chilly purpose. "What good would Christianity be if there weren't some impossibilities." My God, I thought, isn't he talking now about monsters and magic and late nights in mead halls and fairies in country lanes? No, surely he wasn't. Against the slight sobs of the woman, he was saying, "Surely you're complicating the issue. You believe or not. It's an act of will."

"I'm thirty-five years old and I'm miserable," she warbled hoarsely, taking up her drink.

Harry came back quickly: "Before you began to blubber you looked less than twenty-five." Then he pinched her neck gently, as if she were his son, and patted her back. She leaned against his side, and he kept patting.

She gave us full, slack kisses when she left, and Harry gave her a copy of the wartime broadcast talks of that brisk pilgrim C. S. Lewis. I felt I could never explain to her that Harry hadn't been cruel, which meant that I could not explain to her who Harry was. But I now think that even in her rage at his reasonableness—or was it reasonableness? —she was much less critical of Harry than I was. I think she suddenly loved him—and not least for the way he talked.

"No neurotics for me," said Harry when she was gone. I'd had his theories about women before: "Let my wife darn my socks, cook my dinner, bear my children, and stay home when I go for a drink." Perhaps one was to pass to the conclusion that other people's wives could go round the bend.

I had drunk enough. But in those three hours I had been unable to say enough, the opportunities had slipped by me. And I knew this, just as a choking clot of words came up out of my mouth. I turned on Harry and, hating his control, I lost mine. The barrage ended with my loud formula: "Mary on the Cross or a wife in a Cotswold hamlet! You don't feel a bloody thing!"

As if making an unpleasant discovery, he said, "You've never had a numinous experience." Then he went round the room turning out the lights. "Also you're confused about the Crucifixion." All the lights were off. I saw Harry's outline only waist-high, for he now stood in the dark in his eternal bathrobe, warming his behind before the last coals.

I said, "You made that woman feel like an old maid."

He answered, with an overt conceit I hadn't seen in him before: "She liked me, I think." Then he said, very clearly and portentously, "Have you ever thought of what it might

230

mean not to marry? Imagine the work one would get done."

I could have taxed him with his own pronouncements when he began seeing Wanda. He thought her a marvel. One part of my mind thought her an ordinary, intelligent, self-absorbed, maudlin, half-educated war-mare, schizoid some of the time, and acting the rest.

His last weeks at the university it seemed that Wanda was with Harry all the time, though this was rather an illusion. He stopped writing letters, gave up reading except for the little he did with Wanda, suspended the studies he planned to continue when he returned to Oxford in June. When we were alone he spoke of Wanda as if she were The American Girl, puzzled and wild, skeptical but born yesterday, comrade and invalid. He admitted she was not unlike an art student he had known during one of his infrequent visits to London. The fact that he spoke so calmly of the battle he said he was slowly winning, the battle for Wanda's obedience and trust, showed him to be more embattled than he knew. Three weeks before Harry was to sail, he reported to me that Wanda had taken to walking into his classes in midhour, staring at him, then after a few minutes leaving. Almost every morning, now, between Harry's eight and eleven o'clock lectures, he and Wanda sat in the new coffee house that three students had founded after a summer in New York and that featured lobster buoys, fish net, cable-spool tables, and posters advertising Virginia City, Jane Avril, and *Operation Abolition*. Twice—or so I heard—Wanda marched out angrily, Harry laughing at her, students watching closely. When I came home one afternoon to find them seated on the daybed, she with her face against his shoulder sobbing, he gave me a sad frown as melodramatic as it was controlled.

She hated his interest in the workings and the past of the Oakes estate, his interest in my study of the Oakes documents, his research on the Thorntons, even his little digs at the Oakes chapel—"the chapel perilous," as he called it. I studied it with Harry and Wanda one day around sunset. She was desperate that I'd invite myself along for a walk in the meadow. When, with fragile humor, she called Harry a hermit-specialist and a chauvinist-historian, he answered by proving her ignorance of the American Civil War. Then we stopped to examine the chapel, a low granite box, perhaps thirty by fifteen, its little windows boarded but for the peak

231

of each arch. She interrupted Tindall's parody of a guide's spiel on New England Medieval by proposing that we break into the chapel and that I marry them on the spot. But Harry said it wasn't Halloween and if we broke in we'd ruin the relations he and I had with Andrew, ruin Harry's two years at Indian Farm. Moreover, he guessed we'd find nothing important inside. Suddenly Wanda strode off, down the little hill. Then she headed up toward the driveway and her old Packard. She didn't answer Harry's calls. If she'd had trouble starting the motor, Harry would have found her exit "lovely" rather than, as he said, "tedious."

In the house they often read Reynolds' *Discourses* together, bickered over the definition of classicism, fought to the point where Wanda would howl adenoidally that Harry showed less imagination than Sir Francis Bacon. Once, in the middle of her angry oration, as Harry smiled back firmly, tolerantly, she began to weep. "England and America can never understand each other," she said. To which Harry replied that she was indulging in clichés and that the truth was, she felt she knew him very well. They would sit with the *Oxford Book of English Place Names,* and Harry would amuse Wanda by comparing half a dozen nearby towns with their namesakes: Wickham Market, Epping, Portsmouth. "Is there a Blue Bridge in England?" Wanda asked dreamily. Harry didn't know. They would sit with Mencken's roll of Puritan names, and Wanda's giggling would become hysterical as Harry attached some of the longer ones to members of the university administration. The president's special assistant for political affairs, Harry called "Fly-Fornication Farrell." She called him "And It Came To Pass" Tindall.

Ten days before he was due to sail, the three of us had supper at home. Andrew came in to thank Harry for some plans Harry had drawn up. Convinced that the estate and the Oakes family had fallen into corruption, Harry had offered Andrew detailed projects for renting parts of the pasture to two neighboring farmers, for thinning sections of forest and selling the wood, and even for dividing three-quarters of the remaining land into plots on which cottages might be built. After the usual inquiries about travel connections and the work Harry proposed to do at Oxford, Andrew gave us a rather abrupt good night. He would call on us before Harry finally left.

During coffee Wanda set herself to mold a mask on

Harry's face, pressing it out of a ragged sheet of aluminum cooking foil gently from his steep forehead down over the long descent of his nose to the base of his chin.

"This is the ideal way to make a sculpture," she said. "You can't really see what you're doing."

When she finished the last ridges and depressions, she stood on the radiator and propped the effigy on the curtain rod above the window. "Now Harry is history," she said.

Then we were sitting before one of Harry's high fires. On the basis of months of experience, Harry had written an essay entitled "Domestic Pyrotechnology," discussing several ways to make a fire, as well as the behavior of various woods. Before he submitted the essay, he was, as he said, letting it sit.

I watched the triangle of charcoal that coated the sloping back of the fireplace. Wanda asked how many different lists Harry had made in order to expedite his departure. Then she asked him about his home, as she had before.

"People have got to pump each other," she said. "There's just no time, no time at all. Ten years go by and you never bother to ask the simplest questions of someone you're always seeing."

Harry was quickly back at her. "I would argue that the best friendships need a certain mystery or economy. The point is that—"

But here Wanda broke in with a cry that stopped him. The cry was really a call, and she had called Harry's name. Then she asked him again to tell about his home. And he did.

"Currington doesn't stop. It was always a driving town. It manages better than the town nearby down the water, where my father was born. Down there they used to make sailing ships long ago, wooden sailing ships. Not so long ago they made steel rails, and they got iron ore from Spain and Africa. Now the harbor is silted up. You might see a trawler chance scraping in and out every night and morning, but nought else except skiffs and a long-in-the-tooth school mistress who paddles a kayak on Saturday. When we were nine or ten my father would let my friend Jaro and me come with him when he went. He still saw two widower cousins. They met in a pub two corners up from the dock, and while they were sucking up their bitter—there's a Wandaic Americanism—and not saying much, Jaro and I hopped around on the decks of whatever ships were in. But even then the American and Baltic trade had dropped off, and the West Indian too. They say that in 1920 you could walk across the harbor on ships' decks. Now, with the silt, you could almost walk across the harbor itself." Harry was describing the town nearby, but not his home, Currington.

Wanda asked, "Where is Jaro?"

"He's dead," said Harry. He saw that the fire had gone into itself, showing only brief peaks of yellow. So he rose to lift and jab and lever the two big sticks of locust. He seemed even taller as he bent in toward the hearth, probing with Andrew Oakes' great cast-iron fork.

I knew that now Harry was going to give us the chronicle of Jaro's death. Jaro had been his best friend. I wanted to leave the room. It was a stupid impulse. I told myself I objected to Harry's calm way of telling and retelling this dreadful story. But I suspected my impulse wasn't this simple. As for Wanda, she wanted more and more of Harry. She would never see him again after he sailed, except perhaps in his orderly, illegible letters, of which she knew there would be few. She could seem horsey and gauche marching around the living room, trying, with her loud bursts of critique, to drown out the beloved millennia she heard in her record of "The Peacock Variations." But though she was almost untouchable because, as she told us openly, and to Harry's embarrassment, she was sexually quite dead, she could also be the curled virgin demurely welcoming, softly answering. Now she opened to the promise of a story. There was no false reverence for its being a story of death. With how much condescension I could only guess, I loved Harry as he stood there before the fire, "sorting out" his facts (as he would say), getting the sequence clean. As he hesitated, looking at the hearthstone, then at the fire, then about the room, and when at last he bent to sit down on his favorite stump, he might have been preparing some cogent "Prolegomenon" (one of his favorite words, by the way).

"Jaro began Oxford for me, instructed me, prepared me. The summer before I went up, I wrote him several pieces to which he applied ordinary Oxford standards of literacy. He cut them to shreds. He urged me to work up Scott, for I should certainly be asked by one old interviewer to speak about Scott's novels, particularly because I wanted to read history. I think Jaro told me what not to talk about at sherry parties, and I think I took his advice. He gave me a hundred tips. I had managed to get into his college. The year I went up, he won a great history prize, and it was thought that even if by a miracle he should not get himself a first the next year, he'd still be invited to take the All Souls examination and would in the natural course of events be elected.

"Jaro's father was a Czech Jew who, in 1936, emigrated to England with the understanding that his wife and son would follow. Jaro's mother was—is—a Pole, not Jewish. After the old man emigrated—for he could see what was coming—the mother had trouble emigrating westward and instead took Jaro home with her to Cracow. She was working class. Cracow was a small provincial place. She found herself almost an outcast, finally gave up hunting for a job and thought of moving to Warsaw, where no one would know she'd married a Jew. But somehow she stayed, and Jaro went to school and spoke Polish—he was a natural linguist—and read everything from Burke and Volney and Herodotus and Herzl to Peruvian archeology. In a corner of his room at Oxford hung what he claimed was an Andean quipu, a mnemonic device, a kind of abacus the Incas webbed by knotting bits of rope or string in many different ways. He and his mother came to England in '38. He and I had a passion for history and the sort of appetite for reading that's considered abnormal in America. He knew so much that it was a pleasure to hear him destroy Vico and Spengler and, later, Toynbee. I must be mixing up my chronology. He was eleven, no, twelve, in 1938. He saved his pencils till they were sooty stubs. The time in Currington we can skip. We studied the Thirty Years' War together, and with all his languages he read Tieftrunk in Czech, state papers in Swedish and Polish. The Thirty Years' War obsessed him. He was fascinated by exactly how people die, i.e., how, physically and emotionally, they go through the last process of dying.

"My first clue that Jaro was in trouble came just before Christmas, his last Christmas. Word had gone round that Clarendon Press would publish Jaro's prize essay. Six men of his year, acquaintances rather than friends, walked to his boarding house after the pubs closed and sang "Good King Wenceslas"—two verses of it. Jaro banged open his third-floor window and told them quietly to belt up. Thinking he was being funny, they went ahead with the next verse, but he stopped them, shouting that he would throw himself into the street if they didn't pack it in and go home. Their first reaction: a very convincing act. Then they saw he was serious. And sober. He had only begun to drink six months before—quite carefully and purposefully, indeed, to relax himself.

"I heard of this only after the new year. Jaro stuck in Oxford right through the holiday and, as I heard from Mrs. Landino in her Italian English, Jaro had stayed in his room except to take two meals a day with her. Most strange, for Jaro loved to get things straight by walking, always walking. He would even try to get lost, by wandering absorbed into sad little residential streets and consciously not waking up until he had, as it were, found his way into a spot he was totally unfamiliar with. He had found that it was now almost impossible to lose himself in Oxford. But this is irrelevant.

"In January he met me in the High two afternoons a week. Extraordinary! Only two afternoons, and then just for tea—after which, back he went either to Landino's or Bodley. He studied his own symptoms of panic; he studied the fact that he could *be* coolly fascinated with his own panic. He said he wished he could now embark on the study of psychology. He was so taut that I tried to lure him out of himself by proposing, with a pretense of seriousness, that he abandon history, with the school's examinations less than four months away, and begin a whole new three-year course in psychology. He took my seriousness seriously. He spoke a good deal about valves and glands of the mind. I'm certain he was faithful to his materialism. He seemed delighted by the different pressures and reactions produced by his eagerness to get a first. First, first, first!

"January 18. I stopped at Landino's in the evening. Jaro's door was locked, his light on, umbrella by the door. He wouldn't answer.

"January 21. He was out, or so I thought. Mrs. Landino insisted I take coffee with her. She stared and stared at me. I eased the silence with questions about Jaro. She knew nothing. He was studying.

"Involved as I was in my own work, I saw nothing of him till February; it was the eighth. I found him reading. He was hospitable but cold. Four days later I saw him at Bodley from a distance. He waved. But as I moved toward him past the readers' tables, he rose and disappeared, and when I got to his place, he was gone. A volume of an encyclopedia lay open at his place, an odd thing for him to be reading. Somehow he got out of the library before I could find him.

"February 15. Mrs. Landino showed me two letters that had come for him—one from Cumberland, one from Sussex. He'd left them on the hall dresser and, when she had finally taken them into his room, he had returned them to the hall.

"February 21. He met me for tea. Seemed cheerful. February 28. Tea again. This time, Houdini. I thought he was mad to waste his time getting excited about the final plan Houdini made to get in touch after he dematerialized.

"March 4. Receiving no answers to three notes, I stopped by. He told me he was going to sell his books and go to America. He said his tutor was backing him, and so was Mrs. Landino. March 5. I spoke to his tutor, who informed me he had told Jaro to see a doctor. I went to see Jaro, but found only Mrs. Landino, whose fears had increased since Jaro had spent the morning sitting on the doorstep and had refused to speak to her. March 6. I think I have the dates right. Jaro gave me tea in his room. Accused me of surrendering to Oxford, manufacturing a new personality, putting myself in a mental strait jacket. When my father once yelled at me in the middle of an argument, 'Oxford has changed you,' I answered that it wouldn't be much of a place if it hadn't. But Jaro was worried about himself, not me.

"March 8. I found a note in my room inviting me to a small party which was to begin promptly at seven. I thought he'd been seeing only me among his few friends. There was a girl in London, an almoner, an extremely fine girl who'd been to university and had studied sociology. Her parents lived in Surrey. I don't think she figured in this. Jaro didn't have many friends. I felt suddenly that afternoon that Jaro must now have passed through the worst sort of dull depression, but passed *through* it. His note was almost gay, though strange and awkward. I know it verbatim: 'Why worry about firsts or seconds or poet's thirds? Come to my party at seven sharp. Supper. I'll tell you what I'm embarking on. Surely I know enough history for three or four examinations!' "

Harry stood up and revived the fire. I had, of course, heard the story before. And I still wondered whether Harry was cold in his heart or simply capable of extraordinary control. He went on, slowly.

"This is very simply what happened. I went to him on time. I paused in the silent hall to read a one-word message tacked to his door: 'DISTURB.' My knock wasn't answered.

237

When I pushed open the door, I stood for several minutes. I gazed at the incredible neatness of the room and at Jaro. He was dressed only in a vest—you call it an undershirt here —and he had hanged himself with that Peruvian rope abacus, from the fixture in the center of the ceiling. How it held him I don't know. There's no need for details. It was an odd costume. The ceiling was low. I found myself looking past him at a fine, fine old map on the wall—Cracow, its seven suburbs and the ancient inner town. I think he contrived a slow strangling, without even a slight drop.

"And that is the story. March 8."

Harry about-faced to the fire. Perhaps because of an air current he created, the flames unwound upward, reaching into the chimney so that the blue and orange crests rose out of sight for a moment. Wanda was on her feet.

"Have you *sorted* everything *out?*" she cried. "That was a stunning performance. Out of this world." She was speaking fast. It was hushed about the house. The peepers had long since given up their doppler-like complaint and were subdued in their light sleep stuck up in and on the boughs and trunks of our trees. The whippoorwill duet had come on at eight-forty as usual up near the main house, and from the lilacs to the forsythia and back again the two birds had exchanged what Harry called their "musical and amorous telegraphy" until, an hour and forty-five minutes later, it suddenly and on schedule had gone off the air. Now, in the full quiet, Wanda was speaking on and on, harshly.

"You reduce your friend's last days to a printed, dated summary—able, straight, without mistake and unmistakably yours. I bet you even remembered to make a carbon. What'll you do if someday after you've typed one of your monstrous chronologies you discover that the carbon reads differently from the original?"

She took two paces to the hearth and did a very pathetic thing. She tilted Harry's water color of the deer.

And then she was out of the door, bounding and stamping across the board floor of the barbecue. Just as quickly, her sounds ceased, and I thought she must be out on the path, perhaps heading for the garage. But as Harry reached the door I heard her heavy movements again, and heard Harry call, "Put down that ax!" Then I heard her pound across the floor, and again the sound ceased, and I knew she was out in the dark.

Harry was after her, still wearing over his clothes his old brown bathrobe like a friar's habit at the waist.

Helpless, I ran after Harry, and not because I wished to help but because I wished to see. Also, I ran because, even as I saw on the barbecue floor the pine crates Harry had built to transport his books back to England, crates so big they seemed fixed forever to the floor, I had come suddenly to believe that Harry was indeed going to leave America and sail home.

Light from the moon, a fairly large moon, I think, cleared the path before me as I raced blindly up toward the main house, toward the garage and the stone wall that separates the home curve of the driveway from the long pasture. Words bumped in my head as I sprinted across wet grass and across the earth of the vegetable plot that Andrew had just had roto-tilled. Words. Words of Harry's: "America like Elizabethan England. America the symptomatic. America a mish-mash of melodrama and fatigue. Hunted hunters." But were these Harry's clichés, or clichés I in my imagination had given him to say?

"Stop!" I heard his call somewhere ahead. "Stop! Come back! Wanda!"

And then I was at the wall, gasping, hesitating, and for a moment thinking, "It's their funeral, not mine." I stared after them, now embarrassed.

Down the pasture under the absurd moonlight Harry drove on, his motion at this distance a faintly bobbing glide almost as smooth as a plane's far trace up the sky. I thought I could see Wanda beyond him.

Then I followed them, followed fast. And the turf was dim under me and the runway floods at the SAC base spread a busy island of light the other side of the bay.

"Wanda! Wanda! Don't!" Shouldn't she have called back to him, "Heathcliff! Heathcliff!"

The crushing crack of ax on wood rocketed back to me as I rushed past the children's graveyard and its group of high trees. Again the ripping crack and now with a metallic rattle. And the crack again.

And then, as I veered up toward the chapel's silhouette on the hill, down the back of which Harry had studied skiing, his deep "No!" mixed with the crying, sighing groan of a new voice.

Like a snapshot in the scrapbook of those nightmares in

239

which I come on a crucial scene and cannot enter it, a tableau met me at the chapel door. After the shock of felling Andrew, Wanda—for I took her to be the guilty one—had knelt to help him. She turned toward me, seeming to forget her victim. It seemed to me that I was aware of only one thing: that, arriving too late, I could not know precisely what had happened. The ax, in Harry's right hand, hung down, blade outward. Andrew lay quiet on his back across the chapel doorway. One knee twitched from side to side. So far as I could tell, he had been hit just past the beginning of the collarbone—in fact, as it turned out, in the left shoulder blade, deep. Aiming to get through the door, Wanda had sliced three wounds in the wood, framing clumsily, but never touching, the ornate pin-tumbler lock. She had continued her fourth stroke even though Andrew, rushing silently round one side of the chapel, had tried to stop her. I studied Harry, who was staring at Wanda—long-boned and platinum-haired under the moonlight—and she now returned to Andrew and the mortal mess of blood and shirt over and around the place where the ax had come down. Before she broke their incredibly lifelike tableau, they seemed to me, in my despair at losing them by arriving late, an indestructible waxwork, warmed by the moon almost out of the past and into the present.

Ensuing agreements, explanations, surgeries, poses—these I omit. I have to make an arbitrary end somewhere.

Andrew remains at Indian Farm. He will not find much strength in his left arm. No one else knows of the incident. Harry refused to discuss it even with me. He did "promise" Andrew that never before or on the night of "the chase and the siege" (Harry's words) had he contemplated violating the chapel. No doubt Andrew received this peculiar "promise" about the past without thinking that the past, like the future, is always changing. But he received Harry with as active a grace as his hospital bed allowed.

Harry had nothing to say as we drove the thirteen miles home from the hospital in Blue Bridge. And after he shut the door of his room he remained incommunicado for three days. The opening of the university exam period had hushed the town. When I came home from work the first day of Harry's seclusion, I rapped my knuckles lightly on his door. He failed to answer. Then I heard his voice say quietly, dimly, that if I didn't mind he must be by himself. These three days he cannot have eaten more than four or five eggs —hard-boiled, judging from the shells—and drunk, aside from water, more than a quart of milk. This nourishment he must have taken when I was either out or asleep. Then, the night of the third day, he appeared in my room, pale and, as it seemed, ready.

"Why didn't you tell me I'd been stupid to Wanda?"

"Stupid when?" I asked, afraid.

"Almost always, from the start. I ought to have been tender, but I thought she'd scorn tenderness."

"She'd have pretended to be amused by it," I answered.

"But you saw she couldn't take the pressure I put on her."

"But I couldn't tell how she'd get at you."

"But you knew her, you must have known her. Why didn't you help me?"

I retreated into my answer—one of the nastiest things I've said: "Harry, it was too good a show to interrupt it."

He accepted this. If he was puzzled, it wasn't by the possibility that in my answer I unveiled my own plight.

With a certain conscious formality Harry said, "I have just come to know two things: I am not in *love* with Wanda. But I was." He didn't introduce these two facts, if they were facts, with his customary "a" and "b."

Wanda hasn't paid Indian Farm any more visits. If Harry had chosen to tell me about his last talks with her, I'd have asked him not to. Forty-eight hours before we left for his New York sailing, two of his students—lean, towering stubby pioneer types—visited him to propose that he spend the summer driving to Mount McKinley with them. It was a Thursday night, and Harry took out his various anxieties cleaning his shoes, i.e., using his time profitably, while we all talked. The students had brought a case of ale. One of them drank most of it. He spoke of his present project: He was writing a novel about a writer who was himself writing a novel about a novelist's ambition to be a good teacher. Explaining this puzzle to us, his own attention tired. He began to tell of the school of creative writing he had studied at the preceding summer. "Twice a week," he said, "I played seven-card stud with four guys and every one of them had published." Shortly after midnight he and his friend shook hands with Harry, nodded their thanks to me, and bade us good night. Later I learned that Wanda had driven west with them.

Tindall married well, and according to his pattern, or the pattern as I have imagined it: the daughter of an Oxford historian. My most recent information is that Harry is engaged in manuscript analysis. With some angling of my eyes, I can read Harry's latest letter. It races across the blue airmail page with neat and illegible authority. I can break his script because I've had months of practice with his *t*'s and *m*'s and *i*'s and *o*'s and *a*'s and *e*'s. I read his writing more and more easily. I am his court paleographer and can translate what he writes in his occasional letters to Marcus. In his letter to me he says that he and Anselin flew to Vienna for the exhibition of international Gothic, that they hired a car and drove off into the wine country near the Czech border and then—two words aren't immediately clear—lost themselves on a "wild ride" through an almost roadless air-force base. He wonders if I'll come "put up with" them in the house they've rented near Oxford, out near the Wychwood. He'll take me bookhunting, pub by pub, and show me the spot in the wood where the ceremonial slaying occurred nine years ago. "Trying to live up to their historical heritage," he says of the unidentified folk who were apparently responsible for the precise and wrenching fashion in which the young farmer was sacrificed. Harry has a supply of heel ball, which he uses to take brass rubbings. He always looked forward to rediscovering those small parish churches. I hear his voice pronouncing the diphthong as in "say" when he cites Betjeman's "indispensable" guide: "Betjeman says that. . . ." And leaving the kitchen, forgetting I'm still at the trestle table, Harry automatically flicks off the light. Harry knew the cool, solid, smooth stone of parish church floors. My own unstable mind, veering here and there, would feel those smoothnesses when Harry allowed modestly that if someday he had to come back to America to teach, he hoped to get onto one of the "great foundations" (by which he meant "university"). In the above-mentioned letter Harry comments on my decision to leave the house and the state. "It's high time. I approve. Your feelings must surely make a sufficient epitaph to our years at Indian Farm."

Just before I left, Wanda phoned me from her mother's house upstate. Wanda was on vacation from New York City, where she now works as a draftsman. She has saved enough to take a few months off and give full time to wood sculpture. From two over-exposed pictures she has since sent me, I judge that she does monumental, macabre witticisms—for example, a Ruth made out of a barrel topped by a head with five faces painted on it and standing powerfully but without direction on several sets of good slim legs. Over the phone Wanda asked me how I'd punctuate a cable with which Harry had surprised her and which her mother had sent on to New York a month before. It read: "HAPPY BIRTHDAY LOVE LETTER FOLLOWS HARRY." No letter yet.

She also gave me a full account of her rooming house on West One Hundred and Thirteenth Street, and of a very tall Danish boy who inhabits the room next to hers, entertains her at two in the morning with medical photographs in the Manhattan hospital where he is a night file clerk, and takes his exercise, alas, by trotting lankily along the wide ledge atop the wall that runs round the roof of their building, eleven stories above Broadway.

Wanda, who has found in New York the labyrinth she always desired, thinks of Harry Tindall as a prototypically cultivated, pathologically well-organized, and dearly amusing English gentleman. Marcus, who recently caught a fraction of a roentgen when he failed to note the red warning light over the entrance to the basement den of the little university reactor, continues to associate Harry with nightingales and Tudor beams. Andrew, whose senatorial forebear (if I chose) I could now prove was secretly proslavery, looks forward calmly to Harry's first book and has added Harry's Indian Farm proposals to the family files in the west room. I hear that a rising undereditor of the *Mohawk Listener*, learning of Tindall's blueprint for reorganizing the university's history courses, has initiated inquiries into "certain influences" Tindall may have had on the history department and on the university in general. Wanda, Marcus, Andrew, and this editor are, of course, correct in their beliefs and suspicions. They have encircled Harry, or Harry's ghost, and have fixed him in the glare of their headlights. What they see there is what they want to see. But what they want to see is there.

Like Henry of Navarre, Tindall seems to be a greater figure seen from a distance than when regarded close at hand. Yet, lest I confuse, I must add that the distance between Tindall and me—quite apart from the fact that I did pay him a visit—seems to have decreased since he departed. And the days, like my linked words, seem to diminish that famous ocean which for two years separated his enchanted England and his enchanted America.

the canal street hypnotist

David, listen: It's imperative you restore to memory five what you took out yesterday. Harry was to have come to the fraternity masquerade as Theseus and, though it would have done some small violence to what a certain sort of small mind might term "the facts," Wanda was to have accompanied him and was to have been dressed as Antiope. Make no mistake: Theseus was warned by an oracle that, should he find himself greatly afflicted in a foreign country, he must found a city and leave behind some of his companions to govern it. Harry, Theseus—get it? Unh? Unh? (Like Duke and Hercules, on whom it was said that valor was imprinted as on a coin.)

Hey! Listen! Pay attention! Pay—Did I . . . rub you (yuk, yuk!) the wrong way?

I find it so hard not to identify with you—you, my creation.

Ellen pauses, stepping over the stateroom threshold: "Funny, darling, but you've a sort of way of speaking without moving your mouth, like a sort of Peter Brough?"

"Peter Brough?"

"The English Edgar Bergen. And his dummy, Archy Andrews."

Andrews, Andrew. Pelasgian, Pelagius. Often, that second spring, muscle-bound Bobo Paramus drove out to see Harry. Bobo seemed to think Harry liked having a Merrimack Valley All-Conference Guard as an acquaintance. Whenever Harry said anything, Bobo would throw a shadow punch and say "Jesus" and throw back his head and squeal with laughter. What irked Harry most, and finally drew from him a rebuke as killing as it was misunderstood (for Bobo thought Harry was merely giving his English accent some theatrical exercise—and in fact Bobo couldn't imagine anybody wanting to give him a ticking off) was Bobo's habit of quoting Duke Amerchrome. And at last Harry said, *"Mis*ter Paramus" (the *r* rattled and rolled with dreadful precision) "there *is no* logical *connection* between the Pelasgian creation myth and the fifth-century Pelagius whom Saint Augustine attacked, no matter what Professor Amerchrome has said. Now, Mister Parrrrramus, you may go." On which Harry turned to David and offhandedly said, meaning the little screwdriver on the kitchen table, "Hand me the doo-dah firkin." (But Bobo grinned and didn't go, and Harry escaped outside to get kindling.)

The Amerchromes remained impregnable. But David soon saw that the way in—not in to the Amerchromes but in to the center—was via the "I"—the first person, i.e., his own "I."

Yet when he had in fact let go, as if the confessed words were a rush of easy, breathing tears, and had set off toward the center, speaking first person as fluently as if he were gesturing with his hands, he found a new thing: Moving into himself—his "I"—had so swelled it that it all but filled the chronicle's ground, and Harry and Wanda and Andrew and the others had grown small—and paid him no heed.

Well, now he must project into Ellen, project as a real actor. But still, Harry . . . . Harry's but thy factor, good my lord, to engross uproarious deeds on thy behalf!

It is so difficult to look ahead: Unfinished memories (like castles, barnacled castles, seen too quickly from a tourist bus) drag at one's mind.

Ellen has gone to the movies. The sixth day: Time running out, but time here on day hard to measure.

David decides to destroy the ruled card he has accidentally found stuck to a page of "Anglo-American Chronicle": news item, dateline Oxford:

The cobbles in Merton Street are not to disappear. Oxford City Council rejected by 47 votes to 5 tonight its Highways Committee's recommendation that the cobbles should be removed and the road resurfaced with asphalt. The council decided that the cobbles should be taken up, the base repaired, and the cobbles put back. Relaying them will cost £5800, which is £1075

more than the estimated cost of the asphalt. Mr. H.
Tindall argued that the cobbles were of great historic
value. Councillor W. G. White said, "If this is an historical street then I suggest you close the road and make
it into a museum."

Two staterooms away the folk singers are doing "Follow
the Drinkin' Gourd" again. Who are they? David goes out
into the passage and down toward the door of the stateroom
where he thinks the singers are. But now—"Fol*LOWWW* da
dum da dum"—from the suddenly opening doorway steps the
smuggler-man humming. And he shuts the door behind him.

"Got something for you."

"What do you mean?"

"Guess."

"Excuse me," says David and turns back toward his stateroom.

"No, wait." The knowing grin. "What I want to show you
is . . . a Bible!"

From one of the side passageways David hears junior-
year-abroad saying to her companion-silence, "So one of the
wise men tripped over the threshold of the stable and said,
'Jesus Christ!' and Joseph—" a stateroom door closes off the
voice.

David lets scorn and distaste touch his next words to the
blond man: "A *smuggler's* Bible?"

"Exactly," says the man and moves closer. "How did you
know?"

"Excuse me," says David: into the stateroom, keep that
man away.

The truth is that David was upset by Ellen not so long
ago. Ellen is certainly a disturbing influence. "Let's have
four, five, and six," she said.

"Four is sort of ready," answered David modestly and
quietly.

"Come on, let's have them all." There's a . . . grossness
about Ellen's spirit.

Ellen left, then, with four and five—in fact *parts* of David.

Now, forced back into the stateroom, David watches the
door, hears the folk singers, feels trapped by that smuggler-
man. That hypnotist Duke sent David to at the apLewis

Anglo-Welsh Hypno-therapy Clinic on Canal Street didn't understand David's preamble about Spinoza, but said that in any case it was people of weak will not strong who were hard to hypnotize. David didn't believe that. And didn't like admitting to the hypnotist why he'd come. The man—with a rough, drooping blond moustache—said he had to know the purpose of the treatment before he could even consider. . . .

But is it true a weak will mightn't be able to direct the Outer Mind to remain quiescent? What is your problem, Mr. Brooke? and will my hypnosis be succeeded, when I wake, by amnesia? If there's *rapport* between us—But why do you come to me? Oh doctor, would you use the palm-shoulder-blade method to establish magnetic *rapport* so that when—? Do you mean, when my hands are withdrawn the subject will be irresistibly attracted after them—? Yes, that's what I meant—But please now tell me why you're here? How can you tell if I'm faking or not? It's the iris, the iris should roll upward a bit and perhaps the pupil won't contract when a bright light is shone on it, but Mr. Brooke, tell me—Did you say "perhaps"? Yes, I did. You must tell me why you came and what you want. But doctor first *you* tell *me:* Doesn't William James say something about a double consciousness, *das doppel ich,* doesn't Myers say—Hold it, Mr. Brooke—Doesn't Myers say our habitual consciousness may be a mere selection from a sea of thoughts and sensations and that—Please, Mr. Brooke!—And doesn't Myers suggest that at both ends of the subliminal self the spectrum of consciousness is indefinitely extended? Mr. Brooke, please explain why you came.

"I just want you to put me under."

"Why?"

"And then bring me back."

"You're joking."

"No."

"Is it something you're shy about telling me? You want to try to control . . . ?

"No."

"Come on. . . . Smoking? Cheer up! You saw some bull calves castrated one summer and you can't forget?"

"OK. You might work on all those while you're inside."

"While I'm inside?"

"I mean while I'm under."

"Then I *did* guess . . . ?"

"No. I just came here to be hypnotized."

"For what?"

"Out of myself. Please." And his last words—did he say them or were they mere dream-lines scripted onto the type-script of daylight reality: "Does the originality of my request make it seem unfeasible? Please, Mr. Hypnotist, understand/Take me and put me under the Sand." Followed by three dreadful words from that laughing, blond-moustachioed hypnotherapist: "Do it yourself! Do it yourself!" (Or did David put that construction on whatever the man said?) Yet if some way he could hypnotize himself ostrich-style apparently out of his own existence, then he could hypnotize himself into another person, into "another"—thus to love, thus to escape the wild divisions inside him, sub-liminal, supraliminal. . . .

David has turned now to six. I should have urged him to, but lately he seems to be "on manual," seems to be able to do things himself—all, of course, because I've made him such a wonder. Is it my imagination that I find it less easy to see into his mind? I feel less able to speak—i.e., speak in any but David's voice.

But what is he doing! He's changing six. David and I planned, of course, to project into Ellen. But—and I wonder if David didn't take my hint too readily—I did not expect him to change the point of view so sharply—heavens! my dear! David, our lovely lovely point of *view!* supposed to be Ellen's all through! Well, no doubt he is right to act on my hint . . . his voice . . . I feel a slight constriction.

Find Ellen. Is the smuggler-man gone? In the passage David hears the folk singers. Above—on the promenade deck —everyone is outside. Yes! God! He forgot! The sixth night: Cobh, Ireland. The sixth *afternoon;* the ship must have been here for some time. In the lounge, at a bar four newcomers of various sizes—dressed in old suits and large, baggy over-coats—off the Cobh packet come to disembark passengers disembarking in Cobh—are buying cartons of cigarettes and stowing the individual packs all over their persons, all the time looking apprehensively over their shoulders.

David is again in a stateroom passageway. He feels he is
on the wrong deck, though the passageway looks right. But
here's a strange steward: small, bald, with truculent blond
eyebrows. Pass him. This should be the one, but one numeral
of the number seems wrong. Open, open, open it! David sees
into the stateroom and now cannot move. For the smuggler-
man, profile to, is sitting on the edge of a bunk reading to
one of the two boys David has seen together; the boy is in
pajamas. David cannot move; the boy watches him calmly,
thoughtfully; the smuggler-man proceeds:

If you wake at midnight, and hear a horse's feet,
Don't go drawing back the blind, or looking in the street,
Them that asks no questions isn't told a lie.
Watch the wall, my darling, while the Gentlemen go by!
  Five and twenty ponies
  Trotting through the dark—
  Brandy for the Parson,
  'Baccy for the Clerk;
  Laces for a lady, letters for a spy,
And watch the wall, my darling, while the Gentlemen go by!

The smuggler-man turns slowly, and David breaks the
spell and retreats, and rushes away and finds his deck and
finds his stateroom—two levels below.

For the ol man is awaitin' for to carry you to freedom
If you follow the drinkin' gourd.

At last: the stateroom. David finds a ruled card stuck to
six: "Mary Clovis: 'The man built on rock, but a thunderquake came and broke the rock. At the White Tower meetings we did parables during Lent.' " David tears up the card.
From a page of six he removes *"il"*; from his description
of Matthews' musical glasses he removes *"g"*; from Matthews' kitchen shelf he removes Special *"K"*; from the third
part of six he removes *"hihon!"* (as if donkeys brayed in
Italian!); he removes the opening *"j"* of his typewriter's
stammered "jjuniper."

Ellen's hand on the stateroom doorhandle. He hopes it is
Ellen.

VI

ICE CREAM, *INVERTITO*, CEMETERY BY THE SEA

DAVID slept. He needed it.

Ellen leaned to kiss his eyelids lightly, drily, wishing his lids would close all the way and hide that rim of deadish white. Pennies on his lids? Pennies under his tongue? Pennies *on* his tongue to keep it still. Ellen went back down on her elbows, felt the sand part for a second till her funny bones found a hard bottom. Now again she heard that seeming snicker above—ahead? behind? Kids on the thickety bluff? Maybe gulls' afternoon talk rendered by the wind to where she and David lay. The sand's surface was so hilly, the sand seemed deep and abundant.

To her left, along a rocky arm of this small cove, a huge grating caged a fisherman's cave, gear inside, a great rusty boom projecting out over the water.

To her right, where the bluff veered back from the beach, the cemetery rampart began along the landward border of the sand. Beyond, and high on a cliff across a second small cove, a two-story villa stood alone, pink roof tiles over the simple plastered cement walls, the walls sharp blank white in the four o'clock sun. She could make out round the villa low dense macchie bushes, thorny and tangled, and by one seaward corner a small Aleppo pine like a ruffled umbrella.

Between this beach and the hotel the other side of the island, vineyards slanted toward the cliffs, and in the orchards stood silver-gray olive trees Ellen had seen so many times. And round the hotel and, especially, near the white wall on the street side, oleander blooms, sometimes white, usually rose, clustered out of the thick lance-shaped milk-laden leaves. Ellen knew all these, and she knew the lengthy evening schedules of the August Sacra del Mare—the stage by the wharf, the microphone, the gumdrop lights strung over the square, the dressed-up five- and six-year-olds cheek-

251

ing their loud fathers, the grim grandmas all in black at the outdoor tables, the church bells clanging every few minutes with the jogged casualness of harbor bouys, the Neapolitan pop singers who came over from the mainland for the festa, came to do dirty old dialect songs (one that punned on pansy and stomach) and call across the echoing square the yearning doleful joy of *"Mamma so' tanto felice, perchè ritorno a te."*

But this visit was different. Two other years she had come in August, flown to Capodichino from London, taken the tiny steamer from Naples, seen that big white hydrofoil ride past on its bed of foam making for Ischia. She hadn't gone to Ischia or Capri. She had come to *this* island, first with her friend Marie, then two years ago with Mark. (Why had his name had to be Mark! Even the good short Old Testament names were starting to sound insipid: Adam!) And now she was with David; and this island—and this beach—seemed anywhere—Casco Bay, Corfu, Cornwall.

She touched her lips to David's eyelids, now tight shut. What a juvenile face, solemn gob, fine diminishing coat of sand on the hair above his right ear. The poor bugger was probably having another dream about that crowd of his acquaintances all in one bed together. Nothing to do with Mailer's Great American Orgasm. It would all pass, trouble and life. David's dream? Maybe forty cock-proud Italians—forty pubic sheep—leaping up out of oil jars (like the thieves in Ali Baba—no, the likeness was mad) and prodding her away from David, and crying *"Il Duce Ritorna!"* Did David always think her attractive? Must he? This morning, sitting at that tottery table in the port trying to make her lovely soggy after-breakfast rum baba last, she'd felt waves of Davidic jealousy sweeping and foaming toward and through her there where she sat in the sun. Benino, a bit too cocoa-brown and molded and generously handsome (but aha!—*not quite tall* enough!) had lolled tensely at ease. And David, having swallowed his sugarless *cappucino* almost as soon as it came, tried to keep from smoking too steadily, and tried not to seem quite so alert. David hadn't understood that olympic Benino's interest wasn't in her—for Benino saw how she was—but in David himself, his narrow olive slacks, the cowhide sandals she'd bought him in Soho, the loose and skinny long-sleeved blue-and-green-striped jersey from Paris, the absence of a wristwatch (even of a strap's pale print upon the wrist), the absence of flaws she knew

252

Benino wanted to find—flaws he imagined to be American. David knew she had known Benino on her earlier holidays here, but David wasn't sure if Benino was now trying to revive a secrecy, simply move in, or just be grandly Italian, a sweetly muscled host bursting with communicable warmth and sweet brutal readiness. Ellen had seen this easily; and as David and Benino suddenly lurched into Mussolini, and much of David's coiled pique seemed to spring forth disguised by his seeming delight in argument, she had butted in to say she and David were now going to the beach. Not the beach at the base of the hotel's cliff, but the quiet, pebbly beach on the far side of the island. Then Benino had risen, and had posed there in his clogs on the old cobbles, and closed his hand *"Ciao"* to Ellen, and said to David, "You will see it is not only Italy that like a Mussolini. Your Americans also. Without a leader like Mussolini you will not see men working for the nation, you will not see powerful government action. I hear them make speeches in Genoa, in Firenze, but it is in Napoli, right over across the water, you will see the real movement." Then, with another wink of his hand, he sauntered off, almost immediately meeting and embracing and kissing on both cheeks a tall, long-jawed, happy chap called Franco.

On the walk to the beach she and David had had chocolate-frosted *cornettos*. And David had seemed moodily unaware of the three little boys following.

Now she'd like another *cornetto*.

Or she wanted a *Monte Bianco,* firm vanilla showing a conical peak above its coat of chocolate; she and David had at least three ice creams apiece a day here, what with the variety, and the neat, colorful signs picturing the kinds you could have. As she told David, ice cream was so cool it *couldn't* be fattening.

Again she heard the snickers. They were too soft to be gulls, distant gulls; she ought to look back suddenly to see if those three boys following them before had taken up station to watch what happened on the sand.

But she really didn't care. She cared only for herself and David. The word "herself" surprised her for a second. Only herself and David. And in part because of this caring, this beach could be anywhere: Corfu, Casco Bay, Cornwall.

The snickers became voices; yes, they *had* been snickers.

And now Ellen, looking back, heard the voices fading away, sounding eager.

And then she saw the horse. She saw entering the beach beyond the cemetery wall a heavy-bellied gray horse. It had come off the cement ramp at a great slow trot, and now, swaying its belly a little, it was walking to the water. A horse!

Ellen hardly saw the other figures coming onto the beach —a slight, hairy man in his vest and khaki shorts; a young boy obviously tall for his age. The horse was plodding along through the shallows toward Ellen and David. It stopped now, swung its head round at the man and boy. The boy was now in underpants. The man marched with short, stumpy steps; his bare toes turned out, his heels hit hard into the sand.

"David, there's a horse on the beach."

"Ummm? What?" David always woke up too quickly, forced himself to. But this immediate answer? Only reflex alertness. "Mmmmmm."

"David, see the horse."

Sleepily mimicking her: "David, see the hawssse."

But then she felt him come up on an elbow, his cheek by her shoulder.

"Oh, Jesus, it's a horse. Where did he come from?"

"He came down from behind the cemetery."

"Ellen! God!"

She looked down at David's brown eyes.

The man slip-knotted a halter round the horse's neck and led the horse further in. Then the man and boy scooped quick handfuls of water onto the gray flanks and the broad swayback and the hind-quarters.

"They're washing him," said David, who was not fully awake. "Will the salt make his hide itch? Now the boy's going off by himself to swim. The man's still washing the horse. It's really a dappled white-gray. Look, he likes it. Now he's putting his nose right in, look he's sloshing his nose. Now he's looking up out to sea. Now the man's splashing him."

"*I* can see, *can't* I."

"Oh . . . Yes." He'd hardly noticed what she'd said.

Casco Bay, Corfu, Cornwall, here. America, Greece, England, Italy, all the same and nowhere, nowhere. Oh she had to bite his cheek.

The horse threw up its head and made an abrupt, sedate movement back.

254

But the man shouted, and yanked the halter, and the horse stepped unwillingly toward him.

"It isn't a gelding, it's a mare," said David.

The three boys who had followed them were advancing like marauders, yelling at the horse; keeping an eye on Ellen and David.

But David, who couldn't see Benino and the others playing football on the beach—*soccer*—the other beach the other side of the island near the hotel—couldn't see them playing without himself sitting up on his towel hoping they'd ask him to play (which, uncertainly, they *would* do), now leaped up, bowed himself out of his T-shirt, and with a stiff athletic jogging of the shoulders loped magnificently down into the pebbly shallows, where he then stopped, arms akimbo, waiting for the man or boy to grin.

At three this morning David had flipped on their room lights and set out to stalk two mosquitoes. Twice missing them—they kept together—David then stopped and watched them hop, slowly, sporadically, from spot to spot of the ceiling. And as he watched, neither helpless nor, now, on the attack, David had said, "As if they're saved by our not sharing their kind of gravity; look, they seem to hop out toward us, then fall back onto the ceiling." And he'd watched.

If self-absorption was what she hated in David, why did she at times love him for it, too? Love him when he paused on the island in the middle of Edgware Road to study the photograph of Princess Alexandra on the sheet of *Evening Standard* in which the fat man had wrapped David's plaice and chips; love him when she found him one day not in Sainsbury's, where they'd agreed to meet (where the lamb was very good as long as you didn't let them sell you New Zealand), but with three strange men across the road by the demolition area fence watching giant Wates cranes slowly do their towering jobs; love him when, munching digestive biscuits at breakfast, he stopped, arrested in mid-munch by a thought.

Last night, as she was beginning to sleep, he had lit a cigarette and then got up. She had opened her eyes and had seen him in the moonlight chasing mosquitoes by buzz alone. She had opened her eyes and had seen him in the moonlight. And he'd said that thing about gravity, and then he'd come —come *halfway*—back to her with his sweet but disingenuous offer of the story about Sindbad's voyage. Which of the seven voyages was it? Not the last.

But right now he wasn't self-absorbed. She mustn't want him to be attending to her all the time, looking up when she said his name, and saying, with that false gruffness that pretended to hide a tenderness that was in actual fact a mild irritation at being wanted, "What kin I do for ya?"

Here—there—in pebbly shallows David waited. The boys on the sand were shouting something in the island's version of Neapolitan dialect.

Wholly, with mouth and stomach, as if she were craving Black Magic mints or pickled onions, she wanted more ice cream. *Cornetto? Monte Bianco? Coppa Olympia?* David got through them as if he didn't feel the cold—like his American friend who poured soup or coffee down him as if his mouth and throat were lined with hide.

Gelati.

She made a cone of sand, a volcano. Looking up she met David's eyes. *Good boy!* He *had* been watching.

II

Through the little arches along the low terrace wall Ellen looked at the bay glimmering way below. For some minutes the late light seemed to clarify David's face and Signor Giusti's. But now dusk appeared on their cheeks and deepened their eyes. The odor of oleander came across her face, tinting the air and bringing to mind the feather-warm rose of blossoms. Hot olive oil from the hotel kitchen mixed with the old air of other meals. Oleander and olio and the mild sweet rot of old peaches and pomodori in dustbins and gutters and under the evening trees.

Signor Giusti, the island schoolmaster, acted as host. He owned a half-interest in the hotel. He was discussing the oleander with David.

"The Greeks of course knew it as rhododendron. Pliny mentions the poisonous milk in the leaves." He addressed Ellen: "You have been here before, so you know the port."

"Perhaps we go down tonight," said Ellen, slightly awkward, talking, for David's sake, in English.

"At the *cine* you can see the day after tomorrow *L'Isola del Vigneti e Lava*. It was made—"

"Island of Vineyards and Lava," said David.

"Bravo, bravo," murmured Signor Giusti. "It was made here, right here. The director—"

"But wouldn't *lava* also suggest *lavare?* cleanse? purify?"

About to proceed, Signor Giusti found himself caught in his own pause, and said, dimly, courteously, "No . . . no, no, it is not possible. The director and his people came from Roma two years ago at Sacra del Mare. But the film—the movie—shows little of this island. But see it—it is not so bad—day after tomorrow. Tonight we have"—and Giusti relished the words archly, somehow pruriently—"*Hiroshima, Mon Amour.*" He smiled. (He didn't even know what the thing was *about.*)

Now he went on into small queries—uninterested but probing—about an Inglesa marrying an Americano, about their time in Corfu, about London, was it true that . . . ? and did they see the Greek monasteries on those cliffs at Meteaura . . . ? ("No," said David, "it rained a lot, and we wanted to lie on the beach at Glyfadas.") And was it true that Kennedy would be an unsuccessful *presidente?* and . . . *davvero* Signor Giusti *liked* Americans.

A waiter brought out a portable phonograph and placed it on one of the white iron tables.

"Many people come in the evening to dance here," said Signor Giusti. The night before, from their room, Ellen and David had heard a record now and then; the main sound, when she and he had been listening at all, had been the loud laughter of some local bachelors who hung around the terrace.

"And," said Signor Guisti, nodding toward the man who had just come out and was talking to the waiter, "you will find some American ladies here—if you wish to talk American." (He'd amused himself.) "He"—he nodded at the man— "he is an American but not tourist. He resides on the island many years. I do not think you wish to get acquainted with him." Signor Giusti gave a pedagogical nod, as if to acknowledge that they agreed with him. "That man is not liked."

"*Perchè?*" asked David, absurdly.

"His habits," said Signor Giusti, and then murmured, with the headshake and the raised eyebrows, "what we call *invertito* . . . with the boys, some little boys. I wish he would return home." Signor Giusti relished his indiscretion.

"Elucidate," said David, not ready to reprove.

"It is beautiful from this view, is it not?"

On the bay one motion crossed the darkening quiet. A boy, standing braced admidships, facing forward, rowed toward the east point. There, a few lights of the old prison had come on. Now he suddenly backed with one oar and, swinging his bow around toward the west promontory, began again to push his blades slowly, mechanically, jerkily, gracefully—a method centuries old. He was simply out rowing.

"Ah, now I must leave you . . . *B'na sera, b'na sera.*" Rolypoly old suet pudding!

The American had come up to them. Signor Giusti was talking to an older, Italian couple.

The American's voice came subtly, gleefully. "D' he tell you? I'm one of the island's attractions. Department of exotic attractions. You came so close to me today you should have come all the way. *I* saw you."

"On the beach?" asked David.

"Had my glasses on you all the way."

"Where?" said Ellen.

"The cliff? That villa?"

"Above the second cove?" said David.

"They charge me double what it's worth. In their eyes I was like that American widow who bought a tower in San Gimignano. But I've kept them on their toes."

The man had the lined healthy face of an older man who took care of himself; but he wasn't so old, probably midforties. His crew-cut was fuzzy rather than bristly.

"They hate to think I've got roots here. But I have. The only roots you *can* have; the ones you put down all by yourself."

A bore.

David pressed Ellen's hand twice. Affection? Itch to get away quick? Reflex?

"I never used to come to the hotel. I don't swim at the beach on this side. Very clever of you to come to an island like this. Just dead volcanic rock, no museums, no architecture, just some narrow beaches and a merchant-marine school—fellows here either naval officers or fishermen, pretty prosperous place, don't want tourists—and a prison that's half closed down, and loads of vegetables for local consumption, a few for Naples and Pozzuoli, and vineyards that make two nice edgy wines that don't travel—and then quite a fish-

258

ing fleet. Summer people, Italians; and almost no tourists, even for Sacra del Mare. You here for Sacra del Mare? Well, whether you are or not, you are. Because it begins—"

"No," said Ellen, "I just like the island."

"English girl," the man said. He looked at David. "Where *you* from?"

"New York, you might say." David squeezed Ellen's hand twice.

"Sensitive type, eh? Well . . . Phil Matthews." He nodded.

"David Brooke," said David, and paused. "Oh . . . this is Ellen."

"Of course I did go on and let them think anything about me they wanted. What good is it to let people know the truth about you, they'll still think what they want, or—you know—think what they *have* to. Ha! There you are! Department of After-Dinner Philosophy! And they're glad to think bad of me—because I came and stayed. I see them sitting at their windows disapproving of me, watching, having a ball."

"Disapproving?" said David.

"Come over tomorrow, I'll tell you all about it. Really: come over."

"I think we're going to the movies."

"Now, you mean."

"Yes."

"That's very original, coming a thousand miles just to go to the movies. But tomorrow, honestly, do come to see me. No matter what Giusti said."

"It wasn't clear," said David.

"Public opinion's the same everywhere. Come all the way to Italy, you might as well be back in Antioch, Ohio."

"Perhaps we'll see you on the beach," said Ellen.

Holding out his cigar as if trying to drop the long ash on a special spot on the terrace cement, he tapped it with his middle finger and smiled at Ellen and David—in the dusk the gesture and smile seemed to be some kind of irony, magisterial and adolescent.

"You got to understand my position on this island."

"Why?" said David bluntly.

No unimportant fights now. *Please.*

"Because my position isn't what the islanders think it is. I'm devoted to them, and they don't understand, and it's important that they don't understand, but they feel me."

"How?" said David, irked but only half listening.

Matthews peered back over his shoulder. "This isn't much of a place for discussion. You drop over tomorrow, come in for lunch or a drink. Any time, I'll be in all day. I won't move out of there all day."

"If you don't like the hotel," said Ellen, "why come here at all?"

"Exactly," said Matthews. "Well, I got to keep in the public eye."

"Sorry," said David, "I don't know what you're talking about."

"Exactly," said Matthews. "So you got to come see me tomorrow.'

"We don't know what we'll be doing," said Ellen.

"Then you're coming to see me."

"Look," said David, "why should we?"

"How you going to know this island unless you know the famous American resident Phil—"

"We don't care about knowing the island. Ellen and I want a little sun and salt water and vino . . . and a little ice cream."

"A little love, a little ice cream, a little of the festa?" asked Matthews. "Nothing too much?"

"You're annoying me," said David.

Ellen said, "Perhaps we'll see you on the beach."

Matthews nodded slowly, drew on his cigar. "I'm a reflective man," he said.

David and Ellen moved away, leaving the terrace. At the entrance to the lobby, David slipped his arm around her shoulder and she looked back quickly. Phil Matthews wasn't watching them, was standing looking out through the arch toward the lights of Capri.

III

Human noise in the air. Sun and blue and those little girls across the way. A donkey's hideous squall—once, twice, thrice, four, five . . . . Sand between the toes. The mattress just hard enough.

On her back. Legs apart.

"Ellen, what are those little girls doing over the way?"

"Probably—" she sat up, as David sat up and stood up

naked on the floor—"what they were doing yesterday morning. Combing each other's hair."

"That's a happy start for the day. They're orphans."

"Do you imagine they care?"

"Ellen, you *are* cold."

"Oh, of course I do—I mean, *feel*. You think I don't feel *you?*"

"Do I make love to you?"

"You do, my darling. But you . . . *talk* afterwards. You could be . . . sweeter."

"I'm thinking of you."

"Balls. It's this bloody release you're always talking about. For heaven's sake you can manage *that* all on your *tod.*"

"I want you *too* much."

"Funny, that might be true, too."

"You're the puritan, not me."

"My hair's full of salt."

"All right, *change* the subject."

"That's the point, darling."

"What is?"

"Changing the subject."

"Talk English."

"Getting you off any subject, and onto something . . . oh, something, nothing. You're rigid. And don't stand practically on the balcony in plain view; those children can see."

"I'm going onto the balcony."

"You're joking."

"Just like this."

"Put on a dressing—I don't care, I don't care what you do."

"You never did."

"I *always* did."

"Not care."

"Care."

"I guess I'll shave in this bloody water."

"I don't care what you do."

"But in this heat my face is warm, which makes up for the water, so somehow I can shave almost as well as with hot water."

"You just close me out."

"Um-hum."

"Why do you do that?"

"I don't."

"You *do*."

"Don't."

"I'm going down to breakfast."

"Without me?"

"Oh dear you're a clown . . . like a clown with nothing on but Rise Instant Shave."

"No, are you getting dressed or in a bathing suit?"

"Both. In case of emergency."

She loved to watch him shave. A strip of skin appeared under his left sideburn.

"Wait for me, Ellen."

"Hurry."

Then he was coming to the bed; and he knelt on the floor before her, his elbows on his knees, looking up at her. She knew he saw the archness in the downturned corners of her smile, and knew he knew she wanted him to see. He knew he was being funny with the shaving cream slapped all over his cheeks. But she didn't think it was really funny.

"Now what would be the practical consequences of your being married to Harry Tindall?"

"I'd have to learn to be English. I'd have to learn to wash socks."

"Be serious."

"Why the hell should I be?" Why the hell should she be?

"Or Bobby Prynne?"

"I'd have to learn to fight."

"Don't kid me. Or Duke Amerchrome?"

"Haven't met him."

"I've told you about him."

"So what?"

"Boswell Benson?"

"I'd have to learn to ski. That might not be too bad."

"Peter St. John?"

"Why do you ask me these things? I'll be married to *you*."

"I'm curious."

"No you're not. You're getting at me."

David kneed forward, moved in, embraced her waist.

"Your shaving cream." The farce embarrassed her more even than she resented it.

"Mark."

"You're getting at me."

"Mark?"

Was Mark why David wanted to see the island? What

262

about Mark? David would ask. And what did Mark think of this and what did Mark think of the other, and was Mark an Anglican, and what kind of degree did Mark get at Oxford, and what color hair—exactly—and what kind of people were his aunt and uncle—foster parents—in Sevenoaks, and what did Mark do with Ellen in London, did they go hear that female impersonator in the East End, did she take him to her club in Greek Street, where did they go? As if David could, through her own recollections of Mark, find *her*. Yet she was damned if she'd criticize Mark to David— damned if she'd quote Mark, who was unlike the things he said: On holiday in the sun somewhere one might catch him murmuring phrases like "Parables of sunlight"; he was always enigmatically saying things like, "For several years I've been interested in Annunciation pictures," the words demure, the balanced lucid culture of the civilized university amateur with a top second in P. P. E. Mark had spent a year studying political science (or was it archeology?) at Stanford, had adored New York, now produced education programs for BBC-TV (one of those uncriticizable jobs), and ran a Youth Club in the East End. (He had one of those healthy attitudes toward social work—which, of course, he'd never *call* social work.) When he made love he was careful not to be meticulous; always he was tender, rather too affectionate, always slow and efficient, "preparing his partner" (as the books put it), going ahead nicely without mistakes, never in his hands and legs and toes and the firm pushes and turns and hesitations and the things of the skin, never, never seeming in bed to brag. What, then, had been wrong with him and his straight yellow hair and his bony British body? (That blond hair had a strange gray luster.) What had she wanted, after all? Some Icelander or American? Some spasm of estrangement or ignorance? Better to watch others than oneself.

The door. At the knock, David was up and, with his magic speed, into his dressing gown like a sorcerer, as she called *"Un momento"* and David, too, said, *"Un momento,"* holding the *e* rather long, and stepping to the door. (David was the only person on the island who used the subjunctive! Except maybe Signor Giusti in class.)

"Scusa." The slim girl—the blonde girl who was going to study Robert Lowell at the University of Pisa in the autumn —was handing David a piece of paper. "Signor Matthews."

Horrible slim limbs, long and perfect, yet for all the longness the girl not tall. For a long instant the girl and David grinned at each other: Ellen imagined the flat stomach with its drooping Bikini line dividing the white from the dark, saw the absence of fleshiness at the hips, saw David—

"Oh!" cried the girl, covering her mouth, giggling. And David clapped a hand to a cheek, remembering the Rise, then brought the hand away white, and they both laughed.

To Ellen the girl, blonde and dark eyed, smiling said, *"B'n giorno,"* bowing and turning away down the hall.

Hell.

" 'Just to remind you,' " read David, " 'that I'd like to see you at my place today. Phil Matthews.' "

David tossed the paper toward the bed and, stopped by air, the note floated to the floor. He went to the basin and resumed shaving.

"I could see you undressing her."

David turned round, razor held casually and gracefully out from his cheek. "But we've already seen her undressed. On the beach." He smiled.

"You rather fancied yourself till you remembered you had shaving cream on."

"Fancied *her* not *myself.*"

"I have the soul of Audrey Hepburn."

"*You* undressed her, not me."

Ellen lay down on her stomach, eyes covered in the crook of her elbow. She heard the tiny "hhhhhhhh" cut of the blade stop, and David said, "Oh, can it, Ellen"—called her Ellen when he was naked.

"We both undressed her."

"You can do better than that."

"David." She got up and began to think about looking for her clothes.

"Um-hum."

"Fortunately most of our talk is froth."

"*I* try to make sense."

"Why *must* you always?"

Carefully, slowly—she did everything slowly—awkwardly (she felt), she pulled on her new bathing suit. David was quickly into trunks, khakis, blue shirt.

At the door, David ahead in the hall, she looked back into their room. The sun lit up the torn bed. Beyond the balcony railing the little orphan girls on that roof terrace were combing each other's hair and sewing, the room though sultry and deserted was hers and David's, touched by them in various spots: the high-crowned soft-brimmed straw hat David's cousin from China had found for her at Altman's, David's red hard-cover ledger-type notebook belted with a heavy rubber band, one of the two volumes of Drayton she had given him in London, and in a corner of the open suitcase on the rack the white plastic disc whose emptiness she so emphatically felt—she didn't like that word, "diaphragm." She was a purist prude about . . . emotions.

As she caught up with David at the first landing down—halfway to the next floor—a wildly long dragonfly veered seemingly out of the goldenness of the blindingly bright window, and as it hovered whirring by her neck (almost beyond her view), she cried out once stupidly and David, meeting it expertly, batted the brilliant strangely solid thing down almost to the next floor. Then it zoomed off along the hall.

At breakfast, which the boy served them frowning seriously and depositing the dishes perfunctorily, David seemed to have forgotten what she'd said, and they were bemused, and she slipped a foot out of her sandals and touched the ball of her foot to the cool blue-and-gold mosaic tile. (Late coffee and marmalade in a sunny room. Lately she felt David's words inside her edging aside her own.)

But then after breakfast, in the green, heavy garden by the white street-wall, David said, "Now off you go. You have to go to the hair-dresser, don't you?"

And she couldn't help saying, "Will that be convenient for you?"

And he wouldn't let her get away with that: "Now you put it so, yes. You're impossible today and I think you even know it."

And she couldn't give in and say she was sorry; for she felt he wouldn't do the same. "You use me during the *day, too.*"

"It's not true." He shrugged, and she felt he desperately wanted to reach and stroke her arm the way he did. But he didn't reach, didn't even stare probingly at the point between her eyes just above where her nose began. They stood for a whole minute or two. She heard a Vespa taxi dart past, then a car's more serious motor. A charwoman upstairs in the hotel was singing something—*"Vogliamoci tanto bene*

265

amore mio, Il cuore te dice non lasciami piú .... The clichés
were easy, sweet.

IV

Screw him!

She should go to the *parrucchiere* and have her hair
washed. That was what she'd said she was going to do. Yet
she didn't want to stop in that little dark alcove of a shop.
The *parrucchiere* had been watching the dancers the night
before last, and watching her. Had he thought she was tired
of David? The little *parrucchiere* couldn't be more than
seventeen; he'd been alone working himself up to ask someone. He probably thought her an American; he had heard
David talking to Signor Giusti.

A few minutes ago in the bright hotel garden, when David,
instead of having the last word, had said nothing, she hadn't
wanted to leave him. But she hadn't wanted him to know
this. She didn't want to spend time under the *parrucchiere*'s
drier. He'd have the radio on in the dark shop, and he would
touch her shoulder and her wrist and her chin. It was indeed a tradition, but this little cretin hadn't learned how to
inherit it—if it really was worth inheriting. And he'd stand
close and smile, and want to set her hair—back-brush it and
do the front in some lopsided provocation—and he'd say he
was not actually so keen on *Italian* girls.

Well, she'd forget the greasy salt and the sour smell in her
hair, and she'd take the other route round the island. She
would do that, she would walk past the place where the
hundred steps David had counted descended to the beach-
side restaurant. She would make it on foot all the way round
to the other side of the island where the cemetery was, and
their beach. She should cancel the umbrella and the beach
chair here, because she and David had decided to go now
only to the other place.

The umbrella would by now have been put up and, at their
old spot fifty yards down from the restaurant, one would be
able to smell the dense, impure salt of the warm water and
perhaps the first *calamari* frying for an early lunch. Would
David change their collective mind and go on down, maybe
hoping she'd have gone elsewhere, hoping now for some
sliding, sweaty, sandy soccer? Or would he—Oh Christ she

didn't know what he'd do—or would he come along here behind her, or take the other route she and Marie, and then she and Mark (who didn't really like the far beach) had taken those other summers? She ought to know what he'd do, but she didn't. She felt him behind her.

Past the hundred steps—a jukebox aria audible from below—Ellen found the brown street narrower and now uphill. How to explain to David? She couldn't say don't think, for that wasn't right either.

At least he didn't go so far as that American friend with the asbestos tongue—the one who could swallow hot coffee so fast and who said all men should have a course in firearms instruction—who was always telling in his wife's presence how long they had done it the night before or how, exactly, his wife's insides were made (and that they were getting "mushy"), or how—and this with a tough smile at his doting wife—you only married to get it steady, or how one ski weekend in Massachusetts they fell down and made love in a snowbank. Still, though he was wrong-headed and probably lying, you couldn't say not to think about it. But you thought of the other person. David said it all had to do with release. You projected into the other person in order to release yourself. (David, thank God, didn't think sex funny.) But release was selfish. Well, release out of yourself yes: but, *to* the *other*. Oh, David, only touch, please, only skin and help and going to the other person, to David. Or was that more romantic fancy devoured to fatten up one's secret life?

She'd make it round to the beach, and the cemetery, and maybe even the cliff where that rum chap Matthews lived. Matthews might take her mind off. "So, in this immensity my thoughts drown"—she knew Peter St. John's inscription by heart; it and the leather volume in which he had written it (Wilmott's *Journal*) were their secret from David, for Peter wanted her not to tell David—"and shipwreck is sweet to me in this sea." Peter St. John was a poet, a modest poet, for he insisted she not show his lines to David.

Peter knew David; knew how David would peer at the lines—the way his mind peered at people. But in his reminiscences David often seemed to her to surround the one etched absolutely real person with a setting dim or mad or not to be believed. That flat, for instance, in the rooming house, and those *characters:* The old man was so very clear in David's fidgety, rambling talk, yet also ringed round by such a shadowy, quivering covey of others. She'd so have liked to meet the old man—Pennitt was to have gone off to California with Morganstern to visit Morganstern's wife and children, but one day Pennitt had vanished, leaving only his odd press machine to record his having been there; Pennitt clear in a strange way—his bronchitis (in his hack an echo of distant showering pricks of sound—like part of a load of coal passing down a chute two city blocks away), his skinny arms, his gabble about all those English coins he might have collected. Yet meanwhile, round him, in David's telling, those other roomers weren't to be believed, and so old Pennitt seemed to Ellen a vivid, tired figure invented and manipulated in a murmuring void full of possible shapes. And there existed so many *other* shapes.

David wrote to them. (Peppermint stickum on the envelope flaps!) Now why did he have to write to so many of them. He imagined some future convention of his friends on a Hudson River Day Line steamer; David called himself a "kind of epistemological reuniac," whatever that meant. First, the two foolscap pages about his travels he'd asked her to have run off at the office; he sent that letter to three dozen people, most of them the indistinct shapes. Then, when only his mother answered, he started those chain letters, half a dozen at least. He spoke now of how the letters would be crossing and making a cat's cradle from Jerusalem (where Michael Amerchrome was said to be studying), to San Francisco (where Duke Amerchrome was in hospital). Silly-sod David.

How full of him she was. She felt him forcing every turn. Had she become a new memory he was busy editing? When he loved her he seemed to come *too* close, his mouth inspecting her ribs and her head, near but so feverishly strange. How could that be? Maybe someday she would have become just another one of these memories David started to recount but didn't finish. Maybe she was only in his head. Part of the confection.

What happened to Sindbad the Sailor after he married the native woman? David had stopped talking then. Ellen had had her eyes closed and because of this he had bawled her out for not paying attention. But she'd been wide awake, conjuring an image of D. spread out in the air above her, a predatory, swimming angel.

She would go back and walk with David. That sod, that bugger-bastard, always leaning when he walked, as if on the hunt, hunched and muttering puns; she hadn't really wanted that ominous story about Sindbad; she had wanted David to rescue her with his fingers and all the weight of his body, rescue her so she wouldn't have to be herself any more.

She wanted him for herself, all for herself.

He must give up . . . must give up those shapes he so often, now, talked about, the shapes that sometimes killed him.

Michael Amerchrome was afraid, because of what he'd told David about the father, Duke. He didn't want his father exposed. Duke feared exposure, too, but thought people ought to *believe* him a great historian before they scanned his credentials. Now Julia couldn't get out of her head a casual remark of David's that there aren't any brothers or sisters or fathers or mothers, there aren't any connections, and she now had changed somehow toward David because of that tiny tape recorder David had surreptitiously set going in her room one time she was alone. And what about old Pennitt? A dealer, the associate president of a coin-crank club, had come asking questions; he had got onto Pennitt through a mysterious blond man with a German accent; J. J. Lafayette admitted having spoken to this man, but told David the man had hardly been listening; and J. J. said he hadn't had much to tell anyone about Pennitt anyway, because. . . . And Peter St. John had grown cold, or so David said, cold since Peter had told David a story, which Peter said he never should have told David, a story that put Peter in a queer light. David never told her *enough* about these shapes.

They shook him up now and then. But he was a calmer boy, man—calmer than his first caustic evening in Maida Vale when she'd asked him out. (The connections didn't matter: Harry Tindall, Hugh St. John, J. J. Lafayette's Columbia friend whose girl read psychology at London University.) Ellen had to watch David: just before they flew off to Greece, she had found a scribbling of David's on the desk in her mother's living room (for some reason David loved Formosa Street—pale, dead, unimportant; liked strolling about Maida Vale; liked—she had seen him from a block away when he wasn't looking—liked to spit into the Little Venice canal; liked to sit in the Welsh church off Sutherland

Avenue on weekday afternoons): the scribble had been a pattern of something, or names, some of which she knew; a polygon with names written into slots at varying distances from a little circular center, a kind of designed medal, Peter, Roland, Luke, Marcus, Tom, J. J., Julia, Josie, Wanda, Harry, Hugh, Mary, Mary. . . . Ellen took it away and hid it; at odd hours looked at it; destroyed it; never heard David ask. So? Corfu, Cornwall, Casco Bay, Maida Vale. She must go back along this brown street, find David; maybe he still stood among the tremendous leaves in the hotel garden. Now—she'd been looking blindly into a sandal shop and thinking about David's arms. Well, too much about arms and you became an American footnote—*Art of Love, Craft in Bed, Téchnic of Interpersonal Intercourse;* and on the telly lectures about fertility with naval diagrams of the female, with secret maneuvers of sperm cells up that bay, round that bend, get a little now and get a little then, exploratory naval operations that ended when these fleet vessels, now become fired pellets, came bumping like the Coney Island Dodgem cars against that central island ovum, and the bloody man saying, "The problem now is to. . . ." Ah! all too ugly to be true, they couldn't, couldn't prove it, couldn't.

Turn now in the sun. Steps.

David was making her think, making her thoughts.

"Ellena!"

Benino! She blinked against the sun. Over Benino's shoulder she could see beyond the end of the street to a large garden deep dusty green, and a field beyond, and near the streetside wall a sweet blindfolded donkey stepping slowly round a track, hitched to a pole that turned a wheel that moved some water that. . . .

"You were deep inside yourself, Ellena. You almost bumped into me. You were not in the port this morning. Hey! It is me! Benino! Benino of the Merchant Marine!"

David's words in Benino's voice:

> Tell me, O tell who did thee bring
> And here, without my knowledge, plac'd,
> Till thou didst grow and get a wing,
> A wing with eyes, and eyes that taste?

A poem called "The Queer," and David said the title didn't mean what you might think.

She could think of things *too*. "*Invertito*" reminded her. Benino speaking.

Screw her! Where was she now? Choosing another ice cream, day-dreaming in a sandal shop, mentally muttering that she'd keep her U. K. citizenship, her U. K. passport, while he, here in this solitary lane along the cliffs, was left full of the self she said he was lost in. But he wasn't really thinking about himself; he was thinking only of her, he was bound from ankles to peeling forehead in the winding disparagements of him that seemed the only version of herself she let him have.

Why bother to recite to her? She looked away, as if thinking, but she didn't care, didn't see:

> Sure, *holyness* the *Magnet* is,
> And *Love* the *Lure*, that woos thee down;
> Which makes the high transcendent bliss
> Of knowing thee, so rarely known.

The end of "The Queer"—she hadn't responded to the modern absurdity of the seventeenth-century title.

Last night in the room she had come up to him naked and pretended to zip him open down the front and pretended to open him and then pretended to work herself inside him as if he were a child's one-piece pajama with feet and with buttons you did down the back. But he'd said the space was already taken. She kept burrowing her face into his collarbone, and he kept trying to turn her face up.

Oleanders: David examined the blooms: hairy anthers adhering to a thickened stigma, yes.

Along the high cliff ridge he found, now, an opening gulf of air and ocean and a hazy mass of land not far away. Myrrh and junipers grew toughly along the seaward side of the path; and there was the sea, there but so far below that it was no more real than, say, Matthews' villa, somewhere ahead.

David stepped over off the path; the bushes prickled against his thighs; far down, sun-bright rocks fringed the sea, hills and mountains of a far country seen from a height of hours, days, years.

271

Were suicides merely trying to get somewhere fast? "Small profits, quick returns," Bobby Prynne had said about masturbation, referring also to his own helpless dabbling in the ups and downs of the stock market. He watched prefabs, said he was now holding off for the big moment. National Homes had disappointed him, but. . . .

Would a would-be suicide launch himself into a gulf like this Tyrrhenian, Neopolitan gulf if he could truly construe the miniature terrain of rock below—the cups and slants and cuts and nodes and knives there deep below the path where David stood? But not down, so much as far.

From here you'd never make it out to the water. You'd fall short of the sea, you'd land on a rock—that even hemispheric dark one slicked by spray—wreck your bones with hardly any cracking crunch, the sound barely louder to your own ears in that last fading second of impact than to the ears of someone twenty-five yards down the shore watching; and someone fifty, seventy-five away would hardly catch the modest slap-fleck in the gold-gray sea-washed air. But suicide could only be a prospect, never an experience.

What were you ever released *into?* Ellen didn't like the honest word "release." But what, yes, were you released into?

You looked for a person and touched him and figured him and questioned; but then you got back one day a brand-new look foreign to all you knew; and you knew that even if you had in fact been in that other person feeling what he felt, knowing his impulses and how he contrived to live, you would have been alive only in yourself, a discreetly preserved Robinson Caruso (as J. J. Lafayette called him) performing your own imported rites, reproducing yourself. Wanda Woodrow, now almost a year away, was doing just that: wood effigies of herself, the face now less elegant, now leaner, now more skullish, now lush and orange-brown and moist—parthenogenetic proliferations: Wanda, sitting on a bed, arching back and away in such a way that he couldn't tell if she wanted him to take her shadowy breasts or wanted him to take nothing: Wanda murmuring on and on afterward as she scratched his back, saying she had imagined coming between the two friends Harry and David by taking David in what she hoped would appear to both Harry and David as a catastrophic compromise; but, now that the Englishman had gone back to England, getting into bed with

272

David Brooke didn't matter except as it might in itself matter, and it didn't matter; and David himself never admitting to her what he imagined she guessed and hoped and what would have been a fresh, precise shock for her that might even have turned her to David—the idea that David had come to her because she had been Harry's girl. But he must leave her with her guess and with her sculptures, a mirror-room full of them. Onto the sparsely imprinted sands that had seemed his fate, Crusoe brought eighteenth-century London, self and place cohabiting: each of them both the city and the man. But if he could have thrived on those domestic sands—and he *did* thrive—whence came the roots that made him firm? From that London he never left? From that self that was different from London? From outside? Surely from outside. Or from within?

In David's heart, Ellen now turned and kissed his eyelids, thought him asleep on that beach (yesterday); yet though he'd been deceiving her, how intimate he'd felt them then—intimate as when in his parents' flat in Brooklyn Ellen had packed, and he had watched her madly folding dresses and hipster slacks and the gray highland tweed suit Harry Tindall had had him buy in Tottenham Court Road and which David had never worn because in it he felt large, and she and he had listened to his mother persistently playing the one zigzag bridge in the Bartok again and again until the total piece was far away and this stubborn passage a newly autonomous riddle near and alive.

Where was Ellen? On the hotel beach listening to Benino's proverbs for tourists? A woman with a moustache is always liked. Ha, ha, ha!

Would Matthews have his glasses focused on the cemetery beach? Would he come down if he saw David? Everywhere you went, someone.

But now, only Ellen.

On his left a vineyard was stepped in terraces up a further slope, and small squares of levels made the terracing more detailed. On his right, beyond the bushes and stunted juniper, that deep vista of blue with the few gray and white dots of boats and the hazy form of the island whose name he now hardly knew seemed, like the vineyard, cut away finally and absurdly from his path as if nearness and distance were nothing.

Words—Ellen—seemed the only live thing in his mind.

After some minutes the path descended and he came to the entrance of a lane at the end of whose high-walled passage he could see a dark oblong of housefront where the lane joined a street. Self-absorbed, rot. He was absorbed in thinking about *her!* When he touched her shoulder what was he thinking of but *her?*

At the end of the lane he turned right into the narrow, gently uphill street. The late-morning sun failed to get below the upper halves of the whitewashed houses on his left. Ahead he saw the modest dome of the creamy, weathered church blocking the street's seaward end. A young woman—dark plaits piled back and fixed high by a comb—hair Ellen's color—leaned her elbows on a second-floor window ledge. He wanted to keep answering her stare—stare her down from there—but she was impregnably above him and she had been looking first—though in England and America (now he thought about it) having looked first always put one at a *dis*advantage. On his right a passageway found a court, a corner of which he could see was bright and leafy. Moving now toward the end of the street, he smelled mingled stone and dust and the peaceful dusky scent of hanging salamis and bins of dry pasta. Where *was* everybody? He hadn't even seen one of those great cat-sized rats that ran slowly from a wall and down a few yards to another hole.

And then, as he reached the end of the street, the sun was suddenly all over him and he had reached the level of the church. And the sky spread open above and ahead.

But the street didn't really end here; it became an alley to the left, bending back at more than a right angle. And, either side of the walled, heavy-gated enclosure fronting the silent church, dusty cobbles led round toward the sea behind. The drabness of the church's wide wooden door made the door seem locked. The community of low, packed houses on this side of the island might have been a ghetto, deserted not so much by its tenants as by their voices. He loved hearing his and Ellen's footsteps down these streets.

Now David walked round to the left of the enclosure. Now the church was on his right, and he could see.

Some way behind the church that chalky rampart they had seen from the beach side crossed as if it were a fortification against the beach. Above this wall, a strip of dull violet sea hung chinked with glitter. The other cobbled lane led to the lip of a seaward ramp whose length along the right side of the cemetery was hidden by a dusty white wall. But he took the path ahead, shuffling along through the immense blue glare up toward the bluff—the bluff from which the three boys, according to Ellen, had spied yesterday. And, now, from this rise, he saw the whole cemetery.

It stopped him. It waited complete and settled—laid out from the base of the rock table on which the small church stood, to the sea rampart seventy-five yards away.

The fourth side of the cemetery was bounded by the bluff up which David's path turned. Across from and parallel to this bluff ran the walled ramp leading to the beach, the ramp the big horse had come down.

Six little mausoleums stood like civic landmarks among the coffin-shaped tombs and the brittle headstones that were ornamentally topped like architectural façades. Everything, though cramped and packed, grew together—the yearly increment placed, one imagined, with a gathering and shrewd economy. (Was there room for anyone else to die?) All, cluttered; and yet how like a town, established in a trellis of minute avenues, a continuing town, a city bleached silent, but unbroken by the white sun. City, organ of memory.

The other days, David and Ellen had gone down the seaward ramp, whose wall blocked off a view of the cemetery; and now he remembered Ellen saying he should take a good look sometime.

Again David found words he should have had this morning: "You call me self-absorbed. Yeah, but what about when you were off at Coventry that weekend showing those American students the Jaguar factory; and I forgot you'd gone and I was so used to there being two of us I bought *two* of those big long Dover soles at the fishmonger's instead of one —at six and six a pound. Now what about that?"

Chew the seeds, they're soft, and swallow the whole thing, she'd said—she'd been feeding him grapes on the beach. She wasn't a girl to say, "A penny for your thoughts," like the talkative girl at the drug store soda fountain who was never content to serve him his frosted and let him alone. English girls aren't blasé, John Crosby said, bless his spry formulas; English girls are cheerful but not grossly so, well informed but never pedantic, reasonable in daylight, nuts at night. English girl and Jewish girl and Italian girl and Swedish girl and wild wild gal from ZanziTan: women who have been

275

incontrovertibly proved by explorers and a number of research grunts, to be warmer.

To reach Matthews' villa, visible from here, David had to go out of sight of it, pass round the front of the church again.

Now, taking the ramp, he was cut off from the cemetery. Hot cobbles bulged under his sandals.

When he stepped off onto sand he saw to the left the empty beach and the scraggy curve of the far cove, and the fishermen's cage, and its boom, like part of some abandoned construction work. On his right, way above, a part of Matthews' villa shone pink and white.

Where would Ellen be? By that other route—if she had kept on, which he doubted—could she make it all the way round here?

Sand got in on the flapping heels of his sandals, and he took them off and waded along the crescent of cove that led to the foot of Matthews' Bluff. The path David found led sharply up the steep face, wound through bushes and, before it disappeared, moving out toward the seafront of the bluff, could already be seen to have become at several abrupt rises natural rock stairs.

Halfway up he heard little voices, glints of sound falling upward through emptiness. And he turned to survey the graveyard and beach. As he did so, slightly shaken to see how the bushes dropped almost straight down from the smooth dusty rock step he stood on, he saw Ellen and Benino—they had come through a cleft at the far end of the beach and stood looking at the water—and he knew they couldn't spot him without actually trying—"without actually trying": oh please, keep words far hence! And why shouldn't she be with Benino, hearing him tell her how beautiful she was and how *davvero* he was head over heels . . . in Italian.

Even in motion David's dark-blue shirt mightn't be easily seen in the slope's gray-green growth. David didn't look down again.

Hauling himself up the last steep grade and a high rock step like a cliff, David heard Matthews greet him: "Right on time."

"What do you mean?"

Was Ellen coming?

"Saw you and your wife yakking in the hotel garden— why that must be an hour and a half ago—thought it'd take you about that, along the cliffs. Course, I drove."

"But why did you think I'd come?"

"Everyone does."

In the sun before his door, Matthews looked older and even healthier than last night. He had on gray Bermudas and a white T-shirt with New York A. C. and "P. M." in red across the chest. He was holding a copy of *Time* at his side.

V

At the window, watching Ellen and Benino far away, David heard Matthews say from the armchair, "High-priced view, and all mine." Now Ellen turned toward the near end of the beach, and Benino followed, talking with his hands. From this great picture window one saw on the right the last limits of the Bay of Naples merge with the shining reaches of the Tyrrhenian Sea; on the left, the two coves and the cemetery.

Matthews had led David into the living room, had paused at the window to take a pair of binoculars, and was now deep in a low messy armchair. Benino gripped Ellen's shoulders and kissed her. She turned strongly away. Then she came back into his clutch and they were kissing again. Then she pushed out of his grasp.

"Look at this place," said Matthews, and reluctantly David left the window. "All you need, when you stop to think. Now tonight I run the Chris-Craft into Naples, get a little dose of social life." He winked—oh, come on, how *could* he?—and straightened out his long large legs and crossed his ankles. "My old hunting grounds from the war. Counterintelligence. But most of the time who needs it? I mean the social stuff, the gab and the girls . . . . There's our port here on the other side of the island—saw you there two nights ago, didn't I—get a restaurant meal for a change—course it's strictly Italian, no Chinese—play a hand of whist, take in a show—English with Italian subtitles or Alan Ladd playing Shane with an Italian voice—anything you want. But here in this room, well, you see for yourself. Every piece a comfort, not travel relics. Most of my stuff's right from Antioch. And then, you know, when my brother died I got the divan—now do you know anyone who'd ship a big divan all the way from Antioch, Ohio? You can't beat having your own things."

277

Matthews paused, as if to let David look.

The bottle-green couch was flanked by wing chairs and wicker stools—all in a semicircle facing the picture window. Ellen would be leaving the beach now; or would they be swimming, a provocation? Maybe back by the hotel she'd met Benino by mistake, when she was looking in fact for *him, David*. Or had she set off the bumbling fight this morning in *order* to meet Benino?

"Still considered on the island a peculiar honor to be asked here."

"Peculiar?"

"Oh you heard Giusti last night. I've told the story to Americans; some believe it, others don't; I couldn't care less."

"What story?" Tell a story, tell, Ellen had asked the night before last after he'd abandoned the mosquitoes. And he'd explained how Sindbad the Sailor had taken a native wife and how custom obliged the surviving partner . . . . But David had stopped.

". . . just because I don't go slapping my cook's behind— that was when I—before Marjean came from Antioch. But after the cook left and before Marjean came, when I was here without a companion—if the word doesn't make me sound like a cripple— I didn't do any noticeable tom-catting, and they started making jokes—like what do they use the female for in the *Stati Uniti*, or don't I like Italian girls, or don't I like girls . . . ? You get the picture—I don't have to say it in Italian. And then a couple of kids—today I guess they're in the Pacific, young officers—this was before they went to the naval school—started coming to hear my tapes— I collect comic monologues, Benchley's parody of "Oh, what a rogue and peasant slave am I," a classic of anti-Semitism; Paul Rome's broadcast of the last few minutes of the forty-day suspended-animation burial that California Quaker went through; many more."

Ellen would come soon, he knew it: she would leave Benino, she would guess that David was visiting Matthews, she would come.

"And I bought those kids lilos and I took out subscriptions for them to *Look* and *Time*. Well, one night a little scrawny mama came after them and stood in that door and said, with the tape running like 'lectric, 'You are not *yet* the father here!' I turned off the tape and she said, 'These babies have their own fathers and do not need you to sport with them.' Eh? Eh? Maybe *she* spread tales. I notice the fellows didn't cancel the magazines—three-year orders, too. After that I went on, fished for mackerel, tiddled about with those musical glasses"—David looked over at the table-cabinet where twenty-odd small tumblers were ranged—"had my usual quiet hell of a time. But then one Friday two boys no more 'n ten, eleven, came onto the beach while I was in—and I didn't ordinarily wear shorts, y'know, just peeled off and waded in. They came, stood by my clothing, looked at it, took off their pants, all they had, came in, too. Well, what but a young man and woman, parents of one kid it turned out, came after a while and just then the boys and me are finished splashing and are on the way out of the water and I don't see the woman till—ah, what do you expect! I saw him trying to hide her face behind his shoulder, but she only pretended because she managed to look and she really wanted to. They didn't yell at the kids—well, I was back in the water for comfort—the four of them went off. Two nights later Giusti sees me in the port playing whist and asks me what's going on at that end of the island, chuckles but is making such nasty hints he finds he's got to stop chuckling, and then he goes off, and the whist continues. But the two points are . . . . Lou listening? . . . First, the rumor got all round and no one stopped it—not even the old fellow who drives a cab over in Naples, picks me up occasionally. Second, I found that all this was my place in the world, what my twin brother never had trouble finding. The one thing you're supposed to do."

"*What*, exactly?" Ellen was right: The man was a bore.

"Myself to be, well, an example of misunderstanding, an example to the islanders that they were threatened by what they imagined I was and also by the chance that they might just be slandering me—and they got to know that I wasn't ever going to defend myself. I kept friendly with boys here— even after Marjean came. I am the stranger in the midst, buddy, that is what I am, and I never had found a big thing to do before I found this thing. An island character, yes; also a threat; a doubt; a reputation that invites people to be stuffy and say, there goes the *invertito;* a reputation that also forces people to wonder if it's only a reputation; a status in relation to other people, that's what a person wants. By Jesus it is."

"What's the hardest thing in the world?" asked David, thinking of Ellen's fears and objections.

"Mm-hmm," said Matthews, "sounds like a locker-room gag—well, I came here to this island, and I stayed—"

"To be *properly* selfish," said David, half to himself.

"Mm-hmm, well, I stayed two years, '49-'51, and my brother Jesse died and believe it or not I didn't go home to Antioch—I was afraid to—at the end he'd finally gone into the family business—and well, my sister-in-law Marjean— what a gal!—she came to visit after a few months he'd been dead." Matthews talked in spurts. "Came to visit—because my brother Jesse loved me; and what do you know but she stayed. Taught English at the island school here. Liked the island and the island liked her; and what but she got to like me better and better, thought she was taking care of me (actually I was taking care of her), always saying I looked like Jesse—department of understatement: twins! Liked the island. Never left. Giusti tell you?"

"No."

"Just like him to give you his little version of me and leave out the most important thing of all. Marjean."

"Your sister-in-law?" Where had Ellen gone when she turned down toward the near cove?

"Where *you* been?"

Matthews' wide athletic cheek bones made his grin seem menacing.

"Yes, my sister-in-law, but I feel like she was my sister. No, that don't make a hell of a lot of sense. I mean 'wife.' And those bastards round the port thought she *was* my wife, and I always half thought she might have been another reason I got this *invertito* tag. They thought we'd been separated and that she'd come back to me, and meanwhile I was fooling around being an *invertito*. I baited Giusti and them. I went to the port and always got one or two kids at the table with me having a soda, and letting Giusti and the others know when I had a little afternoon party for the kids. 'Course it still goes on."

"I'm sorry: I don't understand," said David, who hadn't been listening but could tell that even if he had been he wouldn't understand.

"Maybe not," said Matthews. "I was a pretty big sergeant in Naples at the end of the war. Intelligence. Why they call that kind of snooping intelligence, I don't know, but anyway

I just about ran the place, we had cleaning up to do. It was mentally tiring, you understand. Where did I go from there? Just before I got out I was noncom in charge of communications at a base in Georgia. I had responsibility for the Western Union Pony Circuit to Valdosta, Georgia, and the Plan 55 Circuit. I was in a bad way. Got drunk in town there one night and they put me in jail and I called for a writ of habeas corpus and they blinked and then just released me—no judge—no . . . I hated that, do you see? What was I going to do? I had to do *something,* but what?"

"You mean ability?" Better give up on Ellen, contrive an exit.

"As Pop used to say, 'You don't bury your talents in the sand.' "

"In the ground, you mean?"

"Yeah, that's what I mean. He had all the talent in our family and he sank it in gravel and made a million carting gravel; and my twin brother and I got it all when the old man fell out of the attic one evening; he was waiting to show us some scrapbooks he'd found, and when we didn't come, he leaned down the little stairs and then fell and cracked the back of his head and that was it."

Without Ellen . . . .

Matthews put a hand on David's shoulder. "You and your wife want to be here tonight?"

"Want? To be?"

"Stay. Because I'll be over the water." Matthews winked and pinched David's neck. "Be by yourselves. The Matthews Hotel." He shook his head, put his hands in his pockets, and went to the mirror. "Have to scrape off all the little spots and crusts and blemishes before I go on the town."

"You mean you want us to stay here?"

"You know, I do *want* you to, yes."

Oh, quickly find out about Matthews, not whether he was queer or not, but . . . find out anything . . . listen. . . . "You like the expatriate life?" No, it wasn't that.

"I tell you," said Matthews returning and placing a hand on David's shoulder. "Guy came here once and when he left—American he was, with an English accent—he said that Saint Augustine had said, or I think this is what he said Saint Augustine said, 'And men go forth and admire lofty mountains and broad seas, and turn away from themselves.' That happened to me. Well, OK, I never have gone over there to see Vesuvius, but I've got a hill or two and some cliffs right here. And broad seas? Well, I go round the bay, fish for mackerel and shark, but *I* don't go down to Sicily, why the hell should I? I'm known all over the island, so was Marjean. I got private stories about every family here—even the ones back in the middle of the island in the vineyards. The man who left thirty-five years ago to go to Brooklyn, and who came back to retire five years ago—to his roots—and do you know how long he stayed? He got sick of the view. Got sick of the old men sitting in the dark in the bars watching bicycle races on TV, and he wanted to get back to his Italian buddies in Brooklyn. Or the story how they wouldn't bury Marjean in the cemetery? But they did. And I can tell you, money passed hands; of course she was a Catholic. . . .

"Well, she died, you know, died in her sleep, aged forty. I thought I'd lost my life, but then I knew I had my odd place here anyway, irregardless of Marjean. But Marjean really *lived* here: with me and with all them kids. I see girls and boys go away to Milan and Turin and the boys go off to be mates on American tankers, and I *know* them from when they were at school here. Giusti never liked me. When Marjean died I tried to take over her English class but Giusti said he preferred to teach the English himself and said that in the States Marjean was qualified. But I got kids up here to play tapes and fool around with the musical glasses—same as the ones Benjamin Franklin invented—and I kept in touch with the school."

"But what do you *do?*" Ellen, please, not *Benino!*

"Never stop. People coming in here. Last summer there was an American air-force lieutenant over for the day. He'd flown into Naples from Bentwaters Base in England. Hates the service. Comes from Riverside, Connecticut, kept asking if they sailed Quincy Adamses in Naples Bay—now I *ask* you! —and he stood out here and had a lot of things to say about sailing Quincy Adamses all over the Sound with a girl on the tiller and—what was it?—the toughest wind quartering at them in the keenest sunlight in the craziest sort of aloneness. And how much was it to rent a boat here. I invited him to come fish for sharks, but he said I must be crazy and said he was going to sail the fjords before he got out of the service. Said he was going everywhere in Europe before he went home. Now *that's* crazy: I told him you have to settle down in *one* place and get to know the people. Look how they know *me.* First thing after you *get* here somebody tells you, next day you—hey! Ellen"—he waved at the window and David turned to see a ghost of an elbow disappear—"you and your wife come over here first thing. That's how I'm . . . known." He shrugged, smiling.

Then he broke away from David and strode to the door.

Ellen took Matthews' hand. She was asking David something with humorous eyes, she was telling Matthews what a good housekeeper he was, she was at David's side and had taken his hand. "I thought you'd be here."

"Why does everyone *expect* me to come here?"

"Listen, I didn't tell you. Just to show how a thing continues—" Matthews was telling both of them—"only last week I saw two kids on that beach down there—my beach—where you were. They trailed me up here. I knew they were behind me. They'd watched me stand in the cemetery. I try to keep some plants going on Marjean's plot. They'd watched me slope off round the cove; and as I came up my steep path I looked back to see them wandering round the cove, wading, glancing up toward me. Department of Mediterranean Mystery, eh? Dark knowledge of the blood, what *Time* magazine would call—say, I wanted to teach the kids at Giusti's school all about the puns in *Time,* I think those puns are simply great, but Giusti said the kids weren't going to read anything so transitory as *Time* and then he said I wasn't qualified anyhow—so I plodded up here and began to hear the boys behind me, knocking a pebble loose, snickering back and forth. I hadn't seen these kids before. The islanders leave this stretch pretty much alone—picnickers from Naples for the day, maybe a couple of women poking round the cemetery, not many people. You get the fishermen out at that cage above the water—leave their nets and fool around here and sit and talk, I watch them with the glasses. Fairly quiet around here. Well, these boys get up to the top and come over and stand in front of me staring and giggling. Well, I asked them in. And they came in and had cold fish and peppers and a hunk of bread. Watching me all the time. Then they had a look at that stack of *Time,* my set of musical glasses, my cameras, my binoculars, my tape recorder. (I showed them how to run it—sometimes these boys come up unannounced at night and turn the goddamn thing on.) Well, then they made like they were ready to go and then came up in front of me and said it is time for the money now. You may be surprised. I wasn't. Hadn't seen *this* exact routine before, but I understood. I made them explain. In a way, that's part of my pleasure. Some friend, an older boy, maybe one of my alumni, had told them go to the *invertito,* who *likes boys,* and he'll give you *denaro.* And I did."

Ellen: the sunburn freckles on her shoulders, freckles first revealed by the sun but then (now) veiled by the shades of days and days of Greek and Italian daylight.

Ellen was managing to move the three of them toward the door, with words and with a certain way of leaning and now with her hands on Matthews' right and David's left shoulder. "Maybe. We'll have to see. We hate to barge in, and you like to be where your own clothes and toothbrush are."

"Bring your goddam toothbrush. You know, please do come; now I really care. What about a swim now?"

"We have a dinner date in the port," said Ellen.

David followed Ellen out the door, and Matthews pointed the other way by the narrow road he used when he drove, that way that avoided the long descent down the bluff.

"Please come, tonight. Always leave it open anyhow. I'll be gone from the six o'clock boat till tomorrow morning. You couldn't have a nicer—hey, you on your honeymoon?"

Ellen put her head on David's shoulder. "The hotel thinks so. Actually we're not married."

Matthews looked serious as he said, "I'll make your breakfast." He went back inside.

As they walked away, Ellen said, "He had you in there quite a while, I think."

"I didn't hear a word he said."

"Self-absorbed." She squeezed his waist and looked into his face.

"Have to look out for yourself."

"Will you tell me the end of Sindbad tonight?"

"I did tell it."

"You hurried it up."

VI

Benino had on a madras jacket. David saw it as soon as he and Ellen turned the corner into the port square, saw it not merely as more color (to go with the whites and reds and blues of dresses and open shirts) but as a more complex patch, the mixing subtleties of whose plaid stood out with a sharp gauche elegance. There (almost a hundred yards away) at the table where Benino and his girl waited for David and Ellen: a madras jacket. But David, as they had come all the way down the winding alleylike street from hotel to square, had been aware of Benino only as a new absence, like a necessary admission one grimly prepared to make to a superior only to find that, through death or transfer, the crux has been passed over on a wave of circumstances and, though unfaced, lies now safely celled in the past. Yet though a fight made no sense—had made none ever since, three hours ago, David had kissed Ellen and felt a foreignness in her sweet flowing plump bones—still some collision was right. Didn't he have to tell Benino that Benino and Ellen had been seen? Mustn't David tell Benino what Benino was? Yet it didn't matter. Stop trying to judge other Beninos and other Ellens; be satisfied with the Ellen and Benino in oneself.

Ellen released her hand from his and ran it up to his elbow and further, and took his arm. "I hope Benino doesn't tell us how wise and good il Duce was, or any more about how a stinking priest made off with il Duce's fortune just at the end."

"I don't care. Benny's funny." David was walking Ellen very, very slowly; they were between seventy-five and fifty yards now, and the welcoming smile that a moment or two ago Benino had set now seemed a pose for a hesitant photographer—Benino seemed unable to look away or stop smiling. The girl by him seemed not to be able to look elsewhere either, but she brought her mouth only to a sort of overt, amiable concern. Instinct such a censor, so precise a diplomat.

Very slowly David and Ellen walked, and Ellen knew it.

Approach, Benino and girl, approach very slowly. The air mustn't be displaced; keep the natural arrangement of sounds—calls from children clambering on boats where older people were finishing up floats for the festa. Benino's fixed smile. Slowly.

The shower in the bathroom on their floor had no curtain, and the central drain toward which the usually clean, gray-tiled floor gently slanted was clogged, and the fine, soothingly scratching tines of water stayed cold. And David had left his towel in the room at the other end of the hall, and leaving the bathroom he felt his cotton dressing gown from Abraham and Straus sticking warmly to back and forearms.

But he was whistling the hurdy-gurdy tune he had heard at midnight on Greek Street, as they came up out of that after-hours club where Ellen had now let her membership lapse, "Love You in the Morning, Love You in the Evening, Love You the Whole Day Through," and he knew that somewhere in his past he had been prepared for that song, had heard it or had heard something that was like it, or . . . and he was whistling, and he was not trying to circumvent the shower drain or the cold water. If his carelessness came from his edge on Ellen—for he had not mentioned Benino and neither had she, except to say Benino wanted them to eat with him tonight in the port—it was also part of a post-afternoon, pre-dinner forgetting, a gay, skin-tight, sun-turned stupidity—he still felt the sandy shore under his feet, he was falling backward into the tepid buoyant Tyrrhenian salt, he was up to his neck, he was looking up to his left at Matthews, who had come out to his cliff surprised that Ellen and David had decided to swim after all, David was smiling at Matthews wondering if Matthews guessed that he was peeing in the water. Skin-tight-tan-gay whistle, with the dressing gown stuck as if with sweat, and knowing he had an edge on Ellen but not caring.

Twenty-five yards, "Ellena, Davidè," very slowly, de-fiance(?), no, trance(?), maybe, balls(?), two-in-a-bunch (as Morganstern answered his own familiar question, "How they hangin'?"), stomach(?), hunger turning into flower, menu teleprinting down the mind, twenty yards, Benino rising, his girl looking up to him, *minestra*, cold peppers (cool, sweet, limp), "Ellena, you are looking—" individual baby octopi (crisp, tangled), a special *manzo bollito*, "Davidè, why you are not wearing a coat? I look forward to what you wear," *fagiolini*, and Ellen for dessert, a peach, Bel Paese, that edgy white wine then that edgy red, edgy but not sparkling, unexportable, and Ellen for dessert, and she, after all the food, perhaps asking should she have a little strawberry *gelato*, "Davidè, di Michelangelo!" The gibe didn't touch. And what's for dinner, Benino-in-your-mar-velous-madras?

Prosciutto and melon. Benino flickering his lids at the three of them. Benino's girl tall, dark, and handsome. She was hearing little Italian, and though this seemed unfair,

David couldn't—and she didn't—care.

Just as in Matthews' living room this afternoon David had been elsewhere, so now he was far from Benino and close, close to Ellen.

Benino had to ask again for the first bottle. He had known the waiter for fifteen years. Through Matthews' window Ellen had seemed far away, but it wasn't competition that gave her now the strangeness he saw in her shoulders, partly bare, and in the grace with which she slowly turned her head toward Benino and Maddalena and David and the two cocky little boys who passed several times, staring and giggling. The strangeness was in the cemetery and in Ellen's preoccupation with ice cream and in the chalk rampart and in the binoculars Matthews handled while he talked on. And the strangeness had made David feel flippant, and made him want simply to have Ellen beside him, touching him, laughing at him, believing that he sometimes thought himself a fool.

But look here—or did he care?—he had something on Benino, and on Ellen. But might he himself have been in a sense dead when he spied them kissing? dead, and "returned"? and as unable to touch either of them as if he'd surprised them in a dark cream-colored room moving together on a bed? David liked the secret he now had with Benny and Ellen.

Maddalena sipped straight through her *minestra, one* two, *one* two, *one* two. Benino of the raised eyebrows became in David's eyes an imaginary creature fixed and far; sharp creases from corner of nostril to corner of mouth at twenty-five implied male experience, yet threatened in their very incisiveness the filling-out of ten years hence.

"And although I am as well qualified, I am paid one-third less than *Americans* on that ship. That is what your country does to me and to Franco and others from our naval school."

"But," said David, "every summer you're back here with money and you run your boat to Ischia for lunch or Capri overnight. Wouldn't you *rather* work an American line?"

"Yes . . . yes," Benino said with a sickened smile. "But I would not bring American shipmates here. Leave ship at Genoa. Finish with ship." He tipped out the last of the *bianco* into David's glass and waved for more. "Then come home," he said, as if inarticulately, nodding sharply, then with a wink at David and Ellen, tilting his head toward Maddalena, who now took a final sip of soup and restored her hands to her lap. "I would not wish them to visit my mother and father when they leave ship. Those Americans want only one thing anyway. You Americans are materialists." He grinned at his soup and shook his head. He wasn't sure how he wished the remark taken but he felt it had import and sting.

"What do the Italians offer instead?"

"We have great leaders and great poets with great visions."

"So does everyone."

"And civilization!" Benino added.

"What's happened to it?"

"It is here," said Benino, who then apparently as an after-thought placed a palm on his breast—"here, waiting."

"You make good sport clothes and after the war you made a few good films and your food is like a sweet drug it's so good. But what else is there? I can find you islands in Casco Bay, Maine, just as pretty as this."

"What *else,* what *else!* Beauty in women, wisdom in living, *architettura,* painting—"

"They wouldn't let me in the exhibit of erotica in the Naples *museo.*"

"Architecture, sculpture, painting—"

"Balls! There's Fornasetti china—that's quite a lot of fun, and splendid, too. An oval butter dish white and gold showing a hand with rings on all but the ring finger."

"Fornasetti I do not know. Why you come to Italy?"

"I'm a materialist."

"Your American Matthews is a good example of materialist. You are with him all afternoon, yes?" Benino winked at David. "You know what I mean. He cares for his automobile and his boat and his tape recorder and his money. That is all—*almost* all. You were with him, eh?" Benino was smiling as carefully as he knew how. David went ahead with his chicken. Maddalena made an appreciative "Mmmmmm," chewing a bit of breast. The four of them got on with the dinner.

After a few minutes Benino said, "*Invertito.* You see? That is American, eh?" He was pretending to josh. "Introduces sodomy to this island."

"I doubt it, from all the hugging and kissing that goes on between the men here."

288

"You are very American, so American," said Benino, not understanding David's tone. "In Italy we do not fear the heart. We *show*, we *show!*"

"*Grazie*," said Ellen as the waiter put down a quart of mineral water.

"Well, what's wrong with sodomy anyhow?" said David.

Talk had subsided. Benino said something quickly to Maddalena, and David saw Ellen smile; and then she turned to David and made a kiss with her lips.

The four of them were going to have grapes and cheese. (Ice cream, Ellena? No ice cream. How proprietary Benino was trying to be.)

Streetlamps up and down the wharf lit a preview of tomorrow night's *Sacra del Mare* procession—floats crowding close in to the wharf, bobbing on the small swells now and then sent shoreward by a passing boat, floats offering from just beyond the limit of the wharf an audience of great *papier-mâché* heads, huge wild sticks of arms, horrid happy pop-eyes.

For minutes and minutes David watched the floats, and watched the children strolling arm in arm. Benino was arguing with Ellen about Italian *au pair* girls in London. Nine o'clock? Ten, nearly ten.

"Ellena, how you like Italian men?" The big grin again pretended to be easy. Maddalena giggled. Benino hadn't paid her any attention tonight.

"I like *men*," said Ellen, and now laid her head on David's shoulder.

"Careful," said David, "you can't kiss in public. You get a ticket."

"Who *wants* to kiss in public?" said Benino quickly.

"*Men*," repeated Ellen, putting her hand in David's lap. "I like *men*, simply."

But was *he*—"David"—the contraband shrouded in "men"? Probably she wanted to give Benino a polite, ambiguous rebuff. Yet how could one tell?

And what sort of contraband was this secret kiss David held against Benino and Ellen, the secret he "had" *with* them? Benino had been put down without intensity and left on the sand to walk away alone; Ellen had kissed him—*twice* —not because she had to but because for a moment she liked his pop-talk, the almost embarrassing sham of ardor seeming for the moment as warm as the real thing.

"But I think you like Italian men, Ellena."

David had picked up the check before Benino could speak, and had gotten up and was headed inside the restaurant to pay the waiter. "Hold it, Davidè, I pay ... !"

But then David had paid and the three were still at the table. Benino was holding Ellen's hand across the table. Maddalena was laughing.

They all stood as David came back. He nodded at Maddalena.

"Benino, give her a big kiss."

Benino shrugged and smiled. He glanced at Ellen. "Let us all go visit the *invertito*," he said, with an expansiveness meant to end the dinner genially.

"It means 'turned inward,' " said David. "You're an *invertito*."

"And you, Davidè, are a scholar and a gentleman."

"And you are an *invertito*."

"Play with your word. Whatever you mean. You are on holiday. What do I care? All I know is that Matthews is what you in America—I hear it on ship—what you call a 'queer.' A queer up there on the cliff with his musical glasses and his stuffed fishes and his Indian music records daaaa-ooaheeaaaa-ooeeaaaaaah. Ha! I know all about him."

David took a step toward Benino and said, "And what would *you* know about the musical glasses and the sexy music?"

And Benino stepped toward David and said quickly, "I went there *once*, only *once*, years ago. You cannot prove I went there—"

"And Matthews converted you? Put the finger on you?"

"What do you say?" Smiling, Benino turned truculently to Maddalena, as if to display his forbearance. To David he said, "Nothing." Benino seemed to be standing at attention, his legs together, his head gently, gracefully tilted.

"Then what's your proof? Who *knows* about Matthews?"

"*I,*" said Benino in a hushed voice, "am a *man:* And that is more than I can say for certain other people."

In the instant, such a dense sequence of debate passed on through David's mind that the action of seeming to move at Benino, and then Benino's premature action of applying a lifesaver's defense to pull David's elbow across and David around so he could be pinioned from behind, happened very slowly. David felt he had chosen to provoke this premature absurd defense; and he didn't doubt that he had *let* himself be pinioned. So be it: let Benino make himself ridiculous, yet let him be his idea of himself; let him sense that the kissing on the beach had been a failure, yet let him think the whole thing his secret with Ellen; above all, let there be at last for David himself a silly giving-in.

He tried to burst forward, and Benino tightened the embrace. They were about the same height, David taller; Benino's breath blew under David's right ear.

"Stop," cried Ellen, "this is nonsense." And as she uttered the words, and a surprised fixity of alarm and excitement touched her face, Benino let go; and to finish Benino properly, David whirled and stood apparently ready to punch, hoping Benino would now do what, now, he perfectly did: make a bad pretense of calling it all off; shrugging pugilistically; even offering his hand.

Dancing, down the wharf? A combo from Napoli? A café near the church for a beer? A ride to the other side of the island in the car of Benino's pal Franco?

David did not at first doubt that he had let himself be pinioned. But when he went on to wonder if he could have stopped it, he found he didn't care. So the choice of passiveness was working.

"*Grazie,*" said Benino.

"*Benvenuto,*" David said.

"You mean '*Prego,*'" Ellen murmured.

"I mean '*Benvenuto,*'" said David.

Ellen said goodnight, they'd go on back to the hotel; Ellen squeezed him as they walked away from the lights of the little square.

"You could have knocked him down. I felt that."

Had he wanted her to think he could? All he recalled was this renewed wish to be passive, to let Benino think whatever he wanted to think.

"It's irrelevant whether I could have or not." David stopped and gave her a stupid, arch, tender look, calculated but genuine. And the returning archness of Ellen's smile seemed for a second the headiest come-on from the most edibly unknown and yielding tart. Had he put that strangeness into her? caused it?

Ellen was speaking quietly about Benino. "A sweet ass, really, such a fool. And not cool, is he?" Then, "I wish we could go to Matthews' villa."

They walked through the gently uphill turning into a new radius of streetlight. They were getting near the hotel. No word now nothing nor not nor now—no radio, no speeches, no conversations telephonic, homeophonic, stereophonic, radiophonic, or just plain phonic, nor a diaphragm either (he could swear she had taken it out, for she had had that plastic disc container with her and a cake of Pears soap when she came back from the bathroom before she dressed for dinner —she must surely have taken it out), nor any turning tempting word.

As they came to the Vespa taxi with its canopy over the two-wheeled rear, Ellen said nothing, and David asked in Italian for Matthews' villa, forgetting to explain how to get there, and the old man, who had been waiting drowsily, nodded and stepped down once, twice, three times hard to start the little high-pitched engine that sounded like an outboard.

Then they were racing round corners and up cool alleys, taking the route Matthews must take—in any case not the way either Ellen or David had gone today. And finally—it had been only a few minutes—the new-paved narrow road had reached a high level; and feeling a breeze and an openness, and looking into the starry dark to the right, David knew he was looking toward the sea.

VII

Matthews had left two big binnacle lights on in his living room, and instructions about drinks and which bedroom to use; and altogether David felt, as he examined a mounted fish and then the musical glasses in their enclosed mahogany tray (there were twenty-six) and stared out the picture window to the left to see a tiny moving light in the cemetery, that Matthews had known they were coming, had even made them come. A set of dynamic tension springs hung from a standing lamp, several copies of *Playboy* were piled on a table, on top of them a great cut-glass ashtray with N. Y. A. C. in blue across the well.

David had brought a glass of water and tried to play a scale on the glasses, running his finger around the edges. Water here acts like a resin on a bow. He resisted the desire to tell Ellen about the famous woman who had performed on glasses like these in the eighteenth century. After decades of acclaim and seeming centuries immersed in the flowing pellucid solitude of that weird musical ether, her nerves reached off into some new tingling disarray and in a state of physical and emotional collapse, she had to give up the glasses, give up almost everything. Marianne Davies. David wouldn't tell Ellen; for Ellen had heard enough from him. When she went up, and called to him to come, it might have been the first—no, say the *second*—time between them. Though the little act a while ago had made her smile back at him a tart's smile, naively self-conscious, he thought that even though this strangeness was a kind of confection of his, he was facing her for the first time again.

Better to be with someone. Surrounded by the archipelago of the recent and distant past, islands of moments near but unattached. Better to be with someone if this archipelago persisted in the poor mind. The only time he had told Ellen about this feeling, she had said, "Oh it's all linked up if you could only remember properly; don't make such a big thing out of it."

In the bare white room Ellen stood waiting, her hand held out toward the bed to call his attention to the fact that Matthews had turned back the corner of the sheet. (Now, how did David know that Matthews had done it and not Ellen?) On the bedtable were a copy of *Time*, the Blue Guide *Southern Italy*, and a Gideon Bible taken from the Baltimore Central YMCA. On the Bible lay a slip of paper: "Sleep well. P.M."

As David unzipped the back of her dress, Ellen said, "I wonder if he *is*."

Ellen turned and hugged him, and he went on undoing her. He found her newly unfamiliar; found known attributes now excised from her known form. Less familiar, she was more close.

He was tired of trying to discover Ellen, tired of trying to find out why she could never learn to get the radio dial right on the band, why she took brown sugar in coffee, why. . . . You can be warmer if you want, you can be different if you want; but you can't reason, you have to want. Then he would be lost: For if it was wanting, not planning, if it was pulse, not calculation, then what she called wanting was plain accident.

"David."

"Don't say a thing." He switched off the lamp on the bed-table.

For a long time he was afraid that the closer he came to the moment he'd stop kissing her, the less he'd be aware of her body and shape, her actual stomach and hips and hair. And he knew he might lose her.

But in his dream—and it *was* a kind of dream, in which words displaced the received details of Ellen's presence—a foolish thing now occurred. And he loved Ellen for it, as if she were responsible.

Seeing a dark, lone hair lost on the pillow by Ellen's shoulder, he forgot her: Seeing the hair in a dash of moonlight, seeing the color in the hair, in the single hair, David lost sight and sense and name of Ellen and, drawn from the indefinite asking of each surface and each join, he kept his eye on that hair (hers? *yes*) and kept, kept, gave . . . to the exact asking, and neglected both asking and Ellen, and even though in the easy endlessness of simple moving, he kissed her cheek (or rather put his mouth there, even though he thought he had stopped kissing her), he kept, kept, kept his eye on the hair, the hair, and this was everything he thought of: For she's here and there and far and near and more or less and away and will, power the silly dark-brown hair, she will power and he will power and it will power and here and there and away, lie with me, lie with me, *ecco, ecco,* vanishing Ellen, vanillan, strawbellan, frosting, pistachigo frost, only darkness, know thyself and die young, forget thyself and funny the hair, will, away.

Later, he was awake. He watched her face, the break in the solitary mouth, the topographical immensity of the face from a close angle. He feared to touch her, for warm shadows lay about her like a charm, and her breath was the breath of wind in a well.

The night before, he had started to end the story about Sindbad but then—for in his absorption he was slow-witted— he had seen where it would end—the interpretation Ellen would put on it. And so he had become vague and sleepy, and he had said that one day Sindbad and his new wife smuggled themselves onto a ship and got away from the island. But as he had stopped, he had realized that, quite apart from his intentional distortion of the tale, he had made one unwitting mistake. For it was a *country* Sindbad had come to, not an island.

Now David moved again, but easily, toward sleep—and Ellen had not woken—moved toward sleep and Ellen; and the story told itself. And Sindbad's wife died. And he was informed that by the custom of that country he must be buried alive with his dead wife, the strange, foreign wife native to this strange country he had happened to come to. Then indeed what had been promised came to pass: Sindbad was lowered after his wife's body into the great funerary well, and then above him, over the mouth, a great stone lid was placed. Alone in the dark, and for the next few days kept alive among the bones and carrion only by seven loaves and a jug of water, Sindbad waited for the weakness of death. Down that charnel well he found himself trapped in a darkness so foul with rotting shapes that his nausea kept him from being afraid. But then, then, suddenly, before a week had passed, another funeral gave him new fearful chance for life. When a woman was lowered after her dead husband, Sindbad hit her on the head and took her bread and water. And before long Sindbad saw a star at the end of what seemed a long passage. This was in fact a tunnel, and Sindbad resolved to try it. Having plundered the dead of gems and other riches, he now made his way toward that star he had seen at the tunnel's end, alert for the beasts that were necriorous frequenters there, and finally (yes? was it like this?) Sindbad came out into the night, and from the foot of the mountain through which the tunnel had taken him, he looked down upon the whispering sea.

And next day, next day, next day Sindbad got aboard (how did he get aboard?) a passing vessel; and, calling himself a Bagdad merchant (which he was), though hiding his recent connubial identity lest any of the ship's company be citizens of that land and observant of its customs, Sindbad was taken home.

Words . . . "The hour became her husband and my bride."

Almost day? Dark. He felt her rise on an elbow. He knew she was gazing on him. As she rolled over and stood up, he opened his eyes just a quiver to see. Ellen stretched her arms hard out above her, turning her cheek onto her right shoulder and bending at the waist sideways. Her look about the room was a savoring, mental yawn, a wonderful idleness. Now she stretched again and, madly, swayed her behind as if she were dancing. Then Eurynome, having risen from the tossed chaotic bed, thought better of whatever it was she had thought of getting up for and, stepping backward, slowly sat down again. She looked back at David, who closed his eyes in time. She eased back down beside him quietly and then with a slight settling wiggle of her body she got into touch with David, shoulder, arm, thigh, calf, foot.

After a while, David looked at her.

Ellen slept.

« n »

the black box

These last few hours I feel parentheses—or "curves," as they ought to be called—enclosing what I think and say. In some macabre way my own ingenuity and force have caused these parenthetical occlusions. I gave David his independent existence; I guess I'm a fool to expect him to let me have my say. Mind you, I do seem able still to keep him on the job, keep him homing back to our little stateroom.

Doubtless my—just now I find the pronominal diphthong difficult to say—my apparent lack of hold on David is due to my creative blood in him. Surely his surly caprices come ultimately from my own controlling hand. But I'd have sworn his use of two points of view so as to pull back into his own midway through six was not in the first original master plan. Ditto for some curious alterations in Ellen's voice and that field of his reveries in which she moves: *Indeed* (!) David has smuggled a *heroine* into this great stream of remembrance that nears its end.

DB takes my breath away. Whenever I talk right *to* him I feel these parentheses closing me, and I feel some millennial biovegetable metamorphosis identifying me with David.

(All right for *you,* Davey B. Have you ever thought what'd happen if I left you? If the salt lost its savior—if the mad world's heterogenii were to be left unordered and unlaid by our homogenius? Remember the psychic federation to insure the planet against nuclear loss? You regulate me to the status of a parenthesis! *Yes you do!* All right; *don't* listen.)

David unlocks his stateroom door and pushes it in. He crosses the threshold and he stops. He scarcely credits what he thinks he must be seeing. (You *asked* for it, DB!)

Considering how small the stateroom is and thus how short the distance between where David stands and what he is looking at, the several seconds during which he is arrested seem minutes. He ought to be seeing on the stateroom table a great . . . he ought to be seeing on the table his East Lite Box-File (with Lockspring). *But he is not seeing it.* Rather, he is seeing—and he feels right away he knows what it is— he is seeing what the smuggler-man promised. A Bible? Black, magisterial, stipple-grained imitation morocco and, shining across the top, these gilt-tooled letters: HOLY BIBLE.

David moves cautiously to the table. Inspecting the Bible now, he sees that the gilt letters lie within the upper width of a rectangle blind-tooled framelike on the cover.

"God! Where is it! My East—!" He dives for the space under the lower bunk. There he finds only the suitcase Ellen left there. Didn't the man explain once what a smuggler's Bible was, or . . . doesn't David seem to know almost in- stinctively what a smuggler's Bible is? "I knew I'd end up using the smuggler's Bible."

A thin ornate brass tongue clasps the book shut. Is this the man's moist-grinned joke—to take the East Lite Box-File and leave as a present a cumbersome antiquarian relic? On this ship the East Lite Box-File could get taken, stolen, jettisoned as easily as a man could throw himself overboard. The man's card! But David threw it away, in fact overboard. Maybe a clue inside. A key? David lifts the Bible; maybe it's a real Bible; David finds no key underneath. Low and querulous, David says, "My East Lite Box-File"—then whimpers as an afterthought, "with Lockspring."

(I say! Can you see . . .?) In the closet? Nope. On the beds someplace? Ellen's (slatternly) clippings stick out from under her pillow—a German caption—more fashion, more thefts from the ship's library. (But Mister Dear, why not look *inside* the . . . holy . . . Bible . . .? Yuk, yuk!)

(Break the classssssp!) David inserts the shaft of his seven-level screwdriver between the clasp and the gilt edge (which he now sees only simulates pages). The clasp gives, bends; and the tip of the tongue tears from its catch.

A smuggler's Bible is just a box? Yes. David recalls that the man said something about smuggling small objects of value—gems, drugs, watches, tea. (How about a collation of exquisite glass eyes?) In the box (in the box seven days old) the East Lite Box-File has been fitted, and so neatly there's a bare eighth of an inch to spare.

On it lies a pair of keys. Why two? One extra for safety's sake? But the clasp had to be broken! One couldn't get the key without . . . . Inside the Bible's cover is pasted a bookseller's label identifying the article: "A Smuggler's Bible. Used by smugglers on both sides of the Atlantic in the early nineteenth century to conceal small objects of value. Actually a mere box, this 'Bible' could be used to contain any assortment of goods the smuggler could get into it. ca 1820 (?)." Peter St. John referred to one once, but he didn't know very much. Why put the keys inside?

Oh God! The ship is in by now. Le Havre.

(Yesterday David found out the voyage was going to take *eight* days; he'd thought seven. Yuk yuk!) London the eighth day; Le Havre the seventh; Cobh yesterday.

Find the man . . . . *Smuggling!* (Oh, lovely baby; maybe I've dogged you *to* it, but sure you can lead a lad to a manger of hay but you can't make him—sweetheart, I've made you ruler over seven, eight memories; I'll make you ruler over nine, ten, eleven!) David puts the smuggler's Bible into the closet.

"Ellen!" (Wouldn't she, the bitch, come *now!*)

"Stop loving yourself in the mirror, David." (David, did you know that according to Irenaeus the Gnostics believed that the Ogdoad—the double quaternity—was represented by Sophia? Eight? *Listen: eight!*) (Ellen is a disturbing influence, I swear!) (Hear her now . . .) "You're my little projector." "Cut it out, Ellen." "I love you." (The bitch holds out six and seven in a manila folder, and David looks at the folder.) "I was trying for the special essence of each of the people I was projecting into." "I love you. They're wonderful." "And I catch the essence of each?" "They're *so* good!" "The style varies, depending what field I'm (yuk yuk) in." "Your style is really original." "In which memory?" "All through. You're consistent." "But Ellen, I meant in these memories to get the tone of each person—even of *myself* in the seventh—that was the point of each projection." "The *point* of each pro-*jeck*-shun, dahhling?" (Bitch!) "Be serious, Ellen." "Can't you be silly at the same time?" "No: In each part I got a special style proper to the person I was projecting into." "I didn't see *that*. But I think your style's marvelous."

"But Ellen, the style's different in each memory." "Why does it *have* to be?" "I explained that." "I just think it's lovely." "The way my style adapts . . . ?" "The style, period." *"The style?"* "Your constant, consistent, inimitable style!" "It doesn't change?" "Of course it doesn't. It's *you*. You never really fall out of it." "No: Please, don't you see? The memories . . . ." "For Pete's sake, as your mother would say, you *have* a *style!*" "Not *one!*" "Yes." "God, I've failed! You mean I've failed?" "Why should it be different in each part?" "I explained that; surely I—" He has to get away, to find the smuggler-man. "David, dear, how did you get off on your project?" "Off on? The old man in Marylebone Public Library my first trip abroad." Away, away, away, out the door, down the passage, up and out.

But pushing the door David feels God the KAAAAAASH explosion of breakage, a jar a jar a jar(!)—he recalls bumping into his father so to speak as one pushed the kitchen door in and the other pushed it out—"Aiee, aiee! Gott, Gott, Gott, Gott!" The bottom edge of the door, now continuing inward, sweeps the fragments, and the great blond zoologist stares down at David with an enormous private gobbling grin topped by a frieze of frowning wrinkles in the heavy forehead—all David sees on the white tile is water and glass— what on earth was the guy doing in the jar? Away, away, away, away, away!

Ah, good, finally. Le Havre. The plump little shipboard band sends "Auf Wiedersehen" over the pier; across the pier a young billboard painter on a scaffolding four stories high sways hips in time, looking back over his shoulder to make sure the college girls on the starboard side are enjoying him. Then the rhythm of his shimmy is subverted by the slower swing of the plank, and as the plank suddenly swings away from the building and sharply the girls at the rail sing "Ooooooooooooooooooooooo!"—for the painter has had to "bump" to save himself—he regains his footing and, chastened, resumes his performance. The ship is backing, the pier is moving; and there on the pier is the smuggler-man, big and blond, staring up at David. And now, for the benefit of two Havre constables, he calls up, "Have you got the diamonds? *Les diamants sont-ils cachés?*" David looks away embarrassed. Down the rail stand two blond stewards, and

the chief steward, and a reddish-blond man in a dark-blue
T-shirt that, as he turns toward David, David sees to be
emblazoned "Igor." But David has wanted to ask the smug-
gling-man something, a universe of things. He is calling
David. "Hey, should have stuck around last night; I told
that kid the story of the smuggler who has to keep running
from frontier to frontier because he's trapped on a tiny
continent of tiny-tiny nations, and he's on the lam from
border to—" The man has to stop, for he is laughing at the
idea or at some vision; and now, as David, tongue-tied, tries
to conjure up a few questions to ask, the smuggler-man turns,
laughing silently and shaking his head. He follows a porter
down the pier.

But a universe of questions! Ah . . . sure: Matthews
smuggled himself along as a certain version of *invertito* . . .
just as Franklin Benjamin sneaked himself along as Terri's
heterosexual bethrothed when he'd no intention of ever
lifting the verbal veil that hung sacred and bridal between
them . . . and you brought aboard this old box, this smuggler's Bible, pretending you merely meant to use it *playfully*
to hold the manuscripts.

A whiff of (duty-free!) Mitsouko and out of the corner
of David's eye the blue of Igor's shirt, and . . . . ". . . tripped
over the threshold of the stable and said, 'Jesus Christ!' "

"David. Darling. Here you are."

Away, away, away, away. Back to the seventh memory
(Chronicles 7—yuk yuk). To the stateroom. Decides David
to eliminate "NP," for Duke's pedantic shortening of neuro-
psychiatric left the wrong impression—he was a man, not
some monster or god of glibness. And delete "qr," an abbreviation St. John would never use for "quire." The stateroom at last. (We gave Ellen the slip, eh?)

(David, do not forget the black box—i.e., the smuggler's
Bible—and do not forget the smuggler-man's words. You
might try writing . . . this:) David sits and begins to scribble.
(But . . . I don't know what's in his mind; but this is impossible, but it's happened; but didn't I make him? didn't I invent
him?) (write this: Yes, he's writing it, he's even anticipating
my thought, oh you mad Davey here we go again aiee again—
Niagara Falls killed seven barrelers, but you and I are
together, boy, together—we're going to make Grand Canyon,

Old Faithful, Golden Gate, Gotham Skyscrapers, California Sequoias, Niagara, and Mount Rushmore look ordinary—we will make the *eighth* wonder of the New World, the ninth, the tenth ooooooooooooooo, why *ever* finish?! *That's* it, and wonders not just of our parodic America but *round the world* ooooooooooo *that's* it, DB, a memo:)

The smuggler hides or disguises his treasure in order to get it across frontier, past customs, duties; if he did not, he would (a) lose it altogether or (b) pay duty and thus not make so much out of it. If caught, i.e., e.g., if at the frontier—or, say, at three-mile limit—his secrecy is seen through, he may be arrested, fined, imprisoned. Disguising his treasure gives him—or at least saves him at least temporarily from losing—his freedom. Smuggler's Bible like East Lite Box-File with Lockspring.

(Wait, David, I have more. If you dun a smuggler . . . DB I've more. Oh please DB! DBDBDBDBDB!) David tears up paper. (Oh! You memorized it?!) David is saying, "The voice, the voice inside me, how terrible the voice inside!" And he thinks of that day in England in November, 1960, just before he and Ellen sailed for New (yuk!): "How insubstantial the causes of all this . . . the old man in Marylebone Public Library, near Baker Street, London W.1." Ellen enters. "I had to *chase* you! You were talking to yourself." (But my darling dear, you look so queer, Johnny I hardly knew you.) "Damn folksingers next door." "David, I don't hear anything." Singing "The Drinkin' Gourd" and "Johnny I Hardly Knew You." I have to revise seven. (Ellen wanted you to give up all this, but of course, Davey, my decision had been taken, and Lethe's dark breezes were bound for you, Davey, and you knew it, and you knew it was necessary, and you were proud of your will, your clean, hard, good, clear will, will to ride that underground river knowing somehow you'd sometime come up in a new, new world . . . !) (Sssssssst! Now why'd you have to go and change it? Why alter VII from what it was? Was it not my militant creativity gave you a life you now dare claim your own? I'm your *parent*, not some second-class parenthesis. Or (kaa-kaa) I am in any case and in a sense an *avuncular* parent, not (as you and Ellen in your different conceptions imagine) your (yuk-yuk) auntiethesis. Deny *me*, and you deny a world of order, you disorder all our mandala'd experience, you ungather all our quires, desecrate our sortilege, isolate and rent separately (selfish clot) the rooms of the flat we were to share; you now set loose the islands after we've got them rendez-vous'd in a dear bathtub flotilla. Why'd you alter the sequence? Why insist in these letters on crass chronology? And why now must you include your *own* letter (!) that came back because of insufficient postage? And why oh why leave the fugal strategy unfulfilled? Oh Davey dear, I saw this, I *conceived* this stream of remembrance—

Oh Davey dear, you look so queer,
Oh Davey I hardly knew you.

conceived this stream of recollection as a source of new, comiopathic wonder-magic to drug if not cure the orphaned, widowed, impure, and heavy-laden who stop to sip. Hey, let's wear matching captain's caps like smuggler-man! What's your cap size? Lemme in! Yet I feel I *am* in. Lemme *go!* Draw the felt off the crystal balls of your conscious—yet I fear I may be *in those balls*—not a scrier but one of the descried. And you act like I'm a mere component part to be turned on or off, screwed tight or loose. OK if I am in the end (yuk-yuk) incorporated in you . . . then buddy watch out! We planned forty letters exquisitely shuffled to restore the truth. I—wi—OK, go ahead and include that *frightful* letter that got returned, go ahead . . . you . . . shshshshellfish!)

VII

SYMPTOMS OF FUGUE, OR HOW DAVID IN A SENSE FAKED AMNESIA, AND WHAT HAPPENED

British Museum Reading Room
24 Sept.

Dear DB (if that's not premature),

Recent as our acquaintance—dare I say *friendship*—is, I found your leavetaking this A.M. unAmerican to say the least. You seemed to snap shut as soon as I said Fargo and Brooklyn Heights. (Believe me, I don't know anything about Brooklyn Heights. Nor about you either.) And then you had to get away, I felt that. (Which reminds me: I had a real sick but very great young religion instructor my sophomore year who said that that was the point about Christ—he had to get away. Once this prof confessed to me he'd stolen the gag —if it is a gag—from a California history prof, some guy named I think Dutch or Duke or Doc.) Well, this A.M. I confess I followed you, for you'd been smiling at me with a crazy stiffness as if I'd pained you, and I thought you'd gone really tilted. After I mentioned Fargo and the Heights and my uncle the art historian who knew the painter Billy Tell in London years ago, you suddenly said you'd forgotten you had to meet your wife to buy her a bathrobe at Galeries Lafayette in Regent Street (I know the place, that's where I bought my Welsh Mary her birthday dress); and I recall now that just before I brought up Fargo and the Heights and my uncle the expert on pop art, I said do you know that Boston U. grad student who's working on Wenceslaus Hollar's engravings at the BM and plays soccer weekends for the Corinthian Casuals. Then you said very intensely and quietly, "Did you ever study the word 'coincidence'? Let's make an absolutely new start, unconnected." And then it was that I mentioned Fargo and the Heights and my uncle Theodore in Monterey. Well, when you said unconvincingly that you had to meet your wife, I decided I'd trail you. I was worried about you. You got to Oxford Circus tube station, looked over your shoulder, bought a *Standard* and a *New Statesman,* sprinted right at me without seeing me, then hopped a number eight bus toward Marble Arch—you barely landed a toe on the platform and a hand on the pole, and in your other hand the *Standard* and *Statesman* were like a flag for a second till you found your footing. I thought we'd been conversing on friendly terms. But then you cut out, seemingly because you were upset. And there was I planning to give you a two-hour peripatetic course on the aesthetic basis of the Gibbs steeple—Gibbs, as I told you, is my D.Phil. at the Courtauld Institute, whose building, by the way, is one of the perfect things in the West End. Anyway, was it my mention of Fargo and Brooklyn Heights that unsettled you? Or did I bug you with my worries about marrying this Welsh gal Mary? Aren't I honoring you with these private, sub-marital matters?!

Today, when I phoned, your wife said you'd had a slight shock—what is this, English understatement?!—and she said you weren't yourself. She said I might drop you a line. I felt like saying, "Where the hell is he?" But instead, I said I was sorry not to catch you, and hung up feeling like a kid who's been told by his pal's older sister (or mother) that the pal can't come out to play stoop ball today. (Did you ever play stoop ball? There was I, at the Little Red School House, then Horace Mann, playing stoop ball for years while you were probably doing the same across the East River.) But look: During the three long walks we've had—listening to me tell you about James Gibbs, and you tell me about the problem of whether Nell Gwynne really used that bathtub in the mansion in Waterlow Park (you're hepped on Highgate!), and then lounging around those elegant doomed squares—Oxford and Cambridge—where the high Georgians are going to come down—all in all, I thought we got along. You were a bit muttery, but so what? "Total recall," you said half under your breath; "I have total recall, what good is it?" I wrote into my diary a description of you. Sartre, doesn't he say keeping a diary is dangerous? Because you force the truth.

305

Look, I hope you're OK, but I'm afraid I said something. I'm not actually such a bad guy. Well, DB, I'm heading south for a few days. *Ciao, bon appetit,* and see you. Did I bug you talking about Mary? Hope not. Yours, Paul Schoonover.

N. Y. A. C. Here I come.
Sept. 23

Dear Dave,

Remember me? Phil Matthews? Department of "You-Said-Look-Me-Up." That afternoon and the next morning (on the island) you didn't look like you were speaking straight *to* me, but you said this and that about my going some place where I didn't have to make such an enterprise of living, and you gave me those addresses to write—and now I just want to tell you I decided to leave the island—said to myself, now there go two kids who know where they're going whether it's going to be London or New York or even Antioch—*you* don't know, you might end up there—and they're just plain happy, I said to myself. So I did a do-it-yourself psychoanalysis on myself and I jotted down a memoranda saying: "Project for the coming year, get an apartment in Nueva York and sink some money in a tourist agency."

Guess we'll meet up. Can't drop in in London, but see you "when." (Do you know the Columbia Club near Lancaster Gate? It's for U. S. armed servicemen.) I didn't catch what it was you were doing in London. Studying abroad, I suppose. Thanks for the advice, though you probably are amazed to know you gave me, your *elder,* advice, or maybe you just don't recall saying to me and I quote, "Many guys don't have roots in a *place,* what they got to do is drop a plumb bob down into theirselves to find out where their inside roots grow, like they were a pit and they got to find a center of gravity." (Well, Dave you sure are GRAVE!!!!!!!!) I bet you don't even remember talking like that, I guess words come pretty easy to you. Well, maybe I was too busy talking, to let you in, and when you started in, *you* were milling over what *I* said. Well, it was a pleasure to meet you and Ellie, and thanks. Let you in on a secret. I spent that night in the cemetery. I sometimes take a flashlight down in the middle of the night, and that night you and Ellen used the villa I stayed down by Marjean's plot for quite a while, at least till two; then I came on up, but didn't want to disturb you, and hauled open the garage door and drove out, and drove round the island till it was a decent time to come back and cook your breakfast. Boy, you looked rough and Ellie looked full of the Lord's joy—a quick dip would have washed the sand out of your eyes! Anyhow I got the message, and this was one reason—I can't explain it—one reason I knew I had to head for the old country. Dave, you'll always reach me at the New York A. C. even after I move into my own place. Drop me a line if and when you hit town. Best regards to Ellie. (Last time I spoke to her—it was private out on the bluff in the sun while you were tuning the musical glasses—she said you'd love a letter from me.)

> Remember
> Your
> Friend,
> Philip S. Matthews

P.S. I have been tooling round Naples Bay with a Republicans-for-Kennedy sticker on the windshield of the Chris-Craft! Will be home for Election Day!

Office of the Director
Amalgamated Inter-Federo-Unities, Ltd.
TIME-LIFE Building
New York, New York
September 24, 1960

Dr. David Brooke, Ph.D.
7½ Harrowby Street
London W.1
England

Dear Dr. Brooke:
This organization is pleased to note receipt of credentials, including taped recommendation sent under separate cover by our former Lingo-Historiographic Associate, Prof. Roland (Duke) Amerchrome. Unfortunately consideration for the post of Assistant Rhetorical Liaison for the Permanent Political Committee cannot proceed until this office receives in octuplicate your Religion-Arts-and-Crafts Informa-

tional FOLDER. This office would appreciate your remitting said Informational FOLDER relatively soon.

Yours very sincerely,
(Mrs.) Mary Joseph
For the Vice-Director

Oxon.
26 Sept.

Dear D.,

We have, of course, heard from Ellen about your illness. Amnesia?

Please forgive me if I find myself unable to conceive that I am not still some figure in your recollection, some sartorially nefarious pilgrim now and then coming into view walking through the customarily bewitched country of your imagination. While I should like to find words for my sentiments and my apprehensiveness over your condition, I suspect the best letter I can write—curiously, the best even in the message it addresses to your strange and temporary malaise—is the one I would have written anyway.

We could have broached the two matters I had in mind when I came down to the BM Manuscript Room yesterday and today, the two days I allotted to the end of my summer timetable. But because of you we couldn't meet, and I now write (as usual, in haste) hoping neither your doctors nor your wife veto the transmission of this note. By the way, can it be that your mental distraction—no doubt somewhat hysterically identified by Ellen as some species of amnesia—is in part a consequence of inadequate planning? You remember —excuse me, I'm not trying to be witty—you recall the paleographic & genealogical cruces in the Oakes Papers? Those were cruces you might have been careful enough to spot early on; instead you risked some premature (albeit lively) inferences. You always knew it was risky seeing in Senator Oakes' letter of 1849(?) the influence of Hugh of Folieto— the four books of life, written, of course, in Paradise, in the Desert, in the Temple, and from All Eternity, as I remember. What in fact did you ever do with the Oakes material? I recall that shortly before I left Indian Farm, the Oakes work had caused you to be so chaotically engrossed and nervous that, in the words of Duke Amerchrome, you couldn't tell the Son from the Holy Ghost. (Amerchrome: that florid

308

faun lording an exotic Colonial landskip!) But Ellen did say she felt maybe you'd overdone things.

The two matters (*vide supra*) are these: (a) Thornton & Sinclair; (b) Wanda.

There is the most unheard-of, incredibly unexpected connection between Thornton and Sinclair. Do you know a very tightly rolled American named Thomas Fargo? He's been spending the academic season at Christ Church for several years now, and at last looks like working out a viable D.Phil. thesis. Doesn't say much, reminds one of a fresh recruit to the Foreign Office who drops menacing hints about the "movements" in Knightsbridge and Marylebone of the Yugoslav cocktail attachés. But I daresay Fargo is sitting on something solid re: T&S. The cookie crumbles into seven chronological parts. All F. divulges is this: (1) Some years ago Goodspeed's in Boston are offered a nineteenth-century American painting, ostensibly early nineteenth, ostensibly Thornton (in fact right away identified as T. by one of the young men there); the person who brings in the painting is a monk (or so dressed)—a darkly tanned, tall, skeletal monk habited in green and in fact hooded rather fully, drapedly, even menacingly. "Unh? Unh?" he is heard to grunt. (2) This monk leaves the painting at Goodspeed's for appraisal; in the backing Goodspeed's find a letter (ostensibly authentic) dated 1777, from a British grenadier to a fellow-soldier making some remarkable claim (so F. *says*) re: Burgoyne's motives; the monk returns, hears the appraisal, stares stonily at the letter (which F. will argue the monk *knew* was hidden in the backing), says Goodspeed's can have the painting free and he will hold onto the letter—in fact is reported to have said in guttural tones, "The Kingdom is like a treasure hidden in a field. Well, I reckon you'll remember *this* baby, eh? [i.e., the letter] *This* ought to make an M.A. thesis for some kid, unh? Young America calls in unison, 'M.A. us.'" (3) Fargo finds (and I suspect that in the chronology of his own hunt this came first) a letter dated 1834 in a volume of BM tracts (he wouldn't say which)—a letter quite unrelated to the tracts, in fact just stuck in among them—a letter from Rose Thornton to Horatio Sinclair (then sojourning in England) offering him the very painting now in question; she needed the money; she had known Sinclair for some time, especially in connection with certain New England abolitionist activities. (4) In the archives of a London World

Spiritualist splinter group (The Marylebone Poly-Federo-Unifists) F. finds a typed copy of a paper purportedly all but disintegrated at time of transcription, in which our Horatio Sinclair agrees to bequeath his collection of books, manuscripts, and paintings intact as the Sinclair Freedom Library, on condition the MPFU ally themselves with his own New England off-shoot of Garrison's movement. (Fargo doesn't know my "Note" on Sinclair, and, as I bide my time, I'll not disabuse him.) (5) This summer at Walpole, N. H., F. finds a brief account of an illegitimate son of Rose Thornton, a rather backward, luckless chap named Jesse: when Rose died in 1834, Sinclair took the boy in as his foster son: Jesse was devoted to Sinclair, though he knew he wasn't his real father; but Jesse's world seems to have fallen to bits when H. S., abandoning Garrison's abolitionism (instant emancipation, immediate enfranchisement), took up the Lang Seminary Group's "gradual emancipation, immediately begun"; indeed, a few months later H. S. began to support Freesoilism; the young man, for whom Sinclair's never-disguised foster-paternity had been emotionally quite sufficient, left Walpole and, announcing he would search for his real father, set off west. (6) In St. Louis Fargo has already found evidence that one B. J. Thaddeus claimed the painter Thornton as his grandfather (though F. won't divulge more than that). (7) And in South Berwick, Maine, where Thornton's wife and remaining children continued to live after he and Rose ran off, there is an ancient document testifying to a local—and perhaps apocryphal—tale that between the man and his daughter Rose there was incest. What Fargo may make out of all this, I don't know: doubtless some extraordinary speculation which his tutor will then ask him to hedge. What fascinates me is this absolutely clear link between two figures on whom I already had something. If I had the time at the moment I'd do a somewhat longer note presenting the relationship in what I take to be its full simplicity.

Long- and broken-windedly I come to *b:* Wanda. You and Ellen seemed to go off to Greece and Italy too soon for us to have a talk about Wanda. She answers my infrequent letters so quickly and copiously I confess I wonder . . . Anselin and I fly out to Berkeley tomorrow for the beginning of term. We may stop in New York for a day or two, I don't know. I do wish that when you and Ellen get "home"

310

you'd have Wanda for dinner or meet her. Try to find out how she is, and send me a report. I confess I often dream of the two of us; and the great Viking boat we're in is, strangely, you. And we are heading west out a high-walled fjord soundlessly, and Wanda is soundlessly talking to me and I am ignoring her and thinking of the Gulf Stream waters we'll soon be in. Isn't that odd? After all the listening *I* did! Happy days and lonely nights are now happy days and happy nights. A man needs his work and his books around him, and he needs his wife.

David, I've said so little about you. But what could I say? Your letter last week may in fact make a fitting prelude to your present state as described by Ellen. I think I can hazard the supposition that you take the wrong things far too seriously. Life is essentially simple. A man needs to work. To work, he must wear blinkers. The quasimetaphysical ponderings that you seem to have been preoccupied with for so long yield few satisfying answers, and these ponderings have unbalanced you. People are not at bottom riddles. I fear you are infected with this almost absurd contemporary predilection for bewailing what my dear old man here in Oxford (my late confessor) in another context called "the dark apartness." He, in point of fact, meant Hell—with a capital *H*, for he wasn't about to allow Sartre's very Franco-psychological hell. As for your secular and unjustified translation—"the dark apartness" of *humans* one from another—I would argue that you'd do well (a) to expect not quite so much response from others, and (b) to credit what Frost says somewhere (?):

> So Brad McLaughlin mingled reckless talk
> Of heavenly stars with hugger-mugger farming,
> Till having failed at hugger-mugger farming,
> He burned his house down for the fire insurance
> And spent the proceeds on a telescope
> To satisfy a life-long curiosity
> About our place among the infinities.

Why, dear boy, is it vital to gain what you term "community" —community with friends, with foreigners, with "other minds" (as you say), with "America," with the past . . . ? And as for sex, Sirrah, isn't it after all a biological function? (Must say I am appalled at your weird theories concerning

311

the symbolism of genital ingress and retraction—e.g., your certainly wrong-headed thesis that the in-and-out "cycle" "embodies" all the seminal but confining paradoxes within which we live." Anselin takes a much more "understanding" view of your theorizing, though she is understandably shy about discussing it.) I believe you've always tried both too hard and yet not hard enough to "know" people, and at times you seemed to me a sort of pathological "news" gatherer busy missing the point. Have a break. Ring a change or two. Sit down and read some William Golding. (*Lord of the Flies* is the new *Catcher in the Rye*.)

I only hope *I* had no "part" in your present malaise: Ellen wrote that you had called me a myth.

Well, it seems as if, faced with the apparent fact of your mental depression, I've done nothing but speak of myself. Yet do believe that I was, in everything I said, concerned for you—for your prospects and, in fact, your retrospects. I wish I could see you both before we fly to Cal.

A. sends love.

Yours always—and in haste—
H.

28 Sept.

Dear DB,

Rang you up again, but your wife said you were sick, insisted I write, not call. When I can persuade myself I'm not the key figure in the world, I do devote a minute here and there to figuring what's with you. Didn't you murmur something very fast about chain letters that hadn't come back to you; and about the connection between the chain letters and a mystery crash-project you're thinking of beginning; and about how you had total recall of people's words but that it was your peculiar fate to be unable to concentrate on a person talking to you until after the person was done and had gone away? Or did I imagine I heard all that? *Ex post facto* total recall, or something? Well now today your wife says you're sick and fuddled. Has this anything to do with what you said the other day? You said then that your total recall was standing between you and others—and you hated your memory.

Sorry, because I have to discuss my big problem with you. That day we met at the Old Friends in the East India Docks, it was a total accident that when you said their new

312

restaurant, The New Friends, had better Beef and Bean Sprouts, I'd recently been, and had formed a similar opinion. And of course we progressed eventually—after that third bottle of Niersteiner—to my problem. And you said to me wearily, "If you have to ask somebody about it, then obviously you shouldn't marry the girl." And I explained what a complex problem it was, and that I was having a time penetrating to the real her, for she felt she had to try to hide her Carmarthen accent under a pukka English. And you said, the Welsh "puckish musical riding glide" (*sic!*) sounded like a cross between Calcutta and Belfast, particularly in the "dying rise" at sentence ends. As I mentioned, this girl Mary is at LSE doing a thesis on Anglo-Russian (?) policy toward India.

DB, we could have hashed this over on a good bachelor Saturday night at the Imperial Steam Baths (Russell Square). God, the London soot oozes out of you, and they give you cubicles later on, and then early in the A.M. you can order poached eggs and real American-type butter-sopped white toast. I want people to know about this place. I guess I've got a taker in this bulliac from Boston grad school, the one who's always in the Slavonic Periodicals Room. This morning I found him reading a book called *Wisdom, Madness, and Folly;* he offered it to me, but I got troubles I haven't used yet.

Yours, Paul Schoonover

St. Francis Hospital
Frisco
25 September

Dear David,

As a link in three of your reported four chain letters, I have of course heard that you are sick. (Dreadful sorry.) From Bobo Paramus I heard your dear wife had hit you accidentally with The Blue Guide *Athens,* and that you blacked out and when you came to had lost your memory. From Wanda Woodrow, one of my former students whom you may remember, I heard (and she'd heard it from Harry Tindall in fact) that you stared at your eyes reflected in the glass of that giant Rembrandt (the Cornelius) in the Wallace Collection (second-floor wing just opposite Gainsborough's delicious, shadow-lustered Irish matron, if I recall aright) and you turned blank, and didn't know where you were. And third, from Michael (who had it from some University of Maryland European Division teacher he met on top of Mount Kilimanjaro) I heard that news of your father's heart trouble had panicked you. You may be interested to know that I have a contact or two in the medical profession in London, and I think it would be a good idea for me to get in touch with them with respect to you. Frankly, your problem, if all (and I have not listed *quite* all) reports of your illness are true, sounds like a form of hysterical amnesia known as fugue. It would be interesting to me to help you. Of course, awareness and initiative—innardness—are what ultimately count.

I have in fact had to depend on contacts lately, for I too have been sick. I came down with a great case of hepatitis seven weeks back, and it seems not to want to clear up. I was incognito in the hospital, forbidden even to use my dictaphones; but word spread.

You may have heard I sold my life story to *The World* in London for £28,000. Will not *Time* eventually break down and "cover" me? I'm asking *you*. I'm hoping early next year to lobby a world fed study group rider onto the Civil Rights Bill. Will be talking shortly to JFK, and to UWF legislative lobbyist in Washington. You may recall that one of the jobs I had my eye on was the Russian stuff for the Adams project. I'm still trying to crack the Adams Papers people at the Mass. Historical Society. I offered to use my contacts to get relevant stuff lying at present untouched in Petersburg. But the editors want to do it their way. But I plan to exploit my contacts at TIME-LIFE to work my own quick trip to Russia. I want Michael to fly up to Helsingfors from Jerusalem while I fly Icelandic to Finland. Michael and I'll pick up our state guide and head across into Russia. Eventually I mean to force the Adams editors to put my name on the masthead or letterhead or whatever drag they have. I'll get my hands on the Russian dossiers, work them up, then wait for the Adams editors in their snug little Belknap Press to start saying please. Besides my life story for *World*—and it's just going to press—I am working backward into *Noah's Fourth Son* and hope to finish it someday so a critic or two can parse it for me. I want it to be one of the great prewar books. But people here won't let me work. They're always watching me, always saying hepatitis means utter rest. What they don't know is that I smuggled in—taped to my skin—a minute ultra-long-run wire-recorder which, in addition, houses a crackerjack AM wireless.

I know you're unwell *too*. But if you've ever had hepatitis you know how crazy I get here in bed—everything filtered yellow by being in the shadow of my vellum-wrinkled eastern skin. Doctors and nursies think I'm nuts, for each time they arrive in their white sterile costumes to see if I'm less yellow, I say I got hepatitis because I ate too much too fast; to which they answer that my liver deserves a little kindness.

Hell, David, what I think I mean is, Get well soon—it's awful being sick. But get well properly.

Accept illness. Have you read Custance? *Wisdom, Madness, and Folly?* A deep manic-depressive who erected a veritable system out of the dichotomous sentence delivered on his poor guilty human mind. Not *precisely* Manichean; *vide Patrologia.* (I sent my copy of Custance to Bobo Paramus.)

Indeed, from the seaseeds of his inner hemisphere—seeds as numerous as the skystars or the shoresands—he has architected a scheme of contraries most valid in the very fact that most casts doubt on the whole enterprise—viz., in the fact that his erection has been projected out of the shifting sandland of his own stormy authoritative "I"-scape. Read it, David. Read it. The man is English. Goes out of circulation whenever he feels the thing coming at him.

If—as I gather—your present malady *is* fugue—in which case you will not for the moment probably recognize who I am—make of it a designed truth built grain by grain out of your own self: be your own sandman; and like Joseph, you'll gather "corn as the sand of the sea, very much, until [verily] you leave numbering." As is recorded in the Gospel according to St. John, "In my Father's house are many mansions. If it were not so, I would have told you." Space used to be the American dream; it still is, but the true demanding space is that psychospiritous atom Pascal matched against the macro. Yes, db, that Hamlet "within," that Hamlet of the Mind's Long Island, which under scrutiny grows to West Hamlet, East Hamlet, etc., plodes out, then amalgamates.

Verily, my keepers have come: specialist, young resident, male nurse, female nurse, student nurse, barber. . . .
ps amnesia a parody of. . . .

Love Duke

David dear,

Ellen's calls from London told me all I'd be able to know, I suppose, without being there with you in the flesh. She said she *believed* that under everything you were really eager for mail. I only hope that the depression that seems to have hit you wasn't due to your father's condition. He's unchanged—pretty much as I've reported in my letters the last two months. I feel I belong here rather than there; so there's nothing but to keep on posting myself by letter and phone as to your state. Ellen said you're physically OK, though you'd had a slight conk on the head. (If that sounds like a stupid word—"conk"—I may say that terror has in the past once or twice caused in me a kind of levity.) The doctor's tentative report of hysterical amnesia seems somehow not so shaking —hysteria seems such a common word.

Your father takes pills for angina, which he hasn't suffered now for some weeks. You know the fibrositis pains may, in the past couple of years, have been sometimes angina—same paralyzing pain plus a kind of oppression in the neck and arms and back. But of course, as we've known for some years, it is—or was bound to be sooner or later—endocarditis, from that old rheumatic fever thing when your father was a boy—"licks the joints but bites the heart." As he says, he always had a slightly leaky valve. Rheumatic fever can hurt the valve leaflets, but endocarditis is an inflammation of the inner lining of the heart and you can't tell whether it has occurred until the valves stop working properly. He doesn't know, but for years I've had a sort of quiz-program knowledge of the murmurs, and other things like auricular fibrillation. Not that I *really* know. We miss you terribly. Anyhow it's now a diastolic murmur, and it hits him in the shoulder blade now and again. But his spirits are good and he refuses to let Dr. Falco talk to me about him and Dr. Falco doesn't.

Your father gets up early in the morning for an hour or two, then again late in the day. Also reads. It's amusing to see him plowing through the Bible. It was Ann and Dan's Revised Standard up through Deuteronomy, then Halsey gave up and went back to King James, which he also had never really read; and he went back to Genesis all over again, as if it were—well, it is—a familiar story he wanted told just so. David, do you know that Dr. Pelago, whom you so despise, has taken your father up as a pastoral duty, even though Halsey never went much to church. Pelago phoned yesterday, before he came; but somehow I forgot to tell Halsey Pelago was coming. When P. arrived he found H. reading Nahum and smiled frowningly as if he thought H. was trying to impress him. Pelago doesn't understand how really interested H. has gotten. I can hear you snarling, "Interested?" OK, more than "interested"; I hesitate to say exactly. Pelago to H.: "Of course Nahum's warnings not only remind us of the flood and Nineveh, but also foreshadow the destruction of apostate Christendom." H. (nodding and trying to make more than a vague response to P.'s stuffiness): "What I like is the writing—'Thy crowned are as the locusts, and thy captains as the great grasshoppers, which camp in the hedges in the cold day, but when the sun ariseth they flee away, and their place is not known where they are.' " And P. (unsure what H. meant): "It's Christ, of course, who's forecast in the 'Behold upon the mountains the feet of him that bringeth good news, that publisheth peace!' " Then H.: " 'Tidings,' I think, not 'news.' " Against Falco's orders—he knows Halsey's tastes—I made them smoked salmon sandwiches.

Your old Hong Kong cousin Jonni—well, she's mine—is here all the time. Always liked Halsey, and now she sits in the living room all day smoking Camels and telling how glad she is to be out of the Hong Kong heat. It's as if she came home only last year.

And your old acquaintance Peter St. John was here yesterday. It really touched me. I hardly know him, of course; and for years now, I've wanted to know him better. I like his wife; she's a great girl, interested in everything, maybe a bit effusive but I prefer that to moroseness. Anyway, Peter St. John came to give your father a book of pictures of England —expensive, I should think. Your father was out of bed and he was pleased to get the book, and he sat in the chair by the telescope window and turned the stiff glossy pages and made little "Hmph" sounds, while St. John himself threw out a few halting explanations of what the book was; and then I felt he felt maybe he shouldn't have brought such an oldish book—you know, a sort of collector's item—to Halsey, who being sick, probably would have preferred a Wodehouse or *Maigret's Allergy* or those lovely Benchley satires on opera.

We had a little drink. And I was going to read aloud those lines St. John wrote years ago—he's a poet, as you probably know—but I thought that really his wife Sally read me those lines (and let me copy them) in confidence, and afterward she was a little sorry she'd given them—and I thought if I read them out it might disconcert Peter. In case you haven't heard them, they go like this (they seem unfinished):

> Then one twin life will each for each ensue.
> Each in himself and in his dear will live.
> Allow me, love, to let my mind fly wild;
>
> I am always sad—I live discreet—
> And never can I bring myself content,
> Unless I sometime move outside of me.

Goodness, I have to go. I'll write tomorrow. I wonder now if this letter will be given you. But you're an outpatient, aren't you? The actual nature of what is said to ail you, I can't somehow face. Maybe I'll do some reading and in my next letter reel off—or is it "reel out"?—a gang of facts on hysterical amnesia. Dear David, I hope you and Ellen will think of coming home. Do write and tell me the whole thing is a nightmare joke. Sometimes I just want to forget everything.

Halsey, who doesn't know about you, sends his love to you and Ellen. Bobby Prynne sent me a postcard of the Statue of Liberty from Athens; why, I don't know. Oh yes, you'll be amused to know your father thinks Kennedy very quick and witty, though he won't probably vote for him.

Love to Ellen. (She asked me to write, but of course I would have written anyway.)

Love,
Mother

P.S. Word is that your Professor Amerchrome, who is very sick in San Francisco, and by the way was a bit weak even when he addressed Iroquois last spring, is said now to be a strange and unresponsive case. Boswell Benson understands that Professor Amerchrome is "resisting" the doctors.

318

Dear DB,

Broke my trip in Shefford (Beds.) only to be captured by a U. S. Air Force sergeant in the White Hart Inn. He's a tee-totaller and a semiprofessional talker. Should he go back to his wife and daughter? Daughter studying now in New York, wife living in New Hampshire, they wouldn't be living apart if it weren't for his separation from his wife. What should he do? Worked in a brewery in God knows where, could have been a manager and part-owner (according to him) if he hadn't stayed in the Air Force after the war. He dragged me back to this U. S. A. F.-R. A. F. base, Chicksands, and played "Worried Man Blues" over and over again on a very expensive 12-string guitar he bought in Munich and doesn't know how to play.

I give *him* advice on his blooming separation?!

Christ I was in a hurry to get away this morning!

Oh yes. Hope you're better. Soon we will meet again and I will treat you to further chapters of my life story. Oh yes: The night at Chicksands, I got drunk and gave this air-force sergeant the Custance book, you know, *Wisdom, Madness, and Folly*. Remember me to your wife, even though I've spoken to her only by phone.

Yours,
Paul Schoonover

Office of the Director
Amalgamated Inter-Federo-Unities, Ltd.
TIME-LIFE Building
New York, New York
September 30, 1960

David Brooke, Ph.D.
7½ Harrowby Street
London W.1
England

Dear Dr. Brooke:

We acknowledge herewith receipt of your Religion-Arts-and-Crafts Informational FOLDER but cannot accept it in septuplicate—at least, not as a bona fide section of your dossier of recommendation-credentials for the post of Assistant

Rhetorical Liaison for the Permanent Political Committee. This office would wish to remind you that Religion-Arts-and-Crafts Informational FOLDER must be remitted (i.e., submitted) in octuplicate. This office would appreciate your remitting said Informational FOLDER relatively soon.

Yours very sincerely,
(Mrs.) Vera Chronos
For the Associate Director

30 Sept.

Dear Brooke,

Is this chain letter some arch jest of yours? Can't you be funny without being a college girl? At least you've grown a sense of humor, which is a great improvement over that solemn time at Kodak. From someone named Anna Mary Benson—any relation to blond Boswell?—I hear you had a nervous breakdown in London. What a place for it! Tough luck, but of course it is *not* luck. Comes from not being open with yourself. But I hear from my old girl friend Wanda Woodrow (who heard it from, coincidentally, my old night-college Humanities prof., Duke Amerchrome), that you had some amnesia along with the breakdown. Strange, but I don't recall Wanda saying she knew you, but she seemed to assume I knew she knew you; sounds like reactionary obfuscation and triviality. Someone who knows your wife said your wife hoped people would write you.

Well, it's been a long time, hasn't it. And I can't say I've missed you. Yet I don't flinch from confrontation, never did. I never reject contact. You want to talk? Man, we talk.

You know, I gather, that I took Pennitt west. My wife remarried, you know. And the guy died and left her a network of bowling alleys all over Santa Ynez Valley, a Dane. He came from Solvang, as you no doubt recall. Well, I met her again, told her her intellectual scorn had driven me away, asked her if she and the kids would take me back if I secured a part-time job in Santa Barbara teaching drafting. And she burst out laughing—first time I ever heard her laugh like that. Said that *I* had been the one who had the snobbish paranoia about college.

A few days later Pennitt suddenly had money, so we weren't so sorry for him. Claimed he'd had it all the time from New York, but I happen to know he got it from a guy

320

he met. Well, Arabella didn't like the way he was always in and out of the kitchen doing his own meals in spite of the fact that she wanted to cook for him too when she cooked for all of us, and he insisted on having his shelf of the icebox though I don't recall he offered to pay any rent. Well, also, the kids didn't like him always washing laundry in the bathroom and snarling at them when they tried to come in. Anyway Pennitt left. I lost track of him. Of course, I soon became involved in part-time teaching and in administering the bowling-alley complex. Recently I heard from some Cape Cod Portagee named Aranho del Torto (whom I met at a [N.B.:] private showing of pop art in Monterey) that Pennitt had gotten into some sort of smuggling. After that blow-up at Kodak he was never the same. It was as if being forced into the open killed his interest in that sick private thing of his, the press and his special coins no one else had. I never meant to hurt him. He was sick, yes. *Socially* sick! But not because he was involved in the inner evolution of a profit motive; rather, because, as in a capitalist emotional economy —as Amerchrome used to say—Pennitt had never admitted to himself—worked it all out—why he *wanted* to have a unique collection.

One evening a week I teach drafting in Santa Barbara. Me, a *teacher!* But Brooke, *you* taught *me!* I looked at you and saw how you couldn't get through to people, had a personality problem. And I saw that *I did* get through, and I saw that I had a role as a teacher—an open communicator! It was fascinating to see all this eventuate!

Open? Well, you can't tell quite all to those around you, can you? So I let Arabella get fitted for a new diaphragm. But her not knowing about me is an ignorance that helps to keep us close, keep up (paradoxically) *open* with each other! Isn't that fascinating?! Some secrets are necessary.

Brooke, I have not commented on your immediate problem. Have to put that off till another time, another letter.

Amnesia? I'll never believe you don't remember *me!*

You might find some strength and solace in a book your friend Abby gave me: Custance, *Wisdom, Madness, and Folly.* A deep manic-depressive who erected a veritable system out of the dichotomous sentence delivered on his poor guilty human mind.

Remember your ADVERSARY,
Alonzo Morganstern

P.S. I now keep a nightly journal in a red hard-cover note-book a New York friend gave me.

Dear old David,

I write, of course, because it's the least I can do, and because I care. But I write, too, because I don't in point of fact believe in this amnesia of yours that Ian Harper has just told me of (having heard from the Fearons, who got it from your mother, who said Ellen hoped people would write you—when I saw your mother she didn't tell me, or maybe it was before you got sick—goodness, this is a heavy time for her!) I don't believe the amnesia story, and yet I feel a sharp surprise in the report of such a weird setback, and surprise makes me wonder. A blow in the head? Am I crass to broach it so grossly? I'm torn between wanting to disbelieve the report and wanting somehow to write you a letter appropriate to such a strange impasse. Here, I often wondered if *you* remembered *me*—and I thought, Does he know the influence (*foudroyant et fine*) he had on me?—and then Ian Harper comes in yesterday and explodes this bomb about amnesia. Isn't it gross of me that apparently instead of feeling anything, I went to a shelf and looked up amnesia in *The Dictionary of Psychology?* I can't believe you "have" it. Anyway, if in you there is right now vaguely the pang of a loss the nature of which you don't know except insofar as a doctor and your wife and some other people question you and insist and probe, surely this past of yours must be restored to you. Why, I found last night I'd got *myself* into a state: *you* didn't remember *me*, you who had so insidiously much to do with my imagination of myself here in this Brooklyn Heights. This Brooklyn Heights seems a cross (!) between Marylebone, the less forbidding parts of Knightsbridge, and the less theatrical stages of Chelsea and of the posher Hampstead. And there *you* are, in the *real* London. Will you visit my father? He'd like any crumb of attention. He's increasingly interested, he says, in people's voices.

No doubt by the time you receive this very ordinary letter, your momentary spell will have been broken. (When you are quite well, you must chronicle what happened.) But I wanted to tell you how much I am your friend, and say I have a terrific new catalog coming. The Fearons put me on to it in Carmel, N. Y., where they go summers. A rich library of Alexandriana—i.e., the Great (cf. LeBrun). Also some assorted useful Americana, including one dark fascinating letter I'm checking for authenticity. Oh, yes: In the Alexander lot are two incunables that would make your fingertips prickle. Plus some rebacks and a couple of rather nasty cathedral bindings. Actually the Fearons heard about the lot through a Reverend Woolley, the local Episcopal minister, and all he knew was that the library belonged to an absentee (and now apparently "late") artist from Indiana named Billy Tell, that the house was occasionally visited by a friend of Tell's, a tall gaunt man with a long lined face who always wore a U. S. Olympic sweatshirt with a hood and who never stopped in town and whom no one knew. Anyhow I got on to Tell's brother, who arranged to have me see the library and then, in a long phone conversation, accepted my offer, stipulating only that I should sell the library *intacta,* giving it an attractive presentation in my catalog. So I got the library. The Fearons were good to know of it. I had a fine evening with them up there. Sarah has given up fighting what the city planners have in store for the Heights, and she has taken up embroidery (crewel work and diaper fillings and all manner of strange amenities). Quincey is now fully retired and has given in to an ancient yen for the organ. He's installed a cherry-red Mason and Hamlin (originally his brother's in Washington) in the study of the Carmel place; and Sarah got a young Brooklyn Heights designer to make them a small, rather abstract stained glass window—a Noah's Ark that's fat as a ferry boat (and perched on Ararat Point) and you can see right through it and through the silhouettes of all the silent, watching animals gathered tight together. Quincey plays "The Church's One Foundation" at cocktail time, sits very straight and calmly pulls the stop-knobs for the voix celeste and vox humana and the octave coupler.

I will give you, as I close this get-well missive, my translation of the first four lines of the Labé, the sestet of which you'll perhaps recall I "Englished" years ago. Lines 1–4 *seq.* (Sally thinks them too open!):

> Again kiss me, kiss me once more, and kiss:
> Give, now, one of your most mouth-watering,
> Give, give, please, now, one of your most loving:
> And I'll give back four hotter than coals that hiss.

You may be amused—David, I'm intentionally ignoring the report of your amnesia—I hesitate even to write the word—you may be amused to know that, looking up translations of Saint-Amant's *"Sonnet Inachevé,"* I found that somebody at IBM Translation Control Center has in fact done my old Bouchet into practically every language from Cornish to Urdu. As for my essay on the Francus myth, it is just another myth in the literary intercourse between me and myself.

We do not become another. I am not a scholar, any more than you are English, or Mike Amerchrome (did I mention meeting him?) is the son of God. How, then, can I claim to be on firmer ground if I pass myself off as something you (through your own scheme of deceptions) saw in me—that eccentric, caustic sodality of nerves perhaps known through these gentle dangerous streets of Brooklyn Heights as "that odd Englishman"? Well, I *can* be on firmer ground, for the simple reason that Englishman was—is—thoroughly me, insubstantial, yes, but not totally insubstantial. When I write next I'll tell you about my new role on the Heights—"the mysterious tire-slasher"; your mother doesn't believe what's being said about me; she's lovely; what a burden she has at the moment. David, I almost forget you're ill.

Do please look up the old man in Highgate. Combine him with a trip to Marx's grave (with that bulbous bust!) and for heaven's sake don't miss Waterlow Park right there by the cemetery, and the designs of shrubs and the little stone tablet on which are cut verses from Marvell's "Garden." If you can spend time with this new acquaintance Paul Schoonover, you can find an hour to pay the old man a visit, can't you?

Love to you and to this Ellen
I scarcely know,
"Your" St. John

P.S. Now, the comfort of crumpling up and throwing away the first draft and a half of this letter. One takes care how one phrases things to David Brooke.

P.P.S. I got a card from your friend Bob Prynne from Brindisi: a picture of the Empire State Building!

Oct. 4 Chichester

Dear DB, Pictured is bust of poor Chas. I, niche of Chi-

chester town cross. Cathedral ordinary—but original Selsey
marsh foundation of gt. antiquity and center of much historical speculation. Evening cricket on town green in delicate
dying sun. Bishop Henry King left on tomb inside church no
name—only this Latin inscription—oops no space. Am skip-
ping Salisbury because of jazz concert in cathedral weekend
I was to be there.   P. S.

Oct. 2nd

My very dear David,

That I should have heard of your illness from of all people
Mary Clovis hurts me (more than I like to admit). Yet,
how *would* I have been notified? For Ellen doesn't know
me—Ellen, about whom I've heard from your friend the
bookseller (whom I met up in the old apartment one night
when he was visiting a newcomer, a blond man with some
foreign accent). That night I was with Alonzo; I guess I may
as well admit to you that even while *we* were still seeing
each other, I was occasionally letting Alonzo make up to
me. Do you blame? Of course after a time I got sick of
hearing from him how potent he was. I told him I was just
a trophy of his.

But I'd have *been* a trophy of yours gladly. All I wanted
was to be ordered. You imagine I heard your talk with
Pennitt about coins. I never really did. I didn't know any
of that talk then, and I don't now. You imagined I paid as
much attention as you.

I've turned music therapist—a group of disturbed children
eight to twelve years old. Well, why *shouldn't* it be a drug?
No doubt you will say that Peter, Paul, and Mary bastardize
folk singing—or do I dare hear you thinking that? But I have
found that in my new work PP&M draw two or three of my
kids into a serious musical experience for the first time in
their lives.

You don't really have amnesia, do you? Couldn't *I* play
you some records that would bring you back?! That Bartok
violin record, for instance, that you so often played when
we were together. I gather your amnesia is partial. Maybe
there are some things you want to forget. Like when you
said, looking at me, "There are some very pretty girls whose
faces don't look substantial or real enough for you to love

325

them." Well, you never wanted me to be real. That was the trouble.

Very truly,
Abby

P.S. Mr. Pennitt stopped in one night, said he was in "difficulties," and could I lend him ten dollars. He left as security a $20 gold piece. Wasn't that sweet and crazy?

P.P.S. I gave Alonzo a red hard-cover notebook as a going-away present with a picture pasted into it that you took of me with your Argus.

Dear David,

This is the first letter I've written you since you were in camp. (I wrote you a card once or twice from Chicago, and once from Norway.) An old man named Luke Pennitt phoned last week, said he was a friend of yours and would like to pay us a visit. I thought maybe he was being attentive because I'm not well. I was relieved to find that however well he knows you, he certainly wasn't visiting me for altruistic reasons. He had a gimmick for sale for a hundred dollars. A $20 gold piece hollowed out—if you can imagine so small a hollow—with, inside, a minute Swiss watch with a real second hand so tiny it looked like one of the specklike household bugs that got into your encyclopedia last summer. Well, this Luke Pennitt explained and explained. The obverse (?) of the coin is hinged so that when you press a certain edge of the milling (?) the top springs open. And there's the Swiss watch ticking away—though you don't *hear* the ticks. He felt I wasn't going to buy at that price, so he started working on your mother. "It's not as if I was offering a lock of hair in some hundred-franc piece. This here is something rather special." He smokes continuously, coughs a lot, but seems active and well. Funny, but it did my heart good to see an old crook like him in our beautiful apartment.

I didn't buy, and I had to persuade your mother not to, too. But the fellow kept shaking his head and blinking away (he has trouble with his contact lenses), and saying what a buy the coin-watch was, and how *you* would understand its value, and at last he made us take a phone number where he can be reached—someone's apartment named Aranho del

Torto, who Pennitt called his "associate"—a "Portuguese-Italian-German-American" fellow who Pennitt said was a genius under his dyed blond hair and took special pleasure in outwitting Greek, Israeli, and Swiss customs officers. There was a good deal more about this del Torto. Later, after your mother made him a drink, Pennitt called del Torto his agent; and then finally he said del Torto was the man who'd saved him, though del Torto himself wasn't aware of the fact. Well, now I've finally written you a letter and I'll get it out of the house by Quincey, who's coming today. Your mother is so full of you all the time and always talking of the new job you applied for and how you and Ellen are coming back to the States—though she doesn't say what you're doing, and I gather there haven't been any letters lately—that if she knew I'd written you she'd have to read this. No, I don't want her to know—and I tell you herewith—about a certain medical dilemma that is driving Falco up the wall. (He, with his cultivated interests in Bartok and someone called Kitaj; and his gray brush-cut worn a bit longer and therefore in a suave way fuzzy; and that skinny elegant efficient body of his that he's been standing on its hands each morning for forty years—him I can really shake up!) You know about the endocarditis. OK. But I've had a small growth—almost insignificant enough to be called a fungus—for almost a year now in a very dodgy place on (or in) my anatomy, and Falco wants me to get it fixed and says that even if it's arrested, as it seems to be, I'm hiding my pain from him, and says my chances under anesthesia are practically normal. Your mother's still in the dark. I don't want to be operated on.

But just now in this rare letter of mine, it's more than that. Somehow, after all these years of sign language between us—you growing up as free as you could be—we've never taken off the father-son disguises. Maybe you and I can talk soon. What's doing in London? I liked the general lowness of buildings there.

Always,
Dad

P.S. As I'll explain in another letter, having to entertain the Rev. A. Pelago lately has made me feel I've lost my rights.

DB, Talland Church (Cornwall), to which I walked along
the cliffs from Polperro. Detached tower of this hallowed
church overlooks small harbor famed for unobserved smugglers' landings. Porch has wagon-roof like upturned hull of
old boat. Hope yr well.   P.S.

Oct. 7
Jerusalem, Tel Aviv

Dear David,

When you get this I won't be here in Jerusalem any more.
I'm flying stateside tonight, will mail this in Tel Aviv. There's
a Barnard girl here—like me, studying American Lit.—who's
forever playing the "Do-you-know-so-and-so" game. (Not
that *I* know anybody!) Strange, though, that your own co-
ercive game of these chain letters seems to have brought me
together with this girl. Did I know J. J. Lafayette? She says
that in his latest letter to her—which she won't let me read—
he named a Mike Amerchrome. She says she came to Israel
to forget Lafayette. All I know is I got a very evangelistic
letter from someone called Mary Clovis (enclosing a brochure from the White Tower Bible Group) and asking me
to write someone named J. J. Lafayette. Having heard from
Duke that you were making a cult of these letter systems, I
went ahead and wrote this Lafayette care of Bunny's Bar
on Broadway; told him all about what a snooper you are
and how, though you pretend to want to communicate and
connect, basically you are a rat. Actually I had a reply from
Lafayette, though the reply is, of course, *hors-d'oeuvre*,
so to speak, i.e., outside the epistolary chain gang you've
gotten under way.

Are you all right? Mentally, etc.? Duke, who is physically
unwell, writes that you had amnesia or something analogous.
Gave me your London address. If you do have amnesia—and
of course it may be one of Duke's multivocal modes of reference—I think you deserve it—for you always tried to be
Mnemon, the World's Rememberer, often confused with
Memnon the Resolute, whose famous black statue at Thebes
I have heard sing at dawn when the initial rays of the sun.
heat the orifice behind the mouth, expanding the air so it
rushes through the throat. But, as Duke so often said, history

is *not* merely memory's record. And your pretentious exposé of Duke which Trailways Lost and Found returned to—of all people—Duke himself in New Hampshire is as inadequate as the newly waxed palimpsest of an amnesiac's brainpan. E.g., how could you have willfully forgotten about the memoir Duke lent you, the one he appropriated from that public library in southern Maine—*Remarks of Bartholemew James on the Secret Activities of the Pony Express in Early 1861* (St. Joseph, Mo., 1870)? Does not BJ himself tell how his grandfather, Thaddeus Bartholemew, having been found eavesdropping back of Burgoyne's shed at Ticondèroga, was court-martialed, condemned, and mysteriously spirited away? (NB: survival necessitated desertion.) Isn't it obvious that this Thaddeus Bartholemew must be the same as the Thaddeus Bartholemew of the letter Duke cites in his elucidation of Burgoyne and Ticonderoga? (God, David, Duke based two *lectures* on the *Remarks!*) Did you actually, or willfully, forget Bartholemew's *Remarks?* (It was shortly after receiving your so-called exposé—which you told me you would not publish—that Marcus Black showed knowledge of it. However, Duke was in fact planning to take a year or two's leave of absence, and he and Mary left N. H. on their own volition.)

I did mean to write you in New York—i.e., when I was there. For as I turned up at so many spots I kept hearing in my mind what you'd had to say about them—e.g., the transient drabness of the Art Students League lockers, the statue of Kossuth (which I seem to recall visiting when I first met Mary), the smell of chocolate (or did I really smell it?) along Sands Street near the Brooklyn Navy Yard, the half-wit, broken-toothed, black-haired shoeshine man in the shadow of a bank doorway down Montague Street near Fulton, the sense as you pass into Brooklyn Heights that it is a quieter territory and that the harbor, even when you can't see it, is there, waiting for and bordering and distinguishing and magnifying the Heights. Did you know I finally gave up and took a room there? Yes: way down Willow, a sort of fourth-floor attic with tiny long windows through which I'd peek at cars suddenly slowing down as they turned in from Middagh and then accelerating down the narrow aisle of street with cars parked bumper to bumper either side. So many lonely strollers—and shaved in so many different ways

—big and little moustaches, beards Lincolnian and Trotsky-ite, sideburns, mutton-chops. . . . ("Facial hair," as Duke once said, "is coming back. Everything," he once said, "is coming back.") By the way I urge you to read Custance's *Wisdom, Madness, and Folly*. I read Duke's copy.

Sorry you've come down with amnesia, but perhaps it will provide a sort of mental enema.

En passant, though it is now a couple of years since I've seen you, I recall you said the Pony Express whipped Lincoln's First Inaugural from Saint Joe to Sacramento in eight days; well, it was seven days seventeen hours. I just wanted to tell you.

Who knows? Maybe you'll meet in New York (perhaps even Brooklyn Heights).

Michael Amerchrome

P.S. Christmas a couple of years ago I ordered Mary a use-ful gift: a Feather Touch Remote Control TV attachment. With this she could sit as far as fifteen feet away and by merely squeezing the little black mushroom button turn the set on or off—for that matter turn on or off "your phono-graph, humidifier, or fan *while in bed*"! (My italics.) How-ever, by a strange coincidence, just after I placed the order, I had a happy note from Duke saying Mary had taken time off from sanding the bedroom floor, and had installed her own remote control: yes, with lamp wire and a toggle switch she had attached a device that would turn off the sound of the commercials whenever she wanted. So my gift, which I thought so clever, went unappreciated.

October 15th

Dear David,

It's Wanda. Heard from someone named Bob Prynne that you were in Corfu getting over getting married. Then I heard recently from a Peter St. John that you'd had a concussion plus after-effects that looked suspiciously like amnesia. (Whatever that means.) Wanted to write months ago; but never quite got to it; maybe didn't want to enough. Now, it seems strange to be communicating with an old enemy who *suddenly* doesn't remember me. Made me feel guilty about that chain letter you started around; I mean the two chain letters. What a wise guy, Prynne! Asked me to come stay with him for the Portland Rose Festival. (Hasn't ever seen me and my bony hips!) I'd written him a special reply from my part of the chain, for I thought he was funny; as a matter of fact I wrote my regular link in the chain (to Duke Amerchrome) also. Bob Prynne wrote back (after I'd asked *him* to come see *me*—i.e., in NYC); he said he'd see me "en route" but I never saw him nor found out what the route was. Then this man St. John's letter came with the news about you in London, and somehow besides wanting to write the link in the chain—which somehow turned out again to be Duke Amerchrome—he's sick, too, isn't he—I also wrote you. Since that vengeful weekend I gave you in New York shortly after our mutual friend departed for England, I haven't felt quite right about you. I did start a letter to you after receiving the first thing from Prynne; but then I let it sit on my worktable and then transferred it to the top of my Zenith (the one Mike Amerchrome gave me, saying it was stolen goods); then the damned thing ended up in one of my books (a paperback, some new modern theology—"I vs. Thee"). Listen: if you have what they say you have, then maybe you don't know what I'm talking about or whom. Listen: You have no *right* to forget me. Anyway, even though I hated your guts that spring in New Hampshire and hated you maybe a little less when you stayed with me in N. Y., I thought I should let you know I'm sorry you're sick and wonder if you remember that spring in N. H. Well, I never heard of anyone having amnesia in real life.

When I heard recently that our mutual friend is on the faculty at Berkeley, I started thinking again all over again about that spring. About our mutual friend, and about me, and of course (though least) about you. Once, a while back, our mutual friend, in one of his quick letters (signed "in haste"), said he thought you were overworking, and overworking to no purpose. According to H., you worked without a definite plan. God, I'm always doing that, beginning a figure without any stronger notion than that the figure ought to be kneeling and the abdomen ought to be sort of out. Our mutual friend—who's a bastard about letter-writing—didn't say what work you're doing, but I bet it's those endless files on the Oakes family.

You're married now, and an English girl. I might have known. Tell her about me sometime. Draw me! Do a portrait of me out of typed punctuation marks. My father used to do

331

that in the education office at one of the bases where he was stationed.

Marcus Black painted from memory a picture of our mutual friend. Sent it to me. I don't know why he didn't send it to H., but maybe he thought I had some significant role in H.'s life. (Which I did.) How hard you were on H. *and* M. Marcus knew Harry's kind of mind, and Marcus accepted it. You always forgot how much Harry at first relied on Marcus; if their Englishness wasn't really the same, it was an idea their two minds met in. And Marcus loved Harry, and Harry made him laugh, and—what you always tried not to know—Harry respected Marcus' aphorisms and loved him. And Harry loved you. And all you could think of was the significance of Harry's mistakenly singing "Hark the Herald Angels Sing" to the tune of "Men of Harlech" and then "The British Grenadiers" to the tune of "Hark the Herald Angels Sing."

Our mutual friend ought to read this wonderful book by a madman named Custance: *Wisdom, Madness, and Folly.* My father gave it to me this week when he turned up humbly at my apartment on the way to N. H. Thirty days' stateside leave.

Funny, but I sometimes have this dream about that spring at Indian Farm. We three are sitting at that big table in the kitchen and our mutual friend gets up and leaves the kitchen and, as if he doesn't know we're there, he flips off the lights as he walks out into the living room, leaving you and me in total darkness, and I feel your hand on my stomach, and I'm convinced that you hypnotized our mutual friend to go off and turn out the lights. Crazy, eh? Or did it happen?

Watch *Time,* they're doing a small report on my new show. Oh yes: Get well.

Wanda

P.S. Had a card from Prynne from Scotland.

Polperro 17 Oct.
Dear DB,

Hope your troubles are over. We've known each other for only a few days (which is an insubstantial foundation for a friendship), but I felt in our three or four walks that you took a genuine interest in me and my Welsh girl. The way, for example, you asked if I half thought marriage to a foreigner was a necessary test of roots; or if I'd taken her to the concert of Pop Art Music by the American Indian combo at that East End pub; or if we wanted children (and wasn't it better to fight the population explosion by adopting rather than having one's own); or if I had any idea where Tom Fargo was now; or if my girl would like living in the States; all of which indicated to me that you were a genuine listener, involved, really involved. (Yes, and you brought up my uncle the art historian in Monterey, whom I'd mentioned only in passing a few days before!) You do listen; and I told you so. And you bowed your head and shook it sadly, and said, "Yes, I have total recall, I think." Funny, how absently you said that.

Here in this Cornish fishing village I drink away my evenings with a squad of skin divers who spend their days working the sea-urchin shoals. I meet them in The Three Pilchards and they sing American folk songs. "Worried Man Blues," "Reuben James," "This Land Is My Land," "Down By the Riverside." Regarding last-named, I now believe that the Prince of Peace line in Riverside means, peace is waiting at Jordan, but no sooner, and any other peace is a lie you pay for through (as Chaucer said) the nose. When I see you I'll tell you about the lugger Unity, and the famous smuggling ethic here, and how Christian Libby sank a hundred ankers of spirits in a rocky cove to fool the revenue men and a few days later came back and recovered all one hundred.

Yrs., P.S.

Oct. 16

Dear Dave,

Yes, though you didn't seem to listen to what you were saying, what you said made sense. I'd been kidding myself. It was only because of my sister Marjean that I wanted to hold onto the island, she being buried there. I don't believe I ever told you that.

Lunched at Downtown A. C. with a pool-playing pal of mine from Antioch, and he says he knows a Halsey Brooke whose son is in London married to an English girl. This Halsey Brooke is sick, he says. Is it your dad? I hope not.

Didn't hear from my letter to you, but maybe you wrote back to Italy forgetting I said I'd sold my Chris-Craft and

333

shipped out. Sure do look forward to having you and Ellen for dinner when you get home. You said you were going to work for world federalism. Well, did you read in *Time* where this professor Amerchrome is deathly ill in Frisco?

I go to the newsreel theaters a lot. Kennedy and Nixon. You know, Kennedy is *too* smart, isn't he? Too *young*, too. I honestly like Nixon's looks. I feel I know him. But I guess I'll vote for Kennedy, he's so different—like a character!

Met a blond book salesman in the Algonquin bar. Italian. Said the place to live in NYC is Brooklyn Heights. Kept saying it was "utter folly" to live anyplace else. Think I'll see about getting a small house there. Too many people use the New York A. C., if you know what I mean. Do you know anything about Brooklyn?

Anyway, thanks again for getting me out of my rut to come west to see how the New York gals dance the polka. Ha ha!

Your friend,
Phil Matthews

Berkeley
26 Sept.

Dear D.,

How glad we'd be if you wrote now to say you're well. Privately, your mother told me she didn't know how to believe in your reported amnesia. It has been inconceivable to me, too. Forgive me if I say what I have to say on the assumption that your amnesia isn't real.

Two matters: (a) Brooklyn Heights; (b) Tom Fargo.

For your sake and your father's, and, of course, your mother's, we felt we should stop over in New York en route. We put up with my friend the print analyst at the Morgan, and incidentally he gave me a prurient after-hours glimpse of the Morgan's magisterial hoard of Bibles. Imagine seeing those Gutenbergs on your tod in the middle of the night—not to mention getting into those glass cases in which these treasures pass immune through time. For comprehensiveness and condition this collection of Bibles may well be the best.

On Sunday we lunched with your parents, who were eager for news of you. Your mother had met us at the door and whispered not to speak to your father about your condition.

Your father moves quietly, but was dressed and ready for us. His color is good; he had a whiskey before lunch; he wondered how you liked England and (quizzically) how Ellen liked you. Was eager—mainly because of you, I think—to hear what I thought about the famous Amerchrome, whose condition is now mentioned daily in the papers. I told only what I thought would amuse your father, even make him feel that Amerchrome was to your life as one more tile in a gathering mosaic of excitements. He said that, to please you —or what he imagined to be your feeling—he'd probably have to cast a sneak vote for JFK though he'd never admit it to his friends at the Downtown A. C.

After lunch, an old man named Luke Pennitt came to see your father, said he'd been in the neighborhood and felt irresistibly drawn to their—your parents'—flat. Blond Boswell Benson didn't appear, though your mother said he might; but Josie Wrenn did. I, of course, had never met her. Anselin thought her rather aggressively bohemian, and Anselin is, of course, right. (Josie describes her colored friends south-east of Gramercy Park as if they were credentials.) Phoned Wanda from your parents; she was just the same, as full of imagination and oracular wrong-headedness and intensity as ever. Kept fanatically urging me to read a book by some English manic-depressive.

At last we're back in Berkeley. Books around us. Supermarket down the street. Proper pleasures, proper timetable. Anselin prefers separate shops for fish, meat, veg, etc., but I've persuaded her how economical it is time-wise to shop in the supermarket.

Returning thence yesterday, who should we find at our door but Tom Fargo—as usual prim and insouciant. He'd flown over.

Here's why: (God save me from the passion-bound maze of Lincoln scholarship; it's coming to resemble the Arthurian swamp.) Over tea, Fargo led slowly to a question. Here were the steps: He thinks everything hangs on the identity of that monk (remember?); Fargo quizzed a young blond Italian at Goodspeed's who claims he talked to this monk at the time of the picture-dickering—noted western boots below the hem of his robe; Fargo found a librarian in St. Joseph, Mo., who recalls a man who spent several weeks three or four years ago checking on someone named Bartholemew James; she thought this fellow was *scribbling* on two of the mss. he was using, but she was too timid to ask; remembers this chap said he now had to go on to "the Pacific" to the Public Record Office in San Francisco, found scribblings on mss. but didn't know the state of the mss. well enough to judge if this visitor had fiddled them. Fargo has other information he's not divulging. He does go so far as to say he now believes the "monk" is in the Bay area.

Inevitably my mind, muddled by a summer of good Cotswold bitter and an unseasonably balmy season among the Oxfordshire ducks (as idle as *I* am!), imagines some link between Fargo's quarry and my despicable foe Amerchrome. (As you may know, he is now in fact very sick in hospital across the Bay.) Of course, any eductive leap would electrify even A. himself (so sure is he of me). Strange, but last night I dreamt Amerchrome had escaped from hospital and sought sanctuary in Alcatraz. The answer, of course, is that I'd been reading of plans to close Alcatraz.

Well, do come see us. From Hilldale Street I see all three bridges.

Regards . . . in haste,
H.

Office of the Director
Federo-Unities, Ltd.
7½ Pierrepont Street
Brooklyn 1, New York
U. S. A.
October 16, 1960

David Brooke, Ph.D.
7½ Harrowby Street
London W.1
England

Dear Dr. Brooke:

If it were not for a significant organizational alteration, this office would not now reiterate that we are not yet in receipt of your Religion-Arts-and-Crafts Informational FOLDER in octuplicate. However, the former Amalgamated Inter-Federo-Unities, Ltd. (and prior to that, Inc.) has effected a division into Federo-Unities, Ltd. (*vide supra*) and Confedero Unifists, Ltd. Should you desire to continue your application for the position of Rhetorical Liaison to the

Permanent Political Committee, the fact that Dr. Duke Amerchrome, your personal referee, has assumed the Senior Wardenship of Federo-Unities, Ltd. will be in your favor. But this office is advised by Senior Warden Amerchrome that your application will now require an additional recommendation from a party not personally associated with this organization. Please, however, do not neglect to submit your Religion-Arts-and-Crafts Informational FOLDER in, of course, octuplicate.

Yours always,
Anna Mary Selbstein
For the Acting Senior Warden

Oct. 16

Dear David, (recognize Mary's typing?)

The doctor treating you there in London happens to be a friend of mine. In fact, though he doesn't fully understand the fact, I got him his job. He writes me that you complain that certain recent letters you've received pretend to be concerned with your condition but actually devote their bulk to the problems of the letter-writer him- or her-self; also that these co-respondents ostensibly alarmed by *your* amnesia, manifest in their disregard of you in their letters their own real and reprehensible forgetfulness. You didn't tell the doc about those great chain letters you started. *I did* tell him. But écoutez: He had already taken a hint of mine and begun to develop a view that you were, if not·in fact suffering from fugue, showing its symptoms. When asked if preoccupation had ever caused some direct or indirect memory failure, you allowed that while driving a certain road in New Hampshire you had often failed to recall anything you had passed. And, incidentally, you were heard to mutter that you took a loss on Jesus Shane's trailer, and that you wished you hadn't sold it to Amerchrome for his mobile campus tape studio. From which the learned doctor and I infer that you recall more than you admit. Add to this, the evidence of Queen Ella your wife, who claims that for some months you have been subject to sharp and sudden social disappearances—i.e., suddenly you would psychologically absent yourself from a conversation. Add to this your wife's report that on an island in Italy you told her one morning—after you'd stayed the night at the villa of some American—that you could recall nothing

337

of what had happened the preceding day. Add to this, Mary's report that in the letter you wrote her two months ago you claimed, first, that your detective ability to summon total recall had cut you off from people,* and second, that (partly through your efforts to bind people to you) you had created a cat's cradle of relations among them quite independent of you yourself. From this, and certain other informations I possess, I infer that you wish those around you to think that you've been living through the state of disturbed consciousness known as fugue—after which, acts of apparent volition and general normalcy are utterly forgotten. (Is this not an attention-getting device?) You believe you can escape all responsibility—and at the same time, through rejecting memory, reverse the result you imagine total recall indirectly caused—by pretending to have had hysterical fugue and now to be (conveniently) stunned under fugue's usual effect, amnesia. That your condition is not "global amnesia"—i.e., oblivion of the whole of your life—is evident from your lugubrious and not at all convincing allegation that ever since you saw a man commit suicide by leaping from a Brooklyn Heights hotel you had been obsessively frightened by prospective *self*-imprisonment—i.e., imprisonment in the self. Still and all, I believe you do have a degree of genuine amnesia, and I have suggested this to the doc in London. Do you not remember nodding excitedly that fragrant warm afternoon you sat in on a lecture of mine in N. H., when I said, "I have done that, says my memory, I have not done that, says my pride, finally my memory yields"? When recently I came across the statement in a substantial monograph Bobo Paramus wrote and which he asked me to check, I realized that, insulated by my exhilaration that day, I had neglected to identify the quote as Nietzsche's. Of course, I had to correct Bobo's scholarship.

Mary's quite concerned over your fugue, and she half-heartedly refuses to believe you don't recollect her. Mary, you'll like to know, is here (in her sexy white gown), and is thinking of moving in with me even though the hospital brass say nix. She's at work on a children's alphabet book—big jelly-bean-colored letters on contrasting backgrounds. Of

---

*(For, knowing you *had* the power, you neglected present-tense engagements!)

course, with my contacts at Simon & Matheluke I can get it published for her easy. The hepatitis holds; frankly I feel (as an old lady I once knew was in the habit of saying) like the last run of shad. But somehow I shall get out of here alive. Please don't worry about my condition.

Am in touch with Sandy Persons, UWF Congressional lobbyist.

Kennedy is, I believe, a winner; but always he's a *close* winner from now on. Yet, you know, JFK isn't quite right artistically. There's laughter and sinewy diplomacy and a real bastardly manliness in the man. But what I want to know—and my question will appear at the end of my life story to be published anonymously next weekend—is this: Will JFK force America to live through the full apocalyptic parody it is evolving toward? Once you rose (at the Greave Sisters' Humanities Club) to ask what I meant America was a parody *of*. I said: "a promised land." Other answers will be forthcoming in a new testament I'm working up; I have yet to correlate the results of my farewell effort before I left New Hampshire: i.e., a study (through polls that used tapes, visual aids, and lie detectors) of the interactional links between virginity and awareness.

Signing off now. Don't expect to hear from me during re-entry. OK *World-Telegram* Seventh Sporting Final: Let's go to press.

Your old spermafactual multi-farer,
DUKE

P.S. Isn't full (and/or fake) amnesia a parody of one's normal state?

21 Oct.

David dear,

Ellen writes that you insist on staying in the flat and won't go back to the hospital as an outpatient. She wonders if you aren't *forcing* on yourself at least some part of the amnesia. Now, maybe I shouldn't have said that. Don't you remember the docks? The docks that have been replaced by new, clean, more geometrical ones—don't you remember walking down there Sundays with your father? Don't you remember Mr. Pascoli from Naples? It would be so wonderful for you to be here. Your father's murmurs have gotten to be a real fatigue of the muscle, and Dr. Falco told me privately he might ask H. to use an inhalator during the day. Halsey hates the idea. He says next thing it'll be an oxygen tent, making him look like an outer-space experiment. He reads your Bible, takes notes in a red hard-cover notebook, can you imagine! I think maybe Dr. Pelago doesn't understand the kind of religiousness Halsey now has. Yesterday Halsey exploded when P. left: went on and on—why didn't that healthy sun-lamp-tan relent a bit and warm up, why did P. have to give out that big tolerant smile while explaining the Christian paradox of inwardness-sociality. I found him yesterday reading an article in the paper about a heart transplant. He circled it with one of his black Broker's Special Number 2 pencils and handed the paper to me with a laugh. And sometimes I actually think I know what's in his mind.

I had a letter from Bobby Prynne from Anchorage, Alaska, but it's been coming for two months judging from the postmark. The letter describes an exquisite golf course there, and how a cow moose and her calf graze at the edge of the course by a group of tall evergreens. You play ahead, unless the papa moose appears. Usually he stays hidden, but when he comes out he ends the game. Now, just yesterday I had a card from Bobby from Ireland.

Also we have heard from Anna Mary Benson that Prof. Amerchrome is very much worse, isn't responding to treatment. The fear now is not only that his liver is permanently damaged but that he may not pull through at all. Such a dynamic man, when he spoke to us at Iroquois. There he was, hands in his purple sport jacket pockets, elbows sort of out, leaning toward us and poking out his head, and whispering wildly: "The new American philosophy is embrace not select; and the American dream remains the same—a dream that the journey westward continues. The frontier is always there." Now he's flat out in bed; I can't imagine him flat out in bed. The newspapers say he's so enervated he can't lift his hands or feet, and he complains of abdominal pain. Apparently he insists there are stones inside him the hospital people won't remove. Awful of me to think it, but it occurred to me today that they have readymade obits of celebrities in the files of most newspapers, which they can just set up under a photo as soon as the person dies. "Your" Prof. Amerchrome's tribulations take my mind off your father. Lately I've been consciously afraid of interpreting my dreams when I wake up in the middle of the night. I was talking to Peter St. John about dreams the other day, and he was very sympathetic. I reminded him of Prof. Amerchrome's talk to us—for Peter St. John happened to be there that night—and I recalled that A. had quoted the Talmud as saying that dreams which are not interpreted are like letters which have not been opened. And suddenly Peter St. John turned at me and said, "Amerchrome never read the Talmud in his life, he got that quote from Erich Fromm."

Dr. Falco tells me frankly that at this point there ought to be either a decline in your father's condition or an improvement. Time will tell. Your father is calm; I think it's because of his Bible. Yet his being this way disarms me. Remember how you felt disarmed when Halsey was on the right side in the Kefauver drug business, the beginning of it? Please get well.

Love always,
Mother

Dearest David,

As I told you, I'll be away on the Essex coast for two days. (Circumstances almost dictate the phrase "forty-eight hours.") It finally got *to* me, your waking in the morning and silently, deadly looking about the bedroom, then undertaking to be polite. Excuse me if I try to dredge up something from your memory—I just thought maybe sometimes you aren't forgetting as much as you—I don't know what I mean. That's why I told you about the Hindu mandala (or is it Zoroastrian? I forget) that you tacked up in your—our—room at your parents', with the clusters of names in each of the eight sections; and it's why I told you about the tinted little photo of that Mary Clovis you have on the bureau, the one you called a document; and I told you about your father's figure skates hanging like a dancer's feet in the closet; and that crinkled Home Mosaic Harry Tindall made; and the little appreciation of Thornton's paintings which Marcus Black spent a week of his precious Italian holiday writing in a Sienese pensione.

I tried, and I'll try again. But just now I have to be away. And I preferred to say what I have to say in a letter. The doctor says he thinks the symptoms of fugue are partly invented (though he concedes that the concerted *attempt* to

341

simulate fugue is itself a symptom, though not of fugue);
he is a bit suspicious of the completeness of your amnesia.
Dear David, when I had that note from Mark's sister in
Edinburgh saying she'd found a divine new diet, you muttered something from that poem you recited to me in Italy—
"O tell me whence that joy doth spring/Whose diet is divine
and fair." And you said the other day why did I worry so
much about slimming, I was lovely, and a little baby flesh
was good protection. (Cor, Mr. Brooke!) Yet I hadn't said
anything to you about my figure since you began to be ill—
so you must have been *remembering*. Then again, when I
went off to Edgware Road Tuesday afternoon you told
me to see if *Time* was out. Then two days ago, you agreed
courteously to go down the street and buy me Beecham's
Powders for my cold, twenty Woodbines, a book of three-
penny stamps, and the *Radio Times;* and you forgot all three
because you were so preoccupied with that new Simenon
you'd found, and you said apologetically as you came in,
"I bought this Simenon because I know how much Hal—"
but you caught yourself and I know you were thinking of
sending it to your father. But this was so typical of the old
David—your typical forgetting something I sent you for,
and also getting involved in some paperback—that I couldn't
help wondering. And I knew, absolutely knew, that you
recalled at *least* your *father*. But then I thought maybe David
is really under amnesia and I'm intolerant; but I didn't quite
believe it. Can amnesia be halfway? I don't know.

Come back to me. When I think that one reason I put
up with you is the talent you have for *making me* forget,
I stop and wonder if your mind has infected mine. Con-
tagious amnesia!

I love you, but, you know, you *are* a rat!

Yours,
Ellen

P.S. I think you should have taken Harry up on his original
suggestion you go with him to see his family in Currington.
Why were you so jumpy about that invitation?

23 Oct.

Dear David,
    Your mother says you may come back before long. The

World Federalist job—if it materializes—sounds good. I would like to see you. I had trouble breathing yesterday, and Falco doesn't like it. Isn't that a thing to say? I didn't "like" it either. Falco still insists on the other "job" I mentioned. Am I stupid to feel about it the way I do? I heard not so long ago about an old man who developed some benign cancer (how can cancer be benign?) in his prostate and before he knew what had happened they'd done a double hernia and cut off his balls, and there he was. My own small growth I find I can forget about much of the day. I have to fight to keep your mother out of the bathroom with me. She's afraid I'll fall on the tub edge.

She talks a lot about Prof. Amerchrome being sick. It was in *Time* again this week. For her sake, I kid her, tell her she's forgetting about *me*. That appearance at Iroquois last year was *his* night, naturally, but still I couldn't help being impressed when he said one of his big ideas had been given to him by none other than David Brooke: It was you—and apparently you had no desire to use it yourself—who told him about the strange case of the old New Hampshire scholar who couldn't make up his mind what to bequeath. Sinclair, the name was.

Did I tell you your old pal Pennitt came back? It was just when Harry Tindall and his little wife were here. Isn't she perfect? Those dark eyes seem to see and hide everything. Of course, most of what she saw was that specimen of a husband in his cord jacket and those thick English pants that look like Western Frontier Trousers. Harry didn't say much about you, except that he hoped you knew what you were doing going in for the world federalists; he said you'd always had a degree of American evangelism in you, but he said it wittily and nicely. Maybe his phrases turn out too neat for comfort, I don't know. But he's quite a guy. You never told us several things, for instance about the farewell postlude he received the day you drove him down to his New York sailing. Harry says the local clothing merchant phoned up from the University Shop, said, "Just a second, Harry," and then proceeded to play slowly on the organ that's installed by the sport coats that "Going Home" tune from the New World Symphony. And Harry said to us, "The only custom I'd ever given him was once during a sale of underwear."

When Pennitt arrived, Harry and Anselin were beginning

to look a little restive; H. had come forward to the edge of his seat, and she had stopped talking very much but was looking at him fondly and nostalgically. When your mother said that this—Pennitt—was somebody you'd known in the rooming house before you'd known Harry, Harry just nodded agreeably and wouldn't ask questions. He and Anselin had a date to go to the Cloisters so Anselin could see the herbs.

Pennitt lit another cigarette and said quietly could he see me in "the other room" (whichever *that* was). And I knew he was up to getting rid of that coin-watch again; your mother was amazed and delighted that Pennitt had been so rude—you know how she is sometimes, the human parade, etc.—but I think she was also irked. I thought Pennitt must be in bad straits, so I took him into the bedroom, and he said he'd forgotten to tell me that a long time ago you'd told him you'd read about one of these and would love to see a real one someday and would like to own one. He'd lower the price to $80.00, said he'd hoped to terminate the deal that day. Well, I got mad; then he seemed to fall from whatever theatrical pose he'd been bargaining from and now just meekly said he had to leave town for a week and would I hold the coin-watch for him, no obligation. Why did I acquiesce? I don't know. I believe the thing is stolen and/or smuggled. Well, he was an old "friend" of yours. . . . Suddenly I felt badly that the bed wasn't made, and as Anselin and Harry came to the door I took the coin-watch and put it in my bathrobe and quickly wrote a check. And then—how confusing life seems to have to be—I had to hush up the old charlatan for he started to crow about his luck to your mother. He rattled off all kinds of nice things about you, what a good neighbor you were, how interested in people, what a well-rounded character you were, etc. I won't tell you for they'd make you feel smug.

So now I have a secret treasure. Let this letter be evidence of its existence; I hereby bequeath the coin-watch (or watch-coin) to you.

Love,
Dad

P.S. today I felt I really needed to see you. But I'm not sure why. I was looking at some of your effects in your bedroom. I even snooped into some of your notebooks; nothing incriminating. And I wanted to ask you a question or two.

Dear David,

I thought the chain letter you got me into was a real friendly gesture, and I do appreciate it. People to People, as General Ike says. Don't know what was meant by what my correspondent Mr. Harper said about you being unwell, and I don't just understand your kind of chain letter with each person in line worked out by you who started it. When I was a girl—which was a long time ago, Mr. Brooke—we had a chain letter each *new* person chose who he or she'd write to. You use a different system, but that's all right. I do hope you recall your old friend Mary Clovis here at Kodak Hotel. Because I like to be remembered (as I used to say to Mr. Clovis two weeks before my birthday). You were thoughtful usually, which is more than I can say for some others.

Mr. P. came back. Wasn't that odd? After all that trouble about his not ever paying his rent? Well, he said he'd been to California, but I never believed him; more likely he'd done a month in jail for stealing drink from that hotel he claimed to be a bell-man at and was just a bellhop. Driving to California with that Morganstern, I never heard such a thing! You recall the blond man with the German or Irish accent moved into Four just when you were leaving? Well, he didn't last. He was supposed to sell books, but I never saw books in his room when Terri let me in. One evening he stopped me in the hall as if he had something personal to say; but he didn't say a thing for a minute or so; then he tilted his head like he didn't understand me. Then he told me he once knew two men who built houses one on rock one on sand and the house on sand lasted just as long as the house on rock, even longer; and I stopped him and said what'd he mean by telling me that as if it actually happened. It was a lesson our Lord Jesus Christ taught, and this blondie—I *told* him so—was guilty of pelagiarism. (I think he'd heard me speaking of my good work and wanted to get the right side of me.) Well, soon after, the blond man left. And then, just after Jimmy Lafayette went, a new blond man came with a pair of aluminum valises. He'd never leave them by themselves. This man never left his room without those valises; except once or twice he would visit the bathroom and just lock the room and not take those valises with him. If he had used the facilities very much, the icebox and bathroom, etc., he might have had to leave those valises many times. He must have gone to the bathroom at his place of work, if he had a place of work.

He and Pennitt had midnight meetings. I happened to stop by Four and del Torto (that was his name) was saying, "Listen, old man, you haven't got time to play around, the John Armoury will be after us in a week if we don't do some broken-field running." So they had taken guns from one of them armories in Manhattan. And you can believe me, from what I heard from del Torto himself, I wouldn't be surprised to find he's in with some group planning an invasion from Cuba. With a first name like Aranho, what could you expect? Of course, *if* his name *was* del Torto—always a little too charming, if you know what I mean. Not the kind of man Mr. Clovis was. This del Torto, you're never sure he takes you seriously. (Claims his mother's father was Polish and one day in Lodge (?) went out to fix the shutters and went to America instead.) Well well, one day del Torto came to me with a White Tower Daily Prayer brochure I'd had Terri leave in his room, and though he seemed as usual very amicable it seemed to me when he quietly asked me why I'd left it in his room that he was out to scare me. I said I did it for his own good. Then he told me a positively dreadful and untrue story about the wise men and Mary and Joseph and the name of our Lord and tripping over a threshold, and I couldn't say a thing, just looked at his blond moustache (he's a handsome man). I was turning the other cheek. And all I said—warningly as I backed away from him—was, "You better read the brochure, Mr. del Torto, you better read the brochure, I wouldn't pretend to add to what's there!" Oh yes, I did say after the story what Mr. Clovis always said: "A travesty! A travesty!" And guess what del Torto said back to me: I can barely say it, it takes hold of me so devilishly: that Jesus was a travesty of man's natural egoism, of man's human nature. Del Torto licked his lips and grinned at me. I thought of the animal in people. One day I'll get down to finding out who he really was— he's gone away now. He looks a bit like the book salesman. Selbstein said his name wasn't really del Torto; and that he dyed his hair. Well, Mr. S. said never to tell, but the fact is that del Torto would sign his name on his blank checks B. Jesus Shine, and the bank was Provincetown, Mass. But "I will take the stony heart out of their flesh, and will give them an heart of flesh."

I sometimes wonder if I can bear any more. So I was glad to get your chain through Mr. Harper and send it on to the next person, a Michael Amerchrome at a Manhattan address, not only a friendly note but a dozen copies of our weekly prayer Brochure. And just as sure as I know Mr. Clovis is waiting for me, I know that your chain letter was a good thing.

Am so full of joy to be in communication with you, David, again.

Yours in His Fellowship
Mrs. Clovis

P.S. Your shelf is always waiting for you in the icebox. Ha ha!

Oct. 29th

David dear,

Today I feel as if the greatest dark confusing shadows have gone away from me, for your father is better. Suddenly he's come back strong. If I'd written you last night I'd have said just the opposite; he couldn't get comfortable, and this little restless business all day and all evening scared me the way little indicators will. Halsey's condition was such that I even forgot you. I forgot everything. But just now Falco has said in an oddly hectoring tone that if H. keeps up the good work we might be able to take a cruise in December. Too cold to go to the country, but a cruise down south might be good. Of course, Falco told me privately that these mysterious comebacks may be misleading. But I easily forget they may be, and now with good news it's as if the world has come back to this apartment. Josie and Bos Benson and their engagement troubles; poor B-G almost refusing to admit that it's too late for him to be having a *real* girl friend, and squiring a perfectly lovely model, a colored girl, to chamber recitals and Boston play-openings, and buying her pompano at Nino's and getting his friend the wholesale fishing tackle magnet—I think his name is something like Ben Shane—to sail him and his girl around the Sound weekends; and your friend St. John pretending he doesn't enjoy being now again thought to be the mysterious tire-slasher; his last letter to the *Brooklyn Heights Press* had the ending, "Drive anything bigger than a Volkswagen up Willow Street or Columbia Heights at ten P.M. and you risk nicking someone's paint job. Our streets are clotted with cars!" And right after that letter the slasher struck again. The police are reported to know who he is (wouldn't it be funny if it did turn out to be St. John?!), but the Figgises have organized two unofficial patrols that operate on random evenings: they proceed down parallel streets, at least one person on each side of a street. The slasher has even worked Clark Street along in front of the St. George and Towers. And St. John met the Figgises one night, or met Mrs.—for he was reconnoitering the other side—and St. John told her he sympathized with the slasher, though said he felt the slasher should let legal cars alone. St. John told me last week—and I forgot it because I was so upset about your father—that one night he saw Mrs. Figgis approaching—with Mr. F. across the street further back—and Peter waited, then crossed over and stood under a streetlamp ignoring her and pretending to look guilty. Frankly, Ian Harper changed the subject with Peter when it came up in the bookshop the other day, or so Peter told me. And now Peter is afraid people like Ian he really cares for may actually believe he *is* the slasher. Peter and I took a walk—your cousin Jonni stayed with your father—and P. and I walked to the Promenade—where else!— and he told me how he felt about the Heights and I told him how you used to scramble about on that dangerous bluff above Furman Street before they built the Promenade and how you polled the neighborhood to find out how many Lucky Sticks had turned up in Good Humors for something like ten days (because you were so eager to get one) and how when you were seven you stayed out on that dangerous banky bluff for hours at a time watching that three- or four-day fire destroy the Furman Street wharf warehouses, and how in the '38 hurricane our awning got ripped off and you wrote a several-hundred-word description of how it happened (even though you were only in the third grade). Well, I found Peter St. John interrupting, getting in little parallels about his London boyhood; and then he took over the conversation almost as if I weren't there. David, dear, some blue evenings just before twilight, the skyline looks as if it had been constructed, not as a sequence of functional buildings or even (as that writer put it who did umpty-thousand words on the Heights for *Vogue*) as a giant cameo finely silhouetted on a rosy ground—but as a memory—yes, constructed as a memory.

Halsey has come back strong. I guess I said that. Has a tan from being on the roof. Is dubious about a trip (after he gets really well) to Puerto Rico. It's been strange how Halsey has been reading the Bible. He smiles rather grimly and says, "Well, I've got to get through it, now I've begun." *Entre nous,* he really is going rather religious—in his own way, of course, and I'd never speak of it. He enjoys what he reads, though he doesn't like some of the arguments he gets into with Pelago. Thinks Pelago overstresses the idea that the Old Testament is nothing without the New. Friday, Monica and I played him the slow movement of the Bach two-violin that you love so much and that we're going to play in church at Christmastime.

Ellen's been so good to keep us posted.

Cross your fingers.

Love to you both,
Mother

P.S. We had a card from Bobby Prynne from Reykjavik. I assume he saw you. Said he found out too late that he should have been visiting the *north* of Iceland; never saw a map till half an hour before his plane left, which was ten minutes before he wrote the postcard. Card shows fabulous waterfall!

P.P.S. Your pal Wanda left a book here called *Wisdom, Madness, and Folly.* I'm not giving it to your father, it's a disconcerting sort of testament. The author, apparently a manic-depressive, uses his psychosis(?) as a foundation for a whole philosophical and religious system of contraries.

My dear E.,

I can explain better in writing than in speech. This note is an answer to yours, but also to a month of your poignant uncertainties.

Part put on? Yes; but this doesn't answer much.

My loss of memory was part real, part something else. The real was a muggy gray sea of clouds in my mind: e.g., my failure to see what any one of a certain group of acquaintances had to do with any one other member of this group; then my failure to get a letter from Bobby Prynne after I'd written him *seven* letters the last two years; then my not hearing from other people; and then my sense of the impracticability of the new "Confederation after Decentralization" plan the New York-London fed outfit sent me for study—I suspect Duke is behind the plan. Then on top of all this, we had that fight after I said I was suddenly sorry the scare about your maybe being pregnant turned out unwarranted, and you got mad and said we were waiting only because of me, and I at last said, "Oh God, what's it going to matter in a thousand years?" And then I got hit on the head—by the Blue Guide *Athens*, I'm told. But *before* I got hit, the gathering incoherence was already great; and I already doubted the identity of the aforementioned acquaintances.

The beginnings of this last spring caused me to send out those crisscross patterns of chain letters designed to return eventually to me. Well, each one got fouled somewhere, and I became convinced that some cat's cradle of reality existed among these people who were supposed to be my acquaintances but who were in fact utterly out of my life. My talent for total recall was always such that I only half listened to people, knowing, of course, that all they said would stick in my mind. But this behavior helped to cut me off from them. But when the doctor, a reasonable man, was looking at my bump that evening of our fight, I was genuinely suffering from the incoherence aforementioned, an incoherence that debilitated my will to remember. You must believe that, take it on faith.

But also, yes, Ellen, I did *put on* some of the amnesia. But pay heed to the fact that I pulled it off—in the face of seeing people dear to me wonder if they knew me. As the doctor felt my bump, I thought of all these things, and also of the chap Schoonover I met by chance at the British Museum Slavonik Periodicals Room who was madly eager to tell me his life so I'd be as fascinated by it as he. And then, if I remember right, he named certain people I knew indirectly; and I thought that now, having failed to make any community, I must erase the past totally and make a new start. All those people Paul Schoonover's "do-you-know's" represented—I felt unbridgeable distances away from them. And I knew my memory was one reason I'd failed to bring them within the circle of myself. Can you understand that? Finding myself cut off from other people (excised from their lives) and also cut out in part because I was letting reliance on memory let me preoccupy myself with matters other than those immediately confronting me, I thought I would choose to act in a way consistent with this excision.

True, memory and ambition are needed for the full engagement of the intelligence. But: Remember the "wrong" things too keenly and you can't move an inch. Ambition—I mean, really, *action*—requires us to forget.

Through this month I was at first appalled at how in the get-well letters I received the one theme of self-concern overwhelmed the other theme of my health. But then Duke's second letter came.

Duke, though many of his shoveling generalizations are parodies of right inference, is (in spite of himself) right: We are all amnesiacs to begin with, we don't have to become that way. Maybe still the highest life demands the most ruthless and even *amorous* memory; yet everyone—from the hard-headed Tindall down to poor old Hugh St. John (who reads seven newspapers a day—or, i.e., has them read to him) practices the art, or, if you will, takes daily doses of the milk of, amnesia.

Thus we cross from day to day, place to psychic place. Harry, e.g., forcibly forgets the anguish he felt over his friend Jaro's death, the guilt he knows he has reason to feel. Does my father put such things out of mind? This morning, as I was getting ready to "recover" and announce to you by mail my recovery, I thought that I don't know the answer to the question. Dad certainly seems remote—but real.

I return to the project. And I cease trying to pass as what I cannot be or want to be—a total amnesiac.

Self-interested the get-well letters have been; but they have been in a sense Orphean parts of *me* homing in on *my* radiant self. And each day lately I'm scared I'll get a suicide note from someone I've tried to forget.

Please come in the door, I want to kiss you.

D.

P.S. (7:30) I hear "Rudolph the Red-Nosed Reindeer" loudly outside, so must close and dash out and catch the ice-cream man before he drives off to Edgware Road.

P.P.S. Do we not use each other to slip across the frontiers of self-scrutiny as something other than lonely people?

<pre>
                                      November 6
ABZ2468/YXW777   NEW YORK
    29000   17   5   1930

    DBROOKE 7½ HARROWBY ST LONDON W1

    YOUR FATHER DIED THIS MORNING
    LET ME KNOW YOUR IMMEDIATE PLANS
                    LOVE MOTHER

                              Post GPO Office
                              Cable & Wireless
                                    Services

    Enquiry respecting this Telegram should be ac-
    companied by this form. Mark your reply VIA
    IMPERIAL
</pre>

Nov. 4

Dear old David,

At this writing I hear your father has come back strong and that it may not be necessary for him to go into hospital. Which is good news. (Incidence of heart disease is so high!) You've heard, of course, that he's breathing more easily. I can't help wondering what effect your father's illness has had on your own, and I again, of course, hope you are restored to your former self. It's so difficult to believe in a friend's amnesia. It's like admitting—in his sudden ignorance of you—that you are dead and gone. Or changed utterly. Walt Roy told me he feels that he went to sleep (in a sense) when his father died—and is just now starting to wake up.

Do you find Prof. Amerchrome in your memory? That renowned hystereogogue is in all the papers today. Apparently dying in hospital in San Francisco (or did you know that?), Amerchrome has suddenly disappeared. In his bed in hospital were discovered a small pile of raw kohlrabi tubers and a pair of Egyptian (Nubian) stone cuff links he is known to have worn in his pajama sleeves. The papers said that his wife couldn't be reached—but she checked out of her hotel two days ago and has been in the hospital with him much of the time. Also it is reported that Michael Amerchrome resigned from the Hebrew University in Jerusalem a fortnight ago and left the country on an El Al jet for New York. Coincidental? All very strange. Mysteries multiply. Sally, of course, knew through Monica that Mrs. Amerchrome had taken a duplex on Grace Court, and, *entre nous*, day before yesterday Walt found out that a certain piece of furniture being moved into a certain apartment house was in fact for the Amerchromes! In fact, a Turnbull Elevator Stairclimber! Amerchrome's life story is to appear in *The World* Sunday. I'll get a copy at Times Square rather than get my father to mail one. Am I mad to see some coincidence in the coterminous illnesses of your father and Amerchrome?

When I phoned your mother yesterday and she said your father was much improved, I couldn't help hoping it was an omen good for you, there three thousand dimming miles away in God's country. This morning, thinking about you, I wondered if it is possible to face calmly a permanent partial amnesia. Browsing through Van Gogh's letters (the big 3-vol. ed., which has now been sold to Mrs. Fargo for her Oxonian son) I came across this passage: "Have more hope than memories, whatever has been valuable and blessed in your past is not lost, you will meet it again on your path, so don't think about it any more, but go forward." (Or is this just Hammerstein with a Proustian reserve?) Elsewhere Vincent speaks of the twenty-five pounds of oatmeal his father sent him in England and speaks of his "sickly (though noble) longing" for father and home. This is, of course, in the period when he still hoped to enter the Christian ministry. Book prices are up since just after the War. Understandable. Look at the St. George swimming pool prices!

Well, if prices don't come back, people do. Do you recall when I blew up at young Fargo at Iroquois and you conceived so odd a respect for me? You'll be amused to know I met him again, and at Iroquois. Sally made me go. We were invited by Monica, and Prof. Amerchrome spoke. Your mother had dragooned him. He spoke—I think—on world federalism and the strangely rich archives of the London unifist groups. Fargo kept after Amerchrome after the talk, wouldn't let him go; and A. kept saying, "Of course, I've got all the time in the world for you," but kept turning away to some of the others, the Fearons (whom he succeeded in charming) and Ian Harper, with whom he talked squash. At last, with Fargo still trailing him, he came up to me and —which pleased me though I've made peace with Tom— ignored Tom and asked me if I'd ever come across any autograph letters from the Revolutionary War in my snooping through Putnam County. I asked how he knew I'd been up there. He said the Fearons mentioned it. I was going to mention one of the letters from the Tell collection, but I haven't verified it yet and at the moment I rather like having the secret to myself.

When next we meet you will recognize me even though I have put on a stone. Funny, this fat just below the floating rib: when you walk you feel that some of the knitting of your body has broken; but on the other hand, the slight jiggle makes you more fully aware than ever before of the connections among the various parts of your body. (Or is the thought just more of my mental dandruff?)

I try to keep in shape at the St. George pool. Do you recall a Walt Roy? I recall telling you about him. Lately he and I are friendly again and meet regularly for a swim at the St. George. The last two Sunday mornings (early) he hasn't been there. I shouldn't count so much on seeing him. Do you recall that night in '57? You rapped on the window and came in and seemed not to be paying attention to *my* story but to be preoccupied with something of your own. You told me how you felt guilty about sometimes wanting to remake your father in another image yet mainly you felt wronged to have been given so much freedom. I forget. I recall feeling as you told me these things, somehow having been through it all myself—yet not with my *own* father. Strange, eh?

Item: Twenty-five of the Heights' finest—the Figgises, Monica Flower, the Harpers, Mrs. Fargo, the Fearons, several others whom you know—have planned a cruise for early next spring: it is billed by Milbanke Travel Ltd. (New Bond St.), as the Wonder Cruise to the Isles of Greece and the Holy Land. They'll begin in London. But the actual

cruise is "Venice to Venice." They sail on the S.S. *Fantasia*.
Epilogue to *The Seven Pillars*:

> I had dreamed, at the City School in Oxford, of hustling
> into form, while I lived, the new Asia which time was
> inexorably bringing upon us. Mecca was to lead to
> Damascus, Damascus to Anatolia, and afterward to
> Bagdad; and then there was Yemen. Fantasies, these
> will seem to such as are able to call my beginning an
> ordinary effort!

Please look up Father. He'd so appreciate it. Did I tell
you? I bought him the freehold reversion on the Highgate
house.

Love,
Peter

P.S. Oh yes: speaking of secrets: Ian Harper brought in
a book yesterday that I sold two years ago. Has passed
through the hands of several owners. Do you know the
book? Custance, *Wisdom, Madness, and Folly?* Strange
thing is that long ago—cross my heart and hope to die—I
doodled part of my Labé into it. Well, guess what! Someone
—I'll never know who—has added the rest; and it's almost
exactly the same as *my* translation!

as always p.

integration and the man upstairs

(Why the last letter? Sneaky enough you scrapped the initial plan for *forty* Gethseminal epistles; but you might still have *ended* as we planned, viz., i.e., with the November 6 cable! Well, I surely hope you quit fiddling with Memoir VIII—and what's the big secret anyway? You're keeping me from looking at VIII; I'd never have thought you were capable of it. As J. J. Lafayette's pa used to say when J. J. forgot to pass the tzimmes, "What, is my soul a raisin?" You let Ellen read VIII last night, but I don't even get a glimpse of it. Well, I *do* hope you've followed the Revised Standard Master Plan here at the end, in this eighth, or "release," memoir-projection. Here, if you recall, we get inside Halsey Brooke; here we gather, like some octavo's conjugate leaves once sadly severed yet still mysteriously kin, the people of our project in one Juliastic "at home" which will take certain statutory liberties with what some narrow minds will call "the facts," but which will transcend base littoral facticity and fly out into an oceanic truth which, as if after Buddha's Seven Stages of Meditation, leads to the Eightfold Way and its concomitant and coterminous Cessation of Pain. Next quest: For A DOUBLOON! Apprenticeship customarily (!) lasts how long? Sink before you answer! See how easy-going I am, Davey? Even though you don't confide in yours truly as before, I trust in you. Indeed, my dear, this VIII is to be a world like that within the atomic nucleus recently described by the Brookhaven Boys—elegant, even gallant arrangements of the "eightfold way" ("unitary symmetry") which itself represents the strange harmonics of the heavy intranuclear particles. (The effect the BB describe seems like plucking a violin string harder and harder so that higher and higher harmonics can be heard, all mathemati-

cally related to the fundamental note.) (Aren't I a one?!)
Davey, pay tension . . . !)

> On the left foot, peg foot, travelin' on
> Follow the drinkin' gourd.
> Follow the drinkin' gourd,
> Follow the drinkin' gourd,
> For the old man is awaitin'
> For to carry you to freedom
> If you follow the drinkin' gourd.

"Your countrymen don't know when to stop. They've
been singing all night. What's the gourd and who's the old
man? It's all *so* portentous." (Ssstupid Ellen!)

"It's a southern slave song, the drinking gourd is the Big
Dipper pointing north, the old man will help them, he's
probably linked up with the underground railway—and he
has a peg leg."

"Well, it's very mysterious; why not call a spade a spade?"

"The singer had to keep from being understood by the
wrong people."

(You're on the same spot, Davey dear; you must use *your*
gourd if you want to escape Ellen. Do you remember Prospect Park's octagonal paving stones?)

"I'm repacked. Imagine you not knowing it took eight
days to get to London!"

"I wish those bastards next door would shut up. I still
have work to do. What's my East Lite Box-File doing there
on the bunk?"

"I put my clippings in it. Your stuff is in the smuggler's
Bible, where you wanted it."

". . . Ready for the old man . . . ."

"For the last time, who is the old man in London?"

"You wouldn't understand."

"You still fiddling with that last manuscript? We've half
an hour till breakfast."

"You took so long over eight last night."

"Strange, that one. It isn't much of a memory. But it is
your father somehow."

(D. darling, what've you *done* to eight!)

"Time's running out."

(Well, not exactly, not exactly. And whatever have you done to this last?)

"*Is* there any such old man? Is this one of your bloody ruses?"

"Are you implying I made him up? Do I re (call the Old man at the Marylebone Public Library? Of course: I was there. Second floor. I recall his small head and receding face, his long jaw, his back-slanting brow, the sparse straight toneless flax slicked back on his skull. Scraps of paper lay strewn on the table within arm's length, some paper-clipped together. He was scribbling new letters and labels, sorting the old papers (moving one scrap toward the outskirts, another in toward the center, dispersing (as if dispatching) three or four slips previously clipped). He was whispering, there in his heavy coat (once a gray cheviot, now the drab memory of one). He stank—socks, armpits, groin, mildew inside and out, all collaborating to make it the special smell of a true foot-fungus. Oh Davey, she can never understand the occult charm of that man!)

"Look if you're just going to tell this to the mirror, I may as well go up and look at the river bank."

"No, I'm trying to explain. The old man seemed not to have (seen me—even when he briefly beamed up at me. But when I paused at the reference desk to get a Manhattan phone book, I found he'd followed me, had left the periodical room, was standing right by me. And when I went into the study room on the other side of the reference desk, he followed still. And when I pulled out an Ouspensky that'd been misplaced from downstairs—the English go for things like theosophy—he said in an undertone, 'You're interested in that?' He couldn't stop blinking. 'Curious,' I said in reply. 'He's reached you already,' the old man said. 'Oftentimes a spirit-author gets to you before you actually read him.' 'I have a thing I'm sort of working on,' I said. 'Yes, he answered, 'well if you like a spirit-author you can't afford to miss—' he pulled out and unfolded an issue of *Psychic News* —'this. This, and—' he pulled from another pocket—'*Two Worlds*. Geraldine Cummins the famous automatic writing medium. And exposés of how weak ESP is in a mere scientific experiment without a medium. And also you get dis-

cussions of the grave crisis organized spiritualism faces—of
course the SNU (Spiritualists' National Union) was formed
in 1901 out of the Spiritualists' National Federation (1890)
and proceeded to take over the rights and assets of SNF,
and now SNU nearly bankrupt because SNF claims a mo-
nopoly of medium-ship and many members have got out.'
In the upper left corner of the front page of *Psychic News*
I saw the words, 'You will live after you die' and pointed
to them. But as I opened my mouth to speak, my old man
said to me, 'You don't become quote unquote spiritual by
the incidence of passing over from this world to the next.
Death only produces a discarnate entity that then begins an
existence in a less heavy atmosphere. But I urge you to take
these two publications and if you want to try a greater London fellowship I'm very high on the Gethsemane Healing
Band, 39 Tachbrook Street, Victoria.' 'My project,' I started
to say, 'my project—' but the old man broke in, 'I believe
in Union, of course—All Worlds Are One World, we say—
but not via SNU. I *was* working on a what I call a psycho-
pathic language based on breath communication and lip
contact but SNU's problems were so pressing I had to stop
my linguistic work and turn to what you might call administration, and the lovely thing is I find my language material
can be utilized, you see, for my new Universal Spiritualist
Constitution.' 'But,' I said, 'my own project—' and as I returned the Ouspensky to its wrong shelf, the old man said,
'Subscribe.' 'My project—' 'That's it, pro*ject*, accent the right
syllable.' 'Pro*ject*? Into? Out of?' 'Both; and a subscription
to *PN* and *Two Worlds* will help.' 'Yes,' I went on, 'I thought
of projecting into people.' 'Like to see you do it,' my friend
said, 'secret stuff—one day you turn up like an apport in
someone's consciousness.' 'I've been at work on it for years,
for my whole life; now, to fulfill this *project* will take me
many months.' 'Like to see your pro*ject*. Bring it around here
when you're finished. I'm always here Mondays. Monday is
the eighth day, you see. You get the first seven, ordinary creation plus a rest stop; but then comes the breakthrough, the
eighth day—' 'You would like to see my project when it's
finished?' 'Always interested in material for my USC.' A
nimbus seemed to shine from the dandruff all on his shoul-

359

ders, and the slight crust on his eyelashes plus the state
of his whites indicated chronic and untended conjunctivitis,
his alarmed, tender look seemed—"

"Oh God, balls, David, balls—well I hope you can get
your nose out of VIII before breakfast. And by the way,
decide whether you're talking to me or reading that
chapter!"

"And he pulled out two little forms for *Psychic News* and
Two Worlds, and I paid him for two subscriptions, and ever
since, I've been planning to present him with my completed
project."

"Even if he does exist as you claim, does he really matter?
Can you believe you actually did these manuscripts for
him?"

(Isn't that a typical Ellen question? Davey, what's the
matter, you don't believe her insinuation, do you? Have you
forgotten the Scots' sense of "smuggle"? Viz., "to manufac-
ture spirits illegally.")

"Darling, you wrote these memories—even though they
really aren't exactly memories—because you *wanted* to. Not
for someone else!"

"What do you mean, they're not exactly memories?"

"Well, it *is*, mind you, your father, somehow it is."

(But—Bitch!—is it *Our* Father? And now you let me look
and what do I see? Oh no! I had an eighth exact memory
for us. *I*, your dear *I*, via whom you've come to these seven
memories—*I*, your dear Aga-Memnon, gave you seven perfectly divine cities to ease you and make you play ball, and
even—against your coming—prepared an eighth. And what
happens! You go all soppy and substitute in VIII an arrant
fabrication. What has happened to our use of Duke's IBM
Concordance of Words used by *Time*, that magazine of
potentially explosive verbal connections in a splintered
world?)

"Ellen, is the steward on the deck above this one blond?"
"I don't know."

"And that man who chased me and got off at Le Havre?"
"*Brown* hair."

"And called up to me from the wharf?"

"He never called up; I watched him, because I didn't like

him; you thought there was something strange about him and you followed him around the ship."

"Our steward has blond eyebrows, hasn't he?"

"Very blond."

"And that other man always spoke of smuggling?"

"I don't know."

(OK Dave, ask this bitch how come you got the smuggler's Bible, ask her that—)

"But they have been singing that slave song next door?"

"Of course, darling. And you're so bright to know what it means!"

(They were *too* blond, every working one of them!)

"Time's run out. Time for breakfast, and then—"

(No, darling D., we have nine, ten, eleven, twelve—think of all the memories in store for our apostolic future! But what are you doing opening the Bible and fiddling with the dedicatory page, that last glistering irony cum generosity? "Without my *wife's* love and encouragement, I should never have been able to compose these memories, to mint and transmit these pieces of eight." Why X it out? Or are you planning a simple humble one like, "To my wife, without whom nothing"? No? No dedication, at all? Well, darling, maybe that's better. Of course, you might write, "To Ellen, In spite of whom this book was written." No? OK dear.)

"Ellen, come here and kiss me. You're practically home."

(Those fake endearments don't fool me, you bad boy. Am I going to have to take extreme measures? Have I to dose you with castor oil to purge you the way the Pakistani Customs "clear" caravan camels of any suspicion of contraband gold at the frontier?)

"Ellen, like a rocket after the first, second, third, fourth, fifth, sixth, and seventh stages drop away—"

"Rocket sprocket, mmmmmmmm."

(David, a clean hand's better than a dirty woman! I only ask a fair shake!)

"David, wake up, chop chop, *here* I am!"

(So many promises broken: e.g., what happened to the seventeenth-century watch (French) that was to have traveled glimmeringly through VIII? Wind it, and you set

off the moving parts (yuk-yuk) of a minute but grossly entertaining scene visible if you open the back of the watch—yes
yes (remember?), a time-piece mentioned first by Peter St. J.
as having been auctioned at Sotheby's described as *"Scène
plus que galante." Quelle belle* design the eight were, could
have been, could still be. Spenser understood fragments:
"Changed like a garden in the heat of spring/After an eight-
days' absence." But I don't quibble, DB, you chose to do
VIII as—yes, all I ask is you remember I'm thy chief steward
ever keeping the pot hot on the range to feed you my dear
Dave—for wearily I say unto you, a well-fed ship can go on
forever!)

"I'm hungry."

(I am yr devoted Tangerine, ever-ready to use my connections to get you an emergency passport, ready to run you
over to Gibraltar in my private minesweeper with its P38
aircraft engines. What can *she* do for you? Oh by the way,
dearie, on second inspection, I think that in VII your use
of Orpheus was acute—or should I—darling, *dare* I—say,
Orpheus and the Thirty Pieces of Silver (yuk-yuk)? Earlier
I called you my invention. Maybe I better call myself your
intention. I know: We'll meet halfway: for memoir nine,
parody Goliath, and *you* must—yes, I've got it!—you will
turn into the stone imbedding itself in my brow, and we'll
be just like old times. Hey, remember that if the Brookhaven
Boys have found the Eightfold Way, the known particles
are grouped not only into three families of eight but—*terra*-
Billy dictaphone!—also into one family of ten. And *pfut!*
Napoleon got English gold via smuggling galleys of a special
type called a "death"!)

"Ellen, once I thought of killing myself—to get out. But
instead, I chose another way of leaving myself—projecting
into the lives, the consciousnesses of others." (Kaa-kaa:
remember the day we spent in Harry's mind? and saw him
thinking we—i.e., *you*—were, in his favorite phrase, "too light
for heavy work"? And remember *all* our *friends*—e.g., Mary
Clovis, chosen one of the 1376 people to tape-read twenty-
five verses from the Bible (any version) for WFME-FM,
Newark!) (Please! Don't you know me? I'm Yore Old

Eeyore Yore Ol' Gay Donkey, egomorphosed so as to pass unnoticed in that low-lit stable tableau. David! Davey! Aieee! DB—)

"Ellen."

VIII

SMUGGLER'S HARBOR,
OR HALSEY LIVES AGAIN

YOU have before you what you always wanted: a view of the main reach of the harbor between the Narrows, which you can't quite see, and the tip of the Battery, where the East River and the Hudson join.

From behind, you appear to be looking through your blooming telescope. But your head has angled left so both your eyes can look at the near docks. It's Monday, and you dressed before breakfast because thus you seem to yourself to be on vacation rather than in mortal danger. A small ruse and, like so many we use on ourselves, successful—but only in one wing of the mind.

You don't usually make believe.

You seldom told me stories when we walked on Sundays down to these docks you now look at, that border Brooklyn Heights on the west. Did you know I was just as glad you didn't tell stories, and did you know I knew you felt awkward telling them? In you some reserve and doughty nervousness decline to ask extended attention of listeners. And you are "man enough" in your odd way to hate botched or punch-lineless endings. One Sunday afternoon—long before you and my mother went to Norway—you told me about the Norwegian fishermen who hauled up in their net a huge cross; and you told how this cross soon became the emblematic foundation of a tall, plain country church near Bergen; and you told how later this cross disappeared, and how now the congregation are said to believe that the sea was claiming what had come from it. But you never knew I loved the newly rediscovered hesitations you fell into, as again you found the end of the recounted tale a letdown. You never knew I loved your lame, grim smile; never knew, because I didn't *let* you know. Or do I hide the truth in the shades

364

of my private bathos? There you sit now by the window, three thousand miles from me. If you could hear me, you'd groan and say, "OK, OK, let's have the *Sad* music," and you'd hum that famous dripping violin line from the silent film days. "Daaa-daaa-daaaaaa, da-daaa-daaa-daaaaaa."

Now, sick, alone with my mother, you see new warehouses, and you see freighters from Colombia and Norway. The oldest ship in any slip here may well date from the time of our first walks. In my now hungrier imagination it seems to have been the large rusted bollards and the greasy rope fenders that caused the special smell. It was cool, metallic, and machine; it was wet, woven, useful, indestructible, and rotting. You and I gazed up at the red-lead-spotted bow of a Norwegian hull and speculated whether she was soon to go out or had just come in. The immense scale of the docks and the grand dark business of arrivals and departures, we felt more then than later, for our apartment was then three whole streets away from the harbor. And furthermore, we walked those docks—not these that you muse over this Monday morning, for so much of these is new—walked those docks on Sundays only. It had to be Sunday afternoons, for my mother made me go to Sunday school. Then, when I reached the age of twelve, I had to go to regular church. I'd been "taken into" the church, old Dr. Mann with much benediction (with impromptu, almost distracted fluency of scriptual citation—one verse leading to one in another book, Old Testament, New, and back again, so we junior communicants, smelling the chrysanthemums from Weirs and feeling God's carpets formal and slippery under the new leather soles of our best shoes, were kept standing, like those in all the pews behind, a good fifteen minutes extra), Dr. Mann gave me a soft, imitation-calf medium-octavo King James inscribed in the inside of the cover with gilt letters identifying me, the occasion, and the date. True, for a time I enjoyed a smug sense of membership in that church—the full, adult rights; the deferential amusement with which our handsome old colored sexton Abraham honored me when I wasted his time asking him questions; and the Bible itself—i.e. *my* copy, and perhaps, too, the poetic, comforting inevitability of the chapter Dr. Mann always had his communicants class memorize, I Corinthians 13.

But always, I longed to walk with you Sunday *mornings*, walk before anyone else was up, walk the docks.

On our regular Sunday afternoon walks you wore your church clothes. If it was March or April you wore that heavy, black double-breasted overcoat tailored, according to the label on the inside pocket next to your heart, by a tailor with the antique, ghostly name "J. Doblin." As for style, you never ran to a white rim of handkerchief in that coat's breast pocket; but you were a little elegant, certainly, with your white, papery carnation and, until the war, gray spats, and a derby, whose constructed, strong-shelled shape I paired in my imagination with your collapsible opera hat, which I often became madly engrossed in snapping open again and again against my knee. Sometimes I took your hand as, with the hint of a hop in our gait, we marched down Joralemon Street's steep, last block toward the shadowy walls of the dock warehouses.

Are you now regathering some of those Sunday afternoons? Do you recall how if the quiet of the docks was broken at all it was merely increased? Yes: by an old locomotive on overtime, slow-puffing and, with an echoing clash of coupling, hauling three great brown-and-orange freight cars over the worn tracks along the wharves; or broken by my projected voice testing the echo in a waterside warehouse that happened to be open.

Those Sunday afternoons you and I weren't surrounded by identifiers—as we were at the grossly entertaining, endlessly rich circus at the Garden, where every other pair was father-son; or as at Ebbets Field taking a seventh-inning stretch and hoping Higbe could hold his fast ball through the top of the ninth. You made a successful father on those official occasions: You had a simpler scorecard code than Red Barber (if his was shorthand, yours was QUIKRITE); and the second year we went to Barnum and Bailey's you stopped me from intently cracking my new souvenir lion-tamer's whip at people's coattails, and you broke its long handle across your knee—which impressed me. But our walks along the docks were different, alone.

"Halsey? Halsey?" My mother has called across the living room from the hallway arch to your chair near the open piano keyboard.

You have answered . . . . You hardly know what. She doesn't mind your being quiet; you often are. But the possibility that you're lost in a deep daydream rather scares her, as you well know.

"Are you out of the Gospels yet?"

You know some of what's in her mind, for the reverend young Dr. Archibald Pelago (very prematurely going healthy gray) out of the tortuous deeps of his pastoral psychology has passed on what she said: that your new reading makes her happy. She knows how calmly full of disbelief you've been all these years. (Of course, she herself is only a *musical* Christian.) And now—abetted tacitly by you—she thinks she knows what this Bible suddenly means to you. And, not being a deceiver, you have been surprised to discover that you wish to help sustain this delusion of hers.

Yet my Bible does interest you. The Jewishness of the Gospels. The strange and maybe plagiaristic echo of Isaiah in Jesus' words about the stone that would someday make Israel stumble. And the reality of the stories in Samuel. And the ceremonial genealogies.

Do you think of me as you read the inscription on the inside of the cover, or as you pursue the adventures of the misunderstood Joseph? Do you think of me as you again come across the exquisite Jacobean syntax of Paul's precious, absurd words to the Corinthians—"then shall I know even as also I am known"? For memorizing the Twenty-third Psalm you gave me a hockey stick, the blade of which I carefully wound with black bicycle tape one afternoon before self-consciously joining my regular afternoon roller-skate scrimmage on Grace Court.

A week later, feeling generous, I volunteered to go with you to Greenwood Cemetery to hunt up your father's grave. You hadn't gone for thirty years, and when I saw that the thousands of stones were packed together in barely containable captivity, I thought I saw why you'd avoided going. But of course I'd forgotten that Greenwood wasn't always so jammed, was once . . . whatever a cemetery is supposed to be. Coming out, just before we passed the cemetery's arched gate, you said, covering your disappointment, "Cemeteries leave me cold." I think you wanted to hide from me your feeling. Your father's marker designated a plot that, defined on all four sides by other markers and their plots, seemed too small for one man's coffin. Coming out of the subway at the St. George, we met Mr. and Mrs. Fargo, and he whispered croakingly to me out of that perpetually bad throat of his that finally killed him, "And where have *we* been this fine Saturday afternoon?" I said, "To see my father's father's grave"—which for some reason really stopped Mr. Fargo.

Do you recall Cousin Jonni yapping at me about my calling you (in the presence of others) "my father" and the same with "my mother"? "Why can't you just say 'Mother' or 'Father'?" And you reported in my behalf, "It's David's style, for God's sake." You knew I was stiff and strange. You didn't know what to do about it. But I see now that what you did do was good enough, better than I then saw. (I hear myself adding, "Better than I perhaps even ever *deserved*," and you checking my remark quickly and shyly, "No, for God's sake, none of *that* talk; that doesn't get us anywhere. You wouldn't say right out what was wrong with my sententious sentiments, would you!)

Was it another one of those indirect messages you sent me the Christmas I'd driven home from New Hampshire? I thought I wouldn't go to the annual church pageant that Sunday afternoon. I'd forgotten that with the organist my mother was playing the Blitzstein "Carol Fantasia" as part of the prelude. But you didn't remind me of that. You merely tilted your head trying to look quizzical and said, "The pageant ought to be good for laughs. The kids . . . ."

Oh God, it was Pelago's first Christmas at the church, and he didn't let anyone forget. Dr. Mann used to digress—but humanly. Dr. Archibald Pelago, with his heavy horn-rimmed bifocals, his seminarial center-right-left-center-right-center-left-center-right-left delivery, and his coolly hortatory "isn't-it-obvious" exposition of Ideas, produced a businesslike sermonette—what the program (printed for the occasion in green ink) called "Christmas Meditation." You gazed vacantly at the twelve tiny flames jetting from the cross high above the altar—eight for the vertical, four for the crossbar, plus the central flame that was part of both. People had come for the pageant: had come not to hear Pelago's dutiful substitute for a sermon but to see the procession of child-wisemen and child-shepherds, and the tableau.

At your telescope now you hear Pelago's words again and feel my left shoulder brush your right as I reach for the hymnal—something to read. Pelago, always prodigal with words, was saying . . .

And as the drama began mysteriously in the stable to which the wise men had come across wintry desolate sands, so it ends miraculously in the spring, and not the least miraculous fact is that the drama in a sense does not end. Well, now, anthropologists say man has always and everywhere believed that something—a spirit, a soul, a ghost—survives the shipwreck of physical disintegration and continues—at any rate for a time —to exist, near the grave or in an underworld which is, as it were, a socialized grave. . . .

But later, after the pageant and the service and the choir's involved, fruity amen, you said as we came out of the church, "Funny, but I'd be just as glad not to go to Norway with your mother this spring." So maybe you were thinking of Norway as you gazed at the cross.

Sitting here by the window now, you think maybe you'll go brush your teeth. You forgot. You wonder if my mother will stand at your shoulder asking little questions as you bend over the basin, your mouth full of foaming Gardol. You won't go just yet.

Even with the bad back and neck pain and the pounding that mild rainy day in Bergen, you were content by yourself, and because of the mile or two you were apart from my mother, you even felt especially close to her. She had planned the following: a cable car up Mount Ulriken, lunch at the Sport Cafeteria there, then a brief tour of Bergenhus and St. Mary's church (twelfth century), and at last a gay evening by bus including an imitation wedding dinner at an imitation farm in the Fana hills. But you said you'd poke around the jetty and she could have her own fun. But then you did go to Mariakirken (almost as soon as my mother had left (via Number 2 bus) for the cable-car station). You were a quarter of a mile north of the wharf, in Old Bergen, and you couldn't seem to get away from steps—the narrow north-south streets so often became part of their length just that—steps. Your heartbeat grew heavy though not painful. But then, in gathering cramping pain, your back and neck grew stiffly attached. And having zigzagged down and up the main long slope of Old Bergen, you found yourself by chance at the gate of St. Mary's garden, the twin gray towers above the west portal, small-scaled and strong and simple. Julia wouldn't yet have come down from Ulriken. You went into St. Mary's, bought a card (which you later mailed me), and went to sit in one of the folding chairs near the front. You wondered what was wrong with you—this church, Bergen's oldest building, seemed too homelike. Why did people go on trips? You sat for a long while, staring at the ponderous crucifix over the chancel arch. Norwegian? Not especially.

You heard French behind you, several mingled voices entering the place. Through them, then alone, appeared a woman's voice, explaining. You turned round and you saw the guide was Norwegian, a middle-aged woman in local costume, long black skirt, embroidered jerkin, round cap . . . . She led her people down the aisle. You found you still felt winded. You took out the postcard and your gold Mark Cross ballpoint. But you had to look up at that Christ's face like a Greek tragic mask and at the feet nailed so high up the beam that the knees stuck out awkwardly as if set in *rigor mortis*.

Didn't you?

Speak to me.

I want you.

Others can brush God's teeth. I want to see my real father's slight squint as he turns his eyes away from me for a moment.

II

After breakfast Halsey, holding the folded *Times* in one hand, went back to his and Julia's bedroom to get David's Bible. Then, at the telescope by the window, he sat in the hard, black, ample Harvard chair Julia had bought him when they moved into this apartment ten years ago. He squinted into the lens, tilted his end of the cylinder up to lower the view from the sun-silvered gray building on lower Broadway in which his own offices are, to the heli-pier near the west end of Wall.

Monday: A commuters' whirlybird floated in and settled. Julia's steps whispered along the hall carpet; then her humming, which he had not noticed before, stopped as she entered the living room.

No doubt she's cancelled her Monday volunteer teaching at the Settlement Free Music School. (That tall Finnish boy's shyness put everyone off, at the school recital in June; he was afraid to really *play;* Julia said he was OK doing Kreisler études, but give him a piece and he went to pieces.) Why must Julia cancel that lesson? She felt she ought to be here. Because.

Now Halsey edges his head left to look with naked eyes at the near docks. No sport today. Those Saturday afternoon soccer games the young stevedores play seem to broaden the new concrete parking plazas. Those boys place their long kicks like pros, but when a dribble gets caught in a scrimmage of shins, ankles, and insteps, the sudden attempt to break the ball free often becomes a wild lonely pass—the ball bouncing ever decreasing steps independently toward the water, toward some imaginary teammate, as one or two players (in khakis or jeans) sprint toward the brink to head it off. Today, Monday, those boys are working.

Years ago Halsey walked with David down there. Those times they seldom spoke. Halsey has always wished to be a raconteur like Ian Harper's skinny, rusty-faced old father. (At ninety-one Robert Harper lives at Watch Hill, Rhode Island, sits at his window all year long rereading Wodehouse, now and then looking out toward the Sound, which he no longer hears.) When he tells a joke he will insert gratuitous parentheses—in a safari joke about how Nabokov met Hemingway, old Harper includes the scene of a man meeting a lion and kneeling down to pray and opening his eyes to see the lion doing likewise, whereupon—. Halsey has always feared his own stories won't come off. E.g., that Sunday years ago. About that great cross the Norwegian fisherman brought back from the sea, David asked, "How big was it? Were there messages on it? Weren't there initials cut in it?" And then, "How did the cross vanish? Wouldn't there have been a sexton on watch? Where in the church had they *hung* the cross?" Halsey sees a limb of it reaching angled up out of a distant sea.

That Sunday with David, Halsey had his own ending—his own explanation of the tale—but he didn't offer it. "The cross was Christianity." That would have been a punchline. And David, who was nine or ten then, might actually have felt what was meant. Even then he had a fine inquiring edginess in his eye. Has David turned out as free as Halsey hoped?

"Halsey, Halsey?" Julia speaking. She has made their beds and now for a moment wonders whether to do her marketing or keep Halsey company. He watches a crane trail a slack line over a hold and out over a dock. A young man grabs the hook, pulls a yard of line down through the high block. But he just stands there. Is the ship loading or unloading?

"Are you out of the Gospels yet?"

Halsey shrugs, doesn't turn round. But here, in what may be the last months, he mustn't tax her spirit to make her pay for the strange favor he's doing her. It is a favor that succeeds only so long as it is a secret. And for love even more than for married custom, he owes her a modicum of contact.

The ruse seems to have worked. Halsey lets Julia think what she wants. Pelago would not, of course, admit the fact in such words.

Halsey suffers Pelago for Julia's sake, and for her sake Pelago suffers Halsey. And Julia suffers, trying not to think Halsey may die.

Well, he'd have gotten round to reading David's Bible anyway, wouldn't he?

The truth is, Julia's always been a bit more than a musical Christian and he always a good deal less than a mere social one. Julia's heaven is populated, and even the heavenly mountains are served by funicular railways, so one train's descent helps bring the other train up.

He thinks he understands: She fancies her interest in his Bible-reading seems insignificant. But he is the one who is really getting away with something.

At first he merely read. Then, seeing that Julia mistook his motive, he took—and takes—more and more care to conceal it. No fake confessions forthcoming, of course. He couldn't pull them off, and anyway that would be too great a price to pay. No exalted looks, or trembling awe: no *positive* fakery. Just a certain care to let Julia believe what she more and more believes: that in him Christianity has finally "taken."

He wishes she'd be only, say, half so attentive.

He can't help it if he's going to die.

Falco can't *order* the little operation. Falco argues that though the heart will suffer some added strain in the operation, one eventual effect of a successful operation will be a lessening of the original strain. Halsey would prefer not to die in the hospital—Leon Fargo, after that unsuccessful laryngectomy; young Bill Roy, in an oxygen tent. Falco says the growth will start again; eventually Halsey will have to give in. But by then—if Halsey holds out—Falco fears there'll be further problems.

There goes a Moran tug, "M" on the fat stack, unblockable grace and momentum in the bold hull-line-sweep from bow down low amidships. Some go clear to Bordeaux and back on tow jobs. Halsey doesn't look through the telescope.

Now when did they close the docks to ordinary pedestrians? It was while David was in college. And the Christmas David came home from New Hampshire, Halsey forgot and suggested they have a walk there Sunday morning. David said, "Are you kidding?" then felt the emptiness in his tone. "I mean, some port authority's closed them off, haven't they?" So he and Halsey rustled the Sunday *Trib* and *Times* till lunch and then also after lunch till it was time to go to the church pageant.

But next day Halsey did get David on a walk. Not along the Promenade, for David even on a Monday was afraid of meeting old acquaintances he didn't want to talk to. But down Remsen past where the tennis courts used to be, where Halsey once skated in winter. And to Plymouth Church of the Pilgrims on Orange Street, the plain New England meeting house built by that English architect. (What was the name? Halsey wonders—David would remember.) In the courtyard J. Q. A. Ward's statue of Beecher stood portly and dedicated and imperious. Halsey, as if out of ignorance, asked David a question or two: "Which were the abolitionists who spoke here?" David grabbed one of the bars of the gate and started in on Whittier and Wendell Phillips and Garrison, and Beecher's propaganda tour of England in 1863. Whole regiments stopped at Plymouth Church on the way south. What did Lincoln think of Beecher? . . .

To be too good a listener is to encourage that kind of contact. Always faced that kind of contact and sometimes wanted to avert it.

But that day in St. Mary's in Bergen what could one have done to stop the guide leading in those French and sitting them in the choir and lecturing them on that rather oriental pulpit ornamented in tortoise shell and lacquerwork, its steps roped off, and overhead a canopy like a great cap or helm, hanging down from a sphere.

The Norwegian adventure wasn't exactly a vacation, after all; but it taught a lesson. Why do people go abroad? (Can a *question* be a lesson?) Some to study, some to see for themselves. . . . Maybe someone cares about the Hanseatic League or the wooden stave churches. But if not, why travel? The young Craddocks seemed never to be coming home; then suddenly one Christmas they flew in from Uppsala, and stayed. Monica Flower does a new country each year, pressing further into Europe—the bridges of Prague, the big green mountains of Poland. Learn from that wide-screen movie about Australia or from a book like that expensive one St. John gave David on Turkey. In Istanbul they have public secretaries right along the sidewalk with their typewriters. Scribes?

Why trips?

But if a person thinks, doesn't he after a while start asking, What is home?

Some hours north of Bergen Julia and Halsey found a chalet, where they stayed seven days. In the long light evenings they walked down a narrow fjord-side road. They looked up at the high snow and the gantries and cables used to bring milk down in summer. And at a point where a path started steeply at the right, Julia and Halsey would pause to listen to the singing voices up by the public shelter back in at the base of the mountain. American voices—the two young college couples who turned up at the town jetty once a day or so to fill the milk can and buy huge scoops of the Norwegian version of frozen custard. Julia wanted to go up the path and visit their shelter, but Halsey wouldn't snoop. The guitar was clear. They sang "Were You There When They Crucified My Lord?"—with one of the girls singing a verse alone. Then they sang a Japanese or Chinese song that sounded very solemn, intense. And Julia said it was Japanese and had to do with the Bomb, she'd heard Seeger sing it on WQXR.

Well, it didn't sound very Japanese, except the actual words. Sounded no more Japanese than the little Jap boy that Christmas-pageant Sunday who upset the works. (Upset them for only a moment.)

One evening the four Americans sang "Were You There?" and when it was over one of the girls said—it came down to the road to Julia and Halsey barely audible but absolutely clear—"Go, man, go."

"Don't let Dr. Pelago go before I get back. I'm going to Reeves."

Yes, Pelago said that on Monday he'd come by early, he's

374

sneaking out to Staten Island for a quick eighteen holes. He feels it is his duty to come. And as for Halsey, he feels duty-bound to Julia to be receptive. And Julia. . . . She's never thought out her religion. But who has? She sings hymns in a warm, amateur contralto, and she likes the relaxation of the moment when the sexton turns down the lights for Pelago's sermon—Dr. Mann never did that—and she loves being in the choir for the annual Elijah and Creation and Messiah. (Ev-ry va-hal-lley sh-hall be egg-zaw-awl-ted. Makes you almost want to get up there with them.) Well, she isn't blind: She smiles hearing Pelago pronounce "Gawd" and she keeps her eyes open during prayers. If one could put into words Julia's attitude toward Pelago's present dealings with Halsey, it would be something like . . . David could work it all out. Word-boy. It's as if dying and death are a sort of boring retirement and along comes Pelago, skilled hobby-therapist, to keep Halsey going.

If only, Halsey feels, if only someone could now know what is going on. David, for example. Someone to under-stand all the deceptions. Then Halsey wouldn't feel bound so in chains of independence, fearful of moving lest a clink be heard. To seem to confide in Pelago (in correlation with seeming to be moved and excited by the Bible) in order to keep Julia *out* of his own confidence! Love by deceiving. And the idea wasn't even new, which would have been some consolation for loneliness. How long will Falco keep quiet about that little growth? (Halsey can't even feel it most of the time.) Would it keep growing even after death? Maybe it will eventually fill the casket, then like a majestic root grow up through. Halsey thinks maybe he should be laid in the casket—like a baby—on his stomach.

Grow like hair and . . . *teeth?* After death, how one ages! Cremation, of course, is the coming thing.

The front door latches shut. Did Julia say goodbye? Should have told her to bring back a copy of *Time*.

"How can you read it?" David asked. But then he'd sneak *Time* into his bedroom. The other day Halsey found part of a red hard-cover notebook of David's a quarter full of lists of puns from four years of *Time*. Hepped on words. Written when? Long ago. Halsey hasn't had a real talk with David in years.

The Christmas he came home from New Hampshire, he walked around the living room shuffling into and out of his jacket pocket bits and pieces of paper. He was pretty awful that year.

Jonni, the old man-eater, called David on something he'd said.

"OK I got the quote wrong. In the beginning, man was a misquotation. Space, hope, and disparity. Miss Quotation of 19—"

"That, my boy, is a wretched pun," she said.

"Man himself is a bad pun," David answered. "And I don't mean old Dr. Mann."

For a second, that day, Halsey had a feeling he knew what David meant. As for old Jonni, she exploded in a coughing cloud of smoky, bronchitic chortling. She thought David ridiculous.

III

At four she woke me with her nightmare chattering. Mumbled and pleaded, said "David, you *might* have remembered Halsey's *birthday!* David, it isn't true that Hell is other people," then two sobs, then a few small, womanly snores— she needs to lie on her side, not her back—then quiet. David *did* remember my birthday. And Julia never calls me "Halsey" to David. When she starts like that in the night, it's like an explosion, you almost think she's been yakking away underground and suddenly the surface slides off and you hear her talking. It used to scare me.

But she was fine today. Amazing the work she gets through early in the morning. How many miles does she travel from eight A.M. to nine? Fast this morning. Taking vases into the pantry, sticking in half a dozen different kinds of flowers the kid from Frank's delivered. Light purple tulips in the old lime porcelain vase Jonni brought us from Hong Kong. Julie carried that vase back in from the kitchen almost as if she might drop it.

Here *comes* J.

Now behind me. Wondering whether to go out shopping or what.

Will Halsey Brooke keep his strange secret? Or, before he dies, will he confess to his dear wife Julia that reading David's Bible hasn't meant to him what she imagines it has?

Well, I'm tired. And the mail delivery gets worse and

worse, and at eleven, when Jay distributes it, there won't be anything from David anyway. But did I ever urge him to write? He doesn't even seem to keep in touch with Julia. Unless lately he has some nutty new idea she thinks would get me going, upset me. Like Quincey attacking the Japanese business invasion. Well, why the hell shouldn't they come in if they can—their transistors, the Brother typewriter that's underselling even the boys who're underselling Hermes and Olympia. The Japs are good. I wonder if I'll ever get there.

"Halsey? Halsey?"

Have to fly. Too long any other—take the Matson Lines maybe—is it Matson to the Pacific? Those white ships that make you think of a very different world with another language not just different as Italian or Norwegian is different.

"Julie?" I don't turn. I can't take my eyes off these docks. Julie thinks—or does she really think—that I'm looking into the eyepiece of the tele—

"I'm sorry to trouble you, darling. I'm just going out to do some errands. And I have to go to Atlantic Avenue about reupholstering the wing chair, and Dr. Pelago said—"

"I know."

"Yes; well, then, I'll be back by ten or eleven. Do you mind being. . . . Oh, are you out of the Gospels yet?"

"Sure, last week. Ask me anything."

"I'll hope to catch Dr. Pelago, but I'm not sure."

What hair Pelago has! I bet he gets a singe—the only way to stop the ends bleeding. Ought to run for office with hair like that. Edward Stettinius.

Still, Pelago looked pretty weak and vacant when the little Jap boy stopped the show that Christmas. Hasn't got the perfect defense. Nobody has. And that day Pelago had already spoken so long, and everyone was waiting for the children. The little Japanese boy's father was near the front on the right sitting with his wife by one of the balcony pillars. They didn't want to miss a single turn, especially anything that little bugger of theirs did. The father's an aeronautics engineer; really made it after the war. Interned; then moved to the east coast. A lucky one. Well, his little son really made the pageant for us. They didn't even live on the Heights then —lived near Lafayette Avenue, somewhere near Brooklyn Hospital. The Hill section. Then they moved to Joralemon Street near the corner of Garden Place. I should have bothered to know them. Not even Julia—of *all* people—went so far as to entertain them. Still could, though.

The little boy'll be thirteen or fourteen now. They got him into Poly Prep. Which must be a good school, I said in '40, because it's umpty-dumpty percent Jewish. And Julia said she was glad David hadn't heard me say such a thing.

Prettiest when she's sad—doesn't happen very often. At this point David would explain to me *why* I like seeing her sad—complicated reason. The school of hard knocks was nothing to what some of these intellectual young fellows pass through today. There's one point old man Pennitt was dead wrong.

You can be *too* intelligent. I'm sorry that I never did like Stevenson's eyes. I worried about that man. Never let David know I stayed Republican in '52. In '56 came the business about disarmament, so how *could* you vote for Stevenson? Of course Ike's feet weren't really planted in this world either. Smug. Tried to get us through eight years without our knowing they were even passing.

Willkie wrote *One World*. That was a crazy summer he got picked. After '36 I began to feel F. D. R. surrounding us, like God, except not so incredible. Poor Willkie. Willkie knew about people and he had an intellect and by God wonder of wonders, with all that, he knew about money, too. Real leadership potential.

One world was something else again. When Monica's uncle joined the other war-claims judges in Berlin in 1955, the only common language they mustered between them was Latin. And how many people know Latin today?

I should have known what that inscription meant in the Bergen church, St. Mary's. "All our SPES is in the death of the Lord." SPES? A miscarving? And I went through Caesar at Boy's High, too. But I couldn't be sure what SPES meant. And then rather than ask David when I got home, I planned to consult a Latin dictionary in the Montague Street library, but I never did. Even though I don't know what the whole thing means, I remember the thing itself. Isn't that strange? (Like some of the old stories you remember word for word even though you don't quite comprehend the full meaning— stories like where Mole and Rat find Pan in *The Wind in the Willows*, or Christ drives the demons out of the madman who was wandering among the tombs, or the forgetfulness of Siegfried, which broke David's heart when Julie took him and Ann to see it at the Met.) The inscription went, "TOTA SPES NOSTRA EST IN MORTE DOMINI." The guide didn't translate it. Maybe didn't know. But she was pretty sweet, with that deep Norwegian chin and that smiling inscrutability. Norwegians friendly, yes: But who the Christ knows what they're thinking! Maybe nothing. The woman at the chalet, the landlord's sister who always seemed to be remooring the two rowboats—she was inscrutable, too. Except one night when the mackerel chased a thick school of herring all over the fjord and she decided to go out for the fourth time that day, and she said, "I can resist all temptation except the jumping of the fish." I didn't suddenly know what the hell I was doing there on that dock. Might as well have been on Echo Lake looking for a school of white perch at dusk.

People want to get away. That's why . . . . Well, David would say, that's why people won't say "die" but will say, rather, "pass away" or "pass on" or even, like old Bobby Harper, "pass out." David would compare touring and dying. I'd call that far-fetched. I won't buy it.

But there certainly was poetic justice when we got home from Norway. David, who'd never been abroad, knew more about Fantoft stave church near Bergen than we did. Did we know about the thirteenth-century bell that was removed from that church? It had inscribed on it *"Christus vincit, Christus regnat, Christus imperat."* At least he took an interest, even though when we got back he was too full of himself to be excited about our coming home. At one time years ago, I could tell him a few things. When he almost failed physics I explained the two main laws of thermodynamics to him, he was so interested he made some hissing sound when I explained the conservation of energy. But God he was always on his guard. And when I likened heat transfer to banking, he suddenly said in that displeased nasal way of his when he got a hair across his ass, "Translating the subject into your own terms, eh?" All I said was that when you pay money out it doesn't disappear, any more than goods and services disappear. Yet sometimes when most on his guard he'd amaze me and suddenly come halfway, more than halfway, to meet me.

That day of the pageant we suffered through Pelago's "Christmas Meditation" and then the procession came down the aisle and they set up the tableau at the front and kids came up to it, and then the little Japanese boy broke the

silence of the church, and had his say, and in the embarrassment—it was really like a little crisis, everyone felt it and
Amy Figgis must have frozen from shame, though the parents of the little bugger merely grinned at each other—at that
absolutely dead moment after the kid had his say, David
turned to me, smiled, shook his head, and in spite of himself
put his hand on mine where it lay on the old plush of the
pew cushion. Then he quickly looked away. But he forgot
to take away his hand. Then, naturally, he did take it away.

What exactly did David look like at that age? I almost
don't recall.

Get that snapshot in his room.

Get up and have a look in his room.

IV

Heart went out then. David knew. Once he too hoped
religion true, and *I* wouldn't disabuse him. Got to find out
for yourself. Faith, hope, charity. But greatest in what sense?
Greatest is hope, my personal view. Like the man who saw
the lion kneeling praying. But how does a lion kneel? Which
way do their legs bend? Could have asked someone or found
out years ago. David put his hand on mine and looked away.
But by that age, twenty-odd, he was past feeling more than
the memory of that first moment of being cognizant of the
great joke we play on ourselves. But David felt memory of
that far moment then in church just after the little Japanese
bastard had his say, and I felt his hand on mine, my heart
went out, David I will see your picture in your aiee room
no stop neck and shoulders aiee get all the way up Julia
where are you and go to David's room aiee neck joined to
shoulders is it like after they take your head off no not possible brain control-centers no longer connected—stop—heart
—went out out.

Sit back down which burial custom buries them sitting
sit back down a second pain pain go away yes better now
better now. Better better. Better better.

That Christmas David gave me *Atoms and People* by
R. E. Lapp. Different than what he used to. Used to give me,
Julie, Ann books *he* wanted. To read. There on the wharf
down there that young Spic doesn't read. But you can't say
he's better off not reading about what was it solipsism, prob-

380

ably living eight to a room in a dirty brownstone lower Hicks
Street between Joralemon and Atlantic Avenue what's he got
he won't get half a chance David had a big chance and look
how happy he isn't this stevedore aiee again made that perfect lob pass in the soccer day before yesterday but no one
waiting for it aiee please hide away pain come again come
again in somebody else's body Julia come come back my pills
God stop it that young stevedore holding the line under the
crane runs during his soccer games all alert like me years
ago when we won the lacrosse championship and might have
made world champions I racing watchful down the sideline
stick ready for the pass from God what on earth was his
name shook hands like a pro politician. I never knew him
really though we played together. Funny, I don't like people
I don't know. Don't be so glum with new people Julia says
Eeyore the Old Gray Donkey what was it exactly he said
when Christopher Robin asked him to David put his hand
on mine and I knew that both of us aiee without being fully
aiee cognizant in our conscious minds of all the little Jap
boy's statement fully meant Ellen would say nipper then
Nipponese nipper spoke suddenly in a moment of silence
what first happened I'd forgotten David's presence and
Julia's behind up in the organ loft and the organist played
some carols very softly on one of his aiee stop pain pain
hide away aiee neck and shoulders played carols on one of
his special instrument stops is it celeste? and up both aisles
came kids in all different costumes people crunched the old
stuffing in the pew cushions craning around to see seven
shepherds and the wise men and in front of them a joint
company of the heavenly host angels ten eleven twelve years
of age with flashlight candles buy them thirty-five cents each
maybe cheaper in dozen lots while from the front of the
church again aiee hard hard hard neck and shoulders come
back Julia is that young Spic stevedore waiting to load or
unload that Norwegian skow Abraham by one of the doors
at the side at the front of the church let in the holy family
who came and took their stations young Joseph and little
skinny Mary with two smaller kids just standing there in
shepherd's drag and up the steps either side of the altar the
white angels mounted and the shepherds and wise men and
some others came on round the manger and at last the
little Japanese boy not more than four who I heard later
insisted on getting into the show even though he was the

youngest in the Sunday school and practically an infant they fixed him up with regulation shepherd's burlap he came last and then the organ stopped and up in the loft at the rear of the church the choir shuffled and were about to get on with a carol or an anthem aiee please Julia maybe if I get up doing the reverse of what I maybe ought to do maybe the pain will aiee oioioioi please neck please shoulder blade please and please and and the little Nip had worked his way in to have a close look at the manger and then there just as the choir was scuffing and rustling in the silence of the church and I'd forgotten David's presence the little Jap boy no again again aiee oh oo no how long oo long please the the the little Nip said loud as anything I ever heard aiee pills please said, so everyone heard and the man in front of me hunched his shoulders but I didn't hunch my shoulders for I wasn't scared by what the little boy said, aiee Julia come pills please, the little Jap boy who I loved suddenly then so much my heart almost exploded in me, said for all to hear for all even Amy Figgis to hear, said in his incredible husky voice there at the manger at the front of the church, said pointing into the spotlit manger ever after famous on the Heights, said, "It's not a real baby Jesus, it's only a doll!" Oh oh oh oh oh oh oh oh. Help police I won't stand it. Well well well well well well well welllll.

Better. Worst in a week. Won't tell Falco.

Heart went out then to David when he put his hand on mine in humor and knowledge showing leaderly sonship my heart came out to meet him by George.

Maybe get up now. Oh slow slow slow that's great yes nice and very slow, oh slow slow go away, come again somebody else. Yes. Now OK. Where was that snap of David somewhere in his desk the snap of him just the spring of that year of the pageant where. Up and yes apparently safe, eh?

My heart went out. So few good chats. Ellen says have a natter, have a rabbit, is she good for him, bridge between him and me, hands across the sea, hands across between the beds, so hard. Always wanted to wow David, hold his attention, what you going to do, missed chances.

Discussed *Winnie the Pooh* with David once on a bench hard by Penny Bridge what kind of honey and was Pooh bear silly and was Christopher Robin from Brooklyn Heights and on and on, I replying to David's every query and this long

382

before Josie Wrenn came to live here I there on the bench with David now not on the bench but leaning his back against my knees looking out toward the harbor and asking and asking, and I saw the blonde nurse or as Ellen would say, nanny, on the bench across the way musing as she mechanically gently rocked the baby carriage or as as Ellen would say, pram, like one they smuggled whiskey in in some old silent comedy, and she'd slipped a wee bit down onto the small of her back and daydreaming had let her knees open easy wide though her white brogues still neatly together and I saw just such a small space of shaded inside-thigh-skin no more no less and she motionless except for the little rhythm of her rocking and no sign of her slip and David spoke on and on and all I heard as I came back to listening was "Eeyore the Old Gray Donkey, Daddy?" And thinking I guessed what was wanted I said Eeyore finally agreed to come to Christopher's birthday party though he couldn't believe he'd been asked and at last said, "I'll come but don't blame me if it rains," and David said, though he hadn't known why I'd not been paying attention, "That wasn't what I asked, I wish you'd listen to me, what I asked was why does Mommy call you Eeyore?"

Not like the also unanswerable question David asked the night in '43 he came with me to collect Julie at the Navy Street canteen. Didn't bear thinking on. No comeback. Father's got to have a comeback for a son, but. Well, for example did I want him to feel he had to come into the business? Course not. Course that never came up really. Wanted him to feel free. Only binding agreement we had was he was to be an inquiring man free to look at both sides of the coin, be a doctor sailor preacher teacher beachcomber bookseller bomber pilot (though today they're just subexecutives operating switchboards) or the man who rigs the big cross of lilies for the Easter show at the Brooklyn Botanic Garden where you used to be able to hear the Ebbets Field crowd roar out if the Dodgers did something.

That pageant-Christmas first I had faith Pelago wouldn't go on and on and then I had *hopes* he wouldn't and at last all I could do was view charitably his so-called "Christmas Meditation" old Mann would never have said in ultimate historical terms the seven prior covenants culminating in the Davidic were now to be gathered into or crowned by that

New (eighth) Covenant itself founded, as we learn in Matthew, Corinthians, and Hebrews, upon our lord's sacrifice David and I both waiting for the kids to be processed up the aisle never forget Christmas dinner that year with only Jonni with us and afterward I read *Atoms and People* that David gave me and got to the tragic Slotin experiment but Jonni was saying you treat your mother as if her presence here had interrupted some vital project you were on, and David caustic as he at times could be and needing in my view a good and if possible a very good screw, saying to Jonni Are you going to preach family solidarity to me? parent-preachers association? that the child is the child of his mother's body and his father's seed and wow how David went on till Jonni picked up her presents including the carton of Camels I gave her and got on her coat and left for the IRT subway and her residence hotel on East Thirty-eighth Street. Why, all I wanted was to read my Christmas present *Atoms and People* and then Julie without crying—she doesn't cry—told David he'd baited Jonni and then David said what *did* he say I was trying to read *Atoms and People* half thinking of the bad time Julie and I were having together around the time I ogled that nurse near Penny Bridge had it all worked out as neat as the two main laws of thermo. Yes what was it, yes, two worlds in our marriage one was perfect and bound forever the other impossible becalmed. And belief sheer belief could throw you into one or the other at will well thermo's easier and though David scorned my analogy I snooped in his exam papers once and found he'd actually used my bank account analogy so it helped him pass he always proud he always proud and do I bequeath him do I will him pay-as-you-go freedom or what do I will the poor bastard so prodigal with words but then so silent too well I'll always remember for it finalized a certain link between us the Jap kid's blurt and David's look his hand on mine must have a look in his room my heart went out.

V

Yes I better move around, even if I have another attack. Even *with* all the flowers, Julie keeps a nice house. She must have bought four dozen chrysanthemums; how high they stick up. Or did someone send them because of me? Julie knows my feeling there. Well, I can't help it if I'm going to die. "Pass away" gets more ridiculous and weird the more you think. David's right always complaining about euphemism. Is that the word? Yes. (Like a man asking a girl's father for her hand? David thought my example crass.)

But doctors need euphemism to keep you from worrying. Falco may not show alarm but even if I don't know anything about medicine I know what I feel. Fatigue accumulating slowly like drips when the faucet washer begins to go. And I'm remembering too little too slowly. Like some shape is blocking my view. Age takes its toll.

What's in the icebox? I'd love to sneak a bacon sandwich like the one Ellen made me but Julia'd smell fat later. And I'd pay.

What's the cleaner's ticket doing on the counter? It's not for anything of mine. Haven't worn a suit in six weeks.

Three years ago Julie gave Abraham at the church two suits of mine. Over the years he must have acquired a whole wardrobe from me. When he died they laid him out in a black suit Doblin made me. The church paid for the works at Fairchild and of course Julia had to get me to go and when I was standing looking down at Abraham all I could think was whether he had the pants on. David said once, "*That* Uncle Tom!" Nasty boy, my David. Doesn't write, but he gets that from me. Also his dislike of telegrams, cables.

Julia wrote him twice from Norway, then wired him offering him a trip over, we'd pay. She was so enthusiastic she had to write David everything we'd done, were doing, or would do. Cod's tongues for supper and about her first visit to Fantoft stave church near Grieg's birthplace, and then about hearing those American campers sing "Were You There When They Crucified My Lord?" when we went north to that fjord—so after she'd written all to David and the Fearons and a dozen others (she doesn't take pictures but Christ doesn't she buy cards!), I felt there wasn't anything we'd done that the rest of the world didn't know we'd done, nothing private between us. The second time we heard them sing, it was mainly a solo, a high thin womanly voice from the base of the mountain toward us and over the fjord, "Were You There When They Crucified My Lord?" not like Marian Anderson, more like the voice of that colored gal who opens *Porgy and Bess* singing "Summertime" from a balcony high and small and clear-floating, and though I didn't understand what exactly I was feeling I knew, hearing those American college kids sing that Negro spiritual, that I had no home to go home to. I couldn't express it to Julie and I loved her the more for that. Then we walked on up that road beside the fjord and passed several elderly English couples, and each couple were discussing transit—Newcastle to Bergen, Flåm to Balestrand, Vik to—, Voss to—, Sunderland by train to Newcastle to catch the Bergen boat, home fra Newcastle till Sunderland, as I said to muther last night haven't the Norwegians got luvely cold table in morning! Julia told all when we got home.

And now. Yes, the other day she had to tell Quincey I was getting religious in old age. If she only knew. I wonder if she guesses that I was never unfaithful to her even after I told her off that time years ago. Oh I wanted a woman that day with David by Penny Bridge when I ignored him and stared at the drowsy nurse under the sun with the smallest breath of air coming from the harbor. Two open legs, stockings sheer but veiling. Nothing like a leg. But I thought I'd have to pay too dearly for a woman—not *that* one, a *possible* one. Pay what? For it wouldn't have been a quickie, it would have been a real thing. Pay? Pay to my fool sense of right and wrong, and then I'd be able afterward to believe I'd been right.

Tell all? Well, for a frank woman Julia was sneaky with those seven silver native brooches she brought back from Norway, all the tiny discs on each one shaking and turning. I wanted to pay duty. The customs man in New York looked like Pelago. Funny I think of the two of them together. David wouldn't let that pass by, he'd show in some scornful way how the customs men and Pelago actually were alike. Pelago'll be here any time.

Odd about his words, he speaks two different ways. Julie says when he leaves, "*Thank* you for coming. . . ." And he says, "Any time." Doesn't ring true. But then he speaks another language in the pulpit. After the pageant-service that Christmas David seemed to recall Pelago's "Christmas Meditation" word for word and exaggerated everything and hooted and yuk-yukked so loudly and scornfully and made that kaa-kaa sound right on the street so even I felt. . . .

Funny, David's words *quoting* Pelago come to me, not Pelago himself:

> The helpless infant in the manger begins the cycle of redemption that once and forever does away with that deathly underworld which, no less in the Old Testament than in Homer, is a place of gloom from which man shrank—a redemption from which he derives new hope.

The other moment was then almost lost in David's scorn.

I'm getting soft. Pelago's tough. Even that pageant-day a few years ago Pelago had a thick springing head of healthy premature gray hair. Last night I dreamed I was bald; haven't had that one since I was in my thirties. I won't go bald *now*. There are two kinds of people, Ian Harper would say in his positive way. Those who keep their hair, those who don't. What about radiation? That hits the scalp, I guess. Did young Slotin lose his? *Atoms and People* doesn't say. Only that with his trusty screwdriver he moved the hemispheres of bomb stuff too close and the neutron counter screamed and he tore the reacting mass apart. Hospitalization. Blood counts. Christ! Hands and arms swelled to bursting, skin sloughed off. His parents flew in to Los Alamos, and eight days later he died. A young leader. In the war effort. But was it truly an effort to win a war? And for who? David says war is psychologically therapeutic.

How much war feeling was in David's remark to me walking that night to pick up Julia at the Navy Street canteen? If I ever got to the heart of David I'd probably find things I couldn't bear to know.

Glad Josie Wrenn survived the first year she came to us. How much true parental feeling was there that sent her off from the west coast to us on the east?

So many questions that want answering, and we had the experts here with us one time or other, could have—well these questions that remain are partly why we dream, but translated into some other illogical language. (Must ask David about that sort of thing.) It's all subjective, in my opinion. Last night I woke up from *my* dream—baldness—to hear Julia chattering in *hers* to David about not remembering my birth—

387

VI

Ridiculous, he thinks. But Halsey knows her dream puts into its own words her fear that David hasn't ever properly respected his father. Yet in Halsey's opinion, David always felt their muffled battles were an understood surface, a viable ground to meet on.

Halsey hesitates in the kitchen doorway that gives on the hall. Though standing, for a second he feels as if he's just sat down hard on a great irregular crest of scrap iron. He pictures the small rectal growth he has never seen about which Falco has told him—imagines it straining to become smaller, tightening and gathering, hardening into a pure ball.

As if up from the hall—from David's very room—old words of David's come to Halsey's ears: "Get finally into the heart of another person and you risk an explosion. Only reach the center of a person, break into the rock-central blindness and desire, the utter elements of the person, and you risk a blow-up. Avoid the risk and you settle for epistemological impotence." And Halsey recalls his own responding words, more shaken than they sounded: "Whatever you're trying to say, you're hiding it in fancy words." Then David quickly back, scornfully: *"You,* with your 'finalize' and your 'componentwise' and your 'transcontinental shipment-potentialization.'" And Halsey, slowly: "In business you need a terminology. But in your field or in philosophy or whatever you're talking, you'd communicate better, you'd verbalize better if you took Rudolph Flesch's *Plain Talk* to heart." "Rudoph Flush," said David. Words in chain reaction so often in his talk pun their way into new unexpected subjects. . . .

Always unprepared. After nearly sixty-eight years still unprepared, still overly watchful for surprises. He hasn't the right to reject Julia's eternal enthusiasm. But what, for instance, could he do that time listening to those kids sing by the fjord? After "Were You There When They Crucified My Lord?" one of the girls said, "Go, man, go," and Julia turned her face close to Halsey's and in smiling, frowning ecstasy said softly and intensely, "They're Americans!" Well it wasn't exactly that kind of thing that caused their brief separations in Bergen—first, when they arrived from London, then later, when they'd returned from the north in order to take the plane from Bergen. What separated them briefly was Julia's peremptory enthusiasm, her habit of announcing the day's schedule . . . which, even on an ordinary Monday at home, she announces as if it's a fixed itinerary. For years now these moments have come, when Halsey doesn't know what to reply. One Saturday, after she had spoken for three packed minutes, he simply said, "I can't bear you," and left the house. That night at the Heights Casino Lester Lanin played "Day by Day" and Halsey danced with Monica Flower, who wore a short, sleeveless evening dress seemingly made of sea-green film and held on each freckled shoulder only by a dark-blue cord. At those do's he escaped conversation by dancing; but he wasn't a very good dancer. He looked in Monica's eyes for a long time—now he can't recall what color they are—and then as the music stopped he kissed her cheekbone and the moment startled and arrested her and she quickly kissed his lips. And above the murmur Ian Harper's all-purpose punchline could be heard loudly from near the bandstand—"That's what the actress said to the bishop."

Halsey knows two dreadfully different insights into his marriage to Julia: Sometimes her loving energy, even the nervous joy with which for instance she tried to push that Finnish boy to play in phrases rather than note by note, and especially the long unmarked legs with their high knees and long calves, and especially the large oval face with the sharp dark-tinted widow's peak a mark of apparent strength above the high, delicately-rounded forehead—this is a world that convinces him no other exists, i.e., that living without Julia is inconceivable; but then another world blows up inside his anxious mind and he wonders how in the old days even the feverish submissive hands over his bare shoulder blades and his moist buttocks could make him forget the various tiny but constant contretemps parting him from her, her from him. One night during the war—Falco, then a commander, came for dinner—Julia had to try to explain to Falco why Halsey had worked for Willkie, but she expressed herself so well she seemed in the end to be speaking *for* Halsey, in *behalf* of Halsey, as if he'd been incapacitated. Well, actually she didn't get it so right—saying Willkie was their "sort" as well as a kind of Wilsonian idealist. And he had a shaggy Will Rogers look and a friendly rolled *r* in his speech. Was he after all ordinary underneath? Anyway, Julia should not have spoken at eloquent length except for herself—and it was painfully obvious that she was in fact speaking *for Halsey*. She often volunteered Halsey's views. Then that cotton-picking telescope—*she* was the one who'd wanted it, not he. But after once agreeing with her that it might be nice to have one by the living room window, he felt he must mention it now and then, for she so liked the idea. She didn't even understand why he'd gone out with Josie Wrenn that evening in '58. Julia had analyzed the Hopper they'd bought, analyzed it before, during, and after supper; and on the subject of the remote, monumental, "even funereal" brightness of that white house on that hill, she'd been richly precise. But *he* liked the thing as much as *she*—in fact he'd been the one to hear of its coming up for sale. Well, to get away, he went out with Josie up to a class at the Art Students League, and Julia thanked him later for being so fatherly toward Josie. Not that he didn't really rather like being with Josie—dull face, but fine healthy hips. Josie drew the model and Halsey sat or wandered about among the students. He always wondered if Josie noticed the white half-inch of Tampax string the elderly beatnik model had failed to take care of. He couldn't mention it to Julia either.

How much deception! He used to fear planes, but now he doesn't think about it either way. Yet his idiosyncrasy is so much part of Julia's view of him that—except for a secret flight to Chicago when he's certain she won't try to see him off or meet him—he still doesn't fly. And because she seems to love him for the idiosyncrasy, he often calls attention to it. "Against my religion," he says; "I'm a devout coward."

How many times has he deceived her? Yet he fears being liable for her solitude should she ever feel even these quirks give no hint of what he is. So, grimly bemused and amused, he plays along. At least there'll be in her possession some idea of him. Well, well, well: nearly forty years of living together: seems like . . . forty days: H. and J.

He knows he does at times tend to withhold himself (or, as David would say, "refrain from collision"). OK, it's true. Returning from Norway, he feared, not a fine or reprimand from the customs man, but merely the sudden "engagement" if the man poked into Julia's toilet bag and found the seven *søljes*. Julia said, "Dear it's the *cus*tom to avoid paying the duty."

As in Bergen those two times, so it had often seemed to him that through his life two discreet worlds of marital perception alternated: the yes and the no—each as sealed off from the other as two languages seem when the would-be speaker tries to pass from his own to the one he knows only how to read. Worst, Halsey never can *choose,* for the feeling descends or disappears, inundates then evaporates into its opposite as if one element were turning into another. *Yes,* it has been right, all thirty-odd years of it, her wisdom, her body, her manners, her fingers in his; or *No,* the silent anger and angry silence he has so often known after one of her stupid imperceptions, her reliance on haste to get through problems—all this has been the real substance of their troth. Not that there haven't been the neutral, anesthetized moods, the utilarian mood by means of which one passes on from one hour to another.

The last afternoon in Norway he left her enigmatically—knowing she would guess charitably that he was going off to buy her something. He sneaked off to the station to catch the bus to that outskirt of Bergen with the odd name. A little English woman, fortyish and, in a sharp-boned solitary way, pretty—though he at once felt there was no need to check her ring-finger—smiled to him at platform 14, got up into the bus, and asked the driver with plaintive courtesy if this was the bus to Paradis—the stop for the stave church near Grieg's birthplace. Since she'd asked the question, Halsey was able to keep his destination—and perhaps his nationality—secret. And off they went, the only passengers, through a typical Bergen drizzle. Julia had condemned him for not joining her the first time in Bergen on her trip to see this church. "The most exciting thing in Norway by a long shot." But he *had* wanted to see it, and had planned to see it after *she* had. And so that afternoon he—and the English woman—sneaked off to see the Fantoft stave church.

Ellen doesn't emote like Julia. And a good sense of humor. She even laughed when Halsey told her that joke old Robert Harper inserted into the joke about Eisenhower and Kennedy at St. Peter's Gate—a joke he forgot to finish, he was laughing so hard at his parenthetical one: the third of the Magi tripping over the stable threshold and saying "Jesus Christ!" at which Joseph said, "Hey, that's a good name; we were thinking of calling him Fred!" Who was it sculpted Madam Liberty? *Fred* Somebody.

Last December Ellen took Halsey's hand crossing Lexington Avenue to that basket shop; and he said to her, "Marry him, Ellen." Which seemed to amuse rather than irk her, for she smiled and kept looking straight ahead at the solid flank of women advancing from the east side of the street, and she said, "To keep him from going away."

Where?

When old Robinson the elevator man died, the agent's legal eagle happened to come into the building to speak to the new elevator man and said to David, "Old Robinson's passed away, I'm sorry to say." "Where to?" said David, the nasty bastard. Well, he's right. Why in the case of death *do* people forever say, for instance, "Uncle Henry has passed on," or "When did she 'go'?"

Halsey acknowledges that, yes, when a man dies, he does leave life, or life leaves him. But it's still unclear. If life leaves *you*, maybe *you stay*. (There's one for David!) So it's perhaps wrong, this trip idea.

The answer is, people want to get away without—but they don't get away—they think they do or think they may. They won't confess to themselves that maybe there isn't a journey *to* anywhere—maybe there's no *need* for a trip—and to keep themselves happy they persuade themselves that—The Clutching Hand Rides Again—they stow their fright under their—try to get away without—away with—"Pay as you go," one might say, and Julia would call the phrase in that context crass—Willkie, bless his heart, had a fiscal head as well as all the other good ideas. He knew what the Chinese emperor's last surviving economist knew who (after his fellow-economists had been beheaded) saved his neck by telling the emperor there was no such thing as a free lunch.

But if Julia contrives to feel happier by contriving to believe that Halsey has begun to believe the Bible, why not . . . ? Did Henry Ward Beecher's fanny-pinching wreck his work? He needed all that hocus pocus as much as he needed to conceal it. (Great men get away with murder!) Look what he did for abolition. As David says, in 1863 Beecher's speeches in England helped diminish English sympathy for the Confederate states. And Lincoln picked him for the Fort Sumter flag-raising speech April 14, 1865. What deception there must have been in B.'s private life! Imagine Beecher looking down from his pulpit lectern and seeing a dark shiny brim and blond curls and thinking, "What a doll!"

If David knew of this Bible thing with Julia, he'd say,

"Selling out!" What about Pelago himself? How sure is *he?* In his "Christmas Meditation" that Christmas the little Jap had his say, Pelago spoke of evidence:

> Easy it is to insinuate that those who first believed Christ resurrected were merely indulging in a fantasy of wishful thinking. Easy to ask, "Who was in fact *there when* . . . ?" Yet all evidence presses toward the contrary conclusion. In fact the apostles rejected the news when it came to them. Christian faith does not at bottom rest on the tomb but on what has in fact happened to people.

Halsey wonders now—when it's too late—if he shouldn't have preached frank agnosticism to David years ago.

Turning out of the kitchen into the hallway, Halsey recalls again what David said the night in '43 he joined Halsey to go pick up Julia at the Navy Yard canteen. Halsey had been rejected by all the services—history of rheumatic heart, automatic 4F. He recalls asking if David was sorry his father couldn't serve and David saying, "Only if you are." And then, as they walked along Sands Street east from Brooklyn Bridge past sailors' outfitters and a Chinese greasy spoon, Halsey thought out loud—maybe he should go into defense work or get into a war office, but that seemed pointless—and at last David said, "I wish you'd make up your mind what you think. You don't give me any leadership . . . ."

Maybe not. But nobody starts with a clear mind. That Christmas David gave Halsey *Atoms and People*, Christmas Day Halsey was interrupted just as he got to

> . . . the hemispheres came closer and closer, more and more of the neutrons would tend to be caught within the bomb stuff and fewer would be lost through the narrowing air gap. The chain reaction would build up, and, just before it was ready to rip, Slotin would calmly stop the experiment, measure the separation and deduce just how big the critical mass was. He grew quite adept at the experiment . . . . He used two hemispheres that he had worked with before and . . . . Suddenly the counters screamed . . . . Slotin hurled himself forward and tore the reacting mass apart with his bare . . . .

and as he turned the page and was interrupted by a sudden flare-up between Jonni and David, he found two mad equations David had pencilled in a margin—the margin of this gift book. Jonni said, "Are you trying to infer that I don't know what Mao is up to?!" And David said, "You don't even know the difference between 'infer' and 'imply'! For God's sake—!" And Jonni: "You're getting rather sharp, young man!" And David, turning and walking to the hall arch flinging his hands out like a preacher, "God implies; man infers; man is himself one of God's implications!" And all the time—just a matter of seconds—Halsey looked at David's impulsive, messy, intimate scribble in that margin:

(HEMISPHERES) Unite = Disperse
Heart of Matter   = Heart of Person
Atomic Bomb   = Discovery of Apartness, Epistemological Impotence

VII

You are moving toward my room. Now as you approach my door you have that stiffening again—an as yet painless stiffening in neck and shoulder. Discount it. You had a slight seizure a few minutes ago at the window. The door you are moving toward is now Ellen's as well as mine. A return on your investment.

When Ellen took your hand crossing Lexington you didn't know I was right behind you. We were to meet for an expensive lunch at Henry IV, but I happened to see you two on the street an hour early, and followed you. I saw that Ellen's taking your hand made you stiffen slightly. I believe you were thinking, "Now that's a nice thing to do."

"Americans shake hands whenever they can," Ellen said one night to Ian Harper with her self-possessed, retreating smile. And Ian said, "What are you going to do with a hand, anyway?"

Later Ian said to you, "If you're going to marry a foreigner, better it should be English. Look at Peter St. John and Sally; couldn't be better suited." Then Ian said, and you could only guess the implication, " 'Course, Peter's really coining money—which helps."

You open my door. And now, standing alone in my room,

looking at the twin beds, you think of Ellen. She's smaller than Julia, plump, with a very nice pair and a face whose sympathetic watchfulness is crossed by hilarity and fear. You are thinking: She might as well be an American girl, except she actually takes note of what a person says, and she doesn't then right away switch the talk off to herself.

This is a bookish room, but that's not all. My Peruvian *quipu* hangs near a Dartmouth megaphone I stole from my roommate. On the Dodger pennant near the window are pinned twenty-odd old Willkie buttons, including a few of the anti-Roosevelt ones. Why did I keep even the ones I now disapprove of? "THERE IS NO INDISPENSABLE MAN" A pith helmet hangs on a corner of the small mirror; a four-string banjo leans against the wall by my closet; on a lower shelf of one bookcase is a large folder containing a full set of those almost worthless (and non-postal) stamps depicting the '39-'40 World's Fair. You smile, remembering how I walked into this room a year ago and said with loud resignation, "This is the room of an eighteen-year-old."

You take up one of several red hard-cover notebooks that lie on my desk. On page 78 I have written, "Ouspensky habitually introduces his own privately minted ideological coins as if they were real currency. . . ."

(That's pretty clever.) You might try shying that at Pelago (see what he thinks).

Pelago is coming. Why didn't Julia see you'd as soon have 'had her there from start to finish? But you know this is tactics. Or is the term "strategy"? (Once you began Kissinger but gave up—you forget which is which, tactics, strategy, different kinds of bombing.) Julia is, for at least an hour, leaving you "alone with Pelago." You allowed her to think you didn't guess her thoughts. You let her think you really wanted to continue this charade with Pelago, talk about the Bible. (Now you recall what I told you about bibliomancy once, and you think maybe you'll find out what Pelago knows about bibliomancy—try it with the Bible itself.)

You knew, though, that you had to make this concession to Julia. You knew it the day Falco paused and then got a little muddled as he said you might have to have special care in Brooklyn Hospital and asked about your breathing—you knew there was a danger Julia wouldn't know how to deal with the news (and it *was* news, even though Falco didn't spell it out; you knew your own body). And so, seeing Julia's reaction when you started the Revised Standard then went to my own Bible and kept at it—you decided to enable her to think what she seemed now to want to think.

Do you see that this concession of yours is reminiscent of other deceptions? The flying? The telescope? Eeyore is a canny old donkey.

Do you see that you have been smuggling your disguised form through to Julia? For thus she'll at least have in her possession the form itself—or even, you *within* it! Don't you see that this smuggling idea has been close to your consciousness for a long time? Ruses like this one bridge the days. Do you see that? I hope you do; I feel you do. And then in retrospect they disappear like surgical stitches that disappear into flesh.

Well, see Pelago again. And again. (The Young Lady from Spain is one of the few limericks you remember! Old Robert Harper knows a hundred.) Pelago can't do less for you than Falco. See Pelago (*Vide supra!*) And talk back at him, and later on grin when he grips your hand to put a societal, intelligent, man-to-man termination to the interview.

Pelago is going to press the buzzer any second. You hear the dim groan of the elevator passing your floor on its way up.

The price is worth the gain: a kind of peace of mind for Julia. Yes, pay as you go—you've said that so many times. Everyone tries not to pay. And don't a lot get away with it? You squint, as you feel one of my captious contentions puzzling you. You were always suspicious of my words, though you were proud of them, too.

But now, as you dwell on how you're deceiving Julia "with" Pelago, a thousand incidents come together in your mind. You have seen, surely, how we smuggle ourselves out of—you must surely have seen—my precious father, you must surely have seen how we smuggle ourselves out of—

What about Bergen? Remember the day—I've reconstructed it from what you and Julia have told me—remember the last day in Bergen? You took the bus to Paradis, having sneaked away from Julia on the pretext that you wanted to see about getting some of that brown fudgelike goat cheese you enjoyed for breakfast. If you'd told the truth you'd have hurt her. You wanted to see that stave church (for the brochure Julia brought back after *she'd* seen it two weeks before had troubled your imagination); but also you wanted to see the church by yourself, you were tired of Julia. You stopped at the Bristol to get your raincoat, and the friendly blond man at the desk asked you if you liked Bergen and you told him where you were going. And you walked up past the park to the bus station. And at platform 14 you boarded the bus to . . . and you saw, didn't you, that what you were doing (i.e., without Julia knowing) was like smuggling. Yes, I *know* you saw that, and you see it now even more clearly. Take the Virgin Mary. Take Christ himself!

Do you remember, that rainy day, being actually *in* the church at last? Of course you do. Yes, you and your companion the little Englishwoman moved here and there in the shadows of that cramped, unbelievably small church. Your companion had bought a maroon brochure entitled *Fantoft Stave Church*, and she kept trying to read it in the dim light. Then, at last having seen the chancel, she turned.

She met your eye shyly as she brushed past you on the way out—only a few paces from the chancel to the door at the end of the nave. You hardly noticed that she murmured "sorry" to someone as she stepped down to the ground. Then the great door latched heavily and you were alone. Now I feel your shoulders growing round me as I think your thoughts. You looked up to the four bull's-eyes high under the roof—distant portholes giving the only light. You inspected the two beams that, like tight-fitting bolts, connect beam with beam from the forward end of the nave to the back end of the tiny, semicircular, apselike chancel. Somebody tinkered with the great door's bolt, seemed to raise it but then hesitate to pull the door open. Looking upward you thought of a ship's hold. You were peering up through antique superstructure into a vortex of night. The door rattled open, a mote of blindness came into the corner of your eye from the light admitted by the newcomer. Then the door closed. You cared nothing for the newcomer. You felt calm captivity in this inside-out ship—the shingled forest organism of its hull outside enclosing the masts and levels and catwalks of its superstructure, enclosing even the night through which it passed. You thought, What an operation it must have been to build this thing. Crisscross beaming—you felt almost as if you had been built into an ingenious bridge. (Surely, you recalled my once mentioning that in ancient days human

397

beings were in this very manner sacrificed to secure a blessing for a new bridge.)

Then, in the seasoned darkness of that church, you heard —and realized as you heard it, that it was in some peculiar way *not* a coincidence—"Hello, darling. Did I scare you? Isn't it marvelous? The man at the hotel told me you'd come and I just had to see it again. Do you know it's almost eight centuries old and it used to be up in the Sognefjord at a place called Fortun and they moved every stick of it here to these woods. Isn't it marvelous?"

Now you think it might have been a nice gesture to give her a kiss there all alone in Norway. Really you were glad to find yourself trapped by her.

And you are, indeed out of self-interest, glad to make her a little happy now.

You might try out on Pelago this idea you feel all round you. (You do feel it, don't you?) Just as so many people try to pass out of life without paying the full fear, so you now are trying to avoid having to confront Julia with the fact that you are dying. Do you see how people try to smuggle themselves out of life? To pretend to sneak across the mortal frontier—when in fact you stay right here after death . . . . You do see, don't you?

Do you see—do you not see—how Christ was in fact the most remarkable contraband of all time, and was simultaneously himself an arch smuggler? And the Virgin Mary, too? You recall, for an instant, Pelago's "Christmas Meditation":

Into the crude stable had come almost invisibly the greatest treasure of past or future history. And—to coin a somewhat different metaphor—*from* that mean stable went out the greatest news release of all time.

As you, my father, move among my possessions here on a Monday in this musty room, you find two Norwegian postcards stuck in a mounting corner of my genuine Portable Mandala. They're postmarked the same day. The one from my mother pictures the stave church and commemorates her first visit there. The one from you shows the interior of St. Mary's; you wrote a message while actually sitting there. "Dear David, Am about to smuggle myself in among some tourists listening to a hired guide lecture. Hope you'll come

398

and do the last lap of our trip with us. Love, Dad."

I remember everything you ever said to me.

(I even recall that you sang in the steaming shower one Sunday years, years ago. "I know tha-hat-maiee-ree-dee-ee-mur-li-i-veth"; I came in to get a cake of Palmolive and you stopped singing and peered squinting from around an edge of the curtain, steam rising behind you in smothering masses.)

Between the red Florentine leather bookends Julia bought me in Brentano's she has placed: *Winnie the Pooh;* next to it, the *Winnie Ille Pu* Jonni gave me one Xmas; *The Wind in the Willows*; Willkie's *One World*; the World Almanac for 1957; Van Gogh's Letters to Theo; and (out of spite, I bet) the Rudolph Flesch you gave me.

When, a few weeks ago, you took my Bible from there, you pressed the bookends to close the space. After your low-fat dinner tonight you'll ask Julia to read to you from Samuel and Kings. The Old Testament is better on stories. (Sartre's wrong: *God* is other people!) Paul you can get on with yourself. (You will be looking tired just before dinner, even after a drink; so in order to cheer up falsely cheerful Julia, you'll tell her again the joke old Robert Harper tells about the lion who, when the terrified man opened his eyes, was discovered also to be kneeling in prayer—whereupon the man, now amazed rather than petrified, asked, "Oh God, are you pray-ing, too?" To which the lion replied, "No, I'm saying grace.")

On one bookcase, under the owlish Bachrach of me that so strongly suggests Julia's cheeks and chin, you see four Poly Prep yearbooks—*The Polyglot* (!). The top one is heavy-grained white. (How summary and officially real those pages of gravure morgue seemed!)

In the corner of your eye you feel your reflection in the full-length mirror on my closet door. (As if you were snoop-ing on yourself!)

And now—for it is also on that bookcase—you slip off the tiny catch and lift the lid of the great black smuggler's Bible I bought cheap from Peter St. John. And as you find it empty, the buzzer goes at last.

 **BARD BOOKS**

distinguished modern fiction

A SELECTION OF RECENT TITLES

AMERICAN VOICES, AMERICAN WOMEN Lee R. Edwards and Arlyn Diamond (editors)	17871	1.95
THE BAG Sol Yurick	20891	1.95
BETRAYED BY RITA HAYWORTH Manuel Puig	15206	1.65
BILLIARDS AT HALF-PAST NINE Heinrich Böll	32730	1.95
THE CABALA Thornton Wilder	24653	1.75
THE CLOWN Heinrich Böll	24471	1.75
DANGLING MAN Saul Bellow	24463	1.65
THE EYE OF THE HEART Barbara Howes, Ed.	20883	2.25
FERTIG Sol Yurick	21477	1.95
THE GREEN HOUSE Mario Vargas Llosa	15099	1.65
HEAVEN'S MY DESTINATION Thornton Wilder	23416	1.65
HERMAPHRODEITY Alan Friedman	16865	2.45
HOPSCOTCH Julio Cortázar	20487	2.65
HUNGER Knut Hamsun	26864	1.75
LEAF STORM, And Other Stories Gabriel García Márquez	17566	1.65
THE MORNING WATCH James Agee	28316	1.50
ONE HUNDRED YEARS OF SOLITUDE Gabriel García Márquez	34033	2.25
NABOKOV'S DOZEN Vladimir Nabokov	15354	1.65
THE RECOGNITIONS William Gaddis	18572	2.65
62: A MODEL KIT Julio Cortázar	17558	1.65
THE VICTIM Saul Bellow	24273	1.95
THE WOMAN OF ANDROS Thornton Wilder	23630	1.65